DREAMWAKER SAGA 

lucid
REVENGE

Lee Gabel

FRANKENSCRIPT

Frankenscript Press
Box 717, #105 - 1497 Admirals Road
Victoria, BC, Canada   V9A 2P8

Lucid Revenge (Dreamwaker Saga #2)

Cover illustration and design by Lee Gabel

Cover images supplied by DepositPhotos

Body font (ITC Galliard Pro) by International Typeface Corporation
Folios, heads and caps (Zapf Humanist 601) by Bitstream Inc.

ISBN: 978-1-9991856-4-0 (ebook)
ISBN: 978-1-9991856-7-1 (paperback)

Want to join Lee's Reader Group or find out more about Lee and the books he writes? Please go to:
LeeGabel.com/links

DREAMWAKER SAGA  2

lucid REVENGE

Thank you, Internet.
You remembered the 1980s better than I ever could.

Playlist

Keep On Loving You
REO Speedwagon

Black Cars
Gino Vannelli

Panama
Van Halen

Dancing With Tears
In My Eyes
Ultravox

Back In Black
AC/DC

Sweet Dreams
The Eurythmics

Major Tom (Coming Home)
Peter Schilling

Don't Dream It's Over
Crowded House

Head Games
Foreigner

Dirty Deeds Done Dirt
Cheap
AC/DC

Fire of Unknown Origin
Blue Oyster Cult

Burning Down the House
Talking Heads

Devil's Gun
C.J. & Company

Red Skies
The Fixx

Sister Christian
Night Ranger

Jailbreak
Thin Lizzy

One Way Or Another
Blondie

KEEP ON LOVING YOU

CASH'S BODY SLOUCHED uncomfortably against orange vinyl cushions cracked at the seams and worn smooth by past visitors. The chair, and Wynter's hospital room, had become his home away from home since she had arrived at Halston Medical Center two days ago.

His arm lay stretched across the armrest, his right hand on her left. The need to hold her hand or touch her skin was always there, even though the nurses said it wouldn't make any difference.

"Wynter has suffered a mild traumatic brain injury," Cash had heard the doctor tell Nolan and Madeline during the wee hours of Saturday morning, only hours after Wynter fell from the 19th Street Bridge. They had many questions for the doctor and Cash had tried to eavesdrop without appearing obvious about it. From what he was able to piece together, parts of Wynter's brain had shut down in order to heal. She was breathing on her own, which was a good sign, and she showed brain activity, specifically the occasional sleep-wake cycle, which was good but highly unusual. Cash wondered if Ransom was in her head with her, taking care of her.

He better be.

Cash would have rather slept at home, but he couldn't bring himself to leave Wynter's side, even after Nolan and Madeline had insisted he come home with them. He made a pact to inform them if there was any immediate news.

He had worked out a deal with the nurses in the coma ward. Cash could stay as long as he kept out of the way when Wynter needed to be tended to. That meant he could be with her most of the day, except for when nurses needed to bathe her or deal with her catheter. The hospital even supplied him with a wrist band clearing him for twenty-four hour access.

During times when the nurses kicked him out, the best option was to hang out or sleep in the chapel one floor down. Cash disliked being separated from Wynter, but the chapel was better than lying on his bed worrying back at the trailer. The chapel was quiet, even with other people there, and the bench seats were comfortable up to a point. The thin seat cushions made prolonged sitting or sleeping difficult at best.

No matter where he slept, Cash's dreams were always variations of the accident, the arrival of the ambulance and the return trip, played out over and over in vivid detail. Sometimes he saw the events through his own eyes and other times his point of view was removed, like from a concealed security camera. Sometimes the ambulance never made it back to the hospital at all, instead crashing against the overpass supports in a fiery explosion. Those times he woke in a cold sweat, not entirely sure if he had cried out in his sleep.

It hadn't taken Cash long to grow used to the beeps and whirrs of Wynter's monitoring equipment. Soon it became a comfort. But he longed for the day when she would no longer need them.

Quinn pushed through the door to Wynter's hospital room. She deflated a little when she saw Wynter was still unconscious. "Hello... Cash?" she whispered.

Jake popped his head over her shoulder. "Are they awake?" He hobbled in behind her on crutches, his left leg in a cast up to his mid-thigh.

Cash snored in the orange chair, his fingertips resting next to Wynter's forearm. Quinn sidled up next to the chair and ran a finger down his left arm.

"Cash," she whispered in his ear. "Dinner time."

Cash stirred, then sat bolt upright as if he had just been poked with a cattle prod. "What? Is she awake?" He looked at Wynter in her bed, at the gentle beep of the vital signs monitor.

"Hey, dude. You hungry?" Jake eyed him expectantly.

Cash sat up, winced, and shook his head. He ran his hand through his hair and hung his head.

"You got to eat." Quinn crouched low enough to look up at him. "Wynter will be right here when you get back."

A single tear fell and soaked into Cash's jeans. "What if something happens while I'm gone?"

"She's in, like, good hands," Quinn said, then leaned in close to whisper, "You got to keep your strength up if you're going to protect her."

Cash's eyes cleared a little and Quinn detected a hint of a smile. "Okay." He made his way to the door and held it open for Quinn and Jake, pausing to take one last look at Wynter before he stepped out of the room.

Quinn and Cash walked to the twinned elevators at the end of the corridor. Jake followed behind, wrestling with his crutches with every step.

"I hate these things." Jake stepped into the left elevator. "But they do make great weapons." He glanced over his shoulder at Quinn and Cash. "Don't make me angry. You wouldn't like me when I'm angry."

Cash smirked at him. "Thanks for the update, *Dr. David Banner.*"

Quinn rolled her eyes. "The Incredible Dork."

"I love you guys," Jake said as the elevator doors closed.

A minute later the three of them entered the large first-floor cafeteria. Even at seven in the evening on a Sunday, most of the tables were claimed.

Jake held up his crutches. "I'll get a table if someone could bring me a burger and fries. I'll pay you back."

"No problem." Cash felt for his wallet in his pocket and followed Quinn to the rows of hot and cold food trays. "You must have Blue Belle back by now."

Quinn nodded. "I picked her up on Saturday. Finn did a great job. And get this..." Quinn leaned closer and whispered. "Jake helped with the cost. He said I could pay him back after Jezebel pays her fine. Sweet of him, huh?"

"He likes you, Quinn."

Quinn dipped her head to hide her blush, then guided a lock of hair behind one ear. "Yeah, he's cool."

"And Jezebel's going to pay alright," Cash said. "But maybe not her fine." He looked at the trays of food. "Burgers and fries, huh? Not at a buffet."

Each of them grabbed plates and approached the row of hot dishes.

Quinn and Cash found Jake sitting at the table furthest from the food. "Sorry. Slim pickings."

"Same here." Cash set two almost identical plates on the table, one in front of Jake. The plates held healthy slices of lasagna with Caesar salad and garlic toast on the side. "Best I could do."

Jake shrugged. "It's okay. Thanks." He grabbed a knife and fork and dug in.

Quinn placed her plate on the table, then disappeared back toward the food trays.

"Nice move, helping Quinn get her car back."

Jake smiled and spoke through a mouthful of salad. "I may not have a job, but I'm not broke."

Cash picked up a fork and pushed his lasagna around. "Not hungry?"

"Yes and no," Cash said, "if that makes any sense."

Jake nodded. "Well, try and eat something, because if you don't, I will. Then I'll get fat and you don't want that on your conscience, too." His words were out before he realized it and he winced. "Sorry. That came out wrong."

"What came out wrong?" Quinn set down three filled coffee cups with one hand and deposited a handful of sugar packets and miniature creamer tubs with the other.

"Nothing," Cash said. "Jake's just putting his foot in his mouth instead of his lasagna."

"Sorry I missed it." Quinn sat and smothered her scalloped potatoes and breaded chicken fingers with ketchup.

"Hey." Jake eyed her plate, puzzled. "I thought you didn't like ketchup."

"I don't like it on french fries."

"But you're eating potatoes. Those *are* potatoes, right? French fries are potatoes, too."

"You're a genius." Quinn took a bite of scalloped potatoes. "Your point?"

Jake glanced at Cash for backup.

"Hey, don't look at me." Cash squeezed a creamer tub into his coffee, added two packets of sugar, and gave the concoction a half-hearted stir. He took a sip and grimaced. Cash reclined in his chair and sighed. His eyes drifted to the clock on the wall, then to the window below it.

Quinn swallowed and set her fork down. "You alright, Cash?"

"Not really." Cash rubbed his temple. "I can't stop blaming myself."

Quinn exchanged a concerned look with Jake. "It's not your fault."

"I should have protected her."

Quinn reached out and touched Cash's hand. "This is no one's fault except Jezebel's."

"Don't forget Roxy," Jake said.

Cash's right hand went instinctively to his left shoulder, palpating the wad of bandages secured there with medical tape. "Oh, I've got thirteen reasons not to forget her."

Jake grinned at Quinn, then turned to Cash and nodded at his shoulder. "Let's see."

"It'll spoil your appetite," Cash said.

Jake tilted his head at him. "You're looking at two people who have watched *Dawn of the Dead* multiple times... while eating."

"Alright." Cash rolled the cuff of his T-shirt up over his shoulder, then slowly tugged one corner of the medical tape away from his skin. He peeled the bandage back and exposed an angry horizontal gash three inches long, sutured with thirteen neatly tied black stitches. Dried blood dotted the back of the bandage.

"Gnarly." Jake sat up to get a closer look. "That's going to leave a wicked scar."

"Is it deep?" Quinn asked.

"Deep enough." Cash smoothed the bandage back over the grisly line of stitches and rolled his cuff back down. He balled his left hand into a fist to remind himself that his muscles still worked as they should. Cash pushed lasagna onto his fork with his garlic toast and took a bite. His appetite had woken up.

"We got to figure out a new plan," Quinn said.

Cash nodded. "It's like one step forward, two steps back."

"Any ideas?" Jake finished up his plate and looked longingly back at the buffet trays.

"I don't know. Maybe." Cash followed Jake's sightline. "We're going to need more food though. Want a refill?"

"Fuck yeah," Jake said, licking his lips.

Cash turned to Quinn. "Want me to bring back anything?"

"One of every dessert they have, please and thank you." Quinn said. "Good to have you back, Cash. Even if it's, like, a little bit at a time."

Cash managed a small smile and headed back to the buffet. Quinn watched him roam the line-up, collecting seconds.

"I feel so sorry for him."

"I know," Jake said. "I mean it was like she almost died in his arms. I hope she doesn't wake up with brain damage."

"Jesus, Jake." Quinn crossed her arms and looked away. "You sure know how to kill the mood."

"Sorry." Jake's cheeks flushed red. "I didn't mean…"

Cash returned balancing three plates loaded with food. Despite the shadow Jake had cast over the table, the three of them ate until they felt as if they'd burst.

Cash led the charge back to Wynter's room, with hope for a plan and some positive news.

NOLAN AND MADELINE stood beside Wynter's bed, holding each other's hand. Wynter's chest rose and fell in a slow, regular cadence. The monitoring equipment hummed and chirped on the opposite side of the bed, and although its sound was unobtrusive, the screen with its relentless bouncing ECG strip and other fluctuating metrics kept bringing them back to reality: though lucky to be alive, their daughter was still in grave danger.

Madeline smoothed Wynter's fiery hair away from her face, her hand coming to rest on Wynter's shoulder. "My baby." A tear crested one of her lids and she caught it with a quick swipe of her wrist.

Nolan kissed Wynter's head, careful not to disturb the nasogastric tube snaking out of her nose, then removed a necklace from around his neck. The symbol for hope, an eight-pointed star contained within a circle, hung from the bottom of a knotted loop of black twine. He kissed the medallion, then hung it off the corner of the bed.

"Can she hear us, hon?"

Nolan offered a small but confident nod. "She can. She knows we're here."

Madeline wrapped her arms around Nolan and hugged him tight, her tears finding their resting place on the shoulder of his shirt.

Cash pushed through the door to the room. He stopped short when he saw Madeline and Nolan. Quinn and Jake bumped into him unaware.

"Sorry," he said. "We can come back later."

"No, it's okay." Nolan waved them over. "She needs us all here."

Quinn had not expected to see Wynter's parents and tried to maintain a strong front, but once her eyes met Madeline's, her emotional wall crumbled.

"Quinn, darlin'. Come here." Madeline opened her arms and wrapped them around her.

"I'm so sorry, Mrs. LaCroix." Quinn stifled her sobs as best she could.

Madeline patted Quinn's back and rocked her gently. "Shh. She'll be awake before you know it."

Cash stood next to Nolan. "Any change?"

"Doctor says she's stable, maybe on the edge of waking, so that's good. But she's got a lot of healing to do inside." Nolan tapped his temple, then glanced at the cast on Jake's leg. "How long do you have to wear that?"

"For the rest of the summer at least," Jake said. "Sucks, I know."

Nolan regarded the three teens. "What I don't understand is why... Jezebel is it? Why did *she* do this?"

Quinn pulled away from Madeline, wiped her face on her shirt, and exchanged looks with Cash and Jake, and shook her head subtly. Her face twisted into an angry scowl. "She's a psycho bitch. That's why."

"She's hiding out somewhere," Cash said. "Anson would've told us if she'd been caught."

Jake hobbled to the chair beside Wynter's bed and eased himself into it. "We'd have heard about it on the news."

"I hope she and Roxy die in a shoot out." Quinn spat her words out. "Just like Bonnie and Clyde."

"Enough," Madeline said. "It's hard enough being here. I don't want no death and dying talk, no matter who it's directed at." Her eyes scanned the room. "Whoever's responsible will pay eventually."

A nurse popped her head into the room. "Visiting hours end in five minutes."

Quinn grabbed one of Jake's crutches and held it upright. "We should get going. On your feet, soldier." She glanced back at Cash. "You should come with us. Spend a night in your own bed for a change."

"That's a good idea," Nolan said. "We should all do that."

"What do you say, Cash?" Jake pulled himself up onto his crutches. "Come with us if you want to sleep," he said in his best Arnold Schwarzenegger accent.

"Nice one." Quinn and Jake bumped fists.

"Okay," Cash said. "I have to say, that chair was forged in hell."

"I bet." Quinn pulled open the door.

"Before you go..." Madeline curved her arm around Nolan's waist. "Thank you. Wynter's lucky to have such good friends."

"Well, we're lucky too," Cash said. "But I'll be back tomorrow."

"I'm sure you will." Nolan smiled but there was pain and worry behind his eyes. "We appreciate your vigilance."

Cash nodded his head at him and followed Quinn and Jake out into the corridor.

"They're great kids." Nolan watched the door close. "Shall we head out too?"

"Let's wait until visiting hours are officially over." Madeline looked up at him, her eyes misty. "Okay?"

Nolan leaned down and kissed her. "Okay."

They resumed their spots beside Wynter's bed. Nolan kissed his fingertips, then touched the hope medallion he had hung on the bed earlier. Madeline raised Wynter's left hand in hers and ran her fingers lightly across the back of her hand, across the webspace between her thumb and index finger, and spiraling on her palm.

At eight o'clock the nurse entered the room and ushered them out. In the commotion of leaving the room, no one noticed Wynter's eyes open, then close a second later.

ONE OF THE two elevators that served the fourth floor dinged and opened to an empty car. Quinn, Jake, and Cash shuffled inside. Their eyes focused on Wynter's room down the corridor. Between the three of them, only Cash shifted uneasily on his feet.

"Sorry, guys. I can't do this." He stepped forward to leave the elevator, but Quinn grabbed his arm and pulled him back.

"Wait." Quinn's eyes held an intensity that Cash had a hard time meeting. "We know you need Wynter, but *we* need you too. And *you* need *us*."

"Come hang out with us, dude." Jake raised a brow and the corner of his mouth curled in an optimistic grin.

Cash pursed his lips, struggling with the decision. Finally, he sighed. "Okay. Maybe you're right."

And like it was a confirmation of his decision, the elevator doors closed and the three friends descended to the first floor.

The adjacent elevator dinged and its doors slid open. Monty stepped out wearing his usual T-shirt, mirrored sunglasses, and leather jacket ensemble. He peered down the corridor and removed his sunglasses, hooking them into the collar of his shirt.

A nurse passed by and he averted his eyes, pretending to be

interested in the various generic art prints hung between the doors to the rooms. Monty continued down the corridor and covertly peered through the windows to the rooms, most of which had their blinds drawn for privacy.

The nurse entered a room at the end of the corridor and as the door slowly swung shut, voices floated out. Monty quickened his pace and managed to catch a glimpse of Wynter's red hair splayed out against her pillow.

"There you are," he said to himself.

Monty tried to look into Wynter's room. The blinds were angled down, allowing a somewhat restricted view into the room from the corridor, but his attempt was thwarted before it began when he heard voices approach the door. Monty stepped hurriedly across the corridor to a small alcove with three chairs. He sat and hung his head, feigning grief.

The door swung open. Nolan and Madeline stepped out, followed by the nurse. They exchanged thank-yous and walked arm-in-arm toward the elevators. Nolan pressed the down call button. The numbers above the left elevator incremented toward the fourth floor.

Monty stood and ran his hands through his oily hair. He walked quickly toward the end of the corridor, slowing when he was within earshot.

"Do you think that was part of it?" Madeline watched the numbers increase above the elevator. Something was happening on the second floor to delay the elevator's arrival. "Remember, your grandmother jumped."

"Wynter was *pushed*." Nolan's jaw tensed with the words. "There's a difference."

"But that *boy* was with her, according to the minimal details Anson told us," Madeline said. "I'd bet it was the same boy we found in her room." She crossed her arms. "They're hiding things from us, I just know it."

"Who? Quinn and the guys?"

Madeline nodded.

The elevator dinged and the doors slid open. Nolan and Madeline stepped inside, turning around to see Monty standing just beyond the doors. He had his hands in his pockets and his shoulders bunched up against his neck. He hung his head down and looked at the floor.

"Probably. Did you keep secrets from your parents?" Nolan selected the first floor and within a few seconds the door began to slide closed.

Monty's pager went off. He pressed a button on a small black box on his belt, ending the rapid succession of beeps. He shuffled forward. "Wait."

Madeline stuck her hand out and stopped the doors from closing.

Monty entered the elevator and positioned himself in the far corner. "Thanks." His voice was low and strained.

"Floor?" Nolan asked.

"What?" Monty tossed his greasy hair to one side. "Oh. First."

The elevator doors closed, and the car began its descent.

Madeline turned her back to Monty and lowered her voice. "Maybe if we tell them about the *power*, they'd let us in." Her voice hadn't been as low as she thought. Monty had heard every word.

Nolan shook his head almost imperceptibly and motioned at Monty. Madeline took the hint and stood by Nolan's side.

"I hope whoever you're here for gets better soon," Nolan said.

Monty nodded but kept his head down. "Thanks. You too."

The three of them stood in silence for the rest of the trip down. The doors opened on the first floor and Nolan and Madeline stepped forward. Monty followed them out.

"What was that about?" Madeline whispered.

"I didn't want that guy to overhear..."

Monty veered off toward the stairwell, now out of earshot. He watched Nolan and Madeline walk toward the front entrance, immersed in a heated discussion. "I'm one hell of an actor." A smug smile stretched across his lips.

He pulled open the door to the stairwell and bounded up the steps two at a time. Monty emerged back at the fourth floor, and he quickly walked back to Wynter's room. He opened the door and peeked in.

Monty's eyes narrowed. "What's your secret, Red? What's your *power?*" Whatever it was, he knew the power was connected to Jezebel too, somehow. And like it or not, it either started or ended with Ransom. But how could he find someone who had vaporized into thin air?

QUINN HUNG BACK with Jake and followed Cash out the front lobby of the hospital. He was already pacing outside by the time Jake hobbled up to the sliding glass doors.

"What are we going to do about him?"

The pleasant aroma of the buffet still hung in the air despite the cafeteria having closed for the evening.

Quinn shrugged. "What's there to do? He's hurting pretty bad." She placed her hand on Jake's shoulder and stopped him before he stepped out of the main foyer. "He loves Wynter, but she chose someone else. And now she could die. How would you feel?"

Jake's eyes widened under the brim of his Nintendo baseball hat. "He loves her? How do you know that? He didn't say anything to me."

"It's obvious." Quinn managed a weak laugh. "To any *girl,* it's obvious."

Jake watched Cash pace for a moment. "I guess I'd feel pretty terrible." He settled his eyes back on Quinn. "So, it's obvious?"

"Is what obvious?"

"You said 'to any girl, it's obvious,' " Jake said. "I wanted to see if your powers are truly great."

"What are you—" Color rose high on Quinn's cheeks as she felt the weight of his gaze. She punched Jake lightly on the shoulder and tried to hide her smile behind her hair. "Come on, gimp." She walked toward Cash and the covered entrance.

Jake followed as quickly as he could. "Who you calling a *gimp?*"

Quinn threw her arms around Cash and gave him a quick hug. "Let's get you home." She spun around, walking backward and facing Jake. "You too, Hopalong Cassidy."

"What?" Jake crunched his brows together in confusion. "Who's *Hopalong Cassidy?*"

"Ha!" Quinn looked at him surprised. "And you call yourself a movie expert." She spotted Blue Belle and ran toward the little VW Beetle. "You're going to have to look it up."

Jake caught up to Cash. "Do you know who she's talking about?"

"Nope."

Quinn hopped into the driver's seat and unlocked the passenger door for Cash and Jake.

Cash pushed the passenger seat forward and out of the way. "Want to take the back? You could stretch out."

Jake nodded. "Sounds good. Thanks." He crouched and crawled into the back, careful not to bang his cast.

Cash buckled himself into the passenger seat. Quinn started the engine and backed out. She navigated out of the lot and within minutes she had merged with traffic headed west on I94, racing the setting sun.

Cash rested his head on the window and remained silent.

Quinn watched as the hospital and the surrounding buildings in Halston shrunk in her rear view mirror as they moved further west. As the distance between them and Wynter grew larger, the more uneasy Quinn felt, until an unexpected wave of grief took hold of her.

She pulled into the Red River Rest Stop and parked at the first available spot.

Jake craned his neck at his surroundings. "Hey, why are we stopping?"

Quinn gripped the steering wheel and burst into tears.

Jake leaned forward from the back seat. "It's going to be okay, Quinn."

Cash faced her, placed his hand on her right arm, and nodded. "He's right."

Quinn shook her head, swiping at her tears with a trembling hand. "What if it's not? It feels like we're abandoning her."

"We're not," Cash said.

"Give me a second?" Quinn sniffed, grabbed a tissue from her purse, and blew. She opened her door, climbed out, and began to fret again.

Cash glanced back at Jake. "Go to her."

Jake surveyed the back seat. "Give me a hand." With Cash's help, Jake positioned his cast between the front seats, allowing him to sit up. "Quinn?"

She looked back at him. Jake held up his arms, but his eyes said everything that needed to be said. She pushed the driver's seat forward and climbed in the back with him. He placed his left arm around her shoulder and Quinn buried her face in his chest, muffling her sobs.

"You too, dude," Jake said. "Group hug."

Cash didn't argue. He reached across the car and closed the driver's side door. He popped the passenger door open, took the space next to Jake, and pulled the passenger door shut behind him.

Quinn's sobbing faded, leaving three friends sharing their grief together. Any awkwardness had been replaced by emotional exhaustion and soon all three were asleep. Perhaps solace would come in their dreams.

Jezebel had found it entirely too easy to evade Anson and leave the scene at the 19th Street Bridge two nights ago. He was never going to shoot her. Anson would always be more concerned with Wynter and preserving human life. Her falling off the bridge was the best thing to happen to Jezebel that night.

Roxy had appeared more unsettled. "Where are we going to go now? Everyone is going to be looking for us."

Jezebel turned onto a side street in the north side of town. "Should I let you out at your place?"

"Are you crazy? That's the first place the cops will look." Roxy bit at her nails. "My parents are going to freak."

"The cops aren't going to do shit," Jezebel said. "Think about it. It's just like last time. As long as I have Ransom, no one will press charges."

"I don't know about that, Jazz. Last time we only *bumped* their car." Roxy stared at her across the center console. "Anson was talking felony hit and run."

"He's full of shit. As long as no one talks, we're free and clear. And no one's going to talk if I have Ransom." Jezebel traced a snaking fracture along the windshield with her eyes. "Too bad that asshole cracked the glass."

Roxy sat back in her seat and pursed her lips. She reached for the radio and turned it on. Gino Vannelli was singing "Black Cars" on KROK.

"You sure know how to pick them." Jezebel turned right onto Main Street. "Know where I'm going?"

"You're not going home."

"No shit."

Roxy thought for a moment, then turned to give Jezebel a small smile and a nod. Even though Jezebel had not planned her getaway, she always knew exactly where to go. Roxy liked that about her.

Jezebel rolled the Barracuda behind the storage shed at the back of Ollie's MovieTyme and killed the engine. "Give me a hand covering it up."

The two of them unfolded a blue tarp from the trunk and secured it over the black muscle car.

"That'll do until things cool down." Jezebel strolled up to the shed. Only she had keys to the new padlocks on the door. Both girls stepped inside, and Jezebel locked the door from the inside with the padlocks she had used on the outside, but she didn't fully engage the lock loops to ensure an easy escape if needed.

There was only one grimy window that cast a dim glow around the interior during the day. In one corner of the shed lay a worn and stained mattress. Many teenagers before them had used the mattress, but ever since Jezebel had changed the locks, the run down space had been hers to use for whatever she wanted.

On the opposite side of the shed a metal shelving unit stood shrouded with cobwebs. Tools and supplies for drive-in maintenance, long since forgotten, remained stacked floor to ceiling. Curiously, power to the shed had never been cut.

Jezebel yanked a rusty ball chain hanging from the ceiling and the bare forty watt bulb next to it turned on. "Cover the window." She sprawled on the mattress until it sagged completely under her weight. "What's left to eat?"

Roxy positioned a piece of cardboard over the window and opened a cooler that sat next to the back wall. "Not much. A bunch of bags of potato chips and a six-pack of Coke."

"Toss me some."

Roxy handed Jezebel the snacks and took some for herself. "We're going to have to spread this out, don't you think? If we're going to hide out?"

"Relax," Jezebel said between mouthfuls of chips. "We'll make a food run later if we need to." She turned to Roxy. "Want to have some fun?"

"What kind of fun?"

"The Ransom kind."

The last thing Roxy wanted to do was fool around with Ransom. But shooting down Jezebel's suggestion would only make things worse.

"Okay," she said.

The mattress was large enough for both girls to stretch out without touching each other. Jezebel finished her snacks and closed her eyes. Roxy considered staying awake and waiting, but sleep won her over. As it turned out, Ransom had other plans.

IT WAS SUNDAY night, almost forty-eight hours since Jezebel and Roxy had set up camp in the maintenance shed behind Ollie's MovieTyme drive-in. They had run out of food once and had to make a late Saturday night run to Halston for groceries. Instead of the convenience store at Zoey's Fast Fill, they chose a nearby Seven-Eleven.

Jezebel's Friday night plan to bring Ransom out from her dreams had failed. As a result, she had been on the warpath ever since.

"I don't know what the fuck's going on." Jezebel paced back and forth in the small space of the shed. "He's in my dreams but he doesn't come out when I want him to."

"It's like he has free will." Roxy considered her words carefully. "Don't get mad, but look at it from his side. Wynter created him. They'll always be connected. And she might die because of what you did."

Jezebel grabbed Roxy's T-shirt and pushed her against the wall. "What *we* did."

"Yeah, sure. What we did." Roxy locked gazes with Jezebel and pushed back. "Whatever. If I was Ransom, I'd be pissed at you."

Jezebel released her and went back to her pacing. "So, what do you suggest, brainiac?"

"Ransom's in your dreams, so that means that Wynter is still alive," Roxy said. "Let him know that. Be nice for a change. Maybe even apologize."

Roxy prepared herself for a litany of profanity, but instead Jezebel laid down on the mattress and closed her eyes. "Don't wait up," Jezebel said.

But this time Roxy did wait up. Two hours later Ransom drifted out of Jezebel's dreams in a chilled wave of ozone. He wore his familiar white T-shirt, black hoodie, and jeans.

Jezebel rubbed the sleep from her eyes.

"Does it hurt?" Roxy asked. "Like, when you become real?"

"Only if I land wrong." Ransom glanced at Jezebel. "Or when someone *stabs* me, like, with a crowbar."

Jezebel propped herself on her elbows. "I do it out of love."

"Bullshit." Ransom scanned the small space. "Where are we?"

"Oll—" Roxy began before Jezebel cut her off.

"You don't need to know." Jezebel faced him. "And next time you better come out when I want you to."

Ransom's blue eyes shifted to a steely grey. "Or else... what?"

"I'll kill Wynter. For real," Jezebel said with a snarl on her lips.

"What were you just saying about love?" Ransom laughed. "You don't know anything."

"Fuck you."

Roxy leaned against the wall, settling in to watch the festivities.

Ransom crouched to Jezebel's level. "What if I just kill you first. That'd be a permanent solution and I'd be out of your control for good."

Jezebel stood and shook her head. "You're under my control.

If I die, you die with me... romantic, isn't it? Plus, you'd never see Wynter again."

Ransom shook his head and laughed softly. "That's not the way it works and you know it."

Jezebel's eyes shifted between Ransom and Roxy. "If I die, you die too—"

"I'd just go back into Wynter's head," Ransom said.

"And... Monty kills Wynter." Jezebel focused her eyes on Roxy's. "Isn't that right, Rox?"

"Uh..." Roxy stammered, instantly at a loss for words.

"Me and Monty, we have an agreement," Jezebel said. "We'd kill for each other."

Ransom crossed his arms against his chest and gave Jezebel the once-over, in an attempt to determine if she was lying. It was an impossible task.

"Enough with the killing talk." Roxy's eyes were wide with panic and she looked out of breath. "It's boring. Change the subject!"

Jezebel stepped around Ransom, then hooked her finger behind the button on his jeans. "I can't stay mad at you." She popped the button out and unzipped his fly. "But before we get to the fun stuff... I need you to do something for me."

Ransom pushed Jezebel's hand away. "What?"

"I have a plan that's better than selling drugs for Monty. But I need a gun."

Ransom zipped up and buttoned his jeans. "Why?"

"I want to blow this town. Hit the road. With *you*." Jezebel laid a hand on Ransom's chest. "But I need money."

Roxy saw where Jezebel's idea was going. "Bad idea, Jazz."

Jezebel turned and pointed at her, anger alight in her eyes. "Shut up. You're in too deep to disagree."

"Look, I'll give you money," Roxy said. "My parents would never know."

"I'm not talking a few hundred dollars," Jezebel said. "I can't live on that."

"You're talking robbery." Roxy shook her head. "Of what? Stores? Banks? We'd go to prison."

"Only if we get caught, and even if we do, we're juveniles. We wouldn't go to prison."

"We're juveniles for what? Like, one more year?" Roxy paced the floor of the small shed. "Such a bad idea."

"Shut the fuck up."

"So, why do you need me?" Ransom shifted his gaze between the two girls.

"You get the gun. You rob the banks." Jezebel stepped nose to nose with Ransom. "Because you don't die. You're our alibi."

Ransom scowled at her and scoffed. "More like a scapegoat. What if I refuse?"

Jezebel ran her finger down Ransom's jawline. "Wynter has an accident."

"You're such a bitch."

"And you love it." Jezebel unzipped Ransom's jeans again and slipped her hand inside.

"I want a cut," Ransom said. "An even split. Between all three of us."

"Of course." Jezebel kissed Ransom's neck.

"We're really going to do this?" Roxy stopped her pacing.

"Yes." Jezebel turned and glared at Roxy, straight through her. "Unless you want to have an accident, too."

Color drained from Roxy's face as she realized that she had no choice but to follow Jezebel. It was true. She was in too deep. "Where are you going to get a gun?"

"Fun first," Jezebel said.

Ransom held out his hand. "Come on, Rox. Two's company, but three's a party."

Jezebel narrowed her eyes on Roxy.

Ransom turned Jezebel's face to his. "Play nice. We're in this together, remember?" Jezebel resumed kissing his neck, her hand resuming its search inside his jeans.

Roxy stepped behind Ransom and wrapped her arms around his chest. She was surprised by how she had missed his smell, his body. But even the sex that came later couldn't distract her from Jezebel's new plan. Had she thought it through this time? Because like it or not, the two of them were intrinsically linked.

CASH SAT SECOND from the back in his Mathematics 10 classroom. Quinn and Jake flanked him, both looking like extras from *Back to the Future*. Wynter sat in front of him. She wore a white off the shoulder T-shirt and her red hair flowed over her brown shoulders and down her back. Even her hair held beauty and he found it hard to concentrate. Other students he didn't recognize filled the rest of the desks, which seemed a little strange.

Everyone had a test in front of them with a pencil and eraser next to it. Math was not one of Cash's favorite subjects, but he wasn't terrible at it. He knew it would come in handy when he started his own business. Or maybe he'd go into business with Jake and capitalize on his high-tech ideas.

"You have two hours to complete your exam." The words floated from a speaker near the door, voiced by a teacher that he didn't recognize. "Please begin."

Everyone flipped open the first page of their exams in a flurry of paper. Cash read the first question and it stopped him cold.

"Calculate the probability of Wynter dying from her injuries," the question read. "Show your work."

Cash looked around the room. Everyone had their heads down, their pencils madly scribbling across the page, including Quinn, Jake, and Wynter.

Cash looked at the next question: "How many days will Wynter remain in a coma?" And the next, a multiple choice question: "Who is responsible for Wynter's death?" All four choices were "Cash Hawkins."

"What the hell?" Cash flipped the page to reveal the same questions repeated. The entire exam was like this. He turned to the last page and in bold capital letters it read: "CASH IS A KILLER."

"Jake," Cash whispered. "Can I see the first page of your exam?"

Jake made no sign that he had heard him and continued writing.

Cash turned the opposite direction to Quinn. "Are you seeing this? These questions are bullshit."

Quinn's lack of reaction mirrored Jake's. Cash leaned across the aisle and looked at her test. Scrawled across her paper in neat, even cursive were the words "Cash is a killer" repeated over and over again.

Cash tapped on Wynter's shoulder. "Wynter? How can you be answering these?"

Wynter did not react, not even a flinch.

"Wynter?" Cash sat forward in his desk. "I don't care what this says. I'm *not* a killer. I won't let anything happen to you."

Wynter spun around in her seat to face him, her hair flying. But it wasn't Wynter who looked back at him. It was Jezebel, with her brunette hair crimped in spiky clumps and her skin no longer brown but white, her lips pulled back in a scowl to expose teeth that looked a lot like fangs.

She took hold of the sides of his desk and pushed it toward the back wall. Everyone in the room dropped their pencils and twisted in their seats to watch.

"Stay away from her or I'll kill *you*," Jezebel spat. She revealed a switchblade in one hand, the blade glinting under the rows of fluorescent lights.

An arm reached around and wedged itself against Cash's neck.

Roxy's breathy whisper came a moment later. "She means it too, Trashy Cash." She snapped her gum in his ear.

"I'll always fight for Wynter."

The other students, including Quinn and Jake, began to chant, low and quiet at first. "Kill-er. Kill-er. Killed her. KILLED HER." Gradually the volume increased until the entire room vibrated with hatred, all directed at Cash.

"No!" Cash slid out of Roxy's grasp and under his desk. He crawled under the rows of desks and headed for the door.

"Then I'll kill *you!*" Jezebel screeched.

The chant morphed to "Kill him. Kill him." Quinn, Jake, and the rest of the students formed a wall behind Jezebel and Roxy as they descended on Cash.

He reached the door, but the door had vanished, leaving a blank wall in its place. Cash flipped onto his backside, his legs scrambling to get away, but he had nowhere to escape to.

In a blink of his eye, Roxy appeared behind him, her hot breath at his ear. She wrenched his hands tightly behind his back.

"Cash. You don't deserve to live." Jezebel waved the knife blade in front of his face like an admonishing finger.

Quinn leaned in close, almost nose to nose with Cash. "Wake up…"

Jake jammed his head forward close to Quinn's and completed her words. "Time to die."

They smiled at each other as Jezebel pushed them aside and placed the blade tip in the center of his chest.

"Good idea." She pushed the knife into Cash's heart.

Excruciating pain shot through Cash's body as blood blossomed from the center of his chest. He screamed and squeezed his eyes shut. Silence descended on the classroom. His lungs burned with panicked breaths, as he choked against air that felt heavy with moisture, like he was out in a dense fog.

Cash cracked his eyes open. Quinn and Jake sat opposite from him in the back seat of the Beetle, their eyes wide with surprise.

He jerked his head down to look at his chest, his hand searching for a stab wound.

But there was no wound and no blood.

"Dude. Uh... you okay?" Jake positioned himself in front of Quinn like a shield.

Cash's eyes darted around the interior of the car and slowly he convinced himself that it had just been a dream. He swallowed hard. A Coke would have hit the spot right then.

"I had the worst dream of my entire life." Cash sighed, shuddering as he did.

"What happened?" Quinn asked, still perched behind Jake.

"I'll tell you guys later... maybe."

Jake ran a finger down the back window, causing a rivulet of condensation to make a fast track to the bottom. "Jesus, it's like we've had an orgy in here."

"Don't get your hopes up, Casanova," Quinn said in a husky whisper next to Jake's ear.

"Cash, is Quinn smiling? Tell me she's smiling."

Cash looked at him, said nothing, and flashed his eyebrows.

Jake sat up. "What the hell is that supposed to mean?"

Cash shrugged.

"Shit! What time is it?" Quinn grabbed Jake's wrist to look for a watch.

"You know Wynter is the only one who wears a watch," Jake said.

Quinn wriggled out from beside Jake and opened the driver's side door. She stretched and leaned on the side of the car.

Cash jumped out of the passenger side. "Sun rises at six." He looked east and formed a fist. He extended his arm toward the horizon and counted two fist widths until he reached the sun. "It's probably close to eight."

"Shit, I'm going to be late." Quinn used her shirt tail to clear the driver's side window of condensation. "Jake? Be a darling and wipe the back window? And you're also going to have to move your leg. Your cast is cramping my style."

Jake peeled off his T-shirt and wiped the back window. He handed it to Quinn. "Wipe the windshield, but I'm going to need it back."

Quinn's eyes traveled across Jake's chest. For a teenager who sat around playing video games, his body looked surprisingly toned. "We'll see about that..."

"My clothes. Give them to me. Now." Jake spoke in his best Arnold Schwarzenegger accent. "You don't want me to catch my death."

A flashback of his recent dream ripped through Cash's mind. He shivered but Jake and Quinn were too wrapped up in each other to notice. He helped Jake move his leg to the back seat.

"Here you go, Adonis." Quinn tossed back his T-shirt.

"Moist and dirty," Jake said with a devious grin. "Just like I like it."

Quinn rolled her eyes and started the engine. She backed out of the parking stall and merged with interstate traffic heading west.

Cash switched on the radio. Van Halen's "Panama" rocked through the VW's speakers.

"Perfect," Quinn said. "Turn it up."

Cash did, and even though the music worked wonders to lighten the mood, he still found himself reliving his nightmare and his feelings of guilt and inadequacy. Right then and there, he vowed to himself that he would protect Wynter until the day he died.

QUINN ROLLED INTO the last remaining parking stall at Finn's, pulled the emergency brake, and shifted to neutral. She looked at Cash and grinned. "You want to guess what time it is now?"

Cash pretended to think for a moment. "Hmm. Close to nine?"

"Brill! What other secrets do you have up your sleeve?"

"I'll never tell." Cash popped his seat belt off and turned in his seat. "How you doing back there, Jake?"

"My leg is aching, and not in a good way. No offense, Quinn, but I can't wait to get out of this car."

"None taken," Quinn said. "But you might have to suck up to Blue Belle later. She's sensitive."

Cash stepped out of the car and pushed back the passenger seat to let Jake move up front. "So back to the hospital after work? Meet you here?"

"Yup." Quinn extended a thumbs up.

Jake wobbled to his feet and tapped Cash's shoulder. "Don't worry, dude. Wynter's going to be alright. I can feel it."

Cash pulled him into a quick hug and patted his back. "Thanks, man." He walked toward the front of the store where Finn stood waiting.

Jake slid the seat back and ambled into the front, watching Cash. "You think he'll be okay?"

From the VW, Quinn and Jake watched Finn give Cash's shoulder a squeeze and a firm pat.

"Totally," Quinn said. "That's a side of Finn you don't normally see, huh?" Without warning, she leaned over Jake's lap and waved at Finn. Her straight black hair tickled his nose on the way by and he detected a light scent of soap. Jake fought against his urge to sneeze. The last thing he wanted to do was spray spit into her hair.

"Thanks for fixing my Belle!"

Finn stooped and cocked his head to one side as if he couldn't hear, then waved her off and laughed. "Any time, doll," Finn called back. Then he followed Cash into the store.

"Huh. He called me 'doll.' " Quinn moved back across the center console and gazed into Jake's eyes. "What do you think, Jake. Am I a *doll?*"

Jake gulped and swallowed hard. "Yup. In the best way possible." He straightened his baseball hat on his head and snuck a peek at the swell of her breasts under her T-shirt.

"Good." Quinn planted a kiss on his lips and smiled at him. "I'll have you home in five minutes. I just might end up being on time for work."

True to her word, the Beetle pulled up in front of Jake's house a short time after. He didn't care if it had been five minutes. He would have gladly stayed in the car for another hour if he could.

"What are you going to do today?"

"Besides get off this leg, I don't know," said Jake. "I'll definitely keep an eye out for that fucking Barracuda."

"Okay. Are you sure you don't want to go to the hospital tonight?"

"I think I better stay off my leg," Jake said. "It's pretty angry. Thanks for the lift home, Quinn."

"Any time." Quinn found his eyes with hers. "And I do mean *any time*, Mr. Nintendo." She smiled and pulled the brim of his baseball cap down. "Call me later."

Jake slid his crutches out from the back footwell and hobbled up the front walk to his house.

Quinn waved at him and tapped the horn as she made a U-turn in the middle of Mortimer Avenue and headed back to Main Street. After a short detour at home to change into her work uniform, Quinn arrived at Stedford Plaza.

"Note to self. Get a clock for the car," she said to the empty Beetle. The silence spoke back to her all at once as Quinn realized that Blue Belle had never needed a clock because Wynter was always close by with her wristwatch. She looked at the empty passenger seat and burst into heavy sobs. She allowed herself to cry until the tears dried up.

She flipped the visor down and framed it on her face. Quinn pulled a tissue from her purse and dabbed her eyes, her eyelids red and puffy. She was doubly glad she hadn't had time to put mascara on when she changed for work. Fortifying herself with a cleansing breath, she stepped out of Blue Belle and forged a path toward the plaza.

Quinn pulled open the doors to the main concourse and saw that all the stores still had their security gates drawn. She wouldn't be late after all. Still, she hustled through the emptiness toward the food court.

As she passed Shooters, a voice called out from the darkness behind the store's security gate.

"Quinn!"

Startled, Quinn stopped and looked back at the store. "Hello?"

The security gate rippled as Daytona wedged her body through the gap on one side. She waved Quinn over.

"Hey, Daytona."

"Hey." Daytona scrutinized her closely. "How's it going?"

Quinn avoided her gaze as best she could for fear of crying again. It wasn't a reaction she wanted to share with Daytona. "You know how it is when your best friend's in a coma." She paused and Daytona chose to let the silence ride. "It's rough."

"I'm sorry," Daytona said. "Any idea when she'll wake up?"

Quinn had never liked Daytona and she took the question in the worst possible way. "Why? So she can come back to work so you won't have to?"

Daytona took a step back like she had been slapped. "No, I was just curious... *concerned*. Just in case Vinnie asks."

Quinn fanned her face and blinked away any tears threatening to fall. "Sorry. The doctors don't really know for sure. But she's not on a breathing machine, so that's good."

Daytona nodded, then in an unexpected rush, she stepped forward and hugged Quinn. "I'm sure she'll wake up soon. Nothing can keep Wynter down."

Initially Quinn wanted to push her away, but the hug felt good, even coming from Daytona. It was exactly what she needed. And she heard sincerity in Daytona's words.

"Thanks." She pulled away and glanced back toward the food court. "Look, I got to get to work, so…"

"Sure," Daytona said. "But there was something else I wanted to tell you."

Quinn gave her a sideways look. "What?"

"You know who Monty is?"

"Who doesn't," Quinn said with disgust.

"Well, he was sniffing around here yesterday, asking about Wynter."

Daytona had captured Quinn's attention. "What did he want?"

"Said he had some questions about photography that only she could answer," Daytona said. "Seemed shady to me. Thought you'd want to know."

"Thanks. And sorry for freaking out on you."

"No problem."

Quinn squinted into the shadows behind the Shooters security gate. "Where's Hunter?"

"Probably still asleep."

Quinn took slow backward steps toward the food court. "You could do better, Daytona."

"In this town? Yeah, right." Daytona laughed. "At least the sex is good."

"There is that." Quinn turned and quickened her pace. "Later."

An image of Jake with his baseball cap and coy grin popped into Quinn's head, surprising her. Even without knowing if Jake was good in bed, she was certain that Daytona was wrong. Newhaven had its fair share of good guys, and Jake was one of them. Knowing him gave her comfort as she began a day that would be filled with anxiety.

Quinn's thoughts soon returned to Wynter. Would she be out

of her coma by the time she and Cash returned to the hospital? In ten long hours she'd find out but it felt like a lifetime away.

CASH HAD FELT scattered all day, his concentration in short supply. Finn had noticed and so had many Gas N Go customers. It was becoming a problem.

Cash could not wait to get back to the hospital. But as the minutes passed, no matter how hard he tried, his brain cycled back to worry. Had Wynter taken a turn for the worse? Would Nolan or Madeline tell him if she had?

Making his anxiety worse, Finn had checked up on him constantly, which was the complete opposite of what Cash was used to.

Near the end of his shift, Finn took Cash aside. "Son, can't imagine what's going through your head today, but—"

"It's nothing, Mr. O'Connor," Cash began. "I—"

"Bullshit." Finn placed his hands on Cash's shoulders and locked his wise gaze on him. "Shut up and listen. Take some time off, for your friend..." The old man tried to recall the name.

"Wynter."

"I knew it was a season. Bloody hippie names." Finn placed his arm around Cash's shoulder. "You can't be here if your head's over there." He waved his free hand in a random direction. "Understand?"

"It's no problem," Cash said.

"It isn't 'til it is." Finn gripped Cash's shoulder firmly. "Your job'll be here when you're ready."

"Thanks, Mr. O'Connor." Cash managed a small smile. "I think I'm going to be okay though."

Finn shook his head and grumbled. "I hope you're right. But

I'm watching you." He pointed at Cash as he shuffled back toward the garage.

Cash detected a subtle grin from the old man. "Got it."

As if on cue, Quinn rolled Blue Belle into the nearest parking stall.

Finn glanced back at Cash and at the VW through the grimy store window. "Well, if it ain't China doll." He waved his hand at him. "Scram. You're useless today."

Cash locked the register and made his way outside. "Thanks for picking me up, Quinn."

"Sure." Quinn still wore her FreshWhip uniform but there was a pile of clothes strewn in the back seat. "Hop in. We got to make up for lost time."

Cash barely had time to buckle his seat belt before Quinn threw Blue Belle into reverse and backed out of her parking space. She shifted to first, cranked the steering wheel hard left, and Cash was sure he heard tires squealing as Quinn drove toward Main Street and the overpass beyond.

"Holy shit, you weren't kidding." Cash had gripped the door handle without realizing it. "Ever thought of racing professionally?"

"No, but I'll add it to my list of things to do before I die."

Cash watched Newhaven shrink in the side mirror as the little car merged onto I94 East. "Please make sure that's not today," he said to himself.

Quinn blew her bangs out of her eyes. "I've been going mental all day. Couldn't wait to get out of there. How about you?"

"Yeah, I've been worrying all day, too." Cash watched the VW's speedometer edge past seventy miles per hour and felt his anxiety rise. "Think you could slow down a bit? Don't want to get pulled over."

"Oh shit. Sorry," Quinn said. "I didn't even notice. I'm just thinking 'get to the hospital as fast as possible.'" She reduced her speed. "How about some music?"

Quinn flipped on the radio. Ultravox was singing about memories, the advancing storm, and a life gone by. They glanced at each other for a second, then said in unison, "Nope." She switched the radio off.

Quinn and Cash completed the rest of the journey to Halston Medical Center listening to the mechanical drone of Blue Belle's engine. But both of them were thinking about what they'd find at the end of the road.

As BLUE BELLE sped past the seemingly endless grasslands and random shrubs, Quinn's speed crept back up to sixty, then sixty-five miles per hour. Cash had taken on the job to remind her of her lead foot. Quinn could have been a jerk about it, but to Cash's surprise she took his reminders in stride.

Traffic on the rail-straight interstate was sparse at six o'clock in the evening. Quinn could have locked the steering wheel in one direction and had a snooze.

The monotony of the landscape had lulled Cash to nod off a couple of times, and if he could fall asleep, he wondered if the same could happen to Quinn. He doubled his efforts to make sure she stayed awake.

"We should've eaten before we left." Quinn groaned. "Are you hungry?" Before Cash could respond, she answered her own question. "I'm starved. We could hit the cafeteria at the hospital."

Food was the last thing on Cash's mind. His stomach twisted in worried knots. "I'm not really hungry."

"Maybe you'll change your mind by the time we get there."

Quinn's relentless speeding had an upside: they managed to shave almost fifteen minutes off their travel time. At half past six, they found themselves trolling the hospital parking lot for a space. Several minutes later their efforts were rewarded, although the parking space was as far away from the entrance as it could get. Quinn backed into the space and turned off the engine. The smell of warm rubber and oil drifted through the car as the engine ticked and cooled.

Quinn threw off her seatbelt, pushed the driver's seat forward, and crawled into the back. "Got to change. Eyes forward, no peeking."

Cash directed his gaze across the parking lot and wondered how many of the cars in the lot belonged to family and friends of patients. Now he was one of them. His eyes counted up to the fourth floor and scanned the windows for something or someone familiar.

The sound of rustling clothing and the occasional labored breath from the back seat pulled Cash back to reality. He glanced at the side mirror and saw the soles of Quinn's Vans propped against the glass behind him. "You alright back there?"

"Remind me to never buy jeans one size too small again."

"Uh, okay." Cash heard a finalizing *zzzzip* from the back seat. "Why would you do that anyway? Sounds like torture."

"If you have to ask..." Quinn bent herself like a pretzel to get out of the car. "Let's go. Don't forget to lock the door." She grabbed her purse and locked and closed her door. By the time Cash had done the same, she was already weaving her way between parked cars, making a line toward the front entrance.

The significance of Quinn's tight jeans made itself clear as Cash ran to catch up. The denim hugged her hips and legs and accentuated her confident stride. Cash smiled to himself.

Quinn eyed him curiously. "What is it, hot shot?"

Cash shook his head. "Oh, nothing."

"You feel like eating now?"

"Not really." Cash placed his hand on his abdomen. "Stomach's not behaving."

"I got to get something, or I might end up ripping someone's head off."

"This is the place to do it." Cash placed his hands on his neck and pretended to choke himself. They both laughed.

"I'll meet you up there."

"You remember where the room is?"

Quinn gave him a sideways look of disbelief. "Of course. Just because I buy jeans that are too small doesn't make me dumb."

"Just makes you uncomfortable."

Quinn swatted his shoulder. "Go. I'll see you in a bit." She disappeared into the cafeteria.

Cash followed the main entrance to the elevators. The doors opened and a group of people filed out, some stifling their sobs. He stepped into the elevator and chose the fourth floor. As the doors closed he watched the people in the foyer hugging and consoling each other, and in his mind he wished them well.

Cash rode the elevator up alone. When the doors opened to the familiar corridor of the fourth floor, he froze. He could see the door to Wynter's room and the nurses' station nearby, but fear of what he would find held him back.

Would Wynter still be asleep? What if her condition had worsened? What if she wasn't there at all? What if... The questions raged in Cash's head and before he realized it, the doors to the elevator slid closed. Everything felt final and Cash panicked.

He pounded on the doors, then on the open button but the elevator began its descent. Cash hit the button for the third floor. The elevator stopped with a jerk and the doors opened as if by divine intervention.

He stepped out. The entrance to the chapel was only a few steps away. He contemplated going in to catch his breath but his need to see Wynter won out, despite his worries about what he would find. Cash heard the elevator doors close behind him as he made his way to the stairwell.

His footsteps echoed in the small space as he ascended back to the fourth floor. Taking the stairs had gotten his muscles moving and his blood flowing, and had an unexpectedly calming effect. He decided to take the stairs more often.

Cash took a deep breath and pulled open the door to the coma ward.

One step at a time.

Cash proceeded down the corridor until he stood outside Wynter's room. He waved at a nurse he didn't recognize seated at the nurses' station and she waved back and gave him a thumbs up. She apparently remembered him.

He pushed the door open and stepped inside. The same machines, tubes, and wires surrounded Wynter, like she was caught in a web. Her eyes were closed, just as they had been when he left almost a day ago. It appeared that he had worried for nothing.

Cash sat in the familiar orange vinyl chair from hell and placed his hand on hers. To his surprise, her hand was warm. He reclined as comfortably as possible and closed his eyes. Perhaps if he was lucky, he'd be able to sleep.

COOL AIR DRIFTED over Cash's face. It was a welcome change after the ride from Newhaven. Even traveling at sixty-five miles per hour, the wind whistling through Blue Belle's vent window hadn't done much to cool the interior of the car.

Quinn had forbidden him from rolling down the window. "Too much drag," she had said.

His anxiety levels had begun to dissipate once he had seen Wynter and realized she was okay—

Unchanged.

Now he was back, his hand on hers. Cash's world felt right again, his purpose restored. It was as if he was tuned into her life force and nothing bad could possibly happen while he was there by her side.

The breeze kept pulling at him. It no longer felt like the air conditioning he recognized at the hospital. The air took on an organic quality as well as an odor, something different, yet familiar. The antiseptic overtones dropped away and left behind... blueberries?

Cash furrowed his brow and inhaled the cool air flowing over his face. Definitely blueberries, but what—

"Wynter?" He opened his eyes. Directly above, instead of a bank of fluorescent lights and an air circulation vent, lay a vast expanse of blue sky. Long stems of vibrant green grass shot up around his head like cage bars, swaying rhythmically in the breeze. A little too rhythmically.

Cash propped himself up on his elbows. "Wynter?" Instead of a response, the essence of blueberries encircled his head from behind. He rolled over and kneeled, raising himself out of the long grass.

Wynter sat cross-legged, grinning at him, holding a partially eaten blueberry Hostess Fruit Pie. Grass sprouted up around her and through the folds of her white sundress. "I was wondering when you'd clue in. I've been blowing over your face for, like, hours."

"That was you?"

Wynter nodded and took a bite of pie.

"But you're in the hospital." Cash crawled forward until he was able to sit across from Wynter, knee to knee. "You're in a coma. It's pretty serious."

"Relax, Cash," Wynter said. "This is your dream. I'm just visiting."

"My dream..." Cash craned his neck and cast his eyes around wildly. "Where are we?"

"Take a guess."

Cash stood and turned himself around slowly. Eight lines of smooth river rock radiated from where he stood, intersecting with an outer circle thirty feet away. It was just like the medicine wheel at—

"Windspeaker Park?"

"Bingo." Wynter smiled.

God, he had missed her smile.

Beyond the wheel of stone, a river wound its way around the grassy field but never quite encompassed it.

"Where is everything?" Cash waved his hands about. "The trees, the paths... Where's Newhaven?"

"I guess all that stuff didn't make the cut."

Cash sat back down and faced her. "Why am I dreaming about you now? I mean, I've never dreamed about you before."

"What?" Wynter pouted. "I'm devastated."

"No, of course I've dreamed of you." Cash felt his neck burn with embarrassment. "I meant it's never been like this."

"I had to talk to you," Wynter said. "And for a while I couldn't. I think my body had to heal a bit first."

Cash reached forward and took her hands in his.

"You need to stop her, Cash." Wynter's eyes glistened as she focused on him. "You need to stop Jezebel."

"How? I couldn't even keep her away from you."

"You have the power," Wynter said. "To summon."

Cash shook his head. "I don't. I've tried. I can't do it."

"You can." Wynter shook his hands emphatically. "You just need practice."

"What about..." Cash let his eyes drift away.

"Ransom?"

He nodded.

"Stop Jezebel and Ransom will fall in line."

Cash tried to conceal his hurt, freshly exposed again, but Wynter saw it straight away.

"It's all going to work out, Cash," Wynter said. "I promise."

Above their heads the sky darkened to a deep indigo sprinkled with stars. A full moon lit up Wynter's hair from behind like a fiery halo.

Cash found her eyes. "How do I know this is real? This could be just one big bullshit dream."

"That's possible, I guess." Wynter returned his gaze. "Have I ever lied to you?"

Cash shook his head.

"Isn't that enough?"

"No, it's not," Cash said. "You need to tell me something I don't already know."

Wynter fell silent. She nibbled at her lower lip as her eyes worked at a memory. Then a hesitant smile spread across her face. "At the cabin, Quinn had sex with Ransom—"

"I know that, Wynter." Cash grabbed a clump of grass in frustration. "You told me already."

"As I was *saying*, before I was so rudely *interrupted*, Quinn had sex with Ransom... *twice*."

Cash's jaw dropped.

"Yeah. Want to know something else?"

Cash nodded, his throat suddenly dry as sand.

"Quinn doesn't know that I know."

"Then how..." Cash trailed off as he tried to process this new information.

Wynter looked at him expectantly and crossed her arms.

Cash raised his brows. "Ransom?"

She nodded then rocked forward on her haunches. "This coma is doing weird shit to my brain. It's like a bunch of Ransom's memories are my memories now. Remembering *that* one really sucked. Now you need to go. Quinn is waiting for you to spill it." She planted a light kiss on his forehead and covered his eyes with her hands. "You can summon now."

Her whisper drifted with the breeze. Cash took in the scent of her skin, as fresh as the grass that surrounded them, and smiled.

"Hey, Cash?" Quinn's voice echoed like she was speaking through a tunnel. "What's going on?"

Cash opened his eyes to find himself back in the orange chair, his hand still resting on Wynter's, but their fingers intertwined. He looked around the room and stretched, his shoulder joints popping.

Quinn sat opposite him in a chair she had dragged in from the corridor, her stare so intense he could practically feel it.

Cash blinked at her. "What?"

"Spill it," she said.

Back In Black

Cash squeezed past Quinn at the foot of Wynter's bed and paced the small room. The dream had already begun to fade, a fact that frustrated him, but certain details remained.

Quinn followed his movement with her eyes. "She's my friend too, Cash. I'll wait all night if I have to."

Cash turned on her. "What?"

"You know how that song goes," Quinn said. "Sleeping under a spotlight. The Romantics, I think."

Cash returned to the orange chair, sat, and placed his head in his hands.

"I'm on your side. Two heads are better than one."

Cash looked up and revealed eyes wet with tears of anger and frustration, unable to fall. "Have you dreamed of her? Since she fell?"

Quinn shook her head and whispered, "No."

"Her last words to me, back at the bridge, were 'Find me.' " Cash looked at Wynter, the slow rise and fall of her chest and the blips on the vital signs monitor the only indications that she was alive. "I found her, but in my dreams. She says I'm a summoner." Cash squinted through his tears. "What does that even mean?"

"It means that you can bring someone out of your dreams. Create a dreamwaker."

"Just people?" Cash wiped his eyes before the tears had a

chance to breach. "What about other stuff, like money, or animals?"

"The thing is, the person you bring out has to want to come out," Quinn said. "Last I checked money can't tell you what it wants. As for animals, I really don't know." She shrugged. "But remember, as real as it was, it was still a dream."

"No, Wynter was real." Cash locked his gaze with Quinn's. "As real as Ransom. She gave me proof."

"What are you talking about?"

"I know about you and Ransom," Cash said. "Wynter told me a while ago. But..."

Quinn tilted her head at him, alarm showing in her eyes. "But... what?"

"You did it twice with Ransom."

The color drained from Quinn's face.

"I'm guessing from your reaction that you never told Wynter that."

Quinn sighed and hung her head. "No. I was hoping to take that secret to my grave."

"Sorry to burst that bubble." Cash sat forward. "But she was real, Quinn. How else would I know that?"

She nodded. "Ransom always said that his memories were separate from the person he's connected to." Quinn's eyes cleared, as if she had just reached an epiphany. "Maybe that's only when he's in the waking world..."

"I don't know. She did say the coma is messing with her mind. It's all pretty confusing," Cash said. "Still, she knew your secret."

"Did Wynter say anything else?"

"It wouldn't have been Wynter if she hadn't." Cash smiled. "Take a guess."

"Reunite her with Ransom?" Quinn shifted in her seat uncomfortably. "Sorry. She's stuck on that troublemaker pretty bad."

"I know, and in a way, you're right. The answer always involves him."

Quinn followed the dots. "Jezebel."

"Yup. We have to stop her."

"Feels like déjà vu."

Cash nodded. "With one big difference. We have to do it without Wynter."

The two of them turned to look at Wynter, unconscious in her hospital bed, half expecting her to give them a sign, but they were met with silence.

A nurse entered the room. "I'm afraid visiting hours are over for today."

"But I've got clearance." Cash protested and held up his wrist band.

"I know you do, Cash, and we certainly admire your loyalty and dedication." The nurse picked up Wynter's chart and made some notes. "But you need some time away. Keep things balanced." She returned the chart to the end of the bed and placed a gentle hand on his shoulder. "It's not like Wynter's holding you for ransom."

This time Cash's face turned ashen. He looked at Quinn and motioned at the door. "Let's go."

The two of them bolted down the corridor, unsure of their next steps, but certain that they had to leave to find them.

QUINN AND CASH spent the ride home from the hospital immersed in their own thoughts. Despite the need to reunite Wynter with Ransom and stop Jezebel, their talk at the hospital had opened old wounds. Her betrayal of Wynter rose to the forefront of her mind. Her guilt had never left her entirely. Her tryst with Ransom had been so hot, it had permanently burned a spot in her memories, for better or worse. But she couldn't let it happen again. She had made a promise.

After dropping Cash at his trailer, Quinn found herself at home, standing in the kitchen, her brain in a conflicted fog with no memory of making the short drive home. Her stomach grumbled and broke her out of her trance.

She fixed herself a small plate of nachos with hot salsa and real grated cheddar, not that melted Velveeta crap they used at the Starlite, and carried it up to her room. She had her snack half-eaten by the time she plopped herself on her bed.

Quinn cocked her ear to one side and listened for her parents. The silence of the house returned no surprises. Her parents had always been deep sleepers, a fact that would have come in handy if she had any kind of a love life.

She finished her nachos, brushed her teeth, and peeled off her clothes, replacing them with fresh panties and a T-shirt with "Here comes trouble" written across the front.

Dreams aren't real. Everyone has fantasies.

Quinn's spicy snack had made her eyelids heavy. There was something about a quiet house that amplified her thoughts and recent memories. She found them hard to ignore.

How can I break a promise if what I'm doing isn't real?

She lay back on top of the bedspread and was asleep within minutes of her head hitting the pillow. Her exhausted mind made room for the dreams and her memories did the rest.

Quinn stood on the deck of her cabin and looked out across Lake Gilberg, its surface a near perfect mirror reflection of the boxelder maples on the distant shore. The sun warmed her bare legs and back. Her dreaming mind had left some details unaltered. Her clothes were the same as the ones she had fallen asleep in.

She peered down at the front of her T-shirt and read the upside-down words out loud. "Here comes trouble? Ha. Not likely."

"I might disagree."

Quinn felt a shiver move up her spine and raise the hairs on the back of her neck. She would know that voice anywhere, and loved and hated it at the same time. She turned and saw Ransom standing a short distance away in his signature black hoodie and jeans. His feet were bare, and Quinn found herself imagining what he was wearing underneath.

"Ransom!" Quinn cast her eyes side to side without even thinking about it, her guilty conscience making itself known even in her dreams. Nothing but nature surrounded them. "What are you doing here?"

Ransom shrugged. "I don't know. This is your dream. You tell me."

Quinn felt her undeniable attraction to him, yet she resisted. "You can't be here."

"Why?"

"You *know* why." Quinn checked her surroundings again and lowered her voice. "We can't... you know... have *sex*."

Ransom took a step forward and shrugged at her. "We're just talking."

"I promised Wynter I wouldn't—"

"Wouldn't what? Dream about someone? Or fantasize about them?" Ransom narrowed his eyes and studied her. "What you did before to Wynter was real, and *really* bad. But in your dreams, anything goes."

Quinn's mind fought against her promise to Wynter. What Ransom said made sense, but it felt wrong. "Not anything... right?"

Ransom narrowed his eyes seductively and gave her a quirky, lopsided smile.

Her heart melted in an instant. Ignoring her earlier misgivings, Quinn bridged the gap between them and wrapped her arms around Ransom's chest. She closed her eyes and breathed in his essence. He smelled as intoxicating as she remembered. "God, I've missed you."

"Excuse me?" Ransom's voice had changed. It sounded deeper. And there was something else…

Old Spice?

Quinn cracked open one eye and spotted a gold star pinned to the left side of Ransom's hoodie, except the hoodie was tan instead of black and she could see a breast pocket with a pen poking out the top. She felt two strong hands take her by the shoulders and move her backward a step.

"Anson?"

"Yes, Quinn." Anson crossed his arms against his chest. "I'm all for hugs, but that seemed a little too… close for comfort, dressed the way you are and all."

Quinn realized that the hem of her T-shirt ended mid-thigh, barely long enough to conceal her panties. She tugged on the hem self-consciously before Ransom's voice echoed in her head.

In your dreams, anything goes.

Quinn grasped the hem of her T-shirt and pulled it down past her knees. Then her devious nature took over. She stopped and raised the hem up. The T-shirt shrunk in length, became a crop top, and exposed her smooth midriff and her panties below.

"Here comes trouble," she said grinning before she launched herself at Anson.

"Whoa, Quinn." Anson stepped backward, his hands up, palms forward. "Whoa."

Quinn ignored him. "This is *my* dream. I can do what I want." She hooked her fingers into his shirt and pulled it open, sending buttons flying and bouncing across the deck. She ran her hands across his chest. "I just want to fuck you. I'm sure Mercy won't mind. And I won't tell anybody."

She kissed his chest, but instead of skin, Quinn felt fabric brush against her lips.

"What the hell, Queenie."

Quinn backed away and looked up to see Zain staring at her, a mixture of surprise and confusion on his face. Even though the dream was hers to control, it became clear that her subconscious had been fighting her every step of the way.

"What do you mean?"

"I mean, shouldn't you be with someone your own age?" Zain had rollerskates on and alternated his legs, rolling back and forth.

Quinn stepped toward him and slipped one of her hands into her panties. "Don't you want me?"

"I'm at least ten years older than you," Zain said. He rolled backward but his eyes remained focused on her concealed hand moving under the fabric of her panties.

"I like older guys."

"I'm sure you do."

They continued their dance of avoidance, Quinn's one foot forward and Zain's one foot back. "Don't you like young girls?"

Zain shook his head slowly. "Uh, not this young."

"Your eyes say something different."

And this is my *dream.*

Quinn pushed Zain backward. His rollerskates hit the side of a king-sized mattress and they both fell. She straddled his waist and pulled Zain's T-shirt up over his head. But instead of Zain's face popping out of the neck hole, it was Jake smiling back at her, and his leg cast was gone.

Suddenly modest, Quinn pulled at her T-shirt and lowered the hem back to her knees. It shouldn't have mattered. She was horny and physically Jake was a guy just like any other. But it felt different with him there and the realization hit her all at once. She wanted it to be different with Jake.

"Hi." Jake waved at her, wearing a goofy smile. "Does trouble come here often?"

"Most definitely." Quinn smiled, leaned down, and kissed him. "Want to see my room?"

Jake nodded. "Sure."

Quinn inched back up onto her knees and asked Jake to do the same. "Ready?"

Jake smiled at her, taking all of her in with his deep, brown eyes.

"Hold on to me." She kissed him again. "For luck."

"Star Wars?"

Quinn laughed and nodded. Then, reducing her voice to a whisper, she said, "Here goes nothing."

Both of them rocked backward and fell through the mattress, into vast darkness. Quinn could sense the world spinning around them but there were no visual cues she could use to ground herself. Just before dizziness could sink its teeth into her, they landed abruptly, square in the middle of her room.

"It worked. We're here," Quinn said, half amazed. She had actually made a dreamwaker version of Jake. She still straddled his waist and could feel a certain hardness down below his belt line. "Are you feeling dizzy?"

"Maybe a little bit," Jake said, "but in a good way."

"Me too." Quinn leaned down and left a trail of kisses up his chest, along his neck and ending at his lips. "I think we left off right about here."

"I think you're..." Jake let her cut him off with a kiss.

Quinn forgot all about her thoughts of Ransom and the rest of her secret crushes. Jake was it. She had been wrong about him for so long. A dreamwaker version of Jake had certain advantages, but she could hardly wait for the real thing.

JEZEBEL PULLED INTO an alley close to a Pepperia take-out joint in Sanwood, an hour west of Newhaven. The smell of Mexican spices and Italian herbs floated from the open door of the fast food joint.

Roxy twisted in the passenger seat so she could see Jezebel and Ransom. "Jazz, you still haven't told us why we're here." She looked back at the storefront. "It's a long way to come just for pizza."

Jezebel side-eyed Roxy and thrust her hand across the center console as if she was going to throw a punch. Roxy flinched as Jezebel's knuckles sailed past, barely missing her jaw. She popped open the glove box and pulled out a plastic bag that contained a ball of oily fabric.

Roxy cast an uneasy glance at Ransom in the back seat. Jezebel set the bag on the center console, rolled down the bag's edges, and pulled away the shroud. In the center, gleaming in cold blue steel, sat a semi-automatic 9mm pistol.

"Holy shit." Roxy's eyes bugged out.

"Beauty, isn't it?" Jezebel grinned. "Monty better not fuck with me."

"How many bullets does it hold?" Roxy reached out to touch the gun metal and Jezebel slapped her hand.

"I don't know," Jezebel said. "More than Monty's pathetic excuse for a gun."

"Where'd you get it?"

Jezebel basked in Roxy's excitement. "My mom's bedside table holds one less secret."

"Whoa," Roxy said. "That's badass—"

"So, you got a gun." Ransom slouched in the back seat. "What you going to do, rob the place?"

"No." Jezebel picked up the pistol and pointed it at him. "You are."

Jezebel expected Ransom to protest, but he just sat there and stared through her with dead, uninterested eyes. "That's it? That's your plan?" He laughed.

"Got a better idea?"

Ransom shrugged. "Anything's better than committing a felony."

"Shut the fuck up." Jezebel scowled at him. "What do you know?"

"Apparently nothing."

"You got that right." Jezebel sized Ransom up, as if she was having doubts. "Now shut your mouth and listen."

Like most of Jezebel's plans, it was light on details. She removed the fabric and tossed him the empty plastic bag. "You rob the place, the register, and the safe under the counter, then run back down here." She pointed the muzzle of the gun in the direction Ransom should run.

Ransom rolled the plastic bag into a ball. "Don't wave that thing around."

"What do you care?" Jezebel snapped. "You're immortal. Now listen up. You run past us and dump the cash in the car on the way by. We'll pick you up when the coast is clear. Or you can off yourself, but it'd be a shame to lose this gun."

Jezebel admired the gun's clean lines, then pulled the magazine out, confirmed it held bullets, and slammed it back into the grip. She pulled the slide back, loading the chamber and cocking the hammer.

"Ready to rock and roll." Jezebel held the gun out to Ransom but pulled it back when he reached for it. "Don't even think about shooting us. Remember, if we die, so does Wynter."

Ransom scowled at her, took the gun, and placed it in his pocket. He faced Roxy. "Let me out."

Roxy swung open the passenger door and pushed the seatback out of the way. Her concerned eyes met his. "Try not to shoot anyone."

"Yeah," Ransom said, unimpressed. He pulled his hoodie up and strolled out of the alley and into the Pepperia.

Roxy hopped back into the Barracuda, chewing her gum madly. "This is a bad idea, Jazz. I can feel it."

Jezebel ignored her. "I've been watching this place for a while. They make night deposits after they close so they should be flush with cash."

"I hope you're right."

Jezebel gave the idling Barracuda some gas, waking up the engine in an instant. "Our lives are going to change for the better, Rox. You watch."

A shot rang out of the small fast food joint.

Roxy turned to Jezebel in a panic. "Oh, shit."

Jezebel gripped the steering wheel, her eyes sparkling with excitement. "Shut up and keep your panties on."

Two more rapid shots echoed out of the small space, followed by another, before Ransom rounded the building, running straight for the Barracuda. But his approach was more a limp than a run.

His hoodie hung over his left shoulder in shreds, with bits of bloodied flesh and bone exposed through its jagged hole. In his other hand he gripped the pistol.

"Oh my God! Ransom!" Roxy spat her gum out the window. "Jazz, he's been shot."

"Yup. Could've been us."

As Ransom approached the car, Roxy could see the left side of his jeans, soaked red with blood. "Shit, this is bad, this is bad."

"Shut up!" Jezebel eased off the brake and began to roll forward slowly. Ransom handed the gun to Roxy through the passenger window, its hammer cocked for the next chambered round.

"Take it!" he yelled but Roxy recoiled from the gun like it was poison. "Fuck." Ransom dropped the pistol into the footwell, then pulled the plastic bag out of his hoodie pocket and did the same. "Happy?"

"What're you waiting for?" Jezebel yelled. "Go!"

Ransom took a quick glance behind him before limping back towards the dark recesses of the alley. The Pepperia clerk rounded the building, a pump-action shotgun in one hand.

Jezebel slammed the Barracuda into park and pulled herself out of the driver's side window. She pointed in the direction Ransom had gone. "Hey! He went that way!"

"Thanks!" the clerk called out as he raced past. "That fucker's gonna pay."

"Hope you get him." Jezebel slid back into her seat, shifted to drive, and rolled out from the alley. She found a parking space and killed the Barracuda's engine.

"What are you doing?" Roxy stared, her mouth agape.

"Counting the cash, what else?" Jezebel flipped on the overhead light.

"Now? We got to go find Ransom."

Jezebel grabbed the pistol, popped the magazine out, and pulled the slide back, unchambering the live bullet. She dropped it all onto the greasy fabric swatch, then grabbed the plastic bag.

"We got to find him."

"We'll go when the coast's clear." Jezebel pulled a wad of bills out of the bag, her eyes gleaming, and began to riffle through it. "And the coast isn't clear."

Roxy shook her head, slid down in her seat, and crossed her arms. "You really think turning on the light in here is a good idea?"

Jezebel stopped flipping through the bills in her hand. Her jaw stiffened as her eyes met Roxy's. She reached up with a slow, deliberate hand and turned off the overhead light.

"You know what, Rox? You got a point." She turned the ignition and the Barracuda woke with a growl. She backed out of the parking spot and exited the lot.

"What are you doing?"

"Going *home* to count my money."

"*Your* money? I thought it was an even split, between the three of us?"

Jezebel laughed. "Like you did anything except bitch and moan. And Ransom, he's not even real."

"He's real enough to do your dirty work."

Jezebel shrugged as she merged from the on-ramp to the interstate headed east. "Better him than me."

"What if he rats us out?" Roxy saw a flicker of doubt—or worry?—flash over Jezebel's eyes, then it was gone.

"He wouldn't do that," Jezebel said, the cool night air whipping her hair against the headrest. "He loves *Whiner* too much."

Roxy narrowed her eyes. "But what if he *does?* The police are going to be after us."

Jezebel opened her mouth to answer, then closed it again. Ransom confessing wasn't part of the plan. She had banked on Ransom putting Wynter first. She glanced at the bag of money sitting on the center console and hoped it had been the right move.

SHADOWS SHROUDED THE alley behind the Pepperia and surrounding businesses. Despite having no idea where he was going, Ransom was sure of two things: his current body had been mortally wounded and the clerk from Pepperia would catch up to him sooner rather than later.

The wildcard? How he would react.

Moments ago, back at the Pepperia, Ransom had pointed the pistol at the clerk behind the counter and demanded money. He had been in control and knew exactly what to do. The exhilaration of robbing someone energized him, even though he knew it was wrong. The clerk had obeyed and filled the bag with money.

But as Ransom backed out of the joint, he stumbled into a chair and lost his aim. The clerk took that moment of uncertainty to grab a shotgun from under the counter, aim, and fire.

The shot ripped into Ransom's left shoulder, rendering it useless. He raised the pistol in his right hand, aimed, and found that he couldn't pull the trigger. A vision of Wynter toppling backward over the 19th Street Bridge guard rail flooded his mind and he realized he couldn't take a life as easy as Jezebel could.

That kind of experience he could do without. Instead, he aimed just above the clerk's head and fired.

The hanging menu above the clerk's head exploded in a shower of splinters. The clerk flinched as he pumped the forearm of the shotgun and fired another round, this time grazing Ransom's left hip.

Ransom fired one more wild shot into the ceiling before he snaked around the door frame and ran into the alley.

The Barracuda's headlights bored into him like the eyes of a predator lying in waiting. His injuries slowed his progress, but he had run as fast as he could to make the drop.

Once Jezebel had the money, she was gone. Ransom hadn't expected her to stick around, and he knew before the Barracuda was out of sight that he had been abandoned. But he still had to deal with the clerk from the Pepperia as the gaining footsteps of his pursuer grew louder.

His options were limited. He could hide and bleed out, but that might take hours and the alley would be crawling with police a lot sooner than that. There would be an interrogation and that would make his situation, and indirectly Wynter's, more complicated.

He could continue to run, but he found he had neither the strength nor the will to continue. The alley made that choice for him as he turned a blind corner to find a chain link fence separating him from freedom. There was no way he could climb over it with one functioning arm.

Ransom was left with one choice: face the Pepperia clerk. He stood, his back against the chain link fence, and waited for the clerk to round the corner.

In the few seconds he had left, Ransom's thoughts tied themselves in knots. He wanted to do everything in his power to protect Wynter, but the only way to do that involved staying loyal to Jezebel and her insane plan.

The Pepperia clerk rounded the corner. Panting heavily he leveled the shotgun at Ransom. "Where's the money, asshole?"

Ransom raised his hands, palms forward, and nodded back the way they had come. "I tossed it somewhere back there."

"Show me." The clerk eyed him warily in the darkness of the alley. "No sudden moves either."

"I don't have the gun anymore either."

"Shut up and move." The clerk waved the barrel of the gun at him, the end staring back at Ransom like a black, unblinking eye.

Ransom changed his course, shuffling toward the clerk instead of around him. Firing a shotgun from a distance was one thing, but point blank range was quite another. He didn't think the clerk had it in him.

"What are you doing?" The clerk stood his ground. "If you get any closer, I'll blow you in two."

"You'll never find your money if you do that."

"Bullshit. You tossed it somewhere close and you're going to show me where." The clerk positioned himself behind Ransom and poked him in the back with the barrel. "Now move."

Ransom led the way back into the alley. He could see the light of the Pepperia and a small crowd of people forming at the door. Sirens rose up in the night. Police were on their way.

Ransom couldn't be arrested. He wouldn't let them. The only way to keep Wynter safe was to die, and each push forward by the clerk with the barrel of the shotgun reconfirmed Ransom's decision. He spun on his good right leg, grabbed the barrel of the shotgun, and jammed it under his chin, clamping it in place.

"Sorry." Ransom hooked his right thumb into the shotgun's trigger hole and pushed down.

The blast was deafening. Ransom's head disappeared in a spray of bloody flesh and bone. The clerk stumbled and fell backward, glancing his head on a garbage bin.

Ransom's body drifted into a swirling blue cloud before it hit the ground and left the clerk with a story that no one would believe.

Jake had no idea what time it was when he finished saving Pauline from Donkey Kong. Except that it was late. The game room downstairs was the one place in the house, other than his room, where he had a say about the decor.

"No clocks," Jake had told his parents. "They stress me out when I play."

Without the time pressure, he could focus on the importance of game play. If he was going to start his own video game company after graduating, he needed to know his games inside and out.

He had often compared game play to schoolwork. Cash understood Jake's reasoning, but his parents never bought into the idea. They thought it was a big waste of time. They'd change their tune when he became a millionaire.

The midnight munchies had set in. He tossed his controller aside, grabbed his crutches, and walked to the door leading up to the first floor.

"Fucking stairs," he grumbled. Everyone thought having a cast was exciting. Oh, the attention he'd get, filling it with signatures and doodles. No one considered living with one, especially a full leg cast like his. The itches that he couldn't scratch, the funky body odor from his unwashed leg, the fractured, uncomfortable sleep... and stairs, his current nemesis.

One step at a time, fourteen steps in all, brought him to the first floor. He ambled to the kitchen, grabbed a box of Honeycombs from the pantry, and clamped it under his arm. He was about to reach for a bowl when he heard a soft knock coming from the foyer.

Jake stopped and focused on the silence of the house, thinking that his hearing had played tricks on him. But a few seconds later, there it was again.

Knock knock knock.

Definitely not a trick. Jake set the box of cereal on the island in the middle of the kitchen and approached the front door. He peered through the spyhole and saw Quinn standing outside, her arms wrapped around her body. She looked cold, wearing only a T-shirt and denim shorts.

Jake unlocked the dead bolt and pulled open the door. "Quinn? Is everything okay?"

Quinn's face brightened when she saw him. "Now it is."

"What?" Jake shot a glance up at his parents' bedroom door on the second floor. "It's super late, Quinn. I mean, I don't know what time it is but—"

"Shh." Quinn pushed her way through the door, planted her lips on his, and kissed him deeply. She pulled away just enough to speak, her hot breath floating past his face. "I want you, Jake."

Jake rocked back on his crutches, his eyes wide with a combination of surprise and panic. "You want—"

Before he could finish, Quinn had directed him backward toward the staircase that led to the second floor. He struggled with his crutches and hopped on his good leg to keep his balance.

He perched himself on the third step and realized that Quinn had already taken off her shirt and shorts, leaving her in her bra and panties. How she had done this was a question his brain couldn't process.

The sight of Quinn practically naked in the foyer reduced Jake's voice to a low whisper. "Holy shit. What are you doing?"

"I'm doing what I want. And you want it, too." Quinn pushed him back and straddled him. His one-legged jeans, cut to accommodate his cast, lay in a heap at the bottom of the stairs and Jake had no memory of how they had gotten there. Somehow, she had removed them too, bypassing the reinforced plaster holding the bones of his left leg together. The only thing that made sense were his boxer shorts, which were now standing at full attention. Panic, worry, and pure lust collided in his mind as he glanced back up at his parents' bedroom door.

"Lover boy, I'm over here." Quinn placed her hand along Jake's jaw, guided his face toward hers, and kissed him again.

Jake felt her tongue probing his mouth. She tasted like strawberries. He wanted to kiss her back with the same intensity but the image of his parents awake in their room above stopped him. "You can't do this... here. *We* can't do this here."

"Yes, we can." Quinn glanced down at his boxers. "Looks like you're ready to go." She lowered her hips against his and moved against his underwear. "Feels like it, too."

"I want to. God, Quinn, I *want* to... But we can't. Not now."

"Yes. We can. Watch me." Quinn gave him a wicked grin and began to remove her bra.

"Come on, Quinn. I'm serious." Jake swallowed hard. "We're going to get caught. I'm..."

The sight of Quinn's black hair brushing her bare shoulders, her perfect breasts, and the rest of her smooth naked skin sent Jake over the edge. He squeezed his eyes shut as his body tensed and released.

Jake woke with a jolt. The leather sofa in the games room had worked its comfortable magic on him again. "DONKEY KONG's" blocky blue letters stared back at him from the television, casting a dim glow around the room. He was fully clothed, but he sensed a warm stickiness lining the inside of his boxer shorts.

"Goddammit." Jake slumped back onto the leather sofa and sighed. "I'm a virgin even in my fucking dreams." He shut the TV and the NES off, collected his crutches, and began his journey back up to his room.

He paused at the kitchen and grabbed the box of Honeycombs. At least that part of his dream was real.

Once back in his room, he changed into fresh boxers and a T-shirt and stretched out on his bed, munching Honeycombs by the handful. His bedside clock read just after four in the morning. Still fresh in his mind, he replayed his dream of Quinn, but revised it to make sure his parents were gone on a business trip. Yes, that was much better, and he couldn't help but wonder how close his imagination was to the real thing.

WHEN CASH ARRIVED at the Gas N Go, Finn had already opened up. He was sitting behind the register with a newspaper spread over the counter, his grubby coffee mug in one hand.

"I thought I said scram?" Finn spoke without looking up from the paper.

"That was yesterday," Cash said.

Finn looked over the tops of his reading glasses, an accessory he rarely wore in public. "You sure you can keep your head out of the clouds? Matters of the heart can get mighty sticky."

"I think I'll be okay."

Finn nodded. "Alright. I got a brake job waiting in the back." He folded the newspaper up and tucked it under his arm. After an ample gulp of coffee, he leaned forward on the counter and supported his bulky frame with his forearms. "Arrested that girl yet? What's her name?"

"Jezebel?"

"*Jezebel!* Figures."

Cash looked at him, puzzled. "What do you mean?"

"Bah, look it up." Finn took another gulp of his coffee and shuffled to the back door to the garage. "Why haven't they arrested her? She pushed your girl, right? Ran down some kids?"

"She's definitely guilty," Cash said. "But they can't find her. That's what Anson said. Plus, we're not pressing charges."

"What the hell?" Finn paused in the doorway and cast him a dubious glance. "That doesn't make a lick o' sense, son."

"We have our reasons… ones I'd rather not get into if you don't mind."

"Huh. I bet I could find her." Finn pointed to the baseball bat. "Then I'd introduce her skull to Ciara." He waddled into the garage a bit further and disappeared.

"Or maybe I'd take *Killian* out for a spin." Finn's disembodied voice preceded him as he stepped back into the doorway holding a double-barreled shotgun.

"Holy shit." Cash's eyes bugged out. He had never seen Finn's secret weapon before.

"It can drop a grizzly at thirty yards." He kissed the barrel and disappeared once again to put the shotgun back.

"I think we'll let Anson deal with Jezebel when it's time." As if Cash had the power to summon in real life, Jezebel rolled her Barracuda into the gas bay closest to the store and shut the engine off. "No fucking way." He turned to yell back at the doorway to the garage. "Finn, call Anson."

Jezebel laid into the horn.

Finn waddled back into the store. "What's with all the goddamn racket?"

Cash motioned at the Barracuda parked outside. "Call Anson. I'll stall her." He pushed through the door and approached the passenger side of the car. "What do you want?"

"Hey, hot stuff." Jezebel let her eyes wander over Cash's body. "Wanna fill me up?" She held out a wad of bills. "There's more where that came from."

"You're going away for a long time," Cash said through clenched teeth.

"Really?" Jezebel leaned across the center console. "I guess I better get arrested first, huh? We all know *that* isn't going to happen."

Finn emerged from the garage, walking with less shuffle and more intent.

"Anson's already on his way," Cash said.

"Move it, son." Finn didn't wait and pushed Cash sideways. He raised Killian and pointed both barrels through the passenger window at Jezebel. "Get the fuck out of here you good for nothin' hussy."

"Hussy?" Jezebel laughed. "That's a new one."

"Put the gun down, Mr. O'Connor." Cash tried to grab the shotgun, but Finn kept it out of his reach.

"Your business ain't welcome here." Finn rapped the side of the Barracuda with the shotgun barrel. "Come back and I'll blow you to bits. Your precious car, too."

Jezebel's eyes went dark. "You better watch your back, old man." She started the engine and gave it some gas. "Later, Cash."

The Barracuda peeled out of the gas bay, spewing smoke and loose gravel across the small parking lot.

Cash watched the black car fly down the street. "Anson should be here any minute. He'll catch her."

"Didn't call Anson, son." Finn pointed the shotgun at the ground. "It was a job for Killian."

"Mr. O'Connor, you could've shot her."

Finn waved his hand at him. "Nah, this thing ain't loaded, remember? See?" He broke the shotgun open and revealed two live shells, ready to go. He shook them out. "Well, shit. No matter. No one would've missed her."

"That's not the point." Cash locked his eyes with Finn's. "You would've gone to jail."

The old man was back to shuffling as he headed toward the garage. "It would've been worth it."

Cash shook his head, sighed, and walked back into the store. As much as he would have liked to see Jezebel gone for good, there was a right way and wrong way to do it.

Around noon Jake's voice rose up from the doorway of the store. Cash was crouched out of view restocking the chip aisle.

"Hello?"

"Jake?" Cash twisted to look around the shelf.

"Hey, dude." Jake smiled down at him, resting on his crutches. "Working hard or hardly working?"

Cash resumed emptying the box of Hostess potato chips onto the shelf. "I always work hard."

"I know, I know. Just busting your balls." Jake leaned on one crutch to glance into the garage. "Finn around?"

"Probably in the back. Why?"

"When do you take your lunch break?" Jake asked. "We could go to the Plaza. I'm buying."

Cash broke down the empty cardboard box and noted the time. "My lunch break's flexible but walking to the plaza would burn it all up."

"Okay." Jake scanned the shelves as he hobbled through the two short aisles. "Pick your poison and we'll eat outside. I'm still buying."

"Sure," Cash said. "But you don't have to pay."

"I don't mind. You get the next one."

After Cash cleared his break with Finn, the two of them headed out to the curb with a good selection of junk: Cokes, Dakota Style Original Kettle Chips, Tostitos, and Fudgsicles. The ice cream was Jake's idea. Even under the shade of the elm tree out front, they had to eat the ice cream first or risk it turning to chocolate soup.

"Always start with dessert. A rule to live by." Jake tore the wrapper off his Fudgsicle and had finished it before Cash was even halfway. He cracked his can of Coke and ripped into the Tostitos, cramming a handful into his mouth.

Cash watched Jake's feeding frenzy with amusement. "Don't forget to breathe. That's a good rule to live by, too."

"Touché." Jake gulped his Coke and swished it around in his mouth.

"Another rule: Don't do *that*. Especially on a date." In response to Jake's perplexed look, Cash continued. "You know, like you're rinsing your mouth."

"Can't help it. The chips get stuck in my teeth."

"Well, it's kind of gross." Cash glanced at him. "Quinn won't like it."

"Noted." Jake extracted a single Tostito chip from the bag as if he was making a point. "You have any more wicked nightmares?"

Cash closed his eyes and pictured Wynter free of all the medical apparatus that seemed to hold her down like a spider's web. He shook his head and grabbed some chips. "No nightmares, thank God."

"I've been having these super hot dreams of Quinn." Jake turned to Cash, his face drawn and serious. "You think I have a chance with her?"

"Sure, why not?" Cash said. "You're a good guy. You know what you want in life and, like, how to get there. That's more than I can say about myself."

"I've said it before. We need to start a business together. I'll be Wozniak and you be Jobs." Jake's eyes radiated confidence. "Except we do it with video games."

Cash nodded, his lips curving to a subtle lop-sided smile as he pictured some form of success in his head. "But I reserve the right to not be an asshole."

"Thumbs up to that."

The two sat without speaking for a moment, punctuated only by the munching and slurping of junk food consumption.

Cash felt thankful for moments like this, to have a friend like Jake that he could just exist with, without the desperate need to fill the silence all the time.

"You want to come over for dinner? Play some Nintendo?"

Again, Cash thought of Wynter, alone in her bed back at the hospital, her consciousness locked up somewhere in her head. He wanted to see her desperately, but time with Jake was important too. As Finn had so wisely warned him the day before, his head couldn't be here if his thoughts were somewhere else. He decided to check in with Madeline and Nolan instead. Maybe a little break from the hospital would help him figure out what he had to do to bring Wynter back.

"Sure," he said. "I'll come by after my shift. Say around four?"

"Shit, dude, that only gives me, like, three hours to get ready. Think that'll be enough time?" Jake tried to keep a straight face but couldn't do it.

"Just avoid Jezebel and I think you'll be okay." Cash collected the Fudgsicle sticks, wrappers, and the soda cans and placed them in the empty Tostitos bag.

"She's probably hiding like the cowardly bitch she is." Jake pulled himself up using his crutches like it was second nature, toning his shoulders and arms in the process.

"Actually, she showed her face this morning. Wanted to buy gas." Cash picked up the unopened bag of kettle chips. "Finn refused her service and pointed a loaded shotgun at her."

"Shit, no way." Jake's jaw dropped in awe. "Wish I'd seen that. I like Finn. He's badass."

"Yeah, until he ends up painting the parking lot with bits of Jezebel's face."

Jake's eyes lit up. "Ooo. I think I'm going to have to go watch *Dawn of the Dead* again."

Cash chuckled to himself and held up the kettle chips. "I'll bring these with me later, unless—"

"Nah, you better take them," Jake said, trying hard to look suave. "I don't need anything that could minimize the chick magnet potential of crutches."

"Maybe you should go by the plaza on your way home. Work that mojo on Quinn."

Jake pointed at Cash as he flashed a toothy smile. "That's a great idea. Later, dude." He made his way down the sidewalk and waved as he turned down a side street and out of sight.

Cash threw the trash into a garbage can outside the entrance to the store and returned to the counter. He set the kettle chips down, grabbed the phone by the register, and dialed Wynter's trailer.

There was no answer.

But it was just past one o'clock. It made sense that Madeline and Nolan weren't home yet, but not hearing a voice on the other end of the line pressed Cash's worry buttons again.

JAKE APPROACHED THE usual entrance to Stedford Plaza. Moving around on crutches was the pits, but his arms were getting a good workout, and his biceps seemed larger. That's what he kept telling himself. As he pulled open the door, he paused and realized that he'd have to walk past Shooters. Answering Hunter and Daytona's questions about Wynter was the last thing he wanted to do. He was here for one thing only: to talk to Quinn.

He stepped back, walked past the exterior of Minit Prints, and used the doors that entered directly into the food court. The intermingling smells of donuts, pizza and pretzels flooded his nostrils and sent his stomach churning. He could have eaten from all three fast food places and still had room for more.

Jake's eyes settled on the FreshWhip stand in the middle of the food court. Quinn served a lineup of thirsty customers while her boss Deb prepared blender containers and frozen fruit to minimize serving delays. There was always a lineup at FreshWhip. For the longest time, Jake had decided that the long lines were only due to the delicious fruity concoction they served. But that was only partly true now. He saw things differently; saw *Quinn* differently. Maybe Quinn was part of the draw, and he felt a weird twang of jealousy towards the line of customers.

Jake shuffled to the back of the line and waited. Every so often he stole a look at Quinn working behind the counter, always happy to greet customers with a smile. She hadn't realized he was in line yet, and he was fine with that. Surprising her would be nice.

As he waited, his mind drifted, his explicit dreams of the two of them together bubbling to the forefront. It wasn't the best place to replay such personal thoughts, but Jake couldn't help himself. When he felt tingling below his belt, he switched to other thoughts, like how to stop Jezebel. But like a stove burner on high, it took a while to cool down. Next in line, he faced a new task: hiding his imminent erection.

Quinn blinked her long eyelashes in surprise when she realized that Jake was her next customer. She turned her back to him, rubbed her suddenly sweaty hands on her pants, then faced him again, leaning into the counter and raising her shoulders to accentuate her FreshWhip T-shirt in all the right places.

"Hey Jake," Quinn smiled and found his eyes easily. "Um, like, long time no see."

"Uh, yeah." Jake placed his crutches in front of him and twisted forward on his good foot. His cheeks burned but he felt somewhat relieved to see a hint of pink in Quinn's face too. He saw his salvation in the counter's overhang. It would conceal the bulge in his pants nicely. He snugged his body close and forced himself to think of FreshWhip drinks, hoping no one looked too closely under the counter.

"Something wrong with your crutches?"

"What? Oh... No." Jake's mind fought against the devil he had unleashed in his pants. "I'm, uh, just giving my arms a break."

Quinn shifted her eyes temporarily to the customers who had lined up behind Jake, then returned her gaze to him. "What's not to like?"

Jake choked on his own saliva. "Uh, what?"

Deb gave Jake a curious glance.

"What would you like?" Quinn scrunched her brows at him and leaned forward, lowering her voice. "You okay?"

"Yeah, yeah." Jake shook his head, silently cursing himself. He looked up at the menu board. What had looked like an organized list of FreshWhip drinks a moment ago now looked like Greek to him.

Strawberries.

"Tastes like strawberries... Strawberry! Large." Jake's words came out in an inadvertent blurt.

"Um, one large Strawberry Twizt coming up." Quinn exchanged a glance with Deb and stepped away from the counter to prepare Jake's drink.

"Sorry," Jake said. "Didn't get much sleep last night."

Quinn added strawberries, ice, fruit juice, and FreshWhip's secret powder to a blender and turned it on. The mixture swirled like a tornado for a few seconds before she removed the container, but she hadn't waited long enough to let the blender come to a full stop. Strawberry Twizt spilled out the top and painted her T-shirt.

"What's gotten into you?" Deb's question was rhetorical. Anyone could see there was some kind of spark between the two teens.

Quinn shared a quick glance with her boss and mouthed, "I'm sorry." She shook her head, her face red with embarrassment, and handed Jake a napkin. "Did I get any on you?"

"No," Jake said. "At least there wasn't a gremlin in there."

"I loved that movie." Quinn relaxed a bit and poured Jake's drink into a large cup. "But the Santa story? Like, oh my God." She snapped on a lid and added a straw. "That's one-seventy-five."

Jake pulled out his wallet and opened it. To his horror, he saw that he had no money. He had spent it all on snacks for Cash and himself at Finn's earlier.

"Shit. Uh, Quinn?" Jake deflated and felt his face flush red with embarrassment, hotter than before. "Can you spot me two dollars? I'll go to the bank right away."

Quinn cast a quick glance at Deb.

"This better not become a habit," Deb said with a look of disapproval.

"No, ma'am. It totally won't." Jake shook his head emphatically. "I'll pay you back ASAP."

"Chill, Jake. I got it," Quinn said. "But you're going to owe me. Big time."

She winked at him, but even her wink couldn't cool the fire on Jake's cheeks. "Thanks, Quinn." He looked around the food court and spotted an empty chair nearby. Jake sighed. "Can I ask one last favor?"

"Of course," Quinn said with a smile that seemed to glow, the splash of Strawberry Twizt across her T-Shirt long forgotten.

"Would you bring my drink to that table over there?" Jake pointed at the vacant table.

"Yeah, sure." Quinn turned to Deb. "Be back in a flash."

Quinn beat Jake to the table and stood waiting for him, holding his drink.

"God, I feel so useless."

"Sit and enjoy your Twizt, *Mr. Nintendo*. That's an order." Quinn tugged the brim of his baseball hat, gave him a quick kiss on the cheek, and bounded back to the FreshWhip counter.

Jake took a sip of Quinn's sweet concoction. The cool fruit flavor relaxed him as he watched Quinn work. He stretched his Strawberry Twizt for as long as possible without coming off like a stalker. The tempest in his trousers had fizzled out and he realized an important lesson. Nothing kills a mood faster than an empty wallet. But Jake was determined to redeem himself somehow.

OLLIE'S MOVIETYME SAT practically a stone's throw from Monty's house, sitting opposite Sheffield Avenue, deep in southie territory. He passed the defunct drive-in every time he headed home. The area was a well-known hang-out for local kids to party. Having sold thousands of dollars' worth of drugs behind the screen over the past couple of years, today he noticed a new detail that piqued his curiosity.

Monty pulled up behind the storage shed at the drive-in, next to a blue tarp that was a little too small to completely hide the vehicle underneath. Polished chrome rims and black body paint peeked out from under the leading edge. The size and shape matched that of a Barracuda. He was sure of it.

He turned the engine off and glanced at the newspaper on the passenger seat, the headline screaming back at him in black, bold letters. He grabbed the paper and hopped out of the Fiat. Monty strode to the door of the shed to find the lock loops on the exterior were vacant. He pushed on the door but it didn't budge. It was locked from the inside.

He rapped the door with his knuckles. "Come on Jezebel, let me in."

Monty could hear shuffling and hushed whispering from behind the door, but no words in response. He formed a fist and switched to pounding the door.

"Don't make me bust in."

The silence behind the door enraged Monty even more. He leaned back and loaded his legs in preparation to ram the door when a better idea came to him.

He unfolded the newspaper. The headline read: "Brazen Robbery Nets Thieves Thousands." Monty pressed the story up to the small window of the shed.

"You made the front page of the *Sanwood Record*. It'd be a shame if someone were to send an anonymous tip to Anson."

As Monty continued holding the newspaper, he placed his ear on the shed's exterior wall. He could hear frenzied voices, sometimes rising in volume beyond a whisper. His lips stretched into a sly grin knowing that he had gotten under Jezebel's skin.

"Suit yourself." Monty removed the newspaper, adjusted his

sunglasses, and strolled back toward the Fiat, gravel crunching under his shoes. He whistled back. "Anson is goin' to owe me big-time."

He barely had time to get back to his car when he heard the locks rattling on the inside of the shed. Then came the tell-tale squeak of the door's hinges.

Jezebel stood in the doorway with Roxy and Ransom behind her. "What do you want?"

Monty spun on his heels and walked back toward the shed. His eyes zeroed in on the pistol jammed in the front waistband of Jezebel's jeans. "I see you're packin'. What is that, a 9mm?"

"Cut the chit-chat, Monty." Jezebel hooked her thumbs into her front belt loops, close to the pistol. "Get to the fucking point."

Monty raised his T-shirt to reveal his .38 snubnose. "Just in case you're thinkin' of usin' yours." He ran a finger down the hand grip. "It might be smaller and hold less bullets, but it can still blow your head off."

He handed the newspaper to Jezebel. "You're famous." Monty passed her and focused on Ransom. "Or should I say *Ransom's* famous."

Roxy stepped in front of Ransom. "How'd you know it was us?"

Monty motioned at the paper in Jezebel's hands. "Says the thief was male. Also says he *disappeared* into thin air. I only know one person who can do that."

"That wasn't the plan," Ransom said.

Jezebel turned on him. "Shut up!"

"If you had just come back for me, none of this would be happening."

Jezebel pulled out the pistol parked at her waist and pressed the barrel against Ransom's head. "Shut up or *I'll* shut you up."

Ransom shook his head and stepped back into the shadows of the shed.

"You're workin' for me now, whether you like it or not," Monty said, a wide smirk on his face. "Either you sell for me, or you cut me in, or both. Fifty percent to start."

"No fucking way," Jezebel hissed at him.

"Sixty percent," Monty countered.

"Hey," Roxy said. "You can't do that."

He looked at Roxy. "What can't I do? Seventy."

Jezebel pointed her pistol at Monty's head. He had anticipated her move and pulled his snubnose out, aiming it back at her head. They stood in a standoff.

Jezebel gritted her teeth. "Ten percent."

"True, ten percent of your head would be left." Monty stood his ground. "I'll be nice and go back to my original offer. Fifty percent."

The pistol shook in Jezebel's hand. "Twenty."

"My gun's got a hair trigger. If you shoot me, it'll probably go off, takin' you with me."

"Thirty." Jezebel spoke through clenched jaws. "That's my final offer."

"It just *might* be your final offer." Monty slipped off his glasses and hung them on his T-shirt collar. He locked gazes with Jezebel. "Fifty."

"Jazz, just give him what he wants," Roxy said, urgency rising in her voice. "Fifty percent is still pretty good."

"Listen to Roxy." Monty grinned. "It appears she's the smart one."

"Come on, Jazz," Roxy whispered into her ear.

Jezebel sighed and lowered her gun. "Okay. Fifty. But we're not selling your fucking drugs."

Monty tucked the snubnose back into his pants. "That's not up to you. But for now, I'll settle for my half." He held out his hand and beckoned.

Roxy found the bag of money and handed it to Jezebel. She placed half the cash into Monty's hand and dropped the bag by her feet.

"Are you sure that's half?"

Jezebel scowled at him. "Want to count it? You just threatened to kill me. Why would I lie?"

" 'Cause you're a greedy bitch?"

"Then count it."

Monty contemplated the time it would take to count the money and decided to let it go. "I trust you, *Jazz*. Been a pleasure doin' business with you." He walked back to his car and climbed in. "Until next time, I'll be watchin'."

Monty started the Fiat's engine and drove away.

Ransom scoffed as he leaned against one of the shelves in the shed. "Nice negotiating skills."

Jezebel pulled out her pistol, aimed at Ransom's head, and fired. The gun recoiled and struck Jezebel's right cheek, leaving a bloody gouge.

At the same time, the back of Ransom's head burst backward, coating the shelves with a sticky red sheen. The light in his eyes flashed blue, then faded out and all evidence of Ransom drifted away, leaving Jezebel and Roxy alone in the shed.

"Jesus Christ, Jazz. Why the hell did you do that?"

Jezebel returned the gun to her waistband. "I needed to kill something."

Roxy stared at her, shaken and scared. "Holy shit. Please don't do that again."

"It's so convenient though." Jezebel closed the door to the shed, locked it, and sat cross-legged on the mattress. "It's not like I'm killing anything real."

"Sure feels real." Roxy waited for her pulse to normalize. "Hey, did you really give Monty half?"

Jezebel grinned at her. "What do you think?"

Roxy returned a sly smile of her own. "You *are* a greedy bitch."

"You know it." Jezebel dumped the bag of money onto the mattress.

"We're not going to play nice, are we?"

Jezebel laughed and began flipping through the bills.

The rest of Cash's shift passed without incident. On occasion he found himself thinking about his upcoming hang session with Jake, rather than worrying about Wynter. He convinced himself that was a good thing.

Cash found Finn in the garage mid-way through his brake job. The car was up on the hoist and the old man had his tools laid out on the work bench, neat and organized, with pieces of the current brake set next to them.

"I'm heading out, Mr. O'Connor."

Finn looked back at him. "Good. Going to go see Summer, I take it?"

Cash shook his head. "No, just hanging out with Jake."

Finn offered a gruff nod in response.

"Her name's Wynter, by the way."

"Shit. I'm never going to get that right." Finn grabbed a wire brush and began to scrub rust off the rotor mount. "Lock the front and turn on the doorbell before you leave, aye?"

Cash nodded and headed back to the front of the store.

"Son, you going to be in tomorrow?"

Cash glanced back at Finn. "I was planning on it."

"Well, if those plans change, let me know as soon as you can, you hear?"

"Sure thing, Mr. O'Connor." Cash enabled the doorbell and locked the front of the store with his key. He headed toward the Main Street Overpass and the trailer park beyond. Bridges would never be the same since Wynter's accident.

Twenty minutes later, Cash stepped into his trailer. The small air conditioner pumped a weak eddy of cool air into the cramped space, but it was enough to take the edge off the heat. Ernie was already up and in the shower getting ready for work.

"Dad?" Cash knocked on the door to the tiny bathroom, then eased it open a crack. "I'm going to Jake's place."

"Okay, son." Ernie pulled the shower curtain back and poked his head out. "How's Wynter doing?"

"No news. I'm going to change and head out."

Ernie nodded and disappeared behind the curtain. "Say hi to Jake for me."

"Yup. Have a good shift." Cash closed the bathroom door and silently cursed his father for asking about Wynter, even though Ernie was only showing concern. Cash had been successful distracting himself from worry, but now he was back at square one.

He threw on a clean shirt and jeans and was on his way to Jake's house by three-thirty. He had just passed Stedford Plaza when he heard Quinn's voice calling out to him from behind.

"Hey, handsome," Quinn called. "Wait up."

Handsome?

Quinn had never called him that before and Cash wasn't sure if he liked it, considering Jake's interest in her. He stopped and waited for Quinn to catch up before continuing along the sidewalk. He turned and studied her. "Handsome?"

"Just stating a fact." Quinn wore her familiar black and pink FreshWhip uniform. The front had splotches of fruit juice on it. "It's not like I'm trying to jump you or anything." She batted her eyelashes.

"You're a hopeless flirt, you know that?"

Quinn shrugged. "Better than being just hopeless. You going to Jake's?"

"Yeah. Going to play some Nintendo." Cash met her eyes, rich, dark, and slightly exotic. He understood Jake's attraction. "Want to come? I'm sure Jake would love to see you."

"I already saw him today. He dropped by the plaza." Quinn

studied him. "You wouldn't know anything about that, would you?"

Cash shook his head. "All I know is he likes you, Quinn." He thought he detected her cheeks blushing a light pink.

"I'm well aware," Quinn said. "But I'm going to pass tonight. I'm bagged. Had quite the day."

Cash motioned at her shirt. "Blender explode on you?"

"You could say that," Quinn said. "I was obsessing about... Wynter."

"I know how you feel."

Quinn reached Hobbs Avenue and began to break off. "Hey, we've both been thinking about it, but have you come up with anything? You know, like, how to bring Wynter back?"

"Nothing worth mentioning," Cash said.

"Well, I have an idea, but I need to work through it." Quinn took small steps backward. "Call me later... *handsome*."

"Okay... China doll."

Quinn froze and widened her eyes. "*China doll?*"

Cash couldn't tell if Quinn was surprised or angry. His cheeks felt as if they had burst into flames. "Sorry. I meant that in the best way possible."

Quinn tilted her head, narrowed her eyes, and looked a question at him. "I'll take it as a compliment." She studied him a moment longer, which did nothing to cool Cash's face. "Call me later with your idea."

"Okay. Sorry." Cash hurried along Main Street. He could see Mortimer Avenue up ahead. "That's the last time I use one of Finn's nicknames," he muttered to himself.

As the fire in his cheeks faded, Cash wondered what Quinn's idea was. He'd find out soon enough, and hopefully he wouldn't embarrass himself again in the process.

∞

AFTER DINNER, CASH AND JAKE had descended to the games room to continue the Donkey Kong tournament they had begun before dinner. Cash had led the way, followed by Jake as he butt-scooted down the stairs. He had said it was more efficient than navigating the stairs on crutches. It certainly had been less nerve-wracking to watch.

After it was clear Jake was the Donkey Kong champion, they switched to Super Mario Brothers. As much as Cash tried, he couldn't focus on the game. His head swirled with thoughts on everything except the game.

Jake set his controller down next to his crutches. "What's gotten into you, dude?"

"I'm worried... about Wynter." Cash faced Jake. "I talked with her."

"You talked? Wynter's awake?"

"No, I dreamed I talked with her," Cash said. "But she told me things only Quinn knew."

"Like what?"

Cash was almost certain that Jake had no idea about Quinn and Ransom having sex, let alone twice. And Cash wasn't going to be the one to tell him. That was Quinn's job.

"Quinn made me promise to tell no one," Cash lied.

"But you're my best friend."

"A promise is a promise. I'd do the same for you." Cash leaned forward. "But what she said isn't important. The fact that I can talk to Wynter for real, even though she's in a coma... that's important. And..." Cash dropped his head.

Jake waited for an answer from Cash, but none came. "And?"

"I have to bring her back." Cash met Jake's gaze with one of seriousness mixed with despair. "It's all up to me."

"No pressure."

"Tell me about it."

"But we'd help you, me and Quinn," Jake said. "Whatever we can do."

Cash slouched back on the leather sofa. "But it's me who has to sleep and dream and all that. The best person to teach me to pull things out of my dreams is Wynter, and she's in a coma."

"Ah!" Jake held up a finger. "But you can talk to her, right? So can't you get her to teach you while you sleep?"

"I don't know." Cash shook his head in disbelief. "Shit, listen to us. If anyone heard us talking right now, they'd think we were stoned or something."

"I think being able to pull shit from my dreams would be a cool power to have. Just think of the possibilities." Jake's eyes glazed over.

"You can't just pull anything out from your dreams," Cash said. "There's rules."

Jake shook his head and lifted his cast up onto the sofa. "Screw the rules. The first thing I'd pull out would be a suitcase of money. You know, to start my... *our* video game business."

"Pretty sure you can't just ignore the rules, Jake."

"Why not? It's a dream. Anything goes, right?"

"Sure," Cash said. "But that doesn't apply in real life. I'm pretty sure anything you pull out from a dream has to be connected to you in reality somehow."

"What are you saying?"

Cash paused to think of a metaphor that Jake could relate to. "It's like in *The Terminator*. Nothing dead will go."

"Then I'll dream up a suitcase made from living tissue. Long live the new flesh."

Cash did a double take at Jake. "Wait, isn't that a line from *Videodrome*?"

"Good catch, dude." Jake laughed. "There's hope for you yet."

"Well, your suitcase made of living flesh would probably not work. It's not real."

"Real? These are dreams we're talking about," Jake said. "I could pull out Brooke Shields and become an instant chick magnet like you."

"Me? A chick magnet?" Cash laughed.

"Seriously, dude. All the girls I know like you. Even Jezebel and Roxy."

"Now *you're* dreaming." Cash shook his head, but as he did, he recalled his earlier exchange with Quinn and her flirting. Maybe Jake had a point but there was no way he was going to concede.

"You could pull Wynter out of your dream," Jake said. "That shouldn't break any of your *rules*."

The idea was so simple, yet it hit Cash like a ton of bricks. He worked through the rules in his head. Wynter existed in reality, and more importantly, his reality. Plus, Wynter had kissed him, connecting her to him. That had to have some power.

"That's not a bad idea," Cash said.

"You're right, it's a great idea." Jake settled into a self-satisfied smile.

"You're a genius, Jake!"

Jake held his hands in the air. "Finally, he sees the light."

"Look, man. I'd love to stay, but I think I should go."

"Sure." Jake nodded. "You want to test out this idea of mine. Right?"

"Yeah. I think I do." Cash wanted to do something else, too: tell Quinn about Jake's realization. Maybe combined with her idea, whatever it was, they'd have a real chance to bring Wynter back.

"I'll let you know how things go." Cash stood, but Jake remained on the sofa.

"I'm staying down here for a bit." He motioned at the doorway. "I can't face those stairs just yet."

"Want help?"

"Nah, but I expect a full report on my desk in the morning."

Cash laughed. "You got it, chief. Later." He bounded up the stairs, two at a time, pulled on his shoes, and raced down the front steps. Jake's idea might change everything and selfishly Cash hoped it would work. And he had to tell Quinn.

Despite his earlier embarrassment, Cash found himself veering off Main Street and onto Hobbs Avenue. He had briefly considered going back to the trailer to call Quinn, but he couldn't wait that long.

He knew he had the right house when he spotted Blue Belle parked in the driveway. His long strides took him up to the front door of the house. He rang the doorbell before he had a chance to catch his breath.

After a moment Quinn pulled open the door. Not expecting company, she was dressed in sweatpants and a loose T-shirt. "Cash?" She poked her head out of the door and scanned up and down the street. "Are you okay? What are you doing here?"

"You said to call you later," Cash said between gasping breaths. "It's later. We need to talk. It's about Wynter."

"Uh, okay. Want to come in?"

"I'd rather stay outside."

The gears in Quinn's head started to turn. "Wait down by Blue Belle. Give me five minutes."

Cash ran down the front walk to where Blue Belle was parked and placed his hands on his knees. With slow even breaths, he felt his heart rate drop back to normal.

True to her word, Quinn burst out of the front door, now wearing tight jeans and a form-fitting white T-shirt with the Rolling Stones' lips and tongue logo across the front.

"Get in," she said.

Fifteen minutes later, Quinn and Cash slid into a booth at Lucy's Burger Stop. Quinn flagged Rhonda down and ordered a cheeseburger with fries and a Coke.

"I'm starved. Sure you don't want anything?"

Cash shook his head. "I ate at Jake's. Well, maybe a water, please."

Rhonda looked at Cash dubiously. "One... water." She made a point to scribble it down on her order pad. "If you change your mind, just holler." She headed back to the kitchen with their order.

Quinn leaned forward, resting her elbows on the booth's table. "What's going on?"

Cash set his gaze upon Quinn. "I know you've... been with Ransom. Did you pull him out of your dreams?"

Quinn clasped her hands. "I did."

"So, if you could do it, so could I."

"Sure." Quinn furrowed her brow. "What's this really about?"

Rhonda returned with their drinks. "Your meal will be up in a few minutes."

Quinn thanked her.

Cash waited for Rhonda to walk out of earshot. "Tonight, Jake came up with this wild idea. I think it's genius and wanted your take on it."

"Spill. I'm, like, dying here."

Cash took a breath and continued. "Do you think I could pull Wynter out of my dreams?"

Quinn laughed. "You remember when I said I had an idea earlier. That was my idea too, in a nutshell."

"Huh." Cash sat back in the booth. "You and Jake... great minds think alike."

Quinn reached across the table and touched Cash's hand lightly. "You're sweet."

Cash pulled his hand back, either by reflex or by choice. He didn't know which, but Quinn noticed.

"Sorry," Quinn said. "Didn't mean to make things weird. Just being my regular friendly self."

Cash nodded. "So do you think it would work?"

"Maybe. It'd be awesome if it did." Quinn thought for a moment before breaking into a wide smile. "Can you imagine

Jezebel's face when she sees Wynter walking around like nothing happened."

"Yeah, and she'd be a dreamwaker so that bitch couldn't hurt her." Cash narrowed his eyes. "So how do I do it?"

Rhonda appeared and set Quinn's meal in front of her. "Your burger and fries..." She glanced at Cash with mild amusement. "And still a water?"

Cash nodded. "Yes, thanks."

"Okay then. Enjoy." Rhonda hustled back to the kitchen.

"How do I—"

Quinn held up a finger, stopping Cash. "One second." She raised the burger to her mouth and took a large bite. She closed her eyes and sighed as she chewed and finally swallowed. "God, I love Lucy's burgers." She nibbled on a french fry, then pushed the plate toward Cash slightly. "Help yourself, by the way."

"Thanks." Cash picked up one french fry and crunched it.

Quinn sipped her Coke. "Back to your question, how do you pull someone from their dreams. The answer; you don't."

"What?" Cash sat back in the booth, confused.

"The person you want to pull out decides if it happens or not." Quinn took another bite of her burger.

Cash stole another french fry. "Even when it's your dream? And everything in it is made up?"

Quinn nodded as she chewed.

"Weird," Cash said as he munched. "So, the real question is how do I dream of Wynter? I can never seem to dream about the things I *actually* want to dream about."

"I think I know how to find out."

Cash eyed her plate of food. "Well, hurry up and finish."

On any other occasion, Quinn would have taken her time and savored every bite. But Wynter's life was on the line, and she wanted answers just as badly as Cash did. She finished her meal and paid.

Soon they found themselves zooming back toward Newhaven

on I94, Quinn focused on the only source of answers she could think of.

Darkness had settled over Newhaven. The town was more subdued than usual on a Tuesday night in the middle of summer, perhaps due to the unseasonably hot weather.

Gino Vannelli may have sung about black cars in the shade, but Jezebel preferred to take her Barracuda out for a prowl at night. Black on black, she cruised down Main Street, the engine rumbling a low growl. Roxy sat shotgun with Ransom perched on the back seat, leaning toward the center console.

Roxy cast a wary glance at Jezebel. "You sure about this?"

"Don't ask stupid questions." Jezebel glanced at her. "You know how much we made from the Pepperia?"

"You mean what I *stole* for you?" Ransom said.

"Whatever." Jezebel glowered at him through the rear view mirror. "You're the brawn. I'm the brains. Multiply Pepperia by ten times, easy." Jezebel took the Main Street Overpass, the interstate traffic buzzing east and west beneath them. "I've been waiting to stick it to Zain where it counts."

Jezebel turned the Barracuda down Jones Avenue next to Sven Dwarfs Trail'r Park and rolled toward the Starlite SuperSkate sign twinkling in the distance.

"Listen up," Jezebel said. "Ransom, you grab Zain and hold him." She held up her switchblade and engaged the blade. "Use this. Cut his throat if you have to." She retracted the blade with a click and tossed it back at Ransom. He fumbled but eventually caught the weapon and shoved it into his pocket.

Ransom's eyes met Roxy's, both concerned about another one of Jezebel's half-baked plans.

"Me and Roxy will rob the place."

Ransom shook his head. "This is a stupid plan. He knows who we are. How are you going to stop him from calling the police after?"

Jezebel focused on the road ahead with malice. "I know where he lives."

"That's it?" Ransom shook his head. "Jesus. I'm not cutting anyone's throat."

"If you don't, you know what happens," Jezebel said. "Say bye bye to your precious Wynter."

Jezebel pulled over to the curb just past the entrance to the Starlite and cut the Barracuda's engine. The parking lot was empty except for one beat up 1979 Toyota Corolla.

"You'd think he'd drive a BMW or something," Roxy said. "Maybe this place doesn't make as much as you think."

"Shut up." Jezebel looked back at the Starlite in her side mirror. "We'll wait for him up there, just around from the entrance, and jump him." She raised her semi-automatic pistol, popped out the magazine to check the bullets, then slapped it back into the hand grip. "Let's go."

Roxy rolled her eyes at Jezebel's show of bravado, stepped out of the car, and pushed the seat forward to let Ransom out.

"Thanks," Ransom said. "Man, she's full of herself."

"You're just noticing now?" Roxy and Ransom shared a short, subdued laugh.

"What's the hold up?" Jezebel spoke through clenched teeth. "Come on."

The three of them ran up to the side of the Starlite, Jezebel leading the charge. She eased her head around the corner and saw no movement inside.

"Can you see him?" Roxy pushed against Jezebel and tried to look around her.

Instead of a reply, Jezebel raised her middle finger at her.

Jezebel watched the doors and the inside of the rink beyond for motion. Lights in the arena went out, then she saw him. Zain locked the doors to the arcade and flipped a few additional switches, plunging most of the Starlite into darkness.

"Get ready." Jezebel reached to her waist and grabbed the handle of her semi-automatic pistol. She craved the feeling of its cool, steel handle in her palm.

Zain stepped out of the doors, one hand holding a pair of pink rollerskates by their laces and a small leather pouch. He began to dig out his keys from his pocket when Jezebel stepped away from the corner of the wall.

"Freeze, motherfucker." Jezebel aimed the pistol at him.

Zain turned slowly and heaved an aggravated sigh when he recognized Jezebel. "Aw, shit." He jammed his keys back into his pocket.

"Ransom. You're up," Jezebel said, holding her pistol steady.

Ransom rounded the corner and approached Zain. "Drop everything." He locked the switchblade, neon light from the Starlite's sign glinting off the blade.

Zain knew better than to aggravate Jezebel, especially when she had backup. He dropped the rollerskates and the pouch to the pavement. "Look, I don't want any trouble."

"You won't get any if you do exactly as I say." A grin as evil as they come slid across Jezebel's lips.

Ransom stepped behind Zain and held the switchblade against his neck. "I don't want to hurt you," he said in a low whisper. "Just do what she says."

Jezebel kicked at the rollerskates. "Pink? You a flamer?"

"They're for my sister."

"Shut up." Jezebel nodded at Roxy. "Grab the money."

Roxy grabbed the leather pouch by Zain's feet and unzipped it. Her eyes bugged out at the bundles of bills within. "Holy shit."

"Come on, Jezebel," Zain said, making sure not to move. "That's my livelihood."

Jezebel held her aim steady and peeked into the pouch in Roxy's hands. "Where's the rest?"

"I don't know what you're talking about."

"Bullshit." Jezebel stepped up to Zain and placed the barrel of the gun against his forehead. "I know you have a safe in there and you're going to empty it for us. Now move."

Zain protested but felt his skin rub against the knife blade Ransom held to his neck. "There's nothing in it."

"Don't fight her," Ransom whispered in his ear. "You'll regret it."

Roxy pulled open one of the doors to the rink and all four entered. A steady electronic beep broadcast throughout the rink and foyer. A few seconds later a phone began to ring from behind the admission window.

"What the hell is that?" Roxy glanced at Ransom and Jezebel panicked.

"Security is calling," Zain said. "If I don't answer by the eighth ring, they send the cops."

"Move your ass, then." Jezebel forced Ransom and Zain behind the rental counter and next to the admission window.

"Answer it!" Roxy cried. "That's the fifth ring."

Zain reached for the phone but before he picked up Jezebel leaned in close. "No bullshit. I know where you... and your kid sister live. Try anything and she dies."

Zain nearly dropped the handset in his sweat-slicked hand, then brought the speaker to his ear. "Yeah, sorry guys, forgot my deposit." He paused to listen. "Video games... yeah. I won't be long." He handed the handset to Roxy and she placed it back in the cradle.

"Turn off that fucking beeping," Jezebel hissed.

Ransom allowed Zain to turn toward the security keypad on the wall next to the admission window. He keyed in the alarm disable code and the rink fell silent again.

"Finally." Jezebel pointed through a door to the back office and waved her gun toward it. "Now, the safe. And be quick about it." She met Ransom's eyes. "Keep that blade against his neck. I wouldn't mind seeing the asshole bleed." Jezebel glanced back at Roxy and scowled. "Make yourself useful and find something to tie him up with."

Not wanting to disappoint, Roxy scrambled back to the foyer.

Zain balked against Ransom's arm. The switchblade scraped at the skin on his neck and left bloodied marks.

"Let's go." Jezebel locked gazes with Zain. "We both know where it is, now open it."

"I'm telling you, there's nothing in it," Zain said. "Nothing you'd want, anyway."

Jezebel placed the barrel of the pistol under Zain's chin. "I got a bullet that says you're lying."

Zain's shoulders slumped. There was no way he could beat a bullet to the head. "Get your goon to back off the knife for a second. I'm not going to do anything stupid."

"You better not." Jezebel flicked her eyes from Zain to Ransom and nodded. Ransom withdrew the knife and retracted the blade. The hilt remained in his hand.

Zain crouched to the floor and reached under the desk to the safe's permanent location. He spun the combination wheel around and back several times, then pushed the handle down and pulled. The door swung open.

"Empty it on the desk." Jezebel's eyes gleamed with excitement.

Zain removed a stack of insurance papers and set them on the desk. On top of that he placed a checkbook and a small stack of one, five, ten, and twenty dollar bills. He looked back at Jezebel with a look that said, "I told you so."

"What the hell is that?" Jezebel riffled through the bills, her glee melting to disgust.

"Float for the registers," Zain said. "I told you there wasn't much. Might as well take it too."

Jezebel jammed the money into her pocket. "Bring him out." She headed out of the office and ran into Roxy headed in, the leather pouch tucked under her arm.

Roxy held up two long laces. "From his rollerskates. Genius, huh?"

"You actually did what you were asked. That's not genius."

"No, I meant—"

"How are you at knots?"

Roxy shrugged.

"You better be good for your sake." Jezebel led the group back to the foyer. Ransom had placed the knife back at Zain's throat, but it was clear that Zain was in full cooperation.

Jezebel waved the gun toward the seating area in front of the fast food section. Like any other fast food restaurant, the tables and chairs were bolted to the floor. "Tie him under one of the tables. And give me the money."

Roxy handed the pouch to Jezebel and crouched under a nearby table. "Put his back to the support and I'll tie his hands."

Ransom guided Zain to the floor. He glanced at Zain, then shot a concerned look at Roxy. "She's fucking crazy."

Roxy avoided Ransom's gaze. "Shut up." She pulled Zain's arms back around the central table support and secured them with the laces. She pulled the knot tight and Zain winced. "Sorry," she said in a low whisper. "Better than getting a bullet in the head."

Ransom and Roxy stepped away from the table and Jezebel kneeled, leveling her eyes with Zain's.

"You say anything about this to anyone, especially Anson, and your sister dies." She tapped Zain's forehead with the barrel of the pistol. "Understand?"

Zain nodded. "Yes." There was nothing he could do except comply.

"Pleasure doing business with you." Jezebel smiled smugly. "Until next time, have a good night." She stood and ran toward the main doors.

Roxy tugged at Ransom's arm. "Come on." Ransom stood but he kept his eyes on Zain as long as he could.

The three of them ran out of the Starlite and around the corner to the waiting Barracuda. Monty stood in front of the driver's side door, his sunglasses hooked into his T-shirt collar as usual and wearing a smile a mile wide.

"This just might be better than sellin' drugs, eh *Jazz?*" He held his snubnose in his right hand.

"Fuck you, Monty," Jezebel said. "This is my operation."

"And if you want it to stay that way, pay up." Monty beckoned with his left hand. "Fifty fifty."

Jezebel holstered her pistol in the waistline of her jeans and unzipped the leather pouch. She flipped through the bills and was about to pull out a wad of cash when Monty grabbed the pouch and looked inside.

"You did well tonight." Monty eyed the bundled bills and took his version of half. "I'm gettin' used to these paydays. Who's next?"

"Like I'd tell you." Jezebel snatched the pouch back.

"You should, if you know what's good for you." Monty let his gaze travel down Jezebel's body. "It'd be so much better if we worked *together.*"

"Never going to happen."

"Never say never." Monty walked back to his Fiat.

Jezebel's hand went to the handle of her pistol, but Roxy stopped her.

"Don't," she said. "We'll get him some other way."

Jezebel glared at her and pushed her aside, pulling open her door. She dropped the leather pouch in the footwell, sat, and slammed the door.

The Fiat's tires squealed as Monty drove past, waving at them mockingly. The Barracuda's engine rumbled to life like it was going to give chase and eat the little sports car for breakfast.

"Hurry, or she'll leave us behind." Roxy ran to the passenger door and threw it open. Ransom leaped inside and Roxy followed him in.

Jezebel made a U-turn and motored back to her hideout

behind Ollie's MovieTyme, her brain buzzing. Monty had become as big a problem as Wynter and he had to be dealt with.

Sweet Dreams

Zain squirmed under the table, his back against the table support and his hands bound behind him with pink rollerskate laces. He wracked his brain to figure out how Jezebel had discovered he had a sister. He knew Jezebel was smart and dangerous, often a lethal combination, but he had always been careful.

"Until next time," Jezebel had said before hustling out of the Starlite with a few thousand dollars of his hard-earned money. She had acted like nothing had happened, like it would be a regular thing.

No fucking way.

There wouldn't be a next time. Not if he could help it, but first he had to get out of there. If he couldn't lock up within a reasonable amount of time, security would follow up with another phone call. If he couldn't answer, they would send the police. Zain had no doubt that he could come up with a believable story, but he didn't want to tempt fate and possibly endanger his sister's life.

There wasn't much room under the table and if he stayed there all night, he'd be in serious pain by morning. But the more pressing matter was the numbing sensation in his hands due to lack of blood circulation. Soon the numbing would turn to pain and if too much time passed, he would lose his hands. He had to break free.

Zain tried pulling in hopes that the rollerskate laces would break, but the loops cinching his wrists just pulled tighter instead, adding an unbearable throb to his problems.

Using the minimal slack he had built up between each wrist, Zain alternated pulling his hands back and forth in an attempt to build up friction on the laces, but he couldn't keep the laces moving fast enough to maintain heat.

The throbbing pain levels in his hands and around his wrists had increased, fighting for his attention. He concentrated to keep his mind clear, but each time he pulled the laces, the constriction became worse.

In a fog of hurt, Zain experienced a moment of clarity. Working the laces horizontally wasn't working. What about vertically?

Zain shifted his body so the laces restraining his wrists rested against the rounded corner of the table support. He pulled the slack just enough to keep the laces taut and clenched his teeth as the loops bit into the flesh of his wrists.

He raised and lowered his wrists rapidly without pause. Only a small section of the laces maintained contact with the table support, and he soon felt the heat build up between his wrists.

"Come on, you stupid motherf—"

The laces snapped, torn and melted in parts, but the loops still cut deep into his skin. He ran to his office and pulled a pair of scissors from his desk drawer. His hands had turned purple from the lack of circulation and his fingers were numb to the touch, barely responding to his thoughts.

Zain slid the scissor handle onto his right hand and found that he had no strength left to cut through the binding on his left wrist. He forced one blade of the scissors under the tight loops of lace on his left wrist and placed all of his body weight on the handle.

The blades flipped sideways. Too much to cut all at once. He extracted the scissor blade and repositioned it under one strand of lace. This time the scissors sliced through the cord with ease. He felt the laces loosen on his left wrist.

Zain switched the scissors to his left hand and repeated the move on his right wrist. The loops released their tension and fell off his wrists like overcooked spaghetti.

The color in his hands slowly returned to normal, bringing with it intense pain. He worked his hands open and closed to help with circulation, but it was soon clear that only time would be the fix.

Zain feebly collected the checkbook and insurance papers from his desk and returned them to his safe. He kicked the door closed and rolled the combination wheel under his foot.

Jezebel may have been smart in some ways, but she lacked experience. In her haste she had left Zain's keys in his pocket. Lucky for him, he could still lock up. He keyed in the security code and the thirty-second countdown began to beep.

Outside, he worked the keys from his pocket and locked the Starlite entrance. Zain rested his forehead on the glass of the door. Inside he heard the final long beep from the alarm system sound off, indicating the building was now armed.

Safe.

But was his truly safe? Not with Jezebel around.

He glanced at his hands, almost back to their original color. His wrists were a different story. Deep red welts encircled them, leaving him to wonder if they would leave a scar.

He crouched and gingerly lifted the pink rollerskates, tucking one under each arm, and walked to his car. He dropped the skates on the hood, unlocked the driver's side door, then tossed the skates across to the passenger seat. He sat and closed the door.

Zain shut his eyes and breathed deeply. "No, Jezebel, there will not be a next time." His voice amplified in the confines of the car. He placed his hands on the steering wheel. Some of the feeling was back already but his hands and wrists were badly swollen.

In the darkness of his Corolla, Zain worked through ways to beat Jezebel at her own game. He refused to be a victim of her extortion and there was no better incentive to find a solution than knowing he would be keeping his sister safe. That and preventing future theft.

The ideas came fast but one stood out. Despite himself, he smiled, started the car, and drove home, a plan forming in his mind.

QUINN TURNED INTO Sven Dwarfs Trail'r Park and followed the circular road to Cash's pad. The parking space in front of the mobile home was vacant.

"Shit, is it really that late?" Cash searched the VW Beetle's dashboard for a clock. "My dad's already gone to work."

"The night shift must suck," Quinn said.

"Yeah, but it beats living out of a cardboard box."

Quinn pulled into the parking space next to Cash's trailer and switched the Beetle's engine off.

Cash cast his gaze past Quinn and across the grassy field that separated them from Wynter's trailer. "You sure this is a good idea?"

"We have to talk to them sometime," Quinn said. "Might as well be now."

Cash motioned at Wynter's trailer. "The lights are still on."

"Under the circumstances I don't think I'd be sleeping either." Quinn unbuckled her seatbelt and climbed out of the car.

Cash closed his door and jogged to catch up with Quinn. The long, cool grass tickled his ankles under the cuffs of his jeans.

The two of them stood at the base of the steps to Wynter's trailer. Quinn glanced at Cash. "Ready?"

"Sure. What are we going to say?"

"I don't know." Quinn stepped to the landing at the front door. "As much of the truth as possible I guess." She knocked on the door and almost at once footsteps sounded from within.

The front door swung inward, revealing a sleep-deprived Madeline. "Quinn... Cash."

"Sorry to bother you Mrs. LaCroix, but can we talk to you?" Quinn shifted her eyes nervously. "It's about Wynter."

Nolan popped his head around Madeline's shoulder. "Cash? Quinn? Isn't it a bit late to—"

"Come on in." Madeline sent Nolan a knowing look as she ushered Quinn and Cash into the trailer and closed the door. "Want something to drink?"

"No, thanks," Quinn and Cash said, almost in unison.

Nolan directed them to the sofa. "Make yourselves comfortable," he said, taking a seat adjacent. Madeline joined him.

"What did you want to talk about?" Madeline's eyes were upon them, filled with concern.

Quinn looked at Cash. "Do you want to start?"

Cash took a deep breath. "I've talked to Wynter."

Madeline's eyes widened and she shot a quick glance at Nolan. "You did? When?"

"Wait," Quinn said. "Cash, I think you need to back up a bit."

Madeline shook her head. "I don't understand. What do you mean?"

Nolan placed his hand gently on Madeline's knee and addressed the two teens. "Take your time."

Cash looked at Quinn for reassurance and she offered a small smile in response. "Remember when you found that boy in Wynter's room?"

Nolan and Madeline nodded.

"Ransom. That's his name, and he's a dreamwaker." Cash spoke soberly. "He's *Wynter's* dreamwaker. And he was there when Wynter fell off the bridge."

Madeline returned a look of confusion. "What's a *'dreamwaker'*?"

"I'll get to that," Cash said.

Nolan's face hardened. "He pushed her, didn't he?"

"No. Actually he was trying to save her, but Jezebel killed him before he had a chance. But..."

"But what?" Madeline grabbed Nolan's hand.

Nolan leaned forward. "But he's not really dead, is he?"

Cash shook his head. "You already know that Wynter has the power to summon. Did you know that the power can be transferred?"

"Transferred?" Nolan furrowed his brows. "How? I always thought you had to be born with the power."

Quinn jumped in. "We know kissing works." A red flush rose on her neck as she stole a glance at Cash. "And probably blood too. The last person to be exposed to Ransom's... bodily fluids when he's awake has control of him in and out of their dreams."

"And right now," Cash added, "Jezebel has him."

"Goddammit," Madeline said. "Not her again. I don't understand why Anson hasn't arrested her yet."

"She's hiding somewhere," Quinn said.

"But more importantly, we can't press charges." Cash wrung his hands anxiously. "We have to be able to separate Ransom from Jezebel and get him back to Wynter. That's not going to happen if Jezebel's in a jail cell somewhere."

Madeline crossed her arms. "Well, that's no fucking good." Everyone, including Nolan, stared at her like she had grown a third eye in the middle of her forehead. "What? I'm no angel. This is my daughter, goddammit." Her eyes met Cash's. "You said earlier that you talked to Wynter."

"I was at the hospital and dreamed I talked to Wynter, except I talked to her for real," Cash said. "She knew things that were impossible for her to know. Even me, too."

"What things?" Madeline's eyes blazed.

Cash stole a look at Quinn. "Just... things. But what I want to do is be able to *intentionally* dream of Wynter. Waiting for it to just happen takes too long."

"You're talking about lucid dreaming," said Nolan.

"I guess I am. How do I do it? Can you teach me?"

"I used to be able to do it, but I'm out of practice." Nolan stood, his knees cracking, and began to pace the small living room. "It involves being in a deeply relaxed state, but I can't really give you any specifics. It's been so long." He snapped his fingers. "Wait." Nolan walked quickly out of the living room toward the bedrooms.

Quinn looked at Madeline. "Can you do it?"

"The lucid dreaming stuff? Nope," she said. "I guess I don't have mystical blood in me."

"You don't need mystical blood," Quinn said. "I've done it and I'm as far from mystical as they come."

Nolan returned with a book in his hand. "I'm sure you've seen Wynter with this." He handed *Eyes Wide Dreaming* to Cash. "It would do a better job explaining things than I ever could. But what would you stand to gain just by talking to Wynter in your dreams?"

Cash gripped the book tightly. "If I can dream of Wynter intentionally, then maybe she can be *my* dreamwaker. Jezebel wouldn't have an advantage anymore."

"That's brilliant," Nolan said. "If it works."

"It was actually Jake's idea."

"Let me get this straight." Madeline cast a dubious look at Nolan, then to Cash and Quinn. "You'd pull a dream version of Wynter into reality? Is that what you're calling a 'dreamwaker'?"

Cash and Quinn nodded.

Madeline regarded them both. "Then what?"

"We'll figure out that part if I can actually do it," Cash said.

Madeline frowned. "It sounds dangerous."

"Maybe, maybe not." Cash ran his hand across the cover of the book. "But I have to try, right? Plus, it might be the only way to break Wynter out of her coma." He looked at the book's cover, its solitary eye and iridescent green iris, staring out at him.

Cash stood and bolted for the door. "Thanks for the book, Mr. LaCroix. I'll guard it with my life."

Quinn followed him with her gaze. "Where are you going?"

"I got reading and sleeping to do," Cash said. "No time like the present."

"Cash!" Madeline called out, but Cash was already gone. "Quinn, if you talk to Wynter, tell her we love her and that we're waiting for her to find her way home to us."

"We'll keep you posted, Mr. and Mrs. LaCroix." Quinn ran to the door to follow Cash.

"Quinn," Madeline called out. "For God's sake, honey, be careful."

"And if you need backup, call us," Nolan said.

"It's just dreams. What could happen?" Quinn smiled and nodded. "But we will. Promise." Then Quinn was out the door.

Nolan sat forward on the sofa, hands clasped with fingers twisted, and worked his thumbs into the palms of his hands, one side at a time.

Madeline recognized the behavior as Nolan's first response to anxiety. She placed her hands on his. "Can I make you a cup of tea?"

Nolan smiled at her, but he couldn't hide the worry in his tired eyes. "That'd be great."

Madeline hustled to the kitchen and set a kettle on the stove to boil. She had her hands up in the cupboard grabbing two mugs when she felt Nolan slide his hands around her waist and place a light kiss on her neck.

"Thank you." He hugged her and took a seat at the kitchen table.

"Wouldn't you be more comfortable on the sofa?"

"Makes it harder to talk."

Madeline lifted the teapot down to the countertop. "I thought worrying was my deal."

"Do you think we should have stopped them?"

"Do you think it would have done any good?" Madeline looked over her shoulder at him. "Teenagers are going to be teenagers. Plus, they're good kids. Their heads are screwed on right. Not like that... *Jezebel.*"

"Don't get me started on her." Nolan set his elbows on the table and placed his hands together like he was praying, tapping his index fingertips. "You know, I think I'm going to try again."

"Lucid dreaming?" Madeline dropped a chamomile teabag in each cup.

"How did you know?"

Madeline smiled to herself. "You're my husband." She approached Nolan at the table, leaned in, and gave him a long kiss. "I know things." The kettle had begun its whistle. She returned to the stove and poured boiling water into both cups. "Chamomile will help."

Nolan dipped his teabag in his cup. "It would be a gift to be able to talk to Wynter now, as she heals. Find out what she's thinking."

Madeline nodded as she blew on her tea.

"If it works," Nolan added. "If I can even do it again."

"It's probably like riding a bike," Madeline said. "It'll all come back to you."

"Hope so." Nolan took a sip of his tea, infusing it with air to cool it.

Madeline looked at Nolan over the rim of the mug in her hand. "Maybe you can teach me."

"I'll do my best." Nolan reached out and gave her hand a squeeze. He had a gut feeling that his dreaming abilities would return, but there was a seed of doubt in the pit of his stomach, and the seed was growing.

QUINN HUSTLED TO catch up with Cash, already mid-way across the grassy field.

"Hey Cash, wait up."

He glanced over his shoulder but maintained his pace. Quinn joined him at the steps to his trailer.

"I could drive you back to the hospital," Quinn said. "You've got that twenty-four hour backstage pass thing going on."

Cash looked at the plastic bracelet encircling his wrist. "To be honest, I'm too tired."

"Then want some company, instead?" Quinn looked at him expectantly. "I could watch, make sure you don't walk around in your sleep."

Cash raised a brow. "You want to watch me *sleep?*"

"Jeez. Don't make it sound creepy or anything." Quinn deflated. "It's not like I'm going to molest you."

"It's not that." Cash paused to find the right words. "I think I need to try this myself first. Alone. You know?"

"Okay. Call me if you need any help. Wynter's my friend too."

Cash nodded, then unlocked his front door. "Later." He watched Quinn hop into Blue Belle, start the engine, and reverse onto the trailer park's ring road. He waved, then closed the door and locked it.

Even though he liked Quinn as a friend, he felt a wave of relief surge through his body as he heard Blue Belle's engine fade into the distance. She moved a little too fast for his liking. Plus with Jake's professed interest in Quinn, having her spend the night could be misinterpreted too easily. Cash valued his friendship with Jake too much to jeopardize it over a platonic sleepover.

Not a sleepover. A research mission.

He looked at the well-loved book in his hand. *Eyes Wide*

Dreaming by Dr. A. X. Gardner. The green eye on the cover compelled him to open the book, like it knew his deepest thoughts. Instead of reading from cover to cover, Cash chose to focus on just the technical sections on lucid dreaming in hopes that he might save some time. He might get a chance to talk to Wynter tonight.

The trailer was hot, despite the windows all being open. The sun had set almost two hours ago, and the chill of the evening hadn't yet worked its way inside. Cash wished he could raise the roof for a minute or two to let all the warm air escape.

He pulled off his jeans and T-shirt and laid on his bed on top of the covers. The thought of Quinn watching him sleep in just his underwear made him laugh out loud. "Relaxing...? Yeah, right," he said to himself.

Cash flipped on the little bedside light clamped to his bed frame and set the book open on his lap, opened to the table of contents. Chapters seven and eight dealt with lucid dreaming techniques and summoning. He began to read.

Apart from the relaxation and mnemonic techniques, Cash quickly discovered that learning to lucid dream was not going to happen overnight. But perhaps he didn't need to. Maybe he just needed to think of Wynter as he fell asleep and she would come to him, just like at the hospital.

But even being tired, Cash found himself too keyed up. He would picture Wynter's face, her eyes, her hair, and be able to hold onto her image for a moment, but it would fade or morph into someone or something else. Sleep came in fits and starts, but nothing seemed to work.

He rolled over and looked at his cheap alarm clock. It read eight minutes after four in the morning. The digital numbers burned their green outlines into the back of his eyes.

"Fuck..." Cash had no choice but to give up for now. He had at best two hours before he'd need to get up for his shift at Finn's and he needed some unfractured sleep or he wouldn't be able to function. He found as soon as he released himself of his task to lucid dream, he was out like a light. His last thought before sleep took him was one of failure, how he'd disappoint Quinn in the morning, and more importantly, how Wynter was still locked in her own head.

Cash had to find a way.

QUINN ROLLED INTO the driveway of her house and shut off Blue Belle's engine, the hot metal clicking as it cooled. From the lack of traffic noise, she guessed it was close to midnight. Someday she'd remember to buy a little clock for the dashboard.

Crickets chirped from the trees and shrubs surrounding the house. Quinn leaned back in her seat and closed her eyes. Her thoughts floated back through her recent exchange with Cash. The more she thought about it, the more annoyed she became.

Who knows Wynter better than me? No one.

She suspected there was more to the story, perhaps relating to his weird "China doll" comment. She *was* a hopeless flirt, a quality she was proud of. Cash could use some lessons in mellowing out.

The front seats of the Beetle were not designed for slumber and Quinn did not relish sleeping in the back, especially since her own bed was a minute away.

An idea flashed in her brain. "If Cash doesn't want my help, I'll just do it myself," Quinn said to the crickets. "And I know just how to do it."

Quinn rolled up her window and locked Blue Belle. She sauntered up the front walk, let herself in with her key, and engaged the deadbolt behind her.

She ascended the stairs, trying half-heartedly not to make noise but not too worried if she woke her parents. Part of her wanted to wake them. Maybe they would ask where she had been, like most caring parents did. But other than the sound of her footsteps on the stairs and hallway, the house remained quiet. Quinn doubted that they would even get up if they heard something.

She brushed her teeth and headed into her bedroom, her safe haven. Quinn pulled out the drawer at her desk and reached into the back left corner. She pulled out a Ziploc bag of small, dark cubes.

"Zees," Quinn said softly to herself, smiling. In her head she could hear Wynter disagree with her, calling them "winx."

She pulled open the bag, shook a few into her palm and tossed them into her mouth. Quinn re-hid the zees, slipped out of her clothes, and pulled on a cool T-shirt and a fresh pair of panties. She crawled onto her bed and closed her eyes. She didn't know it at the time, but she was doing exactly what Cash was doing back at his trailer. Except Quinn had the help of zees and they were already working their relaxing magic on her.

She pictured Wynter in her head, asleep back at the hospital, and imagined taking a seat next to her in the orange chair that Cash had complained so often about. The monitoring equipment on the opposite side of her bed hummed and emitted a steady pulse of fifty-three beats per minute.

Quinn ran her fingers over Wynter's red hair, today more vibrant than it had ever been. She slid the curls away from Wynter's eyes and tucked them behind her ear.

Quinn leaned in and lightly kissed Wynter's forehead, her skin hot on Quinn's lips. She placed her right hand on the back of Wynter's left. "I miss you so much, Bug."

She returned to the orange chair and sighed. Within seconds the room filled with the scent of freshly baking bread. Quinn stood up and went to the door of the room and peeked out.

In front of her was the storefront for Hot Twists from the food court at Stedford Plaza. The window displayed row upon row of fresh baked pretzels. Next to it were the other fast food joints: Great American Donut, The Cast Iron Skillet, and Pepperia.

"What the hell?" Quinn scrunched her brow. "That must mean…" She turned to look behind her and Wynter's bed and monitoring equipment sat in the middle of the FreshWhip stand. The only remnant of the hospital was the orange chair.

The pulse tone quickened. Quinn watched the number rise to fifty-seven, then to sixty-one and stabilize.

"Bug?"

Wynter's eyelids fluttered, then remained open. She looked around before turning toward Quinn and smiling.

"Oh, Bug!" Quinn wrapped her arms around Wynter's neck and buried her face into her chest. "I was hoping you'd come back."

"I'm not back yet," Wynter said.

Quinn fell back into the chair and stared at Wynter in disbelief. She looked like her old self, bright, with eyes sparkling. Wynter was munching on a pretzel.

"I couldn't resist," Wynter said between chews. "I'm starving. Want one?" She reached down the right side of her bed and retrieved another pretzel.

"Maybe later." Quinn suspected this couldn't be real but at the same time she wasn't one hundred percent sure.

Wynter placed the pretzel on the bed next to her. "You're right. All this…" She waved her hands around her. "It's not real. It's your dream. Pretty bitchin', too. I'd rather be here than the hospital any day." She swallowed her bite, then locked her gaze with Quinn's. "But I'm real, and you can talk to me, just like I talked to Cash before."

Quinn nodded. "It's just so strange. Will I remember this when I wake up?"

"Most definitely. Just like Cash."

"He's probably trying to dream of you right now," Quinn said.

"I know. I could feel you both pulling me. But Cash can't seem to relax, so you won."

Quinn held Wynter's hand in hers and grinned sheepishly. "I had help."

"The winx," Wynter said.

"Zees."

"Agree to disagree."

Both girls laughed.

"You should share some... zees with Cash, because he needs to be able to summon me in his dreams. Ever since I fell—"

"Since you were *pushed*."

"Right. Anyway, ever since then the link between us is mega strong. I can only do so much in his dreams, so I'm going to need your help." Wynter took a bite of pretzel. "He might need something extra, something more natural."

"What do you mean by *more natural?*" Quinn looked at her over the rims of her glasses. "Some other vitamin I need to buy?"

"You don't need to *buy* anything," Wynter said. "More like *give* him something."

Quinn gave Wynter a side glance. She didn't like the direction the conversation was going. "Like, *what* exactly?"

Wynter held Quinn's gaze as she slid her right hand over the bedsheets to her abdomen, then past and lower. If it hadn't been for the sheets covering her legs, Wynter's hand would be resting in front of her panties.

Quinn narrowed her eyes. "Bug, what are you..."

Wynter made a loose fist, touching the tips of her thumb and index finger, and began moving it slowly up and down. She watched Quinn's expression move from confusion to crystal clarity.

Quinn's eyes went wide. "What? You're *crazy!*"

"I'm not," Wynter said, her expression one of dead seriousness. "A hand job would relax him even better than winx, or zees, or any vitamin could. Plus, it wouldn't cloud his mind."

Quinn stood, her mouth agape. "You want *me* to give *your* boyfriend a *hand job?*"

"He's not my boyfriend. Ransom is. But, yes." Wynter relaxed her right hand.

Quinn held her index finger up. "Uh, I call bullshit. Cash is, like, *totally* into you, Bug. And last I checked, Ransom isn't real."

"He *is* real," Wynter said. "I *made* him real."

Quinn was in no mood to argue whether Ransom was real or not. She knew it would go nowhere. Instead, she stared at Wynter, not sure how to proceed. "Have you ever kissed Cash? I mean recently?"

Wynter paused to think, then nodded. "He had just told me that lots of real guys, including him, would love to be my boyfriend."

"Then you kissed him?" Quinn placed her hands on her hips and tilted her head toward Wynter. "You don't think that sent the wrong message? Or at least a confusing one?"

Wynter shrugged, knowing that Quinn was probably right.

"After you fell, Cash was there first," Quinn said. "Do you remember that?"

"Kind of. The fall is a little fuzzy." Wynter's eyes met Quinn's. "So, will you do it?"

"Come on, Bug. This is totally bogus." Quinn sat and pulled the chair closer to her bedside. "Look at it from Cash's eyes. He likes you, probably *loves* you, and you're asking him to let someone *else* do something really personal with him. I mean, a lot of guys are horny bastards and would be all over that, but Cash isn't one of those guys. I don't think so, anyway."

"I get that, but I'm in *your* dream, not his. That means he didn't summon me," Wynter said. "It could take days, maybe weeks for him to learn to dream lucidly, and that's time I don't have. Every day my mind gets a bit worse, Quinn. I can feel it."

"What if it doesn't work?"

"It might not. But doesn't cumming release a bunch of relaxing stuff into the blood? You should know. You're the one who reads *Cosmo*."

Quinn thought about the past *Cosmopolitan* articles she had read and shrugged, shaking her head. "I don't know. Maybe I should tell him to just jack off on his own."

"But the relaxing stuff would be more concentrated if you did it," Wynter said. "Right?"

"I guess so." Quinn shivered. "It just feels so icky."

"Will you try? For me?" Wynter matched Quinn's gaze with her own. "The sooner Cash learns how to do it the better. Summon, I mean."

"Okay. Just one time."

"Promise?" Wynter locked her vibrant eyes on Quinn's.

"I promise," Quinn said with a sigh. "But I'm not doing anything else. It feels too much like past mistakes already."

"It's just one hand job." Wynter nodded, then smirked at the sound of her words. "Maybe two."

Both girls began to giggle.

"But don't get carried away."

"That shouldn't matter, right?" Quinn's eyes twinkled devilishly. "I mean, he's not your boyfriend, right?"

"Well, maybe he is." Wynter blushed, a pink hue mixed with the dark tones of her cheeks. "Just a bit."

"Two boyfriends at the same time?" Quinn teased. "You're developing quite a rep."

Wynter laughed. "Shut up. Want a FreshWhip?" She handed Quinn a cup and a straw.

Quinn sipped some of the sweet, fruity liquid into her mouth. "This is better than I make it." She took another sip and her brows furrowed in concern. "Cash is going to think I'm making this all up just to get into his pants. He's never going to go for it."

"It's simple," Wynter said. "Just tell him something only he knows."

"Simple for you, maybe."

Wynter thought for a moment. "If it comes up—"

"It will."

"If it comes up, tell him '4:08 in the morning.' That's when he gave up trying to dream of me tonight." Wynter shrugged. "But you got to me first anyway, so he really didn't have a chance, even if he was doing everything right."

"If I can dream of you, then why can't I get you out of your coma?"

"I don't know. Something connected me and Cash and it was more than a kiss," Wynter said. "It was never like this before my fall."

"Damn. Can you become a dreamwaker?"

Wynter shook her head. "Not yet. The coma is still too strong. It's stopping me."

Quinn sighed. "So, it's all up to Cash. And the orgasmic power of my hands." She raised a hand to her face. "Oh my God. Jake can never know about this."

"I'll never tell." Wynter reached out and gave Quinn's hand a gentle squeeze. "I got to go, Quinn. Thanks for doing this."

"Don't thank me yet, Bug." Quinn leaned in and gave Wynter a tight hug, the red curls of Wynter's hair tickling her nose. A sneeze was upon Quinn in seconds and in the brief moment she had her eyes closed, Wynter, the hospital bed, Stedford Plaza, all of it, disappeared in a flash of black.

Quinn opened her eyes to the familiar speckled pattern of her bedroom ceiling. She rolled to one side. The green numbers of her digital clock shone back at her innocuously.

4:08 a.m. What are the odds?

Quinn slid under the covers, pulling them up around her neck, and tried to imagine giving Cash a happy ending before sleep overtook her again. It didn't work.

∞

IT WAS TEN O'CLOCK and Jake had just finished an overfilled bowl of Cinnamon Toast Crunch. His dad had left for work two hours earlier and he had spotted his mom in the back yard through the kitchen window when he refilled his cereal bowl for the second time.

He had escorted himself to the games room downstairs and was in the middle of a game of Donkey Kong on his Nintendo Entertainment System when the phone rang. By the third ring he realized that his mom would never pick up. She couldn't hear the phone and probably hadn't taken the portable outside with her.

He hopped to the cordless phone, keeping most of his weight off the cast on his left leg. He raised the handset to his ear. "Hello?"

"Hey, is that you, Jake?" The voice on the other end sounded familiar but Jake couldn't match a face.

"Uh, yeah. Who's this?"

"Come on. It's Zain. Didn't you recognize me?"

"Yeah. Right. Of course. The line was just a little staticky." Jake hoped the lie was good enough.

"Are you busy?"

Jake's eyes shifted to the paused Donkey Kong screen. "Sort of. Why?"

"Sort of?" Zain's filtered chuckle floated from the cordless phone's speaker. "I hope Donkey Kong can wait. I've got a proposition for you."

"What kind of proposition?" Jake knew Zain was a good guy. He had known him for several years, but the direction of this conversation set warning bells off in his head.

"Don't worry. It's nothing weird," Zain said. "I need your expertise with video. I had a run in with Jezebel and I need to set up some new security cameras."

"Jezebel? What did she do?"

"I'll fill you in later. Are you interested? I can pay you."

"Uh, I'm a gimp right now. Got a cast on my leg because of

Jezebel." Unaware, Jake slid a finger behind the top edge of his cast and scratched. "I'll have to ask my mom, but she's pretty cool. If you're okay with that, I'm in. Anything to help get that bitch arrested."

"Yeah, sure. I'll do all the grunt work," Zain said. "If I don't hear back from you in an hour, I'll assume it's a go. I'll drop by to pick you up."

"Okay. Later." Jake set the portable phone on its charging cradle and hobbled out to the back garden. As he expected, Mirielle had no problem with him helping Zain out, as long as he checked in every once in a while. Miri was particularly thrilled when she learned that Jake would be paid.

"Almost like a real job," she had said with a wink. Mirielle had always been easier on him than his dad. Hudson had a narrow idea about what was and wasn't considered a *real job*. Both video and video games didn't fit his definition.

Jake returned to the house and changed out of his pajamas. A shower was out of the question, another unfortunate consequence of Jezebel running him down with her car. Instead, he gave himself a once-over with a soapy washcloth, dried himself off and pulled on his clothes for the day: a white T-shirt with a red JVC logo on the front and a pair of jeans with the left leg cut off mid-thigh.

He stood in front of the narrow floor to ceiling mirror in his closet. "Dorky to the max," Jake said to himself and shrugged. "It's not like I'm trying to impress anyone."

With crutches in hand, he worked his way back downstairs, grabbed his Nintendo baseball hat and sat on the front stoop to wait.

Twenty minutes later Zain rolled up in front of his house. He leaned over the center console and motioned at Jake's T-shirt. "Dressed for success, I see. Hop in."

Zain waited until Jake buckled himself in before accelerating down the street.

Jake noticed the red welts encircling Zain's wrists. "Jezebel do that?"

"Sort of." Zain alternated rubbing his wrists, making sure one hand remained on the steering wheel. "One of her gang did it. Roxy? Don't know who the other guy was." He glanced at Jake. "Ever notice that? Jezebel rarely ever does the dirty work."

"I've noticed." Jake glanced at the cast on his leg. "But she did *that*. Could've killed me and Quinn."

Zain crossed the highway. "Let's make sure the Starlite is the last place she'll want to go. Or else catch her red handed."

Jake nodded. "So, the other guy, the one who was with Jezebel. Did he look kind of like Cash? Curly blond hair, black hoodie?"

"He did." Zain sent him a quick look. "You know him?"

"Sort of." Jake returned his glance and shrugged. "It's a long story."

"I'm always up for long stories, if they affect my business."

"Maybe later." Jake shifted uncomfortably in his seat. "How many cameras do you have?"

"Four, plus the control system to hook them all up." Zain turned into the vacant Starlite parking lot and chose a space near the front door. "This is going to sound lame, but I've had all the tech for months. Just haven't found the time."

Jake shrugged at him. "Why do today what you can put off until tomorrow?"

"Yeah, well that worked great until yesterday took a giant bite out of my ass." Zain shut off the car. "Let's go."

When they got inside, Jake's eyes bugged out. Seeing the Starlite during off hours gave him a surreal feeling. Everything looked subdued and fake.

Zain chuckled at Jake's reaction. "It's amazing how different things look during the day without the mirror ball and specialty lighting." He placed his hands on his hips. "Where do you want to start?"

"You got a floor plan?"

Zain pointed at him and snapped his index finger. "Yes! Let me go grab it." He disappeared into the back office.

Jake hopped along on crutches, reorienting himself and forming ideas. For the longest time he had felt like he was missing something from his life. He still wanted to start a video game company with Cash, but Zain hiring him for his tech knowledge boosted his confidence and gave him options. Knowing that he might also be helping nail Jezebel in a possible future infraction made things all the sweeter.

IT WAS A typical mid-morning Wednesday at the Gas N Go. Finn was busy replacing the muffler of a Ford F-100. He had a couple more repairs lined up for the day to keep him busy until the garage closed.

Cash had just finished a fill-up for an elderly woman and was taking an imprint of her credit card. The woman signed the receipt, took her copy, and pulled out of the gas bay. Cash waved goodbye and headed back to the store.

Considering he was working on two hours of sleep at best, Cash felt pretty good. However, if he stopped moving, he knew sleep would ambush him quickly. He ran through the details of his lucid dreaming attempts from last night, his mind buzzing like he had downed a pot of coffee. He hadn't expected it to take so long to develop the ability or for it to be so difficult. Wynter had made it all look easy.

Ransom slipped around the corner of the station and intercepted Cash at the door. He held Jezebel's semi-automatic pistol in his right hand at waist level, pointed at Cash's gut. "Don't try anything dumb."

"What, like pointing a gun at someone in a small space?" Cash eyed the pistol with caution and did his best to conceal his fear. "You even know how to use that thing?"

"Shut up." Ransom motioned with the pistol. "Get inside and empty the register."

Cash kept the muzzle of the pistol within his periphery and did as he was told. "Jezebel put you up to this, right?"

"Who else?" Ransom grumbled and threw a plastic bag on the counter. "Put the money in this."

Cash shook his head. "Jezebel sure didn't think this through. Why rob a store in the morning when you can wait until later in the day and get away with more?"

"I stopped asking questions after she threatened to kill Wynter." Ransom beckoned with the pistol.

"She made a pretty good attempt already, don't you think?"

Ransom waved the pistol at him. "Just fill the bag. Jezebel will kill me if she doesn't get what she wants. I don't even care about the money. I'll give you my cut."

"Fuck you. I don't steal from Finn." Cash started at the one dollar bills and worked toward the higher bills, placing each stack into the bag. He worked slowly on purpose. "You've been nothing but trouble since you became a dreamwaker."

"A what?"

"A dreamwaker." Cash stopped pulling money out of the register. "That's what we decided to call you."

"Who's *we?*"

Cash squinted at him. "Who do you think? Wynter, Quinn, Jake, and me."

Ransom looked back out the store's window for potential threats. "The money!"

"I know you and Wynter are connected somehow," Cash stalled, despite his heart jackhammering in his chest. "But I'm connected to her too. I talked to her a couple of days ago."

Ransom's eyes flickered with surprise and anger. "You talked to Wynter? How? Is she awake?"

"She just came to me in a dream." Cash grinned even though he knew it was a dangerous move. "I'm going to be the one who saves her."

"What did she say?"

"You really think I'd tell you?"

Ransom forgot about the money and raised the pistol, aiming it at Cash's head. "WHAT DID SHE SAY?"

Cash knew the pistol was the real deal even if Ransom wasn't, but he stood firm, a feeling of invincibility flowing through his body. Or maybe it was the lack of sleep clouding his judgment.

The pistol trembled in Ransom's hand.

"You're not going to shoot me." Cash spoke as calmly as he could manage. "I'm Wynter's ticket out of her coma."

"But *I'm* going to shoot yah." Finn's voice carried across the small store. "Killian don't miss."

Cash and Ransom turned to see the stout man level a double-barreled shotgun at Ransom.

"No, Finn! Wait." Cash held up his hands, his left palm at Finn and his right at Ransom. "Everyone stay cool." He met Ransom's eyes. "Don't do this."

Ransom shifted his gaze between Cash and Finn but didn't lower his pistol.

"Just go," Cash said. "It's not worth it, man."

Ransom looked at the money, then settled his eyes on Cash. There was an understanding between them despite their animosity toward each other, and the common element was Wynter's life. He backed toward the store entrance, holding the pistol steady.

Finn shuffled forward to keep Ransom in his sights, but Cash waved at him. "Stay back," Cash whispered through gritted teeth. "And lower Killian."

Ransom pushed through the entrance. "Sorry. No hard feelings?" He didn't wait for an answer and ran back the way he had come, back around the corner of the station.

Finn trudged to the store entrance. "That *fucker.* Next time I'll blow his 'ead off." He glanced back at Cash. "He didn't get any money, did he?"

Cash leaned on the counter on his elbows, catching his breath and letting his pulse return to normal. "No." With shaking hands he began returning the stacks of bills to the register.

"You know that asshole?"

"Unfortunately, I do." Cash wrung his hands in an attempt to stop them from shaking. "It's complicated, but all you need to know is that he's part of Jezebel's crew."

"That fuckin' hussy." Finn dead-eyed Cash. "If any of them show their face here again, I'll shoot first. Forget about questions."

"I'm pretty sure Ransom's not going to be back," Cash said.

A gunshot rang out from outside. Cash ran around the front counter and pointed at Killian in Finn's hands. "Put that thing away. You're going to get arrested."

Cash stepped out of the store. There was no second shot to narrow down where it had come from and hearing the first shot from inside the store had offered no clues.

Something in Cash's gut told him that Ransom would *most definitely* not be back. Most definitely. That was a Wynter-ism and Cash smiled.

A car pulled into the gas bay and he stepped up the driver's side window, ready to serve them. The day wasn't even half over and the last place he wanted to be was the Gas N Go. The thought of being home in his own bed, dreaming of Wynter and talking with her, carried him through the rest of the day. He hoped he would be able to find her.

SWEAT POURED DOWN Ransom's back as he held the pistol aimed at Cash and backed out of the store. He didn't want to shoot anyone, especially not Cash, but Jezebel had him by the short and curlies. He would not be responsible for hurting Wynter more, even indirectly.

Cash had managed to keep Finn cool, and Ransom was grateful for that. According to Jezebel, Finn was a trigger-happy hothead. He was no match for a shotgun as he had quickly discovered at the Pepperia in Sanwood. Even though he was technically immortal, he preferred not to feel the ripping sting of a dozen pellets tearing a hole in his face, or his chest, or...

"Sorry. No hard feelings?" Ransom burst outside and ran back around the corner of the Gas N Go.

Jezebel will not be happy.

Regardless of his failure and the possible consequences, Ransom felt pleased that no one had been hurt. He raced like the wind down the alley behind the station. Jezebel and Roxy waited for him in their usual seats in the Barracuda, parked a hundred feet ahead, its engine purring.

As he drew near, Roxy popped open her door and beckoned him frantically. "Move your ass!"

Ransom leaped into the back seat and Roxy hopped back into the passenger side, yanking the car door closed.

"Go!" Roxy said.

Jezebel cast a wary glance at Ransom in the rear view mirror and floored the gas. The Barracuda lurched forward down the alley. "Give Rox the cash."

Ransom sat up and pretended not to hear the question.

Roxy twisted around the passenger seat and held out her hand. "Give it here."

Ransom's eyes met Roxy's and she knew in an instant that the robbery had failed.

"He fucking blew it," she said to Jezebel, then back to Ransom, "There's no money, is there?"

"It's not my fault," Ransom said. "The old man pulled a gun on me."

Jezebel slammed her foot on the brake and the Barracuda slid to a stop over the loose gravel in the alley. "Out of the fucking car. Now."

Both Jezebel and Roxy burst out of the car. Roxy pushed her seat forward as Jezebel charged around the back of the Barracuda. "Your ass is grass."

Ransom stepped out of the car. "I told you, I couldn't do anything about it."

Jezebel pulled the pistol tucked at Ransom's waist and jabbed it at his chest. "You had a fucking gun, idiot. Next time use it." She pulled back the slide and chambered a bullet, the hammer cocked and ready.

"Wait!" Ransom held his hands forward. "Wait. Cash said he talked to Wynter."

But Ransom spoke too late. Jezebel pulled the trigger and blew a hole through him. He collapsed on the ground, bracing himself on a nearby dumpster.

"Jesus Christ, Jazz." Roxy stumbled backward in shock. "You're out of control."

Jezebel ignored her and squatted to Ransom's level. She grabbed his shirt collar, pulled him close, and jabbed the pistol's muzzle under his chin. "What did she say?"

Ransom met Jezebel's furious stare with one of calm. He felt peace wash over him and raised his middle finger at her. A wide smile spread across his face and his eyes burned an intense blue. In less than a second, he drifted into nothing.

"Fuck!" Jezebel stood and ran back to the driver's seat. She popped the magazine out, pulled the slide back to unchamber the next live round, and dropped everything into the footwell. Roxy barely had time to return to her seat before Jezebel shifted into drive and continued blazing a path down the alley.

"You didn't have to shoot him."

"You better shut the fuck up or you'll be next," Jezebel said through gritted teeth.

Halfway back to their hideout at the drive-in, a silver Fiat X1/9 zoomed up to their rear bumper and tailed them.

Roxy glanced into her side mirror, then twisted in her seat to confirm through the Barracuda's rear window. "Subtle. Monty's on our tail."

"No shit."

"What are you going to tell him?"

Jezebel responded with a scowl. Neither of them spoke for the rest of the trip.

She pulled into her hiding spot behind the storage shed, threw the Barracuda into park, and grabbed the pistol at her feet. She slid the magazine into the handle and climbed out of the car, jamming the pistol into the front of her pants.

Monty parked behind and exited the Fiat to meet her.

"What do you want, asshole?" Jezebel cussed.

"Easy," Monty said, raising his hands. "That's no way to greet your partner. I just want my cut."

"Well, your cut's nothing."

Monty's eyes darkened. "What are you talking about?"

"The job went bad," Roxy said. "Finn pulled a gun."

Monty shifted his eyes suspiciously between Roxy, the Barracuda, and Jezebel. "Where's Ransom?"

Jezebel stepped forward, a little too close for Monty's liking. "I killed him."

He took a step back. "Well, technically he can't die, can he? You're not as badass as you think." Monty stared at the two girls. "So, there's no money?"

"He's a fucking genius," Jezebel said to Roxy.

"That's a problem." Monty strolled toward the Barracuda, looking through the windows for anything resembling hidden money. "You got one free pass and you just used it up." He walked back to the Fiat. "Next time, my half is comin' out of your pockets." His eyes ran a sleazy line down Jezebel's body. "Or your ass."

Jezebel watched Monty back up and drive away. "I fucking hate him."

"Me, too," Roxy said. "Help me cover the car."

"Do it yourself. I got to think."

Roxy didn't argue. She covered the Barracuda with the blue tarp, then followed Jezebel inside the shed.

Jezebel paced back and forth, her brain buzzing, not about Monty, Ransom's screw up, or even revenge. Instead, she was consumed by Cash's apparent conversation with Wynter. How could that be true? Had Ransom lied to save his own skin? She had to know.

WITH HIS SHIFT at Finn's over and the rest of the day to himself, Cash reclined on his bed with a glass of ice-cold lemonade in one hand and *Eyes Wide Dreaming* open on his lap. Ernie had just finished his shower and would soon begin his breakfast. Cash hoped that it would be oatmeal instead of scrambled eggs and bacon. He wouldn't be able to concentrate with the odor of hickory-smoked bacon seeping into every room in the trailer.

The condensation on his glass of lemonade trickled down and soaked into his jeans. Cash took a sip and began to read.

No sooner had he started when a knock sounded from the front door. "Can you get that, Cash?" Ernie called from the kitchen. "I'm tied up."

Cash heard the tell-tale sizzle rising from the kitchen. He set his lemonade down beside his clock radio, placed the book on his bed, and went to the door. When he unlocked it and pulled the door open, Quinn stood there in jeans and a black *A Nightmare on Elm Street* T-shirt, sporting a grin a mile wide. Cash stuck his head out and glanced at the parking pad. Blue Belle sat right behind Ernie's car.

"You're going to have to park somewhere else." He caught Quinn's eyes flick down his body, so fast as to almost be unnoticeable.

"Well, about that," Quinn said. "I thought maybe we could go visit Wynter. It's been too long."

The smell of bacon hit Cash's nose and his stomach growled in response. "It's been one day."

"Almost two, but who's counting," Quinn said. "If we go now, we'd have most of visiting hours left. It might help you dream of her later."

Cash thought for a moment, then nodded. "Okay. I'll let my dad know."

From the door Quinn watched Cash approach Ernie at the stove. Their conversation was brief but before Cash returned to the door, Ernie handed him something wrapped in paper towel.

Cash slipped into his shoes, jammed his wallet in his front pocket, and joined Quinn on the landing. He held up the folded square of paper towel. "Want some bacon?"

"Um, yeah!" Quinn held out her hand.

As the two of them walked to Blue Belle, Cash handed her a strip of crispy bacon, still warm from the frying pan. Quinn crammed the whole thing into her mouth.

Cash smirked. "Hungry, much?" He took out a strip and crunched on it.

"For bacon? Who isn't?" Quinn eyed the paper towel. "Got any more?"

Cash smiled and pulled out another strip and handed it to her.

"Now we're talking." Quinn gobbled it and wiped her fingers on her jeans. "Let's go." She hopped in the driver's seat and started the Beetle's engine.

Cash ate the last strip of bacon as Quinn backed out. He waved at his dad on the front landing and within minutes, the two teens were on their way, headed east on I94 to Halston Medical Center.

"Ransom tried to rob the Gas N Go today."

Quinn's eyes bugged out. "No way! Tell me more!"

Cash retold the morning's events. With Quinn's questions, it took almost the full drive to satisfy her curiosity for details. And it kept Cash from falling asleep.

"Holy shit. Look." Quinn pointed as she pulled into the hospital parking lot. A black Barracuda with two familiar occupants rolled to the exit of the lot, on their way out.

"What the fuck?" Cash turned in his seat to keep the Barracuda in sight for as long as possible. He would recognize Jezebel's crimped hair anywhere. "What the hell were *they* doing here? Wynter better be okay."

"Let's find out." Quinn found a parking spot and Cash paid for a parking ticket before they rushed to the hospital entrance.

Within minutes they were exiting the fourth-floor stairwell and walk-running toward Wynter's room. Cash poked his head inside. Nothing had changed. It was as if he had never left on Monday.

"Looks like she's okay," Cash said. "What do you want to do?"

"To sleep. To dream."

Cash nodded. He lifted a chair from the alcove across the corridor and carried it into Wynter's room. "Maybe if we're lucky we can both talk to her." He looked at the orange chair. "I'll take the Devil's throne."

They positioned the chairs as if they were watching a movie, in this case Wynter's vitals displayed on the pulse monitor standing opposite.

Both exhausted, Quinn and Cash succumbed to sleep within minutes of closing their eyes and remained dead to the world for close to three hours. Even the occasional visit of the attending nurse failed to rouse them.

At quarter to eight, Madeline placed her warm hand on Quinn's shoulder and woke her. Quinn sat up in her chair and stretched. "Hi, Mrs. LaCroix." She poked Cash in the ribs. His eyes popped open in an instant.

"What? What's the matter? Did you dream?"

"No." Quinn rubbed the sleep from her eyes. "But visiting hours are probably over."

"Shit." Cash realized Wynter's parents were in the room. "Oh. Sorry, Mr. and Mrs. LaCroix."

Madeline stood in front of Nolan, one of his hands resting gently on her shoulder. "We have to stop meeting like this." Her attempt to lighten the mood fell flat. "You've been trying to dream of Wynter?"

Quinn and Cash nodded.

"But no luck, unfortunately." Cash deflated. "It was so easy last Monday. But now there's nothing. I just can't seem to raise her. I hope that's not a bad sign."

"As well as your body, you need to relax your mind and your soul," Nolan said. "It takes practice. Have you been reading Wynter's book?"

"A bit." Cash focused his attention on Wynter's vital signs monitor. The rhythmic beeps and the never-ending data lines, all that technology meant that Wynter was alive but just below the surface, just out of reach, taunting him. "I'll read some more when I get home. I just want to talk to her now."

"It'll come, in time," Nolan said.

"In time…" Cash spoke so softly that no one except Quinn heard him. He pretended to wipe sleep from his eyes, but Quinn saw the truth before his wrists swept his tears away.

Quinn tugged on Cash's T-shirt sleeve. "Come on. I'll drive you home."

The two of them stood, bid their farewells to Madeline and Nolan, and headed down the corridor toward the stairwell.

"Cash!" Madeline called out from behind, closing the distance between them with quick steps.

"What is it, Mrs. LaCroix?"

Madeline pulled him into her arms and hugged him. "I know you care for Wynter. Both of you do," she whispered at his ear.

"Please be careful." She released him but held his shoulders firmly. "The power you're playing with is dangerous."

Cash nodded.

"Tell her we love her," Madeline said. "Tell her to come home."

"I'll do my best."

Madeline smiled and let go.

Cash caught up to Quinn waiting at the stairwell doors. "Do you mind if we take the elevator this time? I'm beat." Cash stretched his arms behind his head. "It's like sleeping made me more tired."

"Totally," Quinn said. "We should get some coffees though, before we go."

"Maybe you should. I'm so tired I can barely think straight."

"What did Madeline want?"

"She wanted me to know how much they love Wynter, as if I don't know already."

The elevator doors slid open and they stepped inside. "We won't let anyone hurt Wynter again," Quinn said.

"I hope we aren't in over our heads." Cash waved at Madeline at the end of the corridor as the elevator doors closed.

"Have a little faith, Cash," Quinn said. "Everything will work out."

The cafeteria on the first floor had closed so Quinn was left with no choice but to use a coffee vending machine stationed near the entrance.

Quinn pressed a couple of buttons on the front panel. "What do you think? Black with extra sugar?"

Cash's mind was elsewhere and answered her on autopilot. "Yeah, sure. Whatever."

Quinn dug some coins out from her purse and plugged the coin slot. The coffee machine whirred to life, grinding beans somewhere within its mechanical heart, deposited a paper cup in the windowed receptacle, and filled the cup with hot brew. She handed the cup to Cash. "How does it taste?"

Cash blew over the surface of the coffee, then took a tentative sip. "It's okay."

"Good enough for me." Quinn set the machine into motion again, withdrawing her cup when the machine finished. "They should make these machines out of clear plastic. So we can watch everything inside."

"I bet Jake would like that."

The two of them found Blue Belle in the parking lot. Quinn unlocked the little car and they continued drinking their coffees sitting inside.

"It actually gets better the longer you drink it."

Cash managed a chuckle. "It's just your taste buds dying."

Quinn was taking larger sips of her coffee now that it had had a chance to cool a little. "So did you dream of *anything* when we were in Wynter's room?"

Cash shook his head. "Never ending blackness. Kind of like this coffee." He took a swig, swallowed, and a shiver ripped through his body. "Ugh. This isn't getting better for me... Wait. Why am I drinking this? Won't this keep me awake later?"

"Maybe. You can dump it," Quinn said. "I don't mind."

"No. I'll finish it." He glanced at Quinn, a small mischievous grin appearing at the corner of his mouth. "Race you."

"Chug coffee?" Quinn studied Cash for a moment before realizing that he meant business. "You're on."

"Okay. Three... two... one... Chug!"

They both raised their cups to their lips and began drinking as fast as they could. Cash was half finished when a shiver stole through him again, causing him to choke and sputter coffee over himself.

He continued drinking as Quinn finished and raised her empty paper cup like a trophy. "I win. No contest."

Cash swallowed the dregs in his cup. "But did we win? Really?"

Quinn turned in her seat and settled her eyes on him. "It's easy to see why Wynter likes you."

Cash shrugged off the compliment. "Apparently that's not enough."

Quinn tilted her head, her black hair cascading off her shoulders. "I talked with Wynter last night."

"You did? What the hell, Quinn."

"Sorry. I meant to tell you sooner, but it was never a good time. And that's... probably why you couldn't dream of Wynter last night."

Cash scrunched his brows at her. "What do you mean?"

"Just like I'm talking to you now," Quinn said, "if someone else wanted to talk to you, they'd have to wait."

"So, what you're saying is I could have been doing everything right last night, but since you were dreaming of Wynter..."

"Yup." Quinn turned on her rueful eyes behind her glasses. "Sorry about that. But I had help." She reached under the driver's seat and pulled out a baggie with a bunch of black gelatin cubes within it.

"Drugs?" Cash instinctively looked over both shoulders.

"No way. Wynter and I made these at the cabin about a week ago. I called them 'zees', but Wynter would say they're called 'winx,' with an 'x.' " Quinn handed the bag to him. "They're made from every relaxing herb we could find, mixed with concentrated Jell-O."

Cash squeezed one of the cubes and it quickly regained its shape. "You eat them?"

"Yeah. They'll help you sleep," Quinn said as Cash handed the bag back to her. "Want to try them? Tonight?"

"My dad probably hasn't left for work yet."

Quinn tucked the baggie into her purse. "If it's okay with your dad, could I hang out at your place for a while?"

Cash hesitated.

"I'll cook you some breakfast for dinner," Quinn said. "To make up for stealing Wynter away from you last night."

"Okay. You're on."

"Me and Wynter talked about something else last night, too." Quinn inserted her key into the ignition and started the VW's engine. "But I think you need some food in you first." She backed out of her parking space and drove out of the familiar exit.

"You're not going to tell me, are you?"

"Food first," Quinn said.

Within a few minutes the little Volkswagen was again zooming west on the Interstate, chasing the setting sun across North Dakota.

"How about some driving music?" Before Cash had a chance to respond, Quinn switched on KROK. Peter Schilling's "Major Tom (Coming Home)" had just started. The song's rapid pounding bass synth intro broadcast from the Blue Belle's dashboard speakers.

"Perfect." Cash slid down in his seat as far as his seat belt would allow. "You've got the magic touch."

"I hope so." There was a little smile on Quinn's lips and her eyes gleamed in the twilight. She eased her foot on the gas and slowly accelerated until the dashed center line dividing the westbound lanes shot past the windshield in time with the beat of the music.

She recalled Cash's hushed words in Wynter's hospital room. *In time.*

But time was a luxury they didn't have, especially not Wynter. Tonight, she would try Wynter's special request. How would Cash react? Would it work or would he freak out? Quinn's head filled with worry. The last thing she wanted was to make things worse.

THE TWO TEENS arrived back at Cash's trailer at half past nine. She parked partway onto the grassy field so she wouldn't block Ernie's little tan Honda Civic.

As they pushed through the front door, the scent of hickory bacon still hung in the air of the small space. Ernie had just finished a lunch of soup and a BLT sandwich.

"Hey, son. Quinn." Ernie nodded at them as he wiped his mouth and began clearing his dishes.

"Hi, Mr. Hawkins," Quinn said.

Ernie pointed at the stove. "There's some soup left. You're welcome to it. Might still be warm." He placed his dishes in the sink and walked to his bedroom. The layout was similar to Wynter's trailer, with the master bedroom and second bedroom sandwiching the small bathroom at the rear. "You guys going to be hanging out tonight?" His voice floated out from the back of the trailer.

Cash glanced at Quinn before calling back, "Yeah Dad. Is that okay?"

Ernie popped his head out of the bedroom door. "You're both responsible young adults who make good decisions, right?"

Cash rolled his eyes, then glanced at the floor. "Of course, *Dad.*"

"Then there's no problem." Ernie disappeared back into the bedroom.

Quinn smiled. "Your dad's cool."

"Thanks," Cash said.

She looked at the kitchen area nestled in one corner of the open plan layout. "How about I get breakfast for dinner cooking? I'll need bacon, eggs, a little milk and some bread."

While Cash collected ingredients from the fridge, Quinn grabbed the frying pan from the drying rack in the sink and placed it on the stove.

"How hungry are you?"

"You going to eat, too?"

Quinn thought for a moment, then nodded. "Sure."

Cash handed her a wad of sliced bacon and removed four eggs from the carton. "Then I'm this hungry."

Five minutes later, with Quinn cooking and Cash on cleanup, Quinn placed a plate of steaming bacon and eggs on the table next to a stack of toast. "And now we feast."

Ernie stepped into the living area and sat to tie up his shoes. "Something smells good." He approached the table, broke off a piece of bacon, and scooped up some scrambled eggs with it. "Tastes great, too. Wish I could stay but I got to go clean the wall farts out of Walmart." He laughed at his joke, then leaned close and lowered his voice. "Be smart." But he meant for Quinn to hear, too.

Cash covered his eyes to try and hide his embarrassment. "Have a good shift, Dad."

"Thanks." Ernie checked his watch, then met Quinn's eyes with his own. "Nice to see you again, Quinn. Your parents know where you are?"

"Yup." She gave him two thumbs up before shoveling in a mouthful of eggs.

"Don't stay up too late."

Cash winced. "Come on, Dad."

"See you tomorrow."

"Dad!"

"Okay, okay," Ernie eased the door closed. "Bye," he uttered before latching the door closed.

Cash walked to the door and waited for a moment before opening it, waving, and closing the door, engaging the dead bolt. He returned to the table and sat.

"Sorry."

"Why? For having a dad that cares?" Quinn sat back in her chair. "I just realized all three of my friends have awesome parents."

"Yours are just different," Cash said.

"Yeah, right. Different like yours rock and mine suck." Quinn went to the stove, picked up the soup pot, and began spooning up the remnants. "Anyway, I don't want to talk about it."

"Okay." Cash shoveled more eggs onto his plate and took a bite of toast. "How about we discuss what you and Wynter talked about last night?" He raised a brow. "I haven't forgotten."

Quinn gulped. "Neither did I. I was just waiting for the right moment."

Cash shrugged and glanced around the trailer. "How about now?"

"Okay." Quinn took the pot to the table and continued to slurp up the leftover soup. One spoonful led to another and another.

Cash watched her finish the soup as he finished his bacon and eggs. Then Quinn started in on the remaining bacon, eggs, and toast. "Are you stalling?"

Quinn looked at him over the rims of her glasses and shrugged, a small grin forming at the corners of her mouth.

"What the hell did you guys talk about?"

"Got anything to drink?"

Cash pulled a glass from the cupboard, filled it with water from the tap, and placed it carefully in front of Quinn. "Don't spill... Now, spill it."

Quinn sighed. "Sorry. I just don't want to make things worse, you know?"

"No, I don't know," Cash said. "Fill me in."

Quinn took a sip of water. She could feel Cash's stare and sighed again. "Normally, it's not hard to talk about but you're a guy, and... I'm embarrassed to... Okay. I'm just going to say it."

Cash sat across the table, enrapt with a touch of annoyance. "And...?"

"You know anything about orgasms?"

Cash sat back in his chair as if he had been slapped across the face. "Uh..."

"You know, getting off, cumming—"

"I know what *orgasms* are." Cash practically whispered the

word even though they were alone. A tinge of pink blossomed around his collar.

"Well, did you know how good they are for you?" Quinn munched on a piece of toast. She had control of the conversation now and took secret pleasure in watching Cash squirm. But she had to make sure she didn't cross the line and make him run for the hills. "When you cum, a whole bunch of good chemicals get released into your blood. It's the best way to relax. And it's all natural."

"Wait..." Cash sent her a confused side-ways look. "You think I should... *jack off*... to relax?"

Quinn stifled a laugh, then smiled. "Kind of."

"Kind of? What? I mean, like, either I do it or I don't."

"I know, but I'm talking about *how*, not *what*." Quinn held Cash's confused gaze even though everything in her body wanted her to burst out in maniacal laughter.

"I know *how* to do it." Cash shook his head, the color of embarrassment high on his cheeks. "I can't believe I'm talking to you about this."

"Yeah, sorry, but there's more than one way to do it."

"What are you talking about?" Cash scrunched his brows together. "And how does it relate to Wynter?"

"You wanted to know what we talked about," Quinn said. "I'm telling you."

"Orgasms? You talked about orgasms?"

"Not just any orgasm... your orgasm."

Cash shook his head. "Ugh. Stop saying that word."

"And how *I'd* give it to you."

"You're not making sense—" Cash's face went beet red. It was hard to tell if he was angry or just super embarrassed. He pushed back on his chair but instead of sliding, it tipped backward and sent him flying.

Quinn leaped from her chair and ran around the table to Cash's side. "Are you okay?"

"I don't know." Cash stared at her, incredulous. "Were two of my best friends talking about giving me a *hand job?*"

"Yes, but only one."

"One friend?"

Quinn couldn't help but laugh. "No. One hand job."

"Let me guess. That'd be you?"

Quinn shrugged and smiled coyly.

"Nope. No way." Cash stood and backed away from Quinn. "Not going to fucking happen."

"But I *promised* Wynter I'd do it."

"So what?" Cash crossed his arms. "You promised in a dream. It's not real but this is. And it's personal, Quinn."

"I know, but time is running out," Quinn said, the urgency in her voice clear. "Wynter can feel her brain getting worse. And if you can learn to summon faster, you'll be able to save her."

Cash's eyes blazed. "Why me? How are you so sure I can save her? Why can't you save her? You hang out with her more than I do."

"I don't know. That's just what Wynter told me."

Cash paced back and forth, then stopped. "Just give me one of those little cube things."

"The zees? They might work, but Wynter wanted me to try the natural way first."

"I say we try the zees first," Cash said.

Quinn sighed. "I guess."

"How do I know you're not just trying to get into my pants?"

Cash had struck an angry nerve in Quinn. "Don't flatter yourself. Besides, I'd never do anything to fuck over my friendship with you or Wynter."

"What about Ransom? You remember fucking *him?*"

Quinn shook her head. "Okay, that was a mistake, but it was also research."

"How is that *research?*"

"Forget it. That doesn't matter right now," Quinn said. "You believe Ransom exists but don't believe me. You know how I know?"

"How?"

Quinn scanned the living room. "Do you have a pen and paper?"

Still puzzled and annoyed, Cash went to a drawer in the kitchen counter and pulled out a black Sharpie marker and a notepad. He handed both to Quinn.

"Sit," Quinn said, then took a seat herself facing him across the kitchen table. She tore off two sheets of paper, handed one to Cash, and rolled the pen to him. "Think back to last night, when you woke up and decided to stop trying to summon Wynter in your dreams. Picture the time on the clock in your room."

"What..." Cash's words faded away.

Quinn took her glasses off, spun around in her chair, and covered her eyes. "I can't see anything you're doing, right?"

Cash nodded, then realized that Quinn couldn't hear a nod. "Uh, right."

"Good," she said. "Write the time down and fold the paper up so I can't see what you wrote."

Cash scribbled some numbers on the paper and folded it in half three times. "Okay, done."

Quinn faced him and slid her glasses back on. "So we agree that there's no way I could have seen what you wrote, right?"

"Okay."

Quinn grabbed the pen and hunkered down over her piece of paper like she was writing a test and shielding her answers from a classroom full of cheaters. She folded the paper once, placed her hand on top, and pushed it across the table.

She looked up at Cash over the rims of her glasses. "How else could I know?"

Cash took her paper and unfolded it, revealing the time scrawled in bubbly cursive.

4:08 a.m.

"What the fuck?" Cash unfolded his own paper even though he knew what it said.

The two of them stared at each other.

"Wynter told me the time," Quinn said finally. "I'm not lying to you, Cash, and that proves it. I didn't want to do it either, but I made a promise. You can even ask her the next time you summon her, hopefully tonight."

Cash's eyes flicked between the two pieces of paper. "Okay. I believe you talked to her. But we're going to try the zees first. If they don't work, I'll let you... you know."

"Give you a helping hand," Quinn said. "Okay."

Cash shook his head slowly in disbelief, then both of them began to laugh. "Let's get going."

Quinn went to her purse and pulled the baggie of zees. She placed three onto his palm.

"Do I chew them or what?"

"I guess so," Quinn said. "Chewing them would get the herbs into your system faster."

Cash tossed the zees into his mouth and began to chew, then grimaced. "These taste like shit. You got to work on that." He swallowed. "How long before they take effect?"

"Maybe twenty minutes or so?"

"Okay. I'm going to lie down in my room." Cash walked around the sofa on his way to his bedroom. "We only get a few channels on TV. If you're hungry, feel free to eat whatever you find."

Quinn looked at the clock on the stove. "It's almost eleven o'clock. I'll give you until two in the morning. Then I'm waking you up."

"That's only three hours."

"It's three, maybe four REM cycles," Quinn said. "Plenty of time to dream and summon Wynter."

"Rem?"

"It stands for rapid eye movement. I've read some of Wynter's book, too, you know." Quinn hustled Cash along. "Go lie down so you can let the zees work their magic."

"Okay." Cash turned into his bedroom. "I think I feel them working already," he called out of the open door.

"Awesome." Quinn plopped herself down on the sofa, content to have gotten the evening started. She looked for a remote control to the TV, then realized that this TV was too old to have one. The realities of Cash's life sunk in.

She switched the TV on, lowered the volume, and turned the dial, searching for something to watch. The *NBC Nightly News with Tom Brokaw* would have to do for now.

Quinn reclined on the well-worn sofa and propped her feet up on the wobbly coffee table in front. The three zees would knock Cash out, but it wouldn't help with deep relaxation, which is what he needed in order to summon.

And in less than three hours, Quinn would fulfill her promise to Wynter.

Don't Dream It's Over

"Shit!" The sole expletive floated out of Cash's bedroom and brought a small grin to Quinn's lips. It turned out that he hadn't needed to be woken up at two in the morning. All the better.

Paula Poundstone had just taken the stage on *Late Night with David Letterman*. Usually, comedians closed the show. Quinn glanced at the clock on the stove and confirmed it: twenty minutes past one.

Quinn switched off the TV and padded in sock feet to the door to Cash's room. Even though the door was ajar, she knocked the doorframe lightly. "Cash? Are you decent?"

A light flicked on beyond the door, followed by the sound of creaking bed springs. "Yeah," Cash said.

Quinn pushed the door open a little more and peeked in. She could see Cash's silhouette against the warm light of his little clamp-on bedside lamp. "Can I come in?"

Cash sat on the edge of his single bed in nothing but his boxers, slumped over in defeat. He looked up at her and waved her in.

"As you can see," Cash swept his arm around the empty room, "there's no one else here. It didn't work."

"Except for me."

"You don't count." The realization of how his words sounded dawned on him. "That came out wrong. I didn't mean—"

"I know what you mean." Quinn sat next to him and shared a moment of silence. "So, are we really going to do this?"

Cash shrugged then turned to her. His irises looked grey instead of his regular blue and the whites of his eyes were bloodshot. "I guess."

"Look, I know I promised Wynter I'd do this," Quinn said. "But if you're totally against it, I won't bother. We'll find another way."

"I made a promise to Wynter, too. I guess this is all part of it." Cash placed his hands on his knees. "I mean what kind of guy turns down a hand job?"

"Only the good ones." At that moment Quinn could see herself falling hard for Cash. She switched gears. "How do you want to do this?"

Cash shook his head slowly. "I have no idea."

Quinn looked around the small room. In one corner beside the bed stood a beat up dresser. That was it. No other furniture. "I'll get a chair from the other room." Her eyes flicked to his legs, then straight ahead again. "You're going to have to take off your underwear too."

Without waiting for Cash to respond, Quinn walked out to the kitchen area and grabbed a chair. She paused at the bedroom door. "Are you ready?"

"Yeah."

Quinn carried the chair into the room. Cash lay in his bed, close to the edge, reclined against his pillow. He had pulled the bedsheet up to his armpits, hinting at the form of his body underneath. She set the chair down close to the mattress, next to his hips, and sat facing him.

"When you're ready, I'll reach under the sheets and... you know."

"Okay, but a couple rules," Cash said. "We need to close our eyes, we can't talk, and we can't enjoy it."

"Well, *you* can enjoy it. It's supposed to be relaxing. Imagine it's Wynter, not me."

"I'll try."

Quinn nodded. "Okay, I'm going to start." She found the edge of the sheet and placed her left hand underneath. "I'm closing my eyes now." She moved her hand up along the edge of the bed until her fingertips found the edge of his bare thigh.

Cash's body flinched ever so slightly but Quinn felt it.

"You alright? Want me to stop?"

"No, it's okay."

With slow and careful movements, Quinn let her fingertips guide her over and up his thigh until they detected his nest of pubic hair. A second later, she found Cash's erect penis and she bit her lip. She hadn't expected him to be hard so quickly. It would make the task easier.

She ran her fingers up his smooth taut skin, then wrapped him in a loose one-handed grip. Quinn slid her hand down, then up, then—

Cash groaned and his body shuddered. Warm, sticky fluid cascaded over her hand. "Oh shit, I'm so sorry."

"Don't worry about it." Quinn removed her hand. "I'm going to open my eyes now."

"Wait." Cash jostled in the bed, moving things around. "Okay, now I'm good."

Quinn opened her eyes and saw that Cash had placed his pillow over his abdomen.

"Sorry. I created a huge mess," Cash said.

"I see that." Quinn looked at her glistening hand. "I'm going to go wash up. Can I bring you a towel or something?"

"Nah, I'm okay."

Quinn stood to go.

"Wait." Cash caught her eyes with his own worried gaze. "Please don't say anything."

Quinn tilted her head at him. "Why? Afraid it'll destroy your rep?"

Cash sighed. "I'm a virgin, Quinn. I don't have a rep. It's just… embarrassing."

"Don't worry about it. Your secret's safe with me." Quinn's eyes lingered on his a little too long. "I promise." She held up her left hand. "Now I got to take care of this before it hardens."

Cash raised his hand to his face but couldn't conceal his nervous laugh or the heat flushing his cheeks. "Sorry. Again."

Quinn walked to the bathroom and washed her hands. She hoped Wynter was right, that this would work better than the zees, because she didn't think she could do that again with her eyes closed. Or without jumping Cash's bones.

Quinn returned to the bedroom to find Cash with his boxers back on and fast asleep. She backed out of the bedroom and eased the door closed to a crack.

She found a cheesy late night movie on one of the half dozen channels that the TV picked up.

"You can do it, Cash," Quinn said to herself. "You can bring Wynter home." She settled into the sofa, watched, and waited.

CASH FOUND HIMSELF lying across the back seat of Blue Belle. Quinn sat in the driver's seat, her face bathed in a flickering blue light. He pushed himself up onto his elbows and his sightline revealed a movie projected on the Beetle's windshield. It wasn't any movie he recognized.

"Quinn? Where are we?" Cash scrunched his brows together. "What's going on?"

Quinn said nothing and continued watching the movie on the windshield.

"Quinn?" Cash pulled himself between the front seats to get

a better look at her. Quinn stared past him, through him, expressionless and unblinking. He waved his hands in front of her face and snapped his fingers. "What the hell. Quinn?"

"She can't hear you."

Her voice was unmistakeable. Cash spun around to see Wynter leaning into the Beetle's open passenger window.

"Wynter?" Cash pushed the passenger seat forward, jumped out of the car, and wrapped his arms around her, the clean scent of her red hair washing over him. "Oh God, Wynter, is it really you?" He stepped back, holding her shoulders and searching her eyes with his.

"It's really me." Wynter smiled and Cash pulled her into another hug. "I've missed you too, but don't break me."

Cash stepped back. "Sorry. It's just that…"

"It's okay," Wynter said. "I'm okay." She handed him a folded pair of jeans. "You might want to put these on."

"What do you—" Cash choked when he saw his bare legs extending down from his boxers. He took the jeans and pulled them on in a hurry. They were a perfect fit.

Wynter smirked. "They look good on you."

Cash ran his hands down the front of the jeans, smoothing out the fabric on his legs. He glanced at Blue Belle and Quinn frozen within. The movie continued to play on the windshield. He scanned his surroundings, blocking the fiery sunset from his eyes with his hand and noting the empty parking lot and the Halston Medical Center in the distance. "This is a dream, isn't it?"

Wynter nodded. "But I'm real. You summoned me."

Cash jammed his hands in his pockets. "Does that mean that you know about…" His eyes flicked uneasily toward Quinn and back.

"How Quinn *helped* you? Yeah. And I *did* ask her to do it. She owed me big-time." Wynter gave Quinn a quick look of appreciation. "Somehow I don't think she minded giving you a hand."

"I didn't want her to do it," Cash said. "I swear."

"I know."

"This is all pretty weird." Cash studied Wynter's face as if it would be the last time he'd see her. "Your mom and dad are worried sick."

"Yeah. Tell them that I'm getting better," Wynter said. "The fact that you're here is proof of that."

"Why not tell them yourself?" Cash kicked at a loose pebble at his feet. "Come out of the dream with me."

"I want to, Cash. Really. But either I'm still too weak or our connection isn't strong enough yet." Wynter thought for a moment, her tongue sticking out over her top teeth, just slightly, just like she always did. "It's probably a bit of both. But I'm getting better every day."

Cash looked confused. "Our connection isn't strong enough? How can you say that?"

"Of all my friends, my connection with you is strongest. Quinn's a close second," Wynter said. "But it could always be stronger."

"Your connection with Ransom is pretty strong." Confusion in Cash's voice mixed with anger. "You want Ransom, is that it?"

"Ransom is a dreamwaker. He can't save me." Wynter took Cash's hands in hers. "Only *you* can save me."

Cash threw his hands up. "So, what am I here for? I mean I love talking to you, but if you can't be a dreamwaker, what's the point?"

"You need to find another dreamwaker. For practice. To know how it feels," Wynter said. "And afterwards you need to tell my parents that you can summon."

"Another dreamwaker? Who would that be?"

Wynter shook her head. "Only you can decide. But it has to be someone with a strong connection to you."

"I had a… cat when I was younger." Cash's eyes went distant. "His name was Fonzie, you know, from *Happy Days?*"

"Summoning and dreamwaking doesn't work with animals, unfortunately."

Cash's eyes searched the horizon beyond the hospital. "I had a…" His voice faded away.

"An old girlfriend? You probably had lots." Wynter tried to bring Cash back with her smile. It didn't work.

"What? No. I had a…" Cash's eyes thickened with tears. "I had a sister. A long time ago." He sighed and his whole body shuddered. "Man, I haven't thought of her for so long." Cash sat cross-legged on the asphalt and Wynter lowered herself to join him.

"What was her name?"

"Sierra," Cash said. "She was my twin sister." He picked up a pebble from the ground and tossed it back and forth. "She was six when she died. Hit and run. They never caught the guy, either."

"Oh my god." Wynter took Cash's hand. "I'm so sorry."

"Thanks." Cash closed his eyes, then hung his head and smiled wistfully. "She loved Keds. Never left the house without them on her feet. I can still hear the sound of her running—"

A pitter-patter of quick moving feet on pavement rose from behind him. Before Cash could turn around, he felt a pair of young arms reach around his neck.

"Cashmere!" Sierra flung herself onto Cash's shoulders.

Cash's eyes bugged out and he twisted his body around to make sure what he heard matched what he saw. "Sierra?"

She peeked over his shoulder. "You got it, Pontiac!" A six-year-old Sierra rolled in front of him and sat, matching his cross-legged position. Her cornsilk hair hung long and straight, flowing around her shoulders and almost obscuring the white imprint of Rocky Balboa on her black T-shirt.

Cash remembered her shirt like it was yesterday. Sierra loved *Rocky* (she saw the film in the theaters three times) and wore that shirt almost continuously until the day she was struck down. White shorts with red seams completed her outfit, with white Keds covering her feet, never with socks. She tilted her head at him. "Where have you been? I've missed you."

"I don't know. I…" Cash looked to Wynter for rescue, but she just smiled at him and mouthed the word *cashmere* with a quizzical look on her face. "I've missed you, too."

"You look different," Sierra said. "Old."

"Yeah, I'm… it's been ten years since your accident. I'm sixteen now."

"Oh." Sierra faced Wynter. "Who are you?"

"I'm Wynter. I'm a friend of your brother's."

"I like winter," Sierra said, fiddling with her laces. "But I like summer more." She looked up at Cash. "Where's Dad?"

"He's at work." Cash took Sierra's small hands in his. "Would you like to see where I live now?"

Sierra smiled and nodded enthusiastically.

Cash glanced at Wynter. "So how does this work?"

"Hold onto Sierra and focus all your energy on being awake," Wynter said. "Sierra exists only in spirit and in your memories, and she wants to go, so there should be nothing standing in your way."

"Okay. Here goes nothing." Cash was about to close his eyes when he leaned over and gave Wynter a full, deep kiss. "See you soon."

Wynter smiled.

"Kissing? On the *lips?*" Sierra scrunched her nose up. "Gross. Billy Bishop tried to kiss me at school. I punched him."

"Good for you," Cash said. "Ready?"

Sierra shook her head up and down. Cash held her hands firmly and closed his eyes. He pictured his own bed in his familiar room and allowed his body to fall backward.

Both of them slipped through the asphalt and Wynter disappeared in a spinning blur. A brief bright blue sky replaced the setting sun, then darkness surrounded him again. A brief odor of ozone mixed with old bacon and eggs tickled his nostrils.

Cash opened his eyes to his room again. "Sierra?" He looked around his room. Sierra was nowhere to be seen. He pulled on his well-worn jeans and a T-shirt from the floor. "Sierra?" he whispered. "Are you here?"

From the foot of the bed, Sierra stood, her hair mussed up and obscuring her face. She huffed it away. "I don't like that game, Cashmere."

Cash fell to his knees and hugged her. "Yeah, sorry about that. It's a little weird, isn't it?"

"Smells funny, too."

Cash glanced at the door to his room, open a crack. The soft sounds of the TV played beyond. "Sierra, there's someone else I want you to meet. Come on."

He stood, pulled his bedroom door open and stepped through.

QUINN FOUGHT AGAINST heavy eyelids. *Murder on Flight 502* was about as good as she'd expected it to be, but it would soon be over. Then what? She glanced at the clock on the stove range. It was almost four in the morning. She rubbed her eyes, knowing that she'd have to work the FreshWhip stand without sleep again.

"Quinn."

The sound of Cash's unexpected voice sent Quinn leaping to her feet, her heart jackhammering in her chest. The adrenaline coursing through her body made sure she was awake and alert. She turned and saw Cash standing in the short hallway to the bedrooms.

"Cash!" Quinn grappled with her panicked breath. "Don't sneak up on me like that. You scared me."

"Quinn," Cash said, his voice smooth and steady. "It worked."

"It worked?" Quinn ran toward him. If the sofa had been in her way, she would have bounded over it. "Wynter's back?" Her eyes searched side to side. "Bug?"

Sierra poked her head around from behind Cash's back. He placed a gentle hand on her shoulder.

"Where's the bug?" she said. "I don't like bugs."

Cash crouched to her level. "Remember Wynter?"

Sierra nodded.

He continued. "This is Quinn. She's Wynter's best friend. Sometimes she calls her 'Bug.' "

"Sometimes?" Quinn smirked. "Try most of the time."

"Just like I call you Cashmere?" Sierra said.

Cash gave her a thumbs up and she did the same, bumping knuckles.

"*Cashmere?*" Quinn glanced at him, her curiosity piqued.

"Because I'm warm and soft." Cash beamed at Sierra, then stood to face Quinn. "And you'll keep that secret until the day you die. Right?"

"Uh, right." Quinn studied Sierra's features, her eyes flicking back and forth between her face and Cash's. "You want to let me in on *this* little secret?"

Sierra crossed her arms against her chest. "I'm not little. I'm *six*."

Cash held up a small photo in a scuffed faux brass picture frame. "Quinn, meet my twin sister, Sierra."

Quinn took the picture and compared it to the girl standing next to Cash. "Amazing." She met Cash's eyes. "But why is she six?"

"That's when she died," Cash said.

"Oh." Cash's direct response caught her off guard. Quinn handed the photo back to him, a puzzled expression on her face. "But... she's a dreamwaker. You can summon people who've died?"

"I guess so."

"I'm not dead." Sierra punched Cash's thigh. "Feel that?"

Cash grunted. "Sure did." He crouched again. "Remember we were talking to Wynter in my dream? Well, I've got a special power to help people in my dreams become real."

"So I'm real?" Sierra held one hand in front of her face and flexed it.

"You're a dream in real form," Cash said. "But if you or I fall asleep, you'll become just a dream again."

"Then I don't want you to ever sleep again." Sierra threw her arms around Cash's neck.

"Why didn't Wynter come with you?"

Cash sighed and looked up at Quinn. "She's still not strong enough."

"But..." Quinn gave him an unsure glance.

"I know what you're going to say," Cash said. "As far as I can tell, a dreamwaker needs to be strong in real life, and have a strong bond with the dreamer. It's better if both are true."

"How does that explain Ransom?" Quinn said. "She just made him up."

Cash stood and shrugged. "I guess he's a special case. And Wynter's the key to all of it." He looked to the door of the trailer. "I need to let Wynter's parents know that I can summon. And I need to do it now."

Quinn hooked her thumb back at the clock on the stove. "It's almost four in the morning. They'll be furious."

"I got a feeling they won't be." Cash grinned at Sierra. "I'll need your help. Want to come?"

Sierra nodded and gave him a thumbs up. He matched it and tapped knuckles.

"Wait." Cash hustled back into his room.

Sierra glanced up at Quinn. "Where's Cashmere going?"

Quinn shrugged. "No idea."

Cash emerged seconds later holding up *Eyes Wide Dreaming*. "Now we can go." He found his shoes at the front door and pulled them on. He opened the door and stepped out into the clean and cool night air. Sierra kept close to Cash. Quinn grabbed her purse and slung it over her shoulder on her way out.

"You decided to come anyway, huh?" Cash stopped to let her catch up before continuing across the field to Wynter's trailer.

"I've never witnessed a murder before," Quinn snickered.

"Ha, ha. They'll be cool with it. You'll see." Cash pointed at the lit windows in Wynter's trailer. "Look. Someone's up already."

Sierra hustled up next to Cash and took his free hand. The sight of their strong yet effortless bond brought an unexpected lump to Quinn's throat and reminded her of Wynter. Quinn's heart ached. Wynter had been the only person in her life that even resembled a sister.

At four minutes to four on a Thursday morning, the three of them ascended the steps to Wynter's front door.

Cash made a fist and knocked. He barely had enough time to step back from the door before it swung open, revealing Nolan in a T-shirt and boxer shorts. His black hair hung around his shoulders and partially shrouded his face. To anyone else, he would have appeared sinister.

A wide smile broke on Nolan's face. "Cash, Quinn, and…"

"Sierra," Cash said. "My twin sister."

"Your twin…" Nolan's voice trailed off as he rubbed his chin and processed the difference in their ages. Sierra looked up at him with wide, curious eyes. He squatted to her level. "Sierra's a beautiful name. Did you know that Sierra is Spanish for 'mountain range'?"

Sierra shook her head back and forth slowly without taking her eyes off Nolan. "I like your hair."

"I like yours, too."

"How long did it take to grow?"

Nolan paused to think. "I've had long hair ever since I was your age. Some say your hair pulls energy and information from the universe like a cat's whiskers. It's an extension of our dreams and the things we do as humans. Protect it."

Sierra nodded. "I will."

Nolan stood and looked at Cash and Quinn. "It's pretty late. What can I help you guys with?"

Cash looked down at Sierra snuggled up against the side of his body. "Sorry to bother you, Mr. LaCroix."

"No, not at all. I was just making some chamomile tea." Nolan's eyes kept returning to Sierra's, as if he could sense her otherworldly life energy.

Quinn thrummed her fingers on the railing. "Having trouble sleeping?"

"You could say that." Nolan stepped aside. "Want to come in?"

"No, that's okay," Cash said. "I just wanted you to know that I was able to summon Wynter tonight. Intentionally. And my sister, of course."

Nolan craned his neck above them to scan the field behind. "Is Wynter here?"

"Unfortunately, no. She's still too weak. Sierra is my dreamwaker this time." Cash looked down at Sierra and ruffled her long hair. She smiled up at him.

Nolan placed his palms together just under his nose, like he was praying, and nodded slowly. "I sense there's more to this story."

"You'd be right, but it's late. That story's going to have to wait." Cash threw a quick look at Quinn. "Wynter wanted you to know that she's getting better. When she's strong enough to leave my dreams, you'll be the first to know. You have my word."

Quinn motioned to the book in Cash's hand.

"Oh! Yeah." Cash handed *Eyes Wide Dreaming* to Nolan. "I wanted to return this."

"Thank you, Cash. Did it help?"

"It got the *job* done," Quinn said.

Cash sent Quinn a quick furtive glance before nodding. "It did."

The kettle began to screech in the kitchen. Nolan ran inside to take it from the heat and shut off the stove. He glanced furtively toward the opposite end of the trailer. "I'm going to have a lot of explaining to do come morning."

"We should go then," Cash said. "I've got some explaining to do myself."

"Bye." Sierra waved at Nolan as she followed Cash and Quinn down the steps to the field. "Don't cut your hair."

"Don't cut yours either." Nolan waved at her with a smile.

Back at Cash's trailer, Quinn took Cash aside. "I'm going to motor. I think you can call this night a success."

"Yeah." Cash stared at his feet and Quinn could sense his embarrassment rising in the early morning light. "Sorry about the... you know. But you and Wynter were right. It was the key."

"I'm glad because it was a *one-shot* deal."

Cash groaned at Quinn's pun.

"It's *not* coming to a bedroom near you," she said. "So you'll have to give *yourself a hand* next time."

"Enough." Laughter overtook Cash's embarrassment.

"What are you going to do now?"

Cash glanced back at Sierra waiting on the front steps and waved at her. "Maybe I'll find a photo album and show her some pictures from the last ten years. If I can stay awake, that is."

"Honestly, that sounds depressingly lame," Quinn said. "Like, how would that work? 'Here Sierra. Let me show you everything that you've missed.' "

"Maybe you're right."

"I'm sure you'll figure something out." Quinn waved at Sierra, walked to Blue Belle's driver's side door, and unlocked it. She pulled out the baggie of zees from her purse and opened it, taking out several cubes. "Hold on to these. Use them as a last resort. Maybe share a few with Nolan." She dropped them into Cash's open palm.

"Thanks."

Quinn gave him a quick hug, then slid into the driver's seat. "Say hi to Wynter for me, okay?"

Cash nodded and Quinn closed her door. A moment later, Blue Belle's engine rattled to life and backed out of the parking space.

He waved then joined Sierra, climbing the steps to his trailer. "How would you like some hot chocolate?"

"Yes, please!" Sierra hopped up and down excitedly.

"Come on."

Once inside, Cash took down a canister of Hershey's Chocolate Milk Mix, spooned some of the powder into a pot, added milk, and set it on the stove to warm up.

Cash poured the hot chocolate into mugs and handed one to Sierra. He knew that it wouldn't be long before one or both of them fell asleep. That was the plan all along. Hershey's hot chocolate had always had that effect on them.

Cash couldn't have Sierra awake when Ernie returned home from work, at least not yet. He couldn't be sure how Ernie would react, but Cash was certain that devastation would be in there somewhere, eventually. Ernie would need to be prepared with a proper explanation. The timing wasn't right.

The two of them settled onto the sofa, sipping their hot chocolates and watching early morning cartoons. Part of Cash wanted to stay awake. He had missed his sister terribly over the past ten years, a realization that hit him hard.

Sitting with Sierra now was magical. Cash didn't want it to end but he had no choice but to let sleep overtake him, with the knowledge that Sierra would be gone when he awoke. Now he had the ability to summon her in his dreams at any time, and knowing this gave his aching heart some relief.

Cash closed his eyes and hoped that Sierra wouldn't see his tears before he slept.

RANSOM TUMBLED OVER Jezebel and knocked Roxy off the mattress. A strong odor of ozone floated to the rafters of the storage shed. He was beginning to really loathe being a dreamwaker for Jezebel. Having sex in her dreams was enough for him. It should be enough for her. Making it real seemed pointless to him now, unless she enjoyed flaunting her sexcapades in front of Roxy.

"Jesus, dude." Roxy pushed Ransom back. "Watch who you land on, for fuck's sake."

"As if I have any control over that." Ransom rolled to his knees and sat on his heels. "But sorry. Did I hurt you?"

"Who cares if she's hurt." Jezebel tugged on the button to Ransom's jeans, unzipped his fly, and thrust her hand under the denim. "She'll get over it. Right, Rox?"

"Whatever." Roxy rolled her eyes and took a seat on the floor, resting her back against the shelving unit. "And I'm not hurt, by the way," she said, brushing cobwebs off her shoulders.

"See?" Jezebel looked down and saw Ransom was already hard. She began to push Ransom's jeans down, but he gripped her wrists and stopped her. Anger flashed red in her eyes. "What are you—"

"Turn around." Ransom's voice was firm and calm as he rose up on his knees.

Jezebel's short-lived anger morphed to wariness, then a sly grin emerged on her lips and she narrowed her eyes at him. "You dirty dog."

Ransom returned a small smile of his own. "That's me." He placed his hands on Jezebel's hips and shifted her around until she was kneeling facing away from him. He looked down at his open fly and saw that he was ready to rock. If he could have changed anything about himself at that instant, it would have been to have the ability to control his physical arousal. His body often had a mind of its own.

Ransom reached around Jezebel's waist and popped the button on her jeans. He unzipped her fly, pulled her jeans down to her knees, then hooked his thumbs into the waistband of her black panties and pulled, letting them slide down her thighs.

He placed one hand on Jezebel's back and pushed her. She fell forward, catching herself on her open hands.

"Watch and learn, Rox." Jezebel dipped her head forward and let her hair spill around her face.

Roxy rolled her eyes and looked around for something to read but the labels to paint cans on the shelf held no appeal. She met Ransom's gaze and they shared a heated look. He winked at her as he pushed down his jeans.

Ransom placed one hand on the small of Jezebel's back and guided himself into her from behind. He moved his hands to her hips and rocked them back and forth, keeping his eyes on Roxy as much as possible without raising suspicion.

Jezebel gasped at his intensity. Ransom moved his hands forward, over her T-shirt, running fingertips over her breasts underneath the fabric. He continued thrusting his hips as he moved his hands to her shoulders, then to her neck and began to squeeze.

It only took a few seconds before Jezebel's pleasure turned to fear. She arched her back and clawed at his hands as Ransom's grip tightened.

Soon he'd be back in Wynter's dreams and Jezebel would be gone for good. Even when Ransom remembered Jezebel's deal with Monty, he didn't let up. He was torn between two intrinsically linked outcomes.

Jezebel tried to speak but couldn't get air through her windpipe. She sent a panicked look at Roxy.

"What the hell are you doing?" Roxy sat forward, alarmed,

then scrambled forward on her hands and knees. "Ransom! Stop! You're going to kill her."

Ransom side-eyed Roxy and sent back a smile filled with evil. With his brain clouded by his desire to see Jezebel gone, he convinced himself that he could save Wynter before Monty got to her.

Roxy leaped toward Ransom and pushed him off Jezebel. He tumbled toward the door to the shed, his jeans rolling at his knees.

Jezebel collapsed onto the mattress clutching her throat and wheezing great gulps of air. Roxy was by her side in a second, turning her on her side.

Ransom stood and pulled up his jeans. He removed the loose lock-loop from the door and tossed it to the floor. One of his hands held his jeans up while the other flung the door open wide. He was out of the shed like a shot, buttoning and zipping up his jeans as he ran.

"Stop him..." Jezebel said, her voice coming out in a hoarse whisper.

Roxy shook her head. "No. Forget it, Jazz. I'm not leaving you."

For once, Jezebel had no issue with Roxy's disobedience. She massaged her neck, taking in large breaths, and sat up. "Page Monty," she said with a scowl.

"You're not going to get him to kill Wynter, are you?" Roxy tried to get a read on Jezebel's face but all she saw was hatred. "That's a bad idea, Jazz."

"Just do it!" Jezebel yelled despite the condition of her throat, which had begun to discolor with bruises.

Roxy stumbled back, her eyes both concerned and afraid. She ran out of the shed in search of a payphone.

Jezebel wiped drool from her lips and stared out the open door, her eyes dark and blinded by hate.

Ransom oriented himself as he sprinted down the MovieTyme access road. It wouldn't take long before he passed the Starlite and beyond that, Wynter's trailer. The thought of seeing Wynter again fueled his pace.

The orange glow of the pre-dawn sun bled along the horizon. Ransom guessed it must be around five in the morning.

A car's headlights breached the corner and drove past him going the opposite direction. Ransom could hear AC/DC blasting from the radio, raspy vocals advertising "dirty deeds done dirt cheap." He continued to run, refusing to look back even though recognition was strong. There was only one person he knew who drove a silver Fiat X1/9.

He heard the car slow and turn around. Moments later, the car's headlights were close enough to cast a stretched shadow of his running legs on the pavement ahead.

Monty pulled up beside him. "Where you running to?" Ransom focused on the road ahead instead of answering. Monty wasted no more time. He accelerated, then pulled a hard right, blocking Ransom's path.

Ransom didn't have the energy to fight this new wrinkle in his unwritten getaway plan. He skidded to a stop, supporting himself on the Fiat's passenger door.

"Who you runnin' from?" Monty said.

"Fuck you." Ransom took large, even breaths and slowly regained his composure.

Monty eyed him slyly and glanced back down the road they had come from. "Runnin' from *someone,* though. They wouldn't happen to be hidin' out at Ollie's, would they?"

Ransom stared back at him. "What do you want?"

Monty shrugged. "Just lookin' for opportunities, man. What do *you* want?"

"To get far away from you."

"Ransom, I'm hurt," Monty said, a pre-dawn twinkle in his eye. "I thought we were friends."

"Nope." Ransom started to walk around the Fiat.

"Wait." Monty threw open the car door and hopped out to intercept him. "Want to make some money?"

"I don't want money."

"Everybody wants money."

"Not me." Ransom stopped and eyed him cautiously. "But how about some info."

"Depends on the info," Monty said, wary of Ransom's every move.

Ransom stepped up to him, nose to nose. He could smell stale beer on Monty's breath. "Do you have a deal with Jezebel to kill Wynter?"

"Shit, you don't waste time."

"Do you have a deal with Jezebel or not?"

"If I tell you, you're goin' to have to do somethin' for me."

Ransom nodded without hesitation. "Okay."

Monty told Ransom what he knew, then handed him a package and told him what he needed done. It sounded easy enough. "We good?"

"We're good." Ransom shoved the package into his waistline at the small of his back and concealed it with the hems of his T-shirt and hoodie.

Monty stepped back and allowed Ransom to resume his sprint. "You cross me and you're fuckin' dead. Wynter too, just like Jezebel said."

"I can't die, remember?" Ransom called back. But he had no intention of crossing Monty. In fact, he was looking forward to following through with Monty's plan.

THE CHAMOMILE TEA hadn't performed as advertised. Nolan stared at the ceiling of the master bedroom, streaks of sunlight drawing diagonal slashes across the walls. He had tried to summon Wynter in his dreams and all he had to show for it was a night of frustration. He would need to leave for work in a couple of hours. One thing was certain. There was coffee in his future today. Lots of it.

A quick *knock-knock* sounded from the front of the trailer, capturing his attention. Nolan raised his head off his pillow and focused on the sounds of silence in the trailer.

The night after Wynter had been admitted to the hospital, Nolan and Madeline had decided to keep their bedroom door open in case something happened in Wynter's room. They both knew it was irrational, but it gave them some comfort. But it also exposed their bedroom to all the normal sounds of a single-wide trailer that no one usually noticed, the creaking in the breeze, the expansion and contraction under the summer sun.

At first Nolan thought the sound might have been the trailer settling or something shifting in the cupboards. Until it happened again.

Knock-knock.

This time Nolan was oriented and knew for certain that he hadn't heard the usual nighttime sounds. There *was* someone at the front door.

He eased himself out of bed and as he padded into the main living area, he automatically closed the door to the master bedroom. Madeline would be up soon anyway, but there was no reason to wake her up too early.

Nolan unlocked the front door and pulled it open. Ransom stood on the landing, wearing his iconic jeans, white T-shirt, and black hoodie. Nolan locked eyes with the teenager in front of him and they both regarded each other warily.

"I know you." Nolan shook his index finger at him. "You're the one who was in my daughter's room that night."

"Yes, sir," Ransom said.

"You ran."

Ransom nodded.

"Why?"

"I was s-scared." Ransom stuttered, his body shivering even in the morning sun.

Nolan glanced to the back of the trailer, then stood to one side. "Do you want to come inside? I'll make a pot of coffee."

"Th-thanks." Ransom stepped inside.

Nolan busied himself preparing the coffee maker. "Have a seat, uh... what's your name again?"

"Ransom, sir."

Nolan watched the young man sit down at the kitchen table, still shaking like a leaf. "You cold?"

Ransom looked up at him, his eyes blazing blue. "I need to see Wynter."

"I'm afraid that's not possible. She's—"

"I don't have much time. Please."

Nolan picked up the phone and dialed. "Cash? Sorry to wake you. I need you to get over here... Ransom's sitting in my kitchen right now."

"Nolan, honey, what's going on?"

Nolan hung up the phone to see Madeline in her housecoat and slippers, shuffling toward the kitchen. Her eyes shifted to the back of the chair Ransom was sitting in.

"Who's this?"

Ransom twisted in his chair to face Madeline. Her eyes went wide with recognition, surprise, and anger, all rolled into one.

"Maddie, this is Ransom," Nolan said. "And he needs to talk to Wynter."

TEN MINUTES AFTER Cash showed up at Wynter's trailer, Quinn rapped frenetically on the front door. Nolan let her in and ushered her to the kitchen table where Cash, Ransom, and Madeline sat.

"I'll stand, thanks." Quinn pointed at the coffee cups on the table. "But I'll have some of that. If I stop moving, I swear I'm going to, like, zonk out."

Nolan poured her a cup of coffee and handed it to her. Quinn gulped half of it and set her cup down. She placed her hands on the table and leaned toward Ransom.

"Where have you been?" She scowled at him. "Probably hanging out with that *bitch*."

"Easy now, Quinn darlin'," Madeline said.

"Why? He's a back-stabber."

"I'm sorry." Ransom glanced at Quinn, then at Cash. "For trying to rob you. For everything." His breath came unevenly. "I'm just so tired. I need to be back in Wynter's head."

"That's impossible because *she's in a coma!*" Quinn slammed her fists on the table. "All because of your stupid girlfriend."

Ransom stood, his legs propelling the chair backward. "She's *not* my girlfriend."

"Okay, time out. Quinn, come cool down." Nolan guided Quinn into the kitchen where he could corral her pacing.

"Ransom, you're not listening," Cash said. "Wynter can't talk to anyone. She's in a coma. And you can't dream because you're a dreamwaker."

"There's got to be something we can do." Ransom's eyes pleaded.

"Let's fuck with Jezebel's head." Quinn broke free from Nolan, grabbed Ransom by his collar, and planted a hard kiss on his lips.

Ransom backed away. "Stop it! I'm not a toy."

"A toy? Wait, what's going on?" Madeline shifted her gaze between the three teenagers in her kitchen. "Now's not the time to be kissing anyone."

"But maybe it *is* the time," Cash said. "Remember, whoever kisses a dreamwaker last can summon them in their dreams."

Cash stood and walked around the table to where Ransom stood. "According to Wynter, I'm the only one who can save her."

"What about us?" Nolan placed his hand on Madeline's shoulder. "We're her parents."

Cash shrugged. "I'm only going by what Wynter told me."

"Hold on a second. Now that Quinn has kissed Ransom, she should be able to summon him in her dreams." Madeline narrowed her eyes at Cash. "Is that right?"

"She should be able to, yes," Cash said.

"And you said you can summon Wynter?" Madeline's gears were turning. She locked gazes with Cash. "So, if you kiss Ransom, couldn't you summon them both in your dreams? Then they could talk."

Cash marveled at the simplicity of Madeline's revelation. "Holy shit, Mrs. LaCroix. You're a genius. Would that work?"

"It's worth a shot," Quinn said.

Cash glanced at Ransom. "You in?"

"If it gets me out of Jezebel's head and closer to Wynter, count me in."

"Okay. No time like the present." Cash took a deep breath, then with both hands he pulled Ransom's face to his and planted a solid, beefy kiss on his lips.

"I think Ransom prefers a little tongue action." Quinn laughed.

Cash gave her a playful shove as his neck and cheeks flooded deep pink. "We're really going to fuck with Jezebel's head now."

"Most definitely." Quinn smiled.

Nolan and Madeline exchanged surprised glances.

"I should split." Ransom moved to the trailer door.

Quinn grabbed his wrist. "Why not crash here, in Wynter's room. I'm sure Mr. and Mrs. LaCroix wouldn't mind."

"No, absolutely," Nolan said. "You'd be safe here."

"And you'd be safe in Cash's head," Quinn added.

"I don't want Jezebel to get suspicious." Ransom looked down at his hand on the doorknob. "Besides, there's something I got to take care of."

Quinn cast him a wary glance. "Can you pretend like nothing's happened?"

"Jezebel's bullshit detector is pretty good," Ransom said. "I'll try."

"No. Do." Quinn squeezed Ransom's wrist. "There is no try." She pulled his wrist up between their faces. "Also, no kissing, fucking, hand jobs, or blow jobs. From *anyone*. And don't get stabbed or shot."

"Got it." Ransom matched Quinn's stare. "You done?"

She let go. Ransom rubbed his wrist, then opened the door and disappeared into the dawn sunshine.

Nolan blinked at Quinn, then cast a wary glance at Madeline. "Teenaged life sure has changed," he said.

Cash tilted his head at Quinn. "Were you quoting Yoda? From *The Empire Strikes Back?*"

Quinn nodded. "See? You're getting smarter every day."

"Can I make everyone breakfast?" Nolan shifted his gaze between Madeline, Cash, and Quinn. "No one's going to sleep now."

"Absolutely," Quinn and Cash said in unison.

Madeline pulled Nolan's cheek in for a kiss. "You're a gem. I'm going for a quick shower," she said, heading toward the bathroom.

Nolan grinned. "Bacon, eggs, and pancakes will be waiting."

"And it's not even the weekend," Madeline called back just before she disappeared into the bathroom.

As Nolan made breakfast, Quinn and Cash talked about how

he would summon two people at once. He realized he had already done it once before, with Wynter and Sierra. But the question remained: could he do it again?

RRANSOM STOPPED UNDER the sign to Sven Dwarfs Trail'r Park and scanned up and down Main Street. No cars or activity in either direction. He lifted the pay phone handset off its cradle. Digging into his pocket, he pulled out a piece of paper and a quarter, and dialed.

Across Main Street, half a block from the entrance to Sven Dwarfs, Jezebel and Roxy had been watching from behind a hedge.

"How did you know he'd be here?" Roxy squinted in an attempt to enhance the detail of what she was seeing.

"Where else would he go but back to his *whiner* girlfriend." Jezebel spoke in a mocking sing-song voice. "Pathetic and predictable."

Ransom shifted uneasily on his feet as he waited for the call to connect. After the third ring, an automated prompt asked for a number. He punched in the digits written on the paper and jammed it back in his pocket. He turned and ran down Jones Avenue, toward the Starlite.

Roxy frowned. "What the hell was he doing?"

"He made a call, then punched in some numbers." Jezebel swatted Roxy's shoulder with the back of her hand. "Use your fucking head."

Things clicked and Roxy's eyes widened. "A pager."

"And who in this town uses a pager?"

"Monty?"

"I'd bet your life on it. Come on." Jezebel stepped out from behind the hedge and ran back to the Barracuda hidden further down the road.

Roxy followed. "Wait? You'd bet *my* life?"

"You don't think I'd bet my *own* life, do you?" Jezebel pulled camouflaging branches off the car and tossed them aside. "Get in."

Less than five minutes later, Jezebel and Roxy parked behind the storage shed at Ollie's MovieTyme and pulled the blue tarp over the car. They squatted behind the driver's side fender, their heads just clearing the hood.

"How do you know he's coming back here?"

"Jesus. Where else is he going to go?" Jezebel shook her head in disgust. "He's a wanted man, plus he's got to suck up to me or Monty kills Wynter."

"But that was only if he killed you," Roxy said. "Did Monty say he would really do it?"

"As long as Ransom believes it, it doesn't matter." The sound of runners on pavement approached. "Now shut the fuck up with the questions and get down."

The footsteps grew closer until Ransom revealed himself in the graveled area behind the storage shed. He made a beeline for the door and tried to pull it open even though it was clearly padlocked from the outside.

Jezebel stood, slid her switchblade from her back pocket, and engaged the blade. Roxy took her position beside her.

The *click* caught Ransom's attention. He turned to face the girls, his eyes on the blade glinting in the morning sunshine.

"Where the fuck were you?" Jezebel hissed.

Ransom held his hands forward, his palms facing forward. "Nowhere."

"Bullshit." Jezebel walked steadily toward Ransom. "You tried to kill me."

"I freaked out. Sorry. I had to get out of that shed. Clear my head."

Jezebel glanced at Roxy and tossed her the keys to the shed. "Well, you better get used to it 'cause we're going back in."

Roxy ran to the door of the shed and popped open the padlock. Jezebel sent her a subtle nod. Roxy tossed back the keys and used the distraction to wrap her arms across and behind Ransom's neck, forming a tight choke hold.

Ransom struggled to get free but was quickly losing his ability to fight. A stack of twenty dollar bills wrapped in plastic tumbled to the ground behind him.

"Holy shit." Roxy kicked the bundle to Jezebel.

"What the hell is this?" Jezebel picked up the bundle, tore through a corner of the plastic, and riffled through the bills.

Ransom gritted his teeth, spitting his words out. "I can... explain."

Jezebel motioned at Roxy and she loosened her hold on Ransom's neck. Jezebel turned the tip of the switchblade around in slow tight circles. "You got some kind of hustle going on behind my back?"

"I was going to tell you. I swear."

Jezebel laughed. "Now you won't have to, because I'm going to cut your heart out." Jezebel closed the distance between them. "Then I'm going to do the same to Wynter."

Ransom had regained some of his strength and began twisting against Roxy's arms. "You bitch! I won't let you."

Jezebel drew a line across her throat with her free hand and Roxy tightened her hold on Ransom's neck again. His struggles waned almost instantly.

"Stop. I... I'll kill..." Ransom's arms swayed lifelessly at the sides of his body.

"You'll kill *who*?" Jezebel placed the tip of the switchblade to the center of Ransom's chest and pushed it into his body up to its hilt. Blood soaked into his shirt in a widening maroon circle.

Roxy had had enough and looked away.

"No." Jezebel hissed her words at Roxy through clenched teeth. "You watch or you're next."

Roxy had no choice but to obey.

Ransom locked his gaze with Jezebel's as he formed a broad smile. His reaction threw Jezebel off guard. "Gotcha," he said.

His eyes glowed blue fire and a split second later he drifted into nothing.

Roxy's face filled with panic. "What the fuck did that mean?"

Jezebel pushed Roxy backward and tried to hide her concern. "Probably nothing. Don't spaz." She headed into the storage shed. "You coming or am I locking you out?" Roxy followed Jezebel into the shed and closed the door.

Across the road, behind a line of garbage cans, the morning sun glinted off a piece of glass, specifically a zoom lens. Monty poked his head up, smiling behind his mirrored sunglasses and holding an SLR camera.

"Ransom, you did alright." He left his hiding place and ran back to where he had parked his Fiat.

Head Games

Roxy woke to find Jezebel's hands wrapped around her neck in a tight grip. She clawed at Jezebel's hands with her fingertips, unable to draw a breath to scream or even utter a word.

Jezebel straddled Roxy's abdomen. "Where is he, you fucking bitch?"

Roxy used her feet to buck her hips up and rolled off the mattress, taking Jezebel with her. She could have smashed Jezebel's neck with a well placed elbow, but Roxy chose to use the change in position to free Jezebel's hands from her throat.

Roxy scrabbled across the dirty floor toward the shelving unit. She held her hands over her neck protectively. "Are you crazy?"

"You did something didn't you?" Jezebel crouched, coiling her legs to leap and attack. "You kissed him, didn't you? Fucking whore! You *kissed* him." She launched herself at Roxy, her arms outstretched.

Roxy rolled left as Jezebel crashed into the shelves, sending half a dozen cans of spray paint clattering to the floor. "Stop! Jazz! Listen to me. If you're talking about Ransom, I didn't do shit, okay?"

"He's not in my dreams anymore."

"That's not my fault." In all the years she had known Jezebel, Roxy had never seen her so hung up on a guy. "I was standing behind him for fuck's sake. Jesus. Mellow out." She pushed herself to the opposite end of the shelving unit to keep some distance between them. "Obviously someone else must've kissed him."

"Fuck you." Jezebel threw a spray paint can at her. "Who?"

"How should I know? He was gone for a while." Roxy spotted heavy tears glistening in Jezebel's eyes, ready to fall, but Roxy knew better than to mention it. It was rare for Jezebel to show any display of emotion other than rage. "Is Wynter out of the hospital yet?"

Jezebel looked away and swiped her tears away with her wrist. "Shit. Maybe she's back at the trailer. That's why Ransom was there." Her eyes went dark again. The vulnerable Jezebel few saw was replaced by the hardened sociopath everyone was used to. "I think we need to pay her a visit. Everyone knows you don't take what doesn't belong to you."

CASH AND QUINN stepped out of Wynter's trailer, their bellies full of Nolan's pancakes, eggs, bacon, and coffee.

"Thanks for the grub, Mr. LaCroix." Cash rubbed his full stomach. "I'll let you know what happens with Wynter and Ransom."

Nolan waved and closed the trailer door.

"Want a lift to work?" Quinn shielded her eyes from the rising sun. "I'm going that way anyway."

"I won't pass that up…" Cash cocked an ear. "Oh, shit."

"What?"

Cash pointed toward the trailer park entrance. "Here comes trouble." A black Barracuda barreled down the access road, a swirl of angry dust sticking to its back bumper. "I'll give you one guess what she wants."

Quinn laughed. "I'd say disappointment is in her future."

The Barracuda skidded to a stop, blocking Nolan's car. Jezebel pushed open the driver's side door and stormed toward the front stoop of Wynter's trailer.

Roxy stuck her head out of the window. "Jazz, the car's still running."

"Shut up." Jezebel trudged toward the trailer. "*Whiner!* Get your whore ass out here! Now!"

Cash moved to intercept Jezebel. "Hey, get the hell out of here! You're not welcome."

"Out of my way, asshole," Jezebel said. "This don't concern you."

"It doesn't concern Wynter either." Cash pushed Jezebel backward. "She's in a coma. Because of *you*."

"Bullshit. She stole Ransom from me." Jezebel pushed Cash back. "So get the fuck out of my way."

Roxy jumped out of the Barracuda to help but Quinn blocked her path, waving her finger at her. "Uh-uh. Back off, shit-for-brains."

"She's not here, you psycho!" Cash pushed Jezebel harder, knocking her onto her backside.

"Oh, you're fucking dead." Jezebel scrambled to her feet. Cash crouched like a sumo wrestler, ready to take the full brunt of Jezebel's wrath.

Jezebel pulled out her switchblade and engaged the blade. She ran at Cash, swiping the sharp tip of the knife back and forth.

Unprepared for her weapon, Cash deked and stretched his body out of the way, narrowly missing contact with her sharp blade.

"That's quite enough!" Madeline charged down the front stoop with a baseball bat. "You almost killed my daughter, and you have the *nerve* to show your face here?"

"Maddie!" Nolan yelled after her. "Stop!"

"Mrs. LaCroix, don't." Cash stepped into her path, but Madeline looked right through him. "She's not worth it."

It was no use. Rage had consumed Madeline. There was no

stopping her. Cash stepped aside to let her pass, then looked back at Nolan. "Sorry."

Jezebel stumbled backward toward the Barracuda, unprepared for Madeline's furious approach.

Nolan ran down the steps after her. "Maddie."

Madeline spun around. "Nolan, honey, you're going to let me have this. Because if you don't, I'll always regret it."

Nolan held his hands up and forward. "Okay, just don't—"

"Mrs. LaCroix!" Quinn yelled. "Look out!"

Jezebel had capitalized on Madeline's momentary lack of focus and leaped toward her, the point of the switchblade leading the charge.

Madeline turned and swung the bat just in time, knocking the switchblade from Jezebel's hand. Weaponless, Jezebel lost her nerve and ran for the Barracuda. Madeline ran after her.

Roxy retreated to the car and jumped in.

Quinn laughed. "And *keep* running, you bitches."

But Madeline wasn't finished. As Jezebel scrambled into the driver's seat, Madeline smashed one of the Barracuda's headlights. Jezebel threw the car into reverse and shot back into the access road, narrowly missing a bat strike to the hood.

Jezebel leaned past Roxy and toward the open passenger window. "You're dead. *All* of you."

Madeline resumed her pursuit. Jezebel floored the gas, the exhaust trailing behind the Barracuda like a dog's tail between its legs.

"That psychopath needs to be stopped." Madeline sent a fiery gaze at Nolan. "We need to get Anson involved. The fact that he isn't is crazy."

Cash stepped toward Madeline, careful to give her space. "We didn't go to Anson because Jezebel still had Ransom in her head. If he had arrested her, we might never reunite him with Wynter."

"He's not in her head anymore. Right? He's in yours. So there's no reason *not* to get Anson involved now."

"Just give us some time," Quinn said. "We'll get Wynter to talk to Ransom first, then we'll figure out a plan."

"Maybe they're right, Maddie," Nolan said. "Give them a day or two before we go to the police."

Madeline gripped the bat handle with white knuckles and shifted her eyes between the three of them. "Give me one good reason why I shouldn't go to Anson right now?"

"Because that's not what Wynter wants," Cash said. "She knows best what will heal her and bring her out of her coma."

"How do you know that for sure?"

Cash approached Madeline and placed a gentle hand on her bat, not to take it away, but to acknowledge her fury. "I know because Wynter told me."

Madeline studied Cash for a moment, then continued toward the trailer. Cash moved to follow.

"Mrs. LaCroix," he said.

Nolan raised his hand. "It's okay."

Madeline shot an angry look at Nolan. "No. It's not okay." She faced Cash.

"We... Quinn and I—"

"And Jake," Quinn added.

"Right. And Jake. We won't let you down."

"I hope you're right." Madeline disappeared into the trailer.

"If you need anything, let me know," Nolan said.

Cash nodded and followed Quinn already walking toward Blue Belle. "Is that ride still up for grabs?"

"Most definitely."

"Thanks."

The two of them hopped into the VW Beetle and Quinn sped out of the trailer park, headed for the Gas N Go.

"Jesus, I feel like a bag of shit," Cash said. "I could sleep for a week."

"Me too, but there's no time."

Cash rolled down the window to let the cool morning air wash over his face. "You think it's going to work?"

"What? Summoning Wynter and Ransom at the same time?"

"Yeah," Cash nodded.

"It has to work." Quinn gave him a quick glance of concern.

"I know." Cash met Quinn's gaze with worry of his own. "But what if it doesn't?"

Neither of them had an answer.

AFTER CASH'S SHIFT at Finn's on Thursday, he returned home and was in bed and asleep before Ernie stepped out of his shower at half past three. He awoke promptly at six the next morning, after over fourteen hours of dreamless sleep.

He stretched and swung his legs out of bed. He walked to the living room and picked up the handset to the phone. Cash noticed that Ernie had cleaned up the dirty dishes he had left in the sink after Quinn's late Wednesday night breakfast. He made a mental note to thank him later.

Cash punched in Jake's phone number and waited as the line trilled in his ear. On the fifth ring, a groggy Jake answered.

"Dude," he groaned. "It's way too early for talking. You in trouble?"

"No. Feeling great actually."

"Call me later, 'kay?"

"Let me guess. Nintendo marathon?"

"Sort of." Jake yawned. "Plus a little Skinemax."

Cash laughed. "You're a real *handy*man."

"Shut up."

"Look, want to hang out tonight? We can meet Quinn at the FreshWhip stand at five and go from there."

"I'm down for anything where Quinn is involved. What's the occasion?"

"I can summon. I just learned how," Cash said, excitement clear in his voice but slightly subdued by the memory of how Quinn had helped him get there. "Plus, I got Ransom in my head."

"That's great, but... Wait... how does *that* work? Don't you have to... *kiss?*" Jake trailed off.

"I'll fill you in later."

"Shit dude. Way to leave me hanging."

"Sorry. Go back to sleep. You're going to need it," Cash said. "See you at five." He could hear Jake's protest as he hung up the phone.

Cash began his day the way he usually did, with a shower and a bowl of cereal. He left a note for Ernie thanking him for cleaning up and was out the door by quarter to seven, eager for the day to be over before it had even begun.

As THE ONLY one without a paying job, Jake made sure he arrived at Stedford Plaza with plenty of time to spare. Getting around town on crutches was a royal pain in the ass.

He made his way to the food court and hid himself behind a pillar so he could watch Quinn work. She greeted every customer with a smile, one that he found himself liking more as each day passed.

Jake imagined walking up to the FreshWhip stand, sweeping her off her feet with a couple of movie quotes, and carrying her back to his room, her arms around his neck, the soft caress of her lips on his neck, and—

Crack!

One of his crutches hit the floor and snapped him out of his fantasy. Everyone in line at the FreshWhip stand turned to look, including Quinn and her boss. His cover blown, Jake rolled with it and squatted on one leg to retrieve the crutch.

He waved. Quinn smiled, offering a small wave back. Jake steadied himself, navigated to a nearby table, and sat, silently cursing himself for not doing that to begin with.

By ten minutes to five, all the FreshWhip customers had been served. Quinn skipped over to Jake's table and greeted him with a quick kiss on his cheek.

"Hey, Jake. It feels like I haven't seen you in, like, forever."

"It's been three days," Jake said, smiling. "But who's counting?"

Quinn glanced at the clock suspended in the center of the food court and swayed her shoulders side to side. "I get off at five. Once Cash gets here, we can split."

"I'll be here." Jake placed his chin in his hand and watched Quinn run back to the FreshWhip stand. If Cash had been there at that moment, he would have said something like—

"Looks like someone's in love." Cash walked up to the table and sat next to Jake.

"It's a definite possibility."

Cash gave Jake a once-over. "You look better than you sounded this morning. Just overtones of a skin flick marathon left."

Jake leaned in and lowered his voice. "Hey, do me a favor and keep that under your hat, okay?"

"I would if I wore one." Cash nudged Jake's shoulder and smiled. "I'm kidding. Of course."

"I just don't want Quinn thinking I'm a perv or something."

Cash nodded. "Your secret's safe, man."

Quinn strolled back to the table, sat, and heaved a sigh that flipped her bangs in the air for a second. "I thought the day was never going to end." She looked at Cash. "Did you tell him what we're going to do tonight?"

Jake's eyes flicked wider, all at once unsure where the conversation was going. "All *three* of us?"

"Mainly just Cash," Quinn said. "But I guess so, yeah."

Jake met Cash's eyes. "What are we going to do?"

"Ransom wanted to talk to Wynter," Cash said, "but she's in a coma, so that's not going to work. So I'm—"

"He's going to summon them both in his dreams so they can talk there." Quinn bit her lip and shrugged at Cash. "Sorry. I couldn't resist."

"It's okay. You and Quinn are there for moral support... and beer." Cash raised a brown paper bag.

"Grain Belt from Finn?"

Cash nodded.

Jake relaxed. "Wait a sec. You said Ransom's in your head. So you kissed him?"

Cash shrugged. "I took one for the team."

"Boy, did he." Quinn fanned at her face. "And that kiss was H-O-T hot."

Cash waved her off. "Don't listen to her," he said to Jake. "She's bullshitting."

"Just calling it like I saw it." Quinn crossed her arms. "Before we get this party started, I got to change."

"How about this," Jake said. "We head to your place, you get changed, then we crash at my place, order some pizza, maybe play some Nintendo or watch a movie, and Cash gets his dream on."

Quinn gave Jake a thumbs up. "I-I-I-I-I like it!"

"Chevy Chase. *Modern Problems*."

Quinn nodded with approval.

"Would your parents be okay with *this*?" Cash held up the beer.

"We'll sneak it in," Jake said, winking. "Quinn, did you drive?"

"Sure did."

"Then let's go," Jake rose on his good leg, grabbed his crutches, and hobbled toward the plaza exit, Quinn and Cash following close behind.

Jake loved to host and on this Friday night he hoped to host an adventure.

JAKE, CASH, AND QUINN holed themselves up in Jake's game room and by eight o'clock had finished off most of two large deluxe pizzas from Pizza Zip and a six-pack of Coke. The beer was held under wraps by Cash until contact with Wynter had been made.

"Donkey Kong smack-down anyone?" Jake held up a controller and raised an eyebrow.

"What about cracking open the beers?" Cash grinned.

"Let's wait until my parents go to sleep." Jake shook the controllers in his hand. "What do you say? Mini-tournament?"

"I'm in," Quinn said. "I'll kick your lily-white ass."

Jake looked past Quinn to Cash. "Dude, want to go first?"

"Excuse me." Quinn grabbed the controller. "*Ladies* first. Where's your manners?"

Jake backed away. "Um, you're right. Sorry."

"So, what are the rules, hot shot?" Quinn smirked and rested her arm on the back of the sofa.

Cash began to laugh as he watched Jake melt under the intensity of Quinn's stare.

"What? What's so funny?"

"Nothing, man." Cash yawned. "Just tell us the rules."

"Uh..." Jake stammered, looking for an answer. "How about we play three games each and total up the points. Or we could do two player mode."

"Either work." Quinn hopped from the sofa. She found the Donkey Kong cartridge, plugged it in, and turned on the power.

Jake raised a brow at her, then grabbed the remote and turned on the TV. "DONKEY KONG" appeared on the screen in blocky blue letters. "You've played before, I see."

"There's a lot you don't know about me, yet," Quinn said. "Let's do single player mode, super difficult." She selected the corresponding game option and began to direct Mario up the ladders and girders, avoiding barrels and flames or smashing them with hammers for extra points. Quinn made it through the first screen of level one with ease.

"I think you've met your match, man," Cash said.

Jake gulped as he watched Quinn continue until she had no more lives left.

"Show me what you got." She dropped the controller into Jake's hand.

"Cash?" Jake looked to Cash at the opposite end of the sofa. "Want to go next?"

Cash yawned and reclined into the cushioned recesses of the leather sofa. "Nah, I'm good for now. I'll play the person with the most points."

Jake started the game and Quinn snuggled into his shoulder, giving play-by-play. Cash watched them interact for a moment, like two peas in a pod, then closed his eyes. With a stomach full of pizza and a soft sofa at his back, he was asleep in minutes.

After Jake completed his game, Quinn was snoring lightly against his shoulder. He moved his arm to place it around her shoulder and she fell sideways, her head coming to rest on his right thigh, narrowly missing banging the top of her head on the cast on his left leg.

Jake gulped and looked for a throw pillow to place on his lap but there were none within reach. The last thing he wanted was for Quinn to wake up next to a tent pole in his pants.

He decided to distract himself by continuing to play but that was easier said than done. He could smell the fragrance of Quinn's hair and thought it might be the same brand of shampoo that his sister Chloe used. Rave? Suave? He couldn't remember but it smelled nice and being reminded of his sister helped tame those parts of his body that had a mind of their own.

In a moment of weakness Jake paused the game to touch her hair and it felt just as soft as he had imagined it to be. Playing Donkey Kong now was next to impossible. He couldn't concentrate. And even though the plan was to have Cash sleep, Jake hoped his wingman would wake up.

CASH FOUND HIMSELF standing on a girder of an unfinished skyscraper, high enough above the ground to make his knees ache and feel like jelly. Looking up made things easier but moving forward or back was out of the question. He was frozen.

Ahead of him there was one ladder going up but nothing going down.

"Whoever built this place is stupid."

"Uh, that'd be you," a voice rose up from behind him.

"Ransom?"

"The one and only." Ransom placed his hand brusquely on Cash's shoulder, making him jump.

"Watch it, man," Cash said. "You almost made me fall. I'm having trouble keeping my balance as it is."

"It's your dream. Make it what you want it to be."

Cash crunched his brow. "Like how?"

"I don't know." Ransom said. "Make the girders wider? You decide. I have no control. I'm just a participant. But I have to say though, I like being in your head better than Jezebel's."

"Thanks, I guess." Cash looked around the iron structure. He guessed he was a dozen or more stories above the ground.

"It's lucky that you don't like torturing yourself. Or there might be fire and barrels being thrown at you from way up there."

Cash looked up to see a platform five girders above him and a smaller one above that. "Like in... oh shit." A light bulb clicked on in Cash's head. "Jake and Quinn were playing Donkey Kong. That must be why my dream's like this."

With slow steps, the toes of his stocking feet hanging off the edge of the girder, he turned to face Ransom. A small red oval sat in the middle of his shirt and at first Cash thought nothing of it. Then he noticed it begin to expand, like blood on fabric. "What's that?"

Ransom looked down at the red patch and shrugged. "Jezebel's last stab at control, but she failed. Otherwise, I wouldn't be in your head. See?" The red oval stain continued to expand, but it also faded away until only his pristine white T-shirt remained.

"Good to know," Cash said. "Now tell me how to change the width of these girders before I shit my pants."

Ransom shrugged. "Just picture it."

Cash narrowed his eyes at him. "Just picture it, huh. Okay." Cash looked down at the girder he was standing on, trying hard to ignore the height, and concentrated. The girder remained unchanged. "It's harder than it looks."

"Relax."

Cash closed his eyes for his second attempt. When he opened them, the girders extended out from his feet and above his head at the same width as before. "Shit!"

"How wide do you want it?"

Cash thought for a moment. "Maybe six feet? Like a sidewalk?"

"How wide is that?" Ransom asked. "Show me."

"It's about yay-big—" Cash extended his arms out from his body and the width of all the girders stretched simultaneously to the distance between his fingertips.

"Holy shit." Despite the girders being wider, Cash was unprepared for the sudden change and struggled to keep his balance.

"Nice," Ransom said.

"But how do I keep the girders this wide?"

"Just believe they're permanent."

"Uh, okay." Cash cocked his head to one side, looked at the widened girder, and dropped his hands. The girder's width remained locked at six feet. "Wicked."

"Now let's get down to business."

"Wait. Let me try something." Cash held his hands out in front of him, touched the fingertips of each hand together, and pulled them apart vertically. A pole grew from the base of the girder to waist height. Then with a sweep of his arm, he dispersed pole copies all around the girders, with chains hanging between them, forming a barrier of safety.

"I'm not as fearless as Mario." Cash surveyed his handiwork with satisfaction.

"Of course, you could just create an elevator," Ransom said.

"Good idea!"

Ransom placed his hand on Cash's chest. "But... maybe you can try that next time. I really need to see—"

"Wynter," Cash said.

"Cash?" The reason for Cash's dream echoed from high atop the steel structure.

"Wynter?" Cash looked up and saw Wynter's fiery locks hanging down around her face from the topmost platform.

"I can't get down for some reason," Wynter called down.

"She's like Princess Peach," Cash said quietly to himself. He turned to Ransom. "We have to 'save' her," he said, air-quoting the word.

"Then let's go," Ransom said. "I'm right behind you."

Cash stood at the base of the white ladder connecting his girder to the one above and looked up. More white ladders materialized, forming a path up to where Wynter waited.

"Jake would love this," Cash said as he ascended the first ladder.

"Next time bring him here." Ransom's voice floated up from below.

"I can do that?"

"You can do anything, really," Ransom said. "It's your dream. But more complex environments take more effort and time to build."

Cash pulled himself onto the second girder level and ran to the next ladder.

Ransom continued. "We're limited to having one thought at a time. But whatever you do, don't let your mind wander. Focus on those you summon."

Climbing the ladders became easier for Cash. "Why?"

"Unexpected things can happen."

The two of them clambered from the third level up to the fourth.

"You're fucking *dead!*" Jezebel, looking like Donkey Kong with a human female face, screamed from the fifth level and began throwing flaming barrels down at them.

Cash and Ransom ducked for cover.

"Unexpected things like this?"

Ransom nodded. "But the dream is still yours. Jezebel isn't welcome so get rid of her."

"Why the hell is she in my dream, anyway?" Cash kept his eyes open for wayward barrels. "I didn't summon her."

"Your subconscious plays a big part in your dreams too," Ransom said. "That's why you need to focus."

"I thought I was."

"Jezebel knows that I'm out of her head and obviously you do too." Ransom hopped out of the way of a flaming barrel, the heat and fire singeing the sleeves of his hoodie.

"Wait." Cash narrowed his eyes at him. "How do you know that?"

"I know everything that you know, but you don't know everything I know." Ransom chuckled at him. "You know?"

"Not really, but thanks for the heads up." Cash peeked up at the fifth level. Jezebel could sense where he was, her aim with the flaming barrels spot on. He looked at the platform where Jezebel stood and hauled himself onto the fifth level. Cash held out his left hand, palm up, and smacked his fisted right hand into it.

The platform Jezebel stood on and the girders directly below exploded in a flurry of little cubes. She plummeted toward the ground, but not before releasing one last barrel.

"Cash!" yelled Wynter. "Watch out!"

Cash clapped his hands together, then peeled them apart. The barrel split down the middle, sending both halves in opposite directions and missing himself and Ransom by inches.

"You're getting good at this," Ransom said. "One more level to go."

Cash ran to the ladder that led to where Wynter stood. He launched himself up and pulled her into his arms. "God, I've missed you. It's only been a few days, but it feels like forever." He kissed her neck without even thinking.

"I've missed you too," Wynter said. "And Ransom."

Cash remembered why he was here and his heart flooded with ache. He released Wynter and stepped aside, jealousy flickering in the back of his mind.

Wynter faced Ransom as he topped the ladder, her eyes wet with tears.

"I'm sorry," Ransom said. "For everything."

"Me too." Wynter rushed him and opened her arms. Ransom stepped toward her and their bodies passed right through each other.

"Whoa," Cash said. "What the..."

"This is new to me too." Ransom tried to hold Wynter's hand, but his fingers floated through her like she was an apparition. "Since we've both been summoned, I guess we can't touch."

For a second Cash was glad they couldn't touch. At least that was something he had that Ransom didn't. But his elation soon evaporated.

"Cash," Ransom said. "Do you mind giving us some privacy?"

Cash nodded and stepped to the opposite corner of the top platform. Curiously, his fear of heights was gone. He stared down at what might have been the ground, but the detail was incomplete.

He looked around the platform. The sky, if he could call it that, was half day, half night, and it shifted between the two states constantly. Cash sensed increasing turbulence and glanced at Wynter and Ransom. They were sitting cross-legged on the far corner of the platform, talking and mirroring their hand movements.

"Cash?" Wynter and Ransom now stood behind him. Cash faced them. "It's not complicated." She placed her hands on Cash's shoulders and leaned toward his left ear.

"Why are you whispering?" Cash asked.

"So only you can hear." Wynter continued sharing her plan.

"But—"

A muscular hand slapped onto the platform from below, the fingers embedding themselves into the metal like it was made of plasticine. The arm pulled Jezebel's Donkey Kong hybrid up onto the platform. Veins stood out on her swollen face and her eyes glowed red and bloodshot.

"You're *dead!*" the abomination screeched and slammed her massive fists onto the platform, shattering it to pieces.

Cash tried to repair the damage with his newfound dream power, but everything disintegrated too fast. All three of them fell toward a half-realized ground, the wind whistling at their ears.

Cash could hear Wynter's plan even though they were falling and slowly drifting apart. He tried to reach for her, but she seemed to always be just beyond his grasp. He looked at Ransom.

"Now you know what to do," Ransom called out at him with a smile.

Then they hit the partially formed ground.

CASH JOLTED AWAKE. He squeezed his eyelids shut, then blinked rapidly like they had grit behind them. Jake's familiar stucco ceiling spread out above him. His back lay flat on the leather sofa, his head squished against the backrest. He looked to his left.

Quinn sat nestled under Jake's shoulder. They stared at him, frozen in either surprise or horror, Cash couldn't tell which. *A Nightmare on Elm Street* had taken the place of Donkey Kong on the TV.

"Holy shit, man." Cash used his legs to push himself up to a sitting position and rubbed his face with his hands. "I just had one hell of a dream."

"Are you okay, dude?" Jake relaxed a bit. "You were flipping out."

"You really freaked the shit out of us," Quinn said.

"Yeah, I'm fine." Cash reached down to the floor, pulled a beer out of the brown paper bag, and cracked the seal. He guzzled the entire can in one go, crushed the can in his hand, and belched.

Quinn grimaced. "Gross."

"I feel even better now," Cash said. "But guys, I did it."

On the TV, Freddy Krueger leaped up from behind a bed and frightened the main character, Nancy. Jake, Quinn, and Cash all screamed.

"Oh my God, turn that off," Quinn panted. "I can only handle so many scares."

Jake reached for the remote control to the VCR and pressed pause, freezing Freddy Krueger leaping from the bed. "What did you do?"

"I summoned Ransom and Wynter, and unfortunately Jezebel too, but they talked." Cash looked at them both with excited eyes. "I have a plan. It's so obvious."

"Wait." Jake held up his hand. "How did Jezebel get into your dream?"

"I guess I wasn't focusing hard enough," Cash said. "Apparently Jezebel was pulled from my subconscious mind. And get this, she had Donkey Kong's body. It was weird."

Quinn frowned. "Did you kill the bitch?"

"I don't think so. She destroyed the whole dream, but not before Wynter told me the plan." Cash looked at Jake. "You would have loved it. It was like I was playing virtual Donkey Kong for real, except the barrels were on fire."

"Virtual video games, huh?" Jake smiled and nodded as his brain started to work. "That's a good idea…"

"But back to the plan," Quinn said.

"Yeah, sorry, I'm a little scattered." Cash took a breath. "It's so simple, you're going to kick yourself. We go to the hospital, and I make Ransom a dreamwaker. Then he… he kisses Wynter." His enthusiasm faltered. "Just like *Sleeping Beauty*."

"Then Wynter just wakes up?" Jake looked dubious. "Just like that? Ransom's kiss is magical?"

"I don't know," Cash said. "I guess."

Quinn crossed her arms. "What if Jezebel gets to you before we can get you to the hospital?"

Cash shrugged. "Then we got to make sure she doesn't get to me."

"That's easier said than done," Jake said. "She managed to fuck up *your* dream. She may be a psychopath, but she's a smart psychopath."

"We're going to have to be careful," Cash said.

"No shit." Quinn reached for the VCR remote.

Cash motioned at Freddy Krueger frozen on the TV. "Did you get any ideas from the movie?"

Jake looked at him with uncertainty. "No. Everybody dies."

Quinn pressed play on the remote and Freddy's relentless pursuit of Nancy continued. "Freddy's like our Jezebel."

"Totally." Jake settled his arm around Quinn's shoulder.

"We could try setting Jezebel on fire," Quinn said. "That would fix a whole bunch of problems all at once."

"I'd like to avoid murder." Cash studied Quinn and Jake in turn. "Besides, we don't have the balls to do something like that."

Jake and Quinn looked at each other, then faced Cash. "Yeah, you're right," they said in unison.

Cash grabbed another beer for himself and tossed one to Jake. "Quinn?"

"No thanks," Quinn said. "Blue Belle doesn't like it when I drink."

Cash nodded, then cracked the pull tab. "Here's to *Sleeping Beauty*." Cash and Jake took a sip.

The three of them settled into the rest of the movie, but Cash found his mind drifting back to when he had held Wynter in his arms during his last dream. At this point, that was all that mattered to him and he would do anything to get that feeling back, even if it meant facing Jezebel.

FIRE OF UNKNOWN ORIGIN

MADELINE WOKE TO find Nolan's side of the bed empty, the mattress cold to her touch. She propped herself up on her elbows and listened. The trailer returned silence except for the ticking clock next to the bed. It read five minutes past six.

"Nolan?" She pulled off the sheets and swung her legs off the bed, fighting the concern welling up within her. "Hon?"

Madeline threw on her robe and the ratty pink slippers that Nolan had given her four Christmases ago. She pulled open the bedroom door and spotted him, still in his pajamas, slumped over the kitchen table. Instead of quelling her fears, her heart skipped a beat.

"Nolan?" Madeline hustled toward the kitchen. As she got closer, she could see the rise and fall of his back and a mug in front of him. Somewhat reassured, she flipped on the kitchen lights.

Nolan groaned and whispered, "No. Turn it off. Please." He waved a hand weakly at her.

Madeline turned the lights off and pulled a chair next to him. "Migraine?" she whispered.

Nolan returned a small nod. It had been at least two years since Nolan's last migraine, but when they struck, they were unexpected and always bad.

"I think it had something to do with trying to summon Wynter," Nolan whispered.

"Have you taken anything for it?"

"Three Advil, with coffee." He pushed the coffee mug aside.

Madeline ran a worried gaze over his face. The veins at his temples stood out in thick ropes. "Think you can make it back to the bedroom? I'll close the curtains and get you a cool cloth."

"And a bucket," Nolan added quietly.

Madeline kissed the top of Nolan's head lightly and hustled back to the bedroom to get it ready. She draped a towel over his head to shield his eyes and guided him back to bed. She laid a cool cloth behind his neck and one across his eyes.

"I'll call the library and let them know you won't be in today." Madeline stepped to the closet and began pulling out clothes for the day.

"Maddie?"

"What is it, hon?" She stepped to his side of the bed.

"Thank you." Nolan licked his dry lips. "I love you."

"Love you more," Madeline said. "There's a glass of water by the bed and a bucket on the floor if you need it. I have to get ready for work, but I'll check on you before I leave." She took his hand and squeezed it. Nolan returned the gesture weakly.

Madeline showered, dressed, and fetched a quick breakfast of toast and peanut butter. She reheated a cup of coffee and transferred it into her travel mug. She returned to the bedroom and sat next to Nolan. "I'm heading out. Feeling any better?"

"Not by much," Nolan said from under the cloth compress.

"Let me refresh those before I go. Keep your eyes closed." Madeline returned from the bathroom a moment later with the two cloths, their chill restored. She returned them to their spots around his head.

"Feels good," he croaked. "Thanks."

Madeline leaned in and kissed Nolan. "Hon, your lips are so

dry. Make sure you drink something. Plus, there's a couple more Advil next to your water."

Nolan nodded.

"I'm going to take the car today," Madeline said. "Take it easy and rest, but call me if you need anything."

"Okay," Nolan whispered.

Madeline kissed him once more and crossed the bedroom, easing the door closed. She grabbed her purse and her travel mug and slipped out the front of the trailer, locking it behind her.

She backed the Reliant onto the ring road and soon found herself on Main Street, crossing the highway. Ever since Wynter's fall, Madeline had avoided the 19th Street Bridge. Main Street took her to the FoodXpress too, but the route was less direct. It was a necessary change until Wynter was home again.

JEZEBEL AND ROXY crouched behind a bush across the field from Wynter's trailer. Jezebel followed Madeline's car with her eyes until she turned out onto Main Street and out of view.

She turned to Roxy. "Go knock on *Whiner's* door."

Roxy furrowed her brows. "Why?"

"Just do it," Jezebel said.

Roxy glanced at Jezebel, uncertain, and set off toward the trailer.

"And don't look obvious about it," Jezebel whispered loudly.

Roxy crossed the field, stepped up to Wynter's front door and rapped with her knuckles. She stood and waited, tapping her foot.

"Run, you dumb bitch!" Jezebel hissed, waving her arm in a fruitless attempt to get Roxy's attention. "Fuck."

Roxy looked back at Jezebel and shrugged her shoulders. Jezebel waved her back with a frantic arm and Roxy casually strolled back to their hiding place.

"Why the fuck did you stay?" Jezebel whacked her shoulder with the back of her hand.

"Hey, that hurt," Roxy said. " 'Don't look obvious.' That's what you said. If I knocked and ran, that would have looked obvious. Suspicious even."

Jezebel realized her error. "Well, good then. Did you hear anything inside?"

Roxy shook her head. "Nope. Why are we doing this anyway?"

"Payback," Jezebel said. "No one smashes my car and gets away with it."

Roxy watched Jezebel's eyes go dark. "Payback, how exactly?"

"Forget it. Let's go."

An hour later Jezebel and Roxy approached the Halston city limits. Jezebel pulled off the highway onto Sheyenne Road and the sign to Zoey's Fast Fill stood out like a beacon ahead. She pulled in front of a self-serve pump and they both stepped out of the Barracuda.

"It seems only yesterday that we were here with Ransom." Roxy smiled dreamily.

Jezebel pulled a red plastic jerry can from the trunk and threw it at Roxy. "Shut up and fill this."

"Jesus," Roxy said. "Who crawled up your ass?" She unscrewed the cap and filled the jerry can.

"Wynter's mom," Jezebel said under her breath.

"What a waste of time." Roxy scowled as she hung up the pump nozzle and screwed the cap back onto the jerry can. "We could've filled this in Newhaven."

Jezebel grabbed Roxy's shirt collar and pulled her nose to nose. "Do you *ever* say anything useful? Go pay for the gas so we can get down to business." She hauled the jerry can into the trunk and slammed it closed.

"What business?"

"Just do it!" Jezebel pulled open the driver's side door. "Or I'll fucking leave you here. And get me a coffee and a donut."

Roxy scowled and raised her middle finger, then trudged off toward the convenience store.

Jezebel slid into the driver's seat and flipped on the radio. "Burning Down the House" by Talking Heads blasted from the speakers. "Fucking new wave shit."

She turned the music off and glanced into the rear view mirror, hoping to see Roxy heading back to the car. No such luck. To pass the time she threw her mind into her plan for...

Sweet revenge.

Wynter's mom would pay, that's for sure. She'd never see it coming. Jezebel wished that she had a video camera to record the entire thing because it would be something to remember.

A righteous act of revenge.

She sneered she played out her plan in her mind's eye. A rap on the window brought Jezebel out of her imaginings.

Roxy held a paper tray with two coffees in one hand and a bag in the other, both branded with the Zoey's Fast Fill logo and tagline, "Empty tank... Empty tummy... Fast Fill!" She had a cake donut crammed in her mouth.

Instead of waiting for Jezebel to help her, she set the bag on the roof of the Barracuda and opened the passenger door. Reclaiming the bag, she sat and handed Jezebel a coffee and the bag. She took the remaining coffee and washed down a mouthful of donut.

Jezebel reached into the bag and pulled out another cake donut. "Where's the jellies?"

"Didn't have any," Roxy said through a mouthful of crumbs.

"Jesus Christ, can't you do anything right?" Jezebel tossed the bag out the driver's side window and started the Barracuda's engine. She drove out from the gas bay and back onto Sheyenne Road.

Jezebel brought the cup of coffee to her lips and took a tentative sip. "Ugh, what is this shit?"

"What? Coffee with two cream, two sugar, just like you like it."

Jezebel tossed the paper cup out the window. "Give me yours."

"But..." Roxy saw it would be no use to fight, especially an hour away from Newhaven. One wrong word and she would find herself walking home. She handed her coffee to Jezebel. "Are you okay? You're acting super mental."

Jezebel tasted Roxy's coffee. "Better." She took a larger sip. "Give me a bite of that."

Roxy broke off a piece of her donut and placed it in Jezebel's mouth. She chewed and swallowed.

"You gave me the moldy one, didn't you," Jezebel said.

Roxy recoiled, insulted. "Hell, no. They were both the same."

"Bullshit." Jezebel glanced at the last bite of donut in Roxy's hand. "Let me taste yours again."

Grudgingly, Roxy dropped the remaining piece into Jezebel's mouth, then sat back in her seat and crossed her arms.

Jezebel chewed. "Yup. You definitely gave me the bad donut."

Roxy shook her head. "I didn't. I swear."

"You calling me a liar?"

"No," Roxy said quietly.

"There's going to be consequences."

"What do you mean? I didn't *do* anything."

Jezebel narrowed her eyes as she turned onto the on-ramp to I94 West. "You'll find out in about an hour."

She turned on the radio, but Roxy tuned it out, instead focusing her attention on the changing landscape out the passenger window.

Fifty minutes later Jezebel arrived back at Sven Dwarfs Trail'r Park. She found Wynter's trailer, pad #7, and parked where Madeline's Reliant had sat just over two hours earlier.

Roxy scanned the central field and the mobile homes encircling it. "Why are we back here? You forget something?"

"Revenge and consequences." Jezebel pushed open her door. "Get out."

"What the hell are you talking about?" Roxy said, but Jezebel was already at the trunk and out of earshot.

Roxy met Jezebel at the back of the Barracuda. Jezebel unlocked the trunk and lifted out the jerry can.

"Wait." Roxy shifted her eyes uneasily between Jezebel and the jerry can. "What are you going to do with that?"

"Nothing," said Jezebel. "It's what *you're* going to do with it."

"No way."

Jezebel pulled up her T-shirt to reveal her pistol resting in the waistband of her jeans. "Yes way."

"You're fucking crazy." Roxy stepped closer and lowered her voice. "You're talking about arson. In broad *fucking* daylight."

"I know." Jezebel smirked. "Exciting, isn't it? That's why we got to work fast."

"Fuck it. I'm not doing it."

Jezebel pulled out the pistol and cocked the slide. "Fine. I'll make it look like an arson-suicide."

Roxy held her hands out in front of her. "Okay, okay. Just tell me what to do."

"Pretty simple, really," Jezebel said. "Just pour gas on all the walls and light it. Technically it's an eye for an eye. That bitch smashed my headlight, so I destroy her house."

Roxy stared at the jerry can, then glanced over her shoulder.

"Don't even think of running."

"Actually, I was thinking that you wouldn't hesitate to put a bullet in my back." Roxy unscrewed the cap to the jerry can.

Jezebel watched her work. "You'd be right."

Roxy set the plug aside, flipped the nozzle around, and tightened the cap again. "I don't have a choice."

"Everyone has a choice," Jezebel said. "You're making the one that keeps you alive."

Roxy eyed the structure uneasily. "So, gas on the walls?"

"Yup. And extra on the front steps."

Roxy struggled to lift the jerry can. After dousing the front steps, she circumnavigated the trailer under Jezebel's watchful eye.

Roxy returned to the front of the trailer and tossed the empty jerry can to one side. Jezebel held out a Zippo lighter.

"Showtime," she said and tossed the lighter to Roxy.

"What the hell are you doing?"

The two girls turned to see Nolan standing on the landing in front of his open front door. He sniffed the air.

"What is that, gasoline?" Nolan shaded his squinting eyes from the bright sunshine. "Jezebel?"

"Fuck, Jazz. I thought the place was empty," Roxy said, panicked.

"Shut up." Jezebel set her worries aside and trained her pistol on Nolan. "Back in the trailer, old man."

"One chance," Nolan said, struggling through the pain behind his eyes. "Leave now, or I call the police."

"Call them." Jezebel matched Nolan's gaze. "There won't be much of you left by the time they get here. Light it up, Roxy."

Instead of blindly obeying, Roxy balked and shook her head. "I'm no murderer."

"Bullshit. You just don't know it yet." Jezebel trained the pistol on Roxy. "DO IT."

Tears welled in Roxy's eyes. "No, Jazz. Please, I can't—"

Nolan ran into the trailer. Jezebel tracked the movement and fired the pistol through the open door. Nolan's body sprawled and slid over the kitchen table, his foot hooking a chair and knocking it over as he sailed by.

Jezebel stormed the short distance between her and Roxy and grabbed her T-shirt. "Light it! NOW."

Roxy shook her head.

Jezebel slapped Roxy's face, then jammed the barrel of her pistol under her chin. "Do it or I'll blow your head off."

Roxy's lips trembled, her cheeks wet with tears. "You're not a murderer, either."

Jezebel gritted her teeth. "Fucking useless." She snatched the Zippo back from Roxy's hand, flipped the top and lit the wick. "You don't know me very well." She threw the lit Zippo at the front landing and fire erupted around the railing and door.

Flames followed the spilled gasoline like a train on a one-way track to hell. Fire licked up the exterior walls and into the open front door, engulfing the entire trailer within seconds.

Jezebel ran back to the Barracuda and hopped in, pushing the gun under her seat. She turned the ignition and the car's engine rumbled to life.

The sound of the Barracuda mixed with the gravity of the situation knocked Roxy out of her daze. She launched herself at the car and managed to pull herself half into the vehicle's passenger window before Jezebel reversed out of pad #7 and floored it toward the trailer park exit.

Roxy twisted in her seat to look back at Wynter's trailer through the back window. A plume of black smoke rose in an angry column. She slumped back in her seat and set her eyes on Jezebel.

"Fucking awesome," Jezebel said, her eyes glued on the road ahead and her lips curled in a grin that personified evil. "Two birds with one stone."

Roxy stared at her and found it hard to recognize anything familiar or comfortable anymore. Jezebel had become her worst nightmare, too. She felt like she had a ticking time bomb on her back, one that she couldn't shake. How could she break free from Jezebel's hold on her and arrive alive on the other side?

∞

CASH WOKE ON the floor of Jake's games room. He unzipped the sleeping bag and stretched his back, his joints snapping, cracking, and popping in sequence. He rubbed his temple.

Jake looked down at him over the back of the leather sofa. "Look who's up." Donkey Kong displayed on the TV with the volume turned down low.

"Got any Tylenol?" Cash groaned. "My head feels like it wants to bust open."

"That'd be upstairs."

Cash looked around the room. "Where's Quinn?"

Jake pointed beside him, his eyes wide. Cash peered around the pleated arm of the sofa and saw Quinn curled up next to Jake, her head on a pillow near the start of his cast. "Slept beside me all night."

"Did you score?"

Quinn stirred beside Jake and he lowered his voice. "Later."

"I'm starving," Cash said. "I need food. And that Tylenol."

"Serves you right for drinking all those beers." Quinn blinked at Cash. "But you didn't puke, thank God."

"My mom would've killed you." Jake set the Nintendo game controller down. "I got toaster waffles and Cinnamon Toast Crunch."

"I'll have the Tylenol." Cash stood and stretched again.

Quinn helped Jake up onto his crutches and led the way upstairs to the kitchen. Cash followed last, slow on the stairs, content to feel the cool linoleum on his sock feet. By the time he reached the top of the stairs, Quinn and Jake were already around the corner headed to the kitchen.

A siren sounded outside, low at first but increasing in volume.

"You guys hear that?" Cash called back.

Jake stuck his head out of the kitchen. "Quiet, dude. You're going to wake up my parents."

Cash pulled open the front door. The siren increased in volume like someone had flicked a switch. He saw a police SUV fly past on Main Street at the end of Mortimer Avenue, the siren shifting in pitch and fading as it passed.

He pictured the trajectory of the SUV in his head and locked his eyes on a plume of black smoke.

His stomach fell. The first thought that entered his head was... *Wynter.*

Cash forgot about his hunger and his aching head. "Guys?" He slipped on his shoes and fumbled his laces tied. "There's something wrong." He turned toward the kitchen and yelled, not caring if he woke Jake's parents. "There's something *wrong!*"

"Jesus, dude." Jake hopped to the front door. "What's your... problem?" He saw the smoke first, then Cash sprinting toward Main Street. "Oh shit. Quinn! Get your keys."

Quinn appeared beside him grinning. "What's up? Where's Cash?"

"He took off, but I think I know where he's going." Jake motioned at the sky. "Look."

Quinn's smile faded and her face fell ashen when she saw the black smoke in the sky. "Oh God," she said as softly as fear would let her. "No."

She slipped on her shoes, grabbed her purse, and helped Jake down to Blue Belle waiting at the curb. The two of them shared a look of fear and concern before the little VW Beetle shot down the street, destination Sven Dwarfs Trail'r Park.

WITH EVERY STRIDE, Cash felt his laces loosen a little more, but it was the last thing on his mind. Even his beer hangover had been temporarily placed on hold by the adrenaline pumping through his veins.

The pillar of dense black smoke guided him like an evil compass, and it had Jezebel's name all over it. Every step filled him with increasing dread, eliminating any other explanation for the smoke, one by one, until the only source was within the boundaries of Sven Dwarfs.

Don't let it be Wynter's trailer. Please.

The neon sign for the trailer park loomed in the distance. Cash slowed but didn't stop. He couldn't. The thought of Nolan and Madeline losing their home, of Wynter losing all her treasures, caused his stomach to turn unexpectedly.

Let it be my trailer.

But the reality of that wish hit him hard. His dad would have been home by now. And Jezebel could have torched his place just as easily as Wynter's. She could have torched them both. Jezebel played no favorites. She hated everyone equally. And if the smoke belonged to his trailer, his dad could already be—

Cash skidded to a stop and vomited into the ditch. He wiped his mouth and tried to rinse the bile from his mouth with saliva. It didn't work. He longed for a Tic Tac to cover the acrid smell of his anxiety.

A fire truck roared past him with lights and sirens engaged. He resumed his sprint across the Main Street Overpass and past the first row of southie housing. Cash entered the front gate of the trailer park and followed the circular access road, his fears realized.

Flames had fully engulfed Wynter's trailer. Even at a distance in the central field, the heat blasting from the fire caused the hair on Cash's arms to curl.

The fire truck had stopped in the center of the field and firefighters scrambled to get hoses and equipment ready.

He looked to his trailer and saw Ernie standing on the front stoop. Relief flooded him and Cash almost burst into tears. Yet across from him, Wynter's trailer, a building he knew inside and out, the home of his only true love, would soon be a pile of ashes and charred twisted metal. Memories and possessions gone forever.

Conflicted, Cash ran to Ernie and wrapped his arms around him. "Dad! You okay?"

"I'm fine, son."

Cash stepped back to see Ernie overwhelmed with emotion too. "Did you see who did it?"

Ernie answered him with a disquieting look.

"It was Jezebel, wasn't it?"

"Look son," Ernie began. "You got to be strong. There's more to this awful tragedy."

"What do you mean, *more?*" Cash spun his head around and scanned the field, past the fire vehicles, until his eyes settled on Anson's SUV. He was tending to someone in the cargo bed. "Is it Madeline? Nolan?"

Ernie shook his head. "I don't know, son. I didn't get too close."

Before Ernie could warn him to stay clear, Cash jumped the railing on the front stoop and raced toward the Suburban. "Anson!"

Sheriff Jacobs peered over his shoulder to see Cash barreling toward him. "Cash, hold up."

Cash looked into the back of the SUV and saw Nolan lying on his back, his legs wrapped with protective bandages. An oxygen mask tethered to a small tank had been placed over his mouth and nose. "Nolan!"

"Easy, Cash." Anson held him back. "He's been through a lot."

"What happened?"

"Not sure exactly," Anson said. "But between you and me, the Fire Chief said he turned on the shower to wet himself down first and escaped through the bathroom window. That Nolan is a smart cookie. His legs were still badly burned and he's suffering from considerable smoke inhalation. Ambulance is on the way."

"Shit." Cash looked back at Wynter's trailer, now little more than a rectangular patch of scorched ground, with blackened remnants of furniture and appliances standing up like headstones. "Jezebel did this."

"What?" Anson eyed him critically. "Are you sure? Did you see her do it?"

"No," Cash said, "but it's obvious, isn't it? Who else would do this?"

"It could be just a random accident."

Cash shook his head. "No way."

"Cash!" Quinn called out from across the field as she stepped out of Blue Belle, Jake hobbling fast to keep up.

Cash ran to meet them. "Wynter's place is gone." He threw his arms around both Quinn and Jake.

Jake surveyed the destruction. "Holy shit."

Quinn spotted Nolan's feet in the back of Anson's SUV. She fell to her knees, covered her face, and began to sob. Jake did his best to console her.

Cash crouched to Quinn's level and placed his hand on her shoulder. "Nolan's not dead. His legs are burned but Anson thinks he'll survive."

"What about Madeline?"

Anson rejoined the group. "Looks like Nolan was the only one in the trailer."

Quinn looked at Cash through red, watery eyes. "Jezebel?"

"Probably, but there's no proof."

"Not yet, anyway," Anson said. "Fire Chief says it's probably arson, but they'll know more after things cool down and they can investigate."

Jake rested on his crutches. "We need to take the bitch down."

"Don't get any ideas." Anson shifted his gaze between the three of them. "Let the evidence speak."

As Quinn stood, a siren rose in the distance. She buried her face into Jake's chest to muffle her sobs.

"That's the ambulance." Anson trotted back to the SUV to check on Nolan.

Jake turned to Cash. "Got any ideas?"

"Yeah, a few."

"We got to figure out something," Jake said. "And fast."

The ambulance rolled along the access road. Cash waved at the driver and directed him to where Anson had parked. "I'm going to ride with Nolan. Can I meet you guys at the hospital? We could make a plan."

Quinn sniffled and faced Cash. "We'll be there."

Anson assisted the paramedics with Nolan. They moved him to a spine board and transferred him to an awaiting wheeled stretcher. Nolan floated in and out of consciousness as the paramedics assessed his pain levels.

"Jez... Jez..." Nolan tried to speak but his throat was too irritated.

"Try not to talk, sir," one paramedic said as she cut open his shirt to expose his chest.

Cash glanced at Quinn and Jake, his eyes wide. "You heard that, right?" They both nodded.

The paramedics replaced the temporary bandages Anson had applied with a sterile dressing from their supplies. They loaded the stretcher into the back of the ambulance, elevating his legs.

"Everyone okay here?" The teens nodded and one paramedic working on Nolan gave Anson the thumbs up. "Good. I'm going to check in with the Fire Chief, then go let Madeline know what's going on."

"Can I ride with him to the hospital?"

One paramedic glanced down at Cash from the interior of the ambulance. "You family?"

Cash looked back at his trailer. Ernie still stood on the front landing, watching the events play out. He shifted his gaze to Jake and Quinn, then back to the paramedic. "As close as he's got right now."

Anson called back to the paramedic, "The kid's alright." Cash looked back at Anson, and they shared a mutual nod.

"You're Cash, I take it?" The paramedic eyed him cautiously, then motioned him inside. "Buckle yourself in."

Cash climbed into the ambulance. "Meet you there," he said to Jake and Quinn. He took a seat on the bench along the wall and pulled the seat belt across his lap. The other paramedic closed the rear double doors and pulled herself into the driver's seat.

The ambulance rocked on the uneven ring road as it left the trailer park. The paramedic in the back attached Nolan to the electrical leads of the cardiac monitor, wrapped his upper arm with a blood pressure cuff and clipped a pulse oximeter to his index finger.

"Why are his legs raised?"

"To prevent edema," the paramedic said. "Swelling from fluid buildup in the tissues." He grabbed a manual resuscitator and attached an oxygen line to it. He held the resuscitator to Nolan's mouth with one hand and began to squeeze rhythmically with the other.

From Cash's spot on the bench seat, he could see through the windshield that they were on the highway already. He scanned Nolan's legs, now wrapped neatly with white gauze. "Is he going to lose his legs?"

"The burns didn't look too bad, maybe second degree, so I'd wager not," the paramedic said. "I'd be more concerned with the smoke inhalation. Trailers like that are filled with materials that create toxic smoke when they burn."

"Do you think he inhaled much smoke?"

"Hard to say." The paramedic scanned the cardiac monitor's display. "Air's getting into his lungs. That's good, but his blood pressure is—"

The cardiac monitor began to beep and the pulse line on the monitor's screen danced erratically.

"Kick it, Jackie," the paramedic called up front. "Patient's crashing."

The ambulance's acceleration pulled at the seat belt across Cash's waist. The driver flipped on the lights and siren.

Cash sent the paramedic in the back a panicked look. "What's happening?"

"Heart attack. Stay put." The paramedic removed two paddles from the cardiac monitor, greased them up with electro-conductive gel, and placed them on Nolan's bare chest. "All clear."

He pressed the thumb trigger and Nolan's back arched for a second, then relaxed. The paramedic brought his hands together and began alternating between five chest compressions and one squeeze of the resuscitator.

Cash watched in horror, powerless to do anything to stop Nolan from dying in front of him. After what seemed like an eternity, the paramedic's body relaxed.

He looked back at Cash, his face serious but showing some relief. "He's stabilized, but he's not out of the woods yet. That smoke did a number on him."

The paramedic picked up a radio handset. "Ambulance twenty-three to Halston Medical for patient report."

"Go ahead, twenty-three," crackled the radio response.

"Currently in route emergent with a male in his late thirties, treated for burns on lower legs, smoke inhalation, and myocardial infarction. Defib at two hundred..."

The paramedic's voice faded out, replaced by throbbing static. Dizziness overwhelmed Cash and everything before his eyes lost its color and vibrancy. Then his world turned black.

ANSON PULLED INTO the parking lot of the FoodXpress and parked close to the front of the building. He exited his seat without his usual lightness of step. He walked to the entrance, the sliding doors parting for him automatically as if expecting him.

Anson flagged down the manager of the FoodXpress. "Jerry, can you point me to where Madeline's working today?"

"Sure thing, Anson. Register five." Jerry's smile melted away. "Everything okay?"

Anson took a breath and made a loose fist. "I'm afraid not."

"What—"

"Not now." Anson turned and saw Madeline in the distance, engaged in lively conversation with a customer. "Could you fetch her for me?"

Jerry hustled over to register five and leaned in to whisper in Madeline's ear. Her eyes found Anson in an instant, her smile of recognition giving way to fear. Anson had seen this reaction too many times in his career. He was never able to conceal that he bore bad news. It was like some unspoken language that everyone understood.

Madeline stepped away from her cash register and approached Anson with cautious steps. He took off his campaign hat and held it in front of his chest, swallowing hard and preparing for the predictable fallout.

Madeline's eyelids were already heavy with tears. "Nolan?"

Anson nodded and motioned to the entrance. "Can I speak to you outside, please?"

Madeline raised her trembling hands to her face. The store had fallen to a hush and the weight of the silence overwhelmed her. She followed Anson outside and wasted no time.

"Is he dead?" Her eyes searched his face for clues to an answer she dreaded.

"What? Oh, God, Madeline. No." Anson placed his hands on her shoulders and felt her shaking like a leaf. He pulled her into an embrace meant to comfort her. "Nolan's fine." Anson glanced at his watch. "He's on his way to Halston Medical at this very moment. His legs were burned and he had some smoke inhalation."

Madeline pulled back. "Burned?"

Anson took a fortifying breath. "There was a fire at your trailer."

Blindsided by the news, Madeline switched one worried look for another. "Is there anything…" She trailed off as Anson shook his head gently.

"There's nothing left," he said. "I'm so sorry."

Madeline reached out for the bench next to the store's front windows and sat down, her head in her open palms. Anson took a seat next to her and placed a hand lightly on her shoulder.

She shook her head. "This doesn't make any sense."

"It's not official yet," Anson said, "But the fire chief thinks it could be arson."

"What?"

"Do you know anyone who might do something like this?"

Madeline's eyes cleared and darkened all at once. "Yeah." She looked at him. "Jezebel."

"Why her?"

"She got in my face a couple days ago, so I took a bat to her car." A hint of a wistful smile appeared on Madeline's face only for a moment. "Felt great at the time but I guess I should have backed off."

Anson sighed. "No one wins when Jezebel is concerned."

"One of these days her luck is going to run out," Madeline said. "And I'll dance in the streets when it does."

Anson clasped his hands and rested his forearms on his knees. "Madeline, are you okay?"

"Well, I'm a little rattled to be honest, but—"

"I meant financially speaking. I know that's a personal question. You don't have to answer, but… Are you insured?"

"Thanks for your concern, Anson." Madeline patted his arm. "We're covered."

Anson nodded and stood. "How about I get you to the hospital? I'm sure you'd like to see Nolan."

"Let me fill Jerry in," Madeline said. "I'll be back in a minute."

Anson hooked his thumb over his shoulder. "I'm parked by the road."

Madeline waved at him and disappeared back into the store. Anson walked back to the Suburban and pulled himself into the driver's seat. He radioed the station to let them know his plan, then sat back and beat his thumb anxiously on the steering wheel.

Newhaven would be a better place without Jezebel, but the girl had a horseshoe up her ass. She seemed to always evade capture and no one pressed charges. Anson vowed to find out why.

JEZEBEL PULLED ONTO the front lawn of her house on Woodpark Avenue and cut the Barracuda's engine. Frankie's Pinto was absent from her usual parking spot, which meant the house was empty.

"I need to change." Jezebel gave Roxy a once-over. "Strip. I'll bring you something to wear." She hopped out of the car and disappeared into the side door to the house.

Roxy released her seatbelt and twisted in her seat, scanning her surroundings for possible voyeurs. On a Saturday morning in south Newhaven, anything could happen. Her surveillance revealed nothing but sunshine and birdsong and the houses adjacent had obstructed views.

She peeled off her T-shirt and sniffed it. The fabric reeked of gasoline. This time Jezebel's idea actually made sense. Roxy slipped off her shoes and wiggled out of her jeans. She rolled the T-shirt and jeans into a ball and dropped them into the footwell. The perfect plan would have included a shower, but Jezebel's plans were never perfect.

Roxy reclined the passenger seat and positioned herself to catch a patch of morning sun. The warmth on her skin led her mind to Wynter's trailer and how Jezebel had lit the trailer on fire with Nolan inside. She pushed the thought away.

A familiar engine revved behind the Barracuda. Roxy cast a glance in the rear view mirror. The ugly, angular lines of a Fiat X1/9 reflected back at her.

Monty!

Roxy instinctively crossed her arms against her chest. She briefly considered pulling on her gas-infused T-shirt but that would have raised suspicion. She leaned against the door, using it like a shield, and propped her arms on the open window.

"Hey Monty," she called out. "A little early for you, isn't it?"

"Foxy Roxy." Monty approached the passenger side of the Barracuda and smirked, letting his eyes slide over her face, arms and whatever else he could see. "Lookin' for Ransom. Seen him?"

Roxy looked at her own distorted image in Monty's mirrored sunglasses and shook her head.

"I got a job perfect for him."

Jezebel stepped out from behind the house wearing a black Metallica T-shirt and black jeans. She carried a plastic bag stuffed with fabric in one hand. "What the hell are you doing here?"

"Need Ransom's help with somethin'," Monty said.

"No idea where he is." Jezebel threw the plastic bag through the driver's side window. The bag hit Roxy's back and rolled next to her seat. "Now get the fuck out of here. We're busy."

Roxy sat back and dug through the clothes. At the bottom of the bag was a pair of pink sweatpants and a white T-shirt with the black capitalized slogan "CHOOSE LIFE" across the front.

"Seriously? Little ironic don't you think?" She pulled on the shirt and slipped on the sweatpants. "Ugh, they smell like they've been up someone's ass for a year."

"Don't wear it, then." Jezebel started the ignition. "I don't give a shit." Through the rear view mirror, she saw the Fiat blocking her path. "Move your fucking shitbox, Monty."

"Don't hide him from me, Jazz."

"Yeah? Or what?"

"We have an agreement. Don't forget that." Monty threw an envelope onto Roxy's lap. "See yah, foxy Roxy." He strolled back to his car.

Jezebel snatched the envelope away from Roxy. "What's this?" Jezebel yelled back at Monty.

"Insurance." Monty pulled open the door to the Fiat. "Don't hide him from me, *Jazz*." He poured himself into the little car, revved the engine, and peeled out onto the street, unblocking the Barracuda and leaving tread scars through the long grass.

"Dipshit." Jezebel tossed the envelope into the back seat and reversed onto the street, steering the Barracuda in the opposite direction Monty had gone. "I'm fucking starving. Want to hit up Lucy's?" She didn't wait for Roxy's answer and instead raced down Woodpark, turning right onto 19th Street.

"Sure, but shouldn't we be back at the hideout?" Roxy raised a brow at her. "Anson's probably looking for us."

Jezebel clenched her teeth. She hated when Roxy was right. Without slowing down, she pulled the steering wheel hard left, causing the Barracuda to slide around one-hundred eighty degrees. "Fuck the hideout. I want some real food."

"Halston again?"

"Or the first restaurant I see."

Roxy eyed the envelope lying on the back seat. "Aren't you going to open that?"

"What, the *insurance?*" Jezebel scowled. "Screw it."

"Then I will."

Jezebel shrugged indifference, instead focusing her eyes on the road. She turned left back onto Woodpark, past her run-down excuse for a home, and toward Main Street.

Roxy unfastened her seat belt and stretched to grab the letter-sized manila envelope. She set it on her lap as she buckled herself back in. "Feels kind of heavy."

Roxy unwound the string from the buttons that kept the

envelope closed and flipped open the top flap. She tilted the envelope and a stack of 4"x6" photos slid into her hand. She flipped through them like a stack of *Wacky Packages* stickers. But what played out in front of her eyes made her eyes widen with every new image.

"Holy shit," Roxy said. "This is bad."

"What?" A flicker of worry flashed across Jezebel's face.

"Pull over. You need to see this."

Jezebel pursed her lips, annoyed that Roxy was directing her choices, even if the choices were appropriate. "This better be good." She pulled the Barracuda to the side of the road.

"Don't think 'good' is the right word." Roxy placed the photographs into Jezebel's beckoning hand.

Jezebel flipped through the photos one by one, each showing in progressing detail her murder of Ransom back at their hideout. However, there were no pictures of Ransom drifting.

Jezebel's eyes went dark and distant, a look Roxy recognized as bad things to come, but she didn't explode. Quite the opposite.

"They double-crossed us, Rox."

Roxy nodded, afraid to say anything that might set Jezebel off.

"Well, game on, motherfuckers." Jezebel pulled out onto Woodpark again.

"What are you going to do?"

Jezebel grinned with malice. "We're going to teach them all a lesson."

CASH SAT OUTSIDE Nolan's fifth floor room, supporting his head in his hands. Two nurses checked Nolan's vital signs and verified his connections to the monitoring equipment as a doctor examined him. Their muffled voices filtered through the wall and blinded window, and he made no attempt to decipher their conversation.

Cash tried to envision the hospital's layout. Wynter was close, one floor down, and even though she was still in a coma, her closeness gave him a small sense of comfort.

Quinn burst out of the elevators, followed by Jake on crutches. She spotted Cash at the end of the corridor.

Cash looked up at the sound of hustling footsteps and wiped his eyes. "Hey."

"Dude." Jake tried to look into Nolan's room through the slivers between the blinds. "How is he?"

Cash stood and wiped his sweaty hands on his jeans. "I don't know for sure. He... he had a heart attack on the way."

"Oh God." Quinn placed a trembling hand over her mouth. She exchanged a worried look with Jake.

"Fucking Jezebel." Jake clenched his teeth. "Two members of Wynter's family in here is two too many."

The doctor opened Nolan's hospital room door and led the two nurses out, all three deep in discussion of treatment options.

Cash tapped the doctor's shoulder and pulled him aside, noting his name tag "Eastman." Quinn and Jake stood right behind. "Doc? How is he? Can we see him?"

Dr. Eastman shared a look with the nurses as they parted in the corridor and turned to Cash. "You rode in with Mr. LaCroix?"

Cash nodded.

"Then you know he had a heart attack, a small one, but serious just the same." Dr. Eastman shifted his gaze between the three teens and settled back on Cash. "We're waiting on some blood tests, but he's stable. We've got him on some IV drugs to help with blood flow and pain, and we've redressed his burns. Luckily, the gunshot grazed his arm and only required stitches."

"Gunshot?" Jake looked as surprised as the others.

"I thought you knew," Dr. Eastman said. "There was a bullet wound in his upper right arm."

Cash ran a frustrated hand through his hair.

"Is there anything we can do?" Quinn asked.

"Best thing? Go home," Dr. Eastman said. "Let him rest. The nurses will contact you if his condition changes."

Cash struggled to accept the doctor's recommendation. "We need to talk to him, doc."

"That's out of the question," Dr. Eastman said. "And before you argue, know that Mr. LaCroix is presently asleep and can't talk now anyway."

Cash sighed. "Okay. Thanks, doc."

Dr. Eastman nodded. "If you'll excuse me, I have other patients requiring my attention."

Cash, Jake, and Quinn moved to the side of the corridor in a huddle as the doctor hustled past them.

"So, do we stay or do we go?" Cash eyed his friends.

"Stay," Quinn said. "Most definitely stay."

Jake nodded. "I vote for staying, too. We need to talk with Nolan, find out what really happened."

"I think I can help with that."

Quinn turned and her eyes went wide as saucers. "BUG!"

Wynter stood in the doorway to Nolan's room, her signature smile faltering under the circumstances. Her red hair cascaded around her shoulders, somehow even more vibrant than usual. She wore sneakers, jeans, and a deep purple hoodie.

Quinn threw her arms around Wynter in a tight hug and kissed her cheek. Tears of joy breached her eyelids. "God, I've missed you." She stood back at arm's length to take her in, then hugged her again.

Words betrayed Cash, both dumbfounded and enamored by Wynter's presence. But she was here, and it was real. His heart swelled.

"Wait." It was Jake who pointed out what the others had either failed or chose not to recognize. "How is this possible? Don't get me wrong, Wynter. I'm happy to see you but… aren't you still in a coma one floor down?"

"I am."

"Then you're a… *dreamwaker?*" Cash kept a close eye on Wynter, fighting against the worry that this was all a trick somehow.

Wynter nodded, crossed her arms against her chest, and leaned against the door frame.

Cash squinted. "How?"

Quinn slapped Cash's shoulder lightly. "She's getting better. That's how. It also means Nolan's awake."

"Have you woken—"

Cash pushed past Jake, pulled Wynter's hoodie up, and took her arm, guiding her down the corridor.

"Hey!" Jake hopped out of the way, swinging his crutches aside. "What's got into you—"

Cash cast a brief but intense stare back at Quinn and Jake. "Her mom!" He said through clenched teeth and motioned toward the elevators at the opposite end of the corridor.

Jake turned to look and saw Madeline and Anson step out from the elevator, deep in conversation. He shared a look with Quinn. "Shit. Shit. Shit."

"I'll be right back. Don't follow me," Cash said as he hustled Wynter around a corner and out of sight. A lock of her red hair trailed around the leading edge of the hoodie.

"What do we do now?" Jake asked.

"Just act normal."

"What's normal?"

Quinn shrugged, then took Jake in her arms and hugged him.

"This is normal, huh?" Jake tried to reciprocate but his crutches kept getting in the way. "I like it."

"Quinn, Jake!" Anson waved at them. "Which room is it?"

Quinn released Jake and he pointed a crutch at the door to Nolan's room. Without a word, Madeline rushed into the room and stood beside Nolan's bed.

"Where was Cash headed?" Anson nodded in the direction Cash and Wynter had left.

Quinn exchanged a brief glance with Jake. "Uh, he was looking for a bathroom."

"The bathrooms are back by the elevators." Anson hooked his thumb back while keeping his eyes on them.

"I guess he forgot," Jake said.

As if on cue, Cash strutted around the corner toward the group.

Anson's gaze flicked between the three teens before settling on Cash. "You find the bathrooms okay?"

Quinn turned to face Cash and made a small "cut it out" sign with her hand in front of her chest, obscured from Anson's field of view.

"Uh, actually no." Cash looked at Anson. "I remembered they were back by the elevators."

"You better go."

"The feeling's passed," Cash said, then added, "I'll remember on the way out."

Anson eyed Cash suspiciously. "You got anything you want to tell me?"

"Actually, yes." Cash moved into Nolan's room, Quinn and Jake following him closely. "But I need to tell Mrs. LaCroix too."

"Wait." Anson grabbed Cash's arm and pulled him back out into the corridor. "Did you see Wynter?"

Cash stared back at Anson, his eyes dark and serious. "No. Did you?"

"I could have sworn that I saw you leave with someone just before Madeline and I arrived."

Cash shook his head. "I don't know who you saw, but it wasn't Wynter."

Anson alternated his attention between the three teens, unconvinced.

"If you don't believe me," Cash said, "just go down to the fourth floor and see."

"I'll take you up on that." Anson motioned at Nolan's room and released Cash's arm. He noticed that his hand had made a mark on Cash's arm. "Sorry... Now what were you going to tell Madeline?"

Cash rubbed his arm as he headed back to Nolan's room. Once they were all inside, Cash faced Madeline. "Mr. LaCroix—"

"Nolan," Madeline said as she quickly wiped a tear from her cheek. "Just call him Nolan."

Cash nodded. "I rode in the ambulance with Nolan. He had a heart attack on the way."

"What?" Madeline raised a hand to her mouth to stifle a gasp and took Nolan's hand with the other.

"As you can see, he's okay." Cash let his eyes roam the length of Nolan's body, ending on his face.

Nolan nodded almost imperceptibly, his eyes conveying gratitude.

Cash continued. "The medics, nurses, and doctors fixed him right up."

"We sure did," Dr. Eastman said from the doorway, his arms crossed against his chest. "Hate to break up the party, but Mr. LaCroix should be left alone to rest."

"I'd like to ask Nolan some questions," Anson said.

"I'm afraid that will have to wait," Dr. Eastman said. "If you give me your phone number, I can have the nurses contact you when he's more rested."

"I'd like to stay. I'm Nolan's wife, Madeline." Madeline's eyes pleaded as she extended her hand. "I won't make a sound. I just need to stay."

Dr. Eastman thought for a moment, then relented, shaking Madeline's hand. "Okay. Only you. The rest of you have to take a hike until visiting hours."

Anson nodded. "Alright. We've got another matter to sort out anyway." He faced Jake, Quinn, and Cash. "After you."

The four of them stepped into the elevator at the end of the corridor and Anson pressed the call button for the fourth floor.

"Why don't you believe us?" Cash asked as the elevator bounced and began its descent.

"It's my job to notice things." The elevator emitted a *ding* and the doors slid open on the fourth floor. Anson stepped out. "I could have sworn I saw you with Wynter earlier."

"I think your mind's playing tricks with you," Jake said as he followed the others out of the elevator.

Cash stopped just outside Wynter's room. "See for yourself."

Anson pushed through the door, his eyes settling on Wynter in her bed, hooked up to a host of different monitoring machines. The gentle blip of her steady heartbeat bounced on the cardiac monitor.

Cash cringed at the familiar sight. It had been less than a week ago that he was keeping vigil in that orange chair from hell next to her bed. A shiver ripped up his back and set the hairs on his neck and arms on end. At that moment he preferred the dreamwaker version of Wynter. Even if she wasn't real, she was real enough.

"Believe us now?" Jake said.

Anson answered him with a doubtful look.

Quinn nudged Cash from his trance-like stare. "We should go."

"Right, yeah." Cash stepped by Anson in the doorway. "You don't need us for anything else, do you?"

"No," Anson said. "Nolan's my priority at the moment. But later I might, so don't go far."

Jake crunched his eyebrows. "Define 'far.' Like as in don't leave the hospital?"

"Stick to Newhaven."

"We can do that." Cash looked to the others. "Right, guys?"

Quinn and Jake nodded, and the three teens headed back to the elevators. Quinn pressed the down call button.

Anson caught up to the group. "Quick question though. Was it my imagination, or did Wynter look better to you?" He slammed a fist on the other call button.

Cash, Quinn, and Jake exchanged looks, then Quinn nodded. "Yeah, she did. Maybe she'll wake up soon."

"Hope so." Anson ran his fingers through hair which still bore evidence of the hectic morning. "I have many questions for her." The elevator going up arrived and he stepped inside the car. "Watch for purple hoodies."

Cash's eyes popped as he looked at Anson. "What?"

A small smile curled at the edges of Anson's lips. "Nothing." The elevator doors began to close. "Keep me posted," he managed to say before the sliding door cut him off.

"He knows," Cash said.

"Of course he does, dude." The down elevator opened and Jake hobbled inside. "He just doesn't know how or why or where."

"We need to catch Jezebel red-handed," Quinn said as the elevator doors closed.

"Something foolproof." Jake faced Cash. "I know you don't like the guy, but we're going to need Ransom."

Cash groaned. "I was afraid you'd say that."

Quinn eyed Cash intently. "Can you summon him right now?"

"What, here?" Cash looked around the elevator. It was bigger than the typical elevator, built to accommodate gurneys.

"Not *here,* dummy, but here, at the hospital," Quinn said. "Like at the chapel. We could *help.* Jake could stand guard and make sure no one else, you know, *comes* inside."

Cash detected a subtle smile on Quinn's lips. Luckily Jake completely missed the subtext. "I think that's too risky."

"Where did Wynter go, anyway?" Jake asked. "She should be part of this plan."

"I'll give you one guess," Cash said as the elevator doors opened.

"I know!" Quinn ran for the entrance to the hospital.

"I'm not chasing her on these." Jake motioned at his crutches. "Not that I even could. Do you know where she's going?"

Cash grinned. "Yeah. Quinn's one smart cookie." He followed Jake out of the hospital. "You should ask her on a date."

"Working on it," Jake said.

Quinn stood beside Blue Belle near the back of the parking lot. She beckoned them, rising up and down on her tiptoes. Then she disappeared behind an adjacent car.

Jake squinted at the VW Beetle. "Dude, what the *hell* is she doing?"

"I don't know. Just hurry up, you dweeb."

"Bite me," Jake said, then both broke out into laughter.

Cash and Jake approached Blue Belle to find Wynter on her back under the VW, with her head stuck out next to the right front wheel.

Quinn sat on the asphalt, her back against the VW's passenger door, her left hand playing with the flowing red hair spilling from Wynter's hoodie.

"Hi, guys," they said in unison.

Cash squatted, amusement on his face, and looked at Wynter upside-down. "You comfortable down there?"

"Not really."

Cash extended his hands and helped both Wynter and Quinn to their feet.

"Quinn says we all need to talk." Wynter looked at Cash, Jake, and Quinn in turn. "Where should we go?"

"Wherever we end up, it's got to be private," Cash said.

"What about the Red River Rest Stop?" Wynter pulled open the passenger door. "We could get some takeout and—"

"I'm down for that." Jake crawled into the back of the VW Beetle. "And I'm freaking starving. Let's go."

Cash followed him. "You heard the man."

Quinn ran around the car and hopped behind the steering wheel. She watched Wynter buckle herself into the passenger seat.

"You don't have to do that," she said. "You're a dreamwaker. You're immortal."

Wynter shrugged. "Old habits."

Quinn started Blue Belle's engine and backed out of her parking space, then slammed on the brakes. "Shit!" She leaned across the division between the front seats, took Wynter's face in her hands, and kissed her deeply.

"What the…" Jake said as he shared a look of surprise and amazement with Cash.

Quinn returned to her seat and smiled. "Come on guys. You know the first rule of dreamwakers. They return to the dreams of the last person to kiss them. I just made sure that Wynter sticks around for a while… at least while I'm awake."

Wynter's cheeks showed a warm shade of brown.

Jake nodded. "Genius."

"Most definitely!" Quinn gave the engine some gas and the Beetle sprang forward.

Together again after what had felt like forever, the four friends embarked on a quest for food to fuel a plan to beat Jezebel at her own game.

THE ELEVATOR OPENED to the fifth floor and Anson stepped out. He replayed the earlier details of his arrival with Madeline as best he could but found the sequence of events fading with time. Still, he had a gut feeling that Cash wasn't being honest with him. And he was positive he'd seen Cash walk away with someone dressed in a purple hoodie.

Could it have been Ransom?

No, his hoodie was black… or was it *really* a dark purple?

Anson had begun second-guessing himself. The color *was* purple, that he knew for sure, and he pushed away the rest for now.

Anson approached the doorway to Nolan's room and poked his head in. Madeline had found a chair and taken her spot next to Nolan's bed. They were holding hands and talking softly with each other.

"I hope I'm not interrupting," he said.

Madeline and Nolan both faced him. "No, not at all." With her free hand Madeline dotted a tissue along her eyelids to catch any tears.

"Look, I know I'm not supposed to be here, but can I ask you a few questions?"

Nolan nodded.

"I'm going to have to act as your go-between," Madeline said. "Nolan can't talk above a whisper due to the smoke irritation."

As if on cue, Nolan picked up a cup of water and took a sip.

Anson took out his notepad and pen from his breast pocket and found a blank page. "Let's go back to the beginning. Why were you still at the trailer today?"

Madeline answered before Nolan had a chance to respond. "He had a migraine. I got him set up in bed before I left for the store."

"When was that?"

"A little after seven, I think?"

Anson's hand jotted notes. "You were alone at the trailer when Jezebel and Roxy arrived?"

Nolan nodded.

"When was that?"

Nolan thought for a moment, then whispered into Madeline's ear. "Around nine-thirty he thinks," she said. "They were arguing."

"About?"

Madeline waited for Nolan's answer, then said, "Who was going to light the gas." She squeezed his hand gently and faced him. "Oh lord, hon."

Nolan tugged on Madeline and she leaned in again. "Jezebel had a gun. He ran back inside but she shot him."

Nolan found his bandaged right shoulder with his left hand and tested its tenderness. "Just a flesh wound." His raspy voice was loud enough for Anson to hear.

"Easy, hon." Madeline looked at Anson. "I think that's enough questions."

Anson nodded. "Okay. According to the Fire Chief, he said you doused yourself in the shower and forced yourself out the bathroom window." He tapped his pen on the notepad. "The medics said that probably saved your life... *and* your legs."

Nolan shrugged. "Can't remember," he choked out.

Anson closed his notepad and slid it, along with his pen, back into his pocket. "Thanks, Nolan, Madeline. I know this was hard."

"You get that bitch for us," Madeline said.

Anson nodded. "I'll do my best." Anson moved to leave, then stopped. "But one more thing before I go." He could tell they were both tired and just wanted some alone time. "Did you happen to see Wynter earlier this morning? In a purple hoodie?"

Nolan's eyes flicked up and locked on Anson's.

"What?" Madeline sat up in her chair. "Wynnie's awake? Why didn't you—"

Anson held his hands up. "Wait a second. She's not awake yet. I just checked. But there was a sighting and I'm following up, wondering if you saw anything. It's probably nothing."

Nolan leaned toward Madeline's ear without breaking his gaze with Anson.

Madeline listened, paused, then faced Anson. "No. He hasn't seen anything."

Anson nodded. "Okay. Thanks folks."

A nurse hustled past Anson in the doorway and glared at him. "You aren't supposed to be here. Doctor's orders."

"Technically, I'm not actually *in* the room." Anson pointed at his feet just outside the threshold to the room. "But I'm going. Got to find the psycho who did this."

Upon hearing this, the nurse softened her gaze on Anson and picked up Nolan's chart at the foot of his bed. "Good, but rules are rules."

Anson shifted his eyes to Madeline and Nolan. "I'll keep you both posted." He saluted with his index finger and headed back down the corridor toward the elevators.

Reading people, deciphering their faces, and knowing when they were hiding something were skills Anson was particularly adept at. And as he pressed the down call button for the elevator, he knew one thing for certain: Nolan knew more than he had admitted to.

Anson exited the hospital. Being in Halston, he couldn't use his radio to contact dispatch. He found a pay phone to notify them that he was on his way back to Newhaven.

"Sheriff, swing by the fire station on your way in." The officer's voice at the other end of the phone buzzed and crackled. "The Chief has a new development on the LaCroix arson case for you."

Anson scrunched his brow. "And that is what, exactly?"

"Didn't say. Dispatch out."

Anson hung up the phone and rubbed his beard, thoughts churning in his head. He located his police SUV and climbed aboard.

"New development, huh?" Anson said to himself as revved the Suburban's engine and pulled out of the hospital parking lot. "Better be good."

QUINN PULLED BLUE BELLE into the parking area of the Red River Rest Stop. She would have preferred a deserted rest stop, but at close to noon on a Saturday five other vehicles were using the westbound side of the facility. She found a parking space as far away as possible and shut the Beetle's engine off.

Wynter held two big white Burger King bags in her lap. She wasted no time doling out the food: a Whopper, large fries, and a large Pepsi for everyone.

"You spill anything and you're dead meat." Quinn focused her attention on Cash and Jake in the back.

"Give us a little credit, huh?" Jake tucked his Pepsi between his legs. "It wouldn't be a problem if there were cup holders."

"I'm not going to drive a minivan just for cup holders." Quinn unfolded her burger and set the fries next to it. She looked at Wynter. "How much do you know? About what happened?"

"I know pretty much what my dad knows." Wynter inserted a straw into her Pepsi and sipped. "Jezebel and Roxy soaked the trailer in gas and torched it... even when they knew my dad was still inside. And—"

Wynter choked on her words, her voice thickening. The reality of what she was saying hit her hard. "I know everything's gone. My books, my camera stuff, my..." She grabbed a napkin and began to sob into it.

Cash reached forward and placed a light hand on her shoulder. "We're going to get her, Wynter."

Quinn scrutinized him. "Don't you mean *them*? Roxy too?"

"We all know Jezebel drives that crazy train," Cash said.

"Doesn't mean Roxy's not guilty."

"No, it doesn't." Cash cast his gaze at the others, one at a time. "So, how are we going to get them?"

The only person eating was Jake. He swallowed his bite and spoke. "Hard evidence."

Wynter wiped her nose and turned toward Jake. "How?"

"If you don't mind being bait, we could get her on video at the Starlite," Jake said. "I could even set up my camcorder for backup." He took a sip from his Pepsi.

Quinn grinned at him, her head resting on the seatback. "I love you, you know that?"

"Um, *what*?" Jake choked and sputtered Pepsi over the front of his shirt and onto the back seat.

Quinn rolled her eyes. "Too bad I have to kill you now. Oh well. It was fun while it lasted."

Jake's eyes widened with confusion. He looked to Cash for help but there was nothing but amusement on his face.

Quinn reached over the driver's seat and poked him. "I'm *kidding!*"

"About which part?" Jake met and held Quinn's gaze.

Quinn flicked her eyes away, suddenly self-conscious, and slid back into her seat. "Uh, all of it." She shared a quick glance with Wynter.

"But back to your idea, Jake," Cash said. "You think the video quality would be good enough?"

"I don't know. Maybe. Between that and my camcorder, we could nail their asses."

"Yeah, could work," Cash said. "What do you think, Wynter?"

The interior of the car fell silent. Wynter sighed. "I just don't want anyone else getting hurt. She shot my dad, so she's got no problem with shooting people."

"We'd have to make sure she only wants you," Quinn said. "And Ransom of course, isn't that right, Cash?"

"Totally. But I can't summon him here." Cash thought a moment. "My dad's home now so my place's out." His eyes contemplated Jake, then Quinn. "Really, the best place would be the Starlite."

"Let me out and I'll make the call," Jake said. "And crack the windows. People are going to think we're fucking in here."

Acting practically in unison, Quinn and Wynter unlocked and pushed open the vent windows. Quinn collected her food in its wrapper and moved it to the footwell. Her Pepsi in hand, she swung open her door and tilted the seatback forward. "Move it, nerd," she said with playful eyes.

Jake handed his burger and fries to Cash. "Dude, no stealing."

"Chill out. I got my own."

Jake sipped his Pepsi and looked up at Quinn. "Help me out?"

She took his Pepsi, placed both cups on the roof of the Beetle, and offered her hand.

Jake took it gladly and used his crutches as leverage to extract himself from the car. "Anyone got a quarter?"

Quinn jammed her hand into her pocket and removed a palmful of coins. Jake plucked a quarter out and headed for the payphone.

"I'll be back," he said in his crappy Schwarzenegger accent.

Quinn shook her head and leaned into the car, smiling. "He's growing on me."

"Like a fungus?" Wynter plucked a french fry and chewed it.

"Yeah, maybe."

"Hey, Wynter." Cash slid sideways on the back seat so he could see Wynter better. "Have you ever been a dreamwaker before?"

"Never."

"Do you think it hurts when you drift?" Cash's blue eyes found Wynter's. "Not when you sleep, but, like, when you die."

Wynter recalled the sound and the carnage when Ransom jumped in front of the eighteen-wheeler. She shivered and nodded. "It must. But it shouldn't last long."

"I guess that would depend on *how* you die," Quinn said.

Cash winced. "You're probably right."

"We're all set." Jake stood hunched on his crutches behind Quinn. "Zain's going to let us in early so we can get things set up. Then we call *Jizz-balls* and wait for her to take the bait."

"What if she's not home?" Cash looked up at him from inside the Beetle. "That's the last place I'd hide after committing arson and attempted murder."

Jake's self-satisfaction melted away. "Uh, shit."

Wynter leaned forward so she could see Jake. "Just page Monty."

Jake sat gobsmacked. "Wynter, you're a genius."

Wynter and Cash exchanged smiles.

Jake reached for his Pepsi on the roof of the Beetle, then hesitated. "Which one is mine?"

Quinn walked her fingertips across the roof of the car. "I guess you got a fifty-fifty chance of sharing my germs, *nerd*." She winked at him.

Jake grabbed one of the cups. "Never tell me the odds."

"Watch your mouth, kid, or you'll find yourself floating home."

Jake laughed and climbed into the back, handing his crutches to Cash. "God, you're good."

"And don't you forget it." Quinn took the remaining Pepsi cup off the roof and sat down. "Let's chow down so we can get those bitches behind bars."

Now that they had most of a plan in place, the food went down fast and easy. Twenty minutes later, the four friends found themselves barreling west on I94. Wynter's head swirled with thought.

How would it feel to touch Ransom again?

The satisfaction of entrapping Jezebel and Roxy.

Would it hurt when she died?

She'd find out soon enough.

At half past noon, Anson turned the Suburban into the Newhaven Fire Department's parking lot. Several volunteers had the department's sole fire truck out in front of the garage and were giving it a good scrubbing. Anson tipped the brim of his campaign hat at them and headed inside.

Being a volunteer-run fire station, Charlie Embers was the only paid employee and had held the job of Newhaven's Fire Chief for the past twenty-three years. Retirement was still several years away, a milestone he flat out refused to consider, and despite his diabetes (Charlie loved his beer, donuts, and Lucy's bacon cheeseburgers) he insisted that the only way to prevent him from working would be for him to drop dead on the job.

Anson found Charlie in his small office finishing up a sandwich and a Dr. Pepper. "Hey Charlie. Was told you got something for me?"

"Jacobs, my boy," Charlie said through a full mouth. He extended a hand and both men shared a firm shake, then washed down his bite with a sip of soda. "Sorry. Lucy's turkey bacon club is the cat's ass. Healthy, too."

"The turkey maybe, but the bacon'll kill you."

Charlie wiped his mouth. "Fuck that. Life ain't worth living without bacon." He stood and moved his portly frame toward the office door. "Walk with me."

Charlie led the way down a short hallway to a locked door. "You're definitely looking at arson. We haven't gotten the official word from the IAAI, they've got a couple guys from Larkinson on their way, but there was evidence of accelerant all around that trailer. After you've been fighting fires as long as I have, you get a nose for that kind of shit."

Anson pulled out his notepad and pen. "What did they use?"

"They?" Charlie eyed him curiously as he pulled out his keys. "You know something I don't, Jacobs?"

Anson considered his words carefully. "We think there were two arsonists."

"Interesting," Charlie said. "Probably retaliating for something, no doubt. Anyway, they used regular, run-of-the-mill gasoline. The IAAI suits might be able to tell you what brand, if that matters."

"It might. Anything to build a case."

Charlie unlocked the door and led Anson inside a small storage room. A folding table had been set up against the back wall. "How'd you like *our* evidence locker?"

"Does the job."

Three Ziploc bags, two small and one large, lay on the table. Charlie picked up one of the small ones. "We recovered one 9mm shell casing, extreme heat damage though. That guy was shot right? The injun?"

"The Native American, yes." Anson turned the soot encrusted casing around in his hand looking for any distinctive markings. "Luckily the bullet grazed him."

"And there's this." Charlie handed him the second small bag. Inside was a Zippo lighter charred black. "Typical Zippo, no distinctive markings except for the 'XO' on the side."

Anson held the bag close and tried to rub the soot off the metal through the plastic. It didn't work. He set the bag back on the table.

"Now, this is a better find." Charlie grabbed the large bag. A melted mound of red plastic sat inside the bag.

"And this is?"

"Best guess, a melted jerry can," Charlie said. "The thing reeks of gasoline."

Anson gave the bag a sniff. The odor of gasoline permeated through the plastic in waves. "Wouldn't all jerry cans smell of gas?"

"Got a point." Charlie sat on the edge of the table. "They thought they could get rid of the evidence by burning it. Idiots." He took the bag from Anson and flipped it over. "Any idea what this means?"

Charlie pointed to a sequence of numbers and letters scrawled in black pen on the bottom. The beginning and ending had been melted away, leaving "46W00."

"Forty-six 'W' zero zero." Charlie handed the bag back to him. "Any ideas?"

Anson squinted at the handwritten numbers and letters. Something about them seemed familiar and itched for connection, but he came up blank.

Instead, he shook his head. "Mind if I take these back to the station?"

"They're all yours." Charlie handed him the bags with the shell casing and lighter in them. "We don't need no goddamn firebugs in Newhaven."

"Thanks, Charlie." Anson headed for the door. Charlie followed him. "No need to walk me out."

"Who says I'm walking you out, princess?" Charlie grinned at him. "I got a sandwich *with bacon* to finish."

Anson laughed and waved. "Keep me posted on the investigators' findings."

"Will do."

Charlie shuffled back into his office as Anson walked through the open garage to his SUV. He examined the black lettering on the melted jerry can again before tossing all three pieces of evidence on the passenger seat.

As he drove back to the station, Anson's thoughts drifted to Nolan at the hospital, with Madeline by his side. He made a mental note to call and check up on them later in the day. Then it dawned on him that Halston Medical Center had become the temporary residence of the entire LaCroix family.

Injured, and now, homeless.

Anson's head filled with rage. One person was behind it all. Jezebel Caine. Except all the evidence he had against her was circumstantial. He looked at the melted remnants of the jerry can. Fingerprints left behind on the plastic, if there were any, wouldn't be viable. If the investigators could determine the brand of gasoline, that might give him a lead, but he didn't hold much hope. The bullet casing found at the scene was useless without a pistol to match it to. And the lighter was a charred mess. That left him with lots of potential clues but nothing certain.

But...

Anson pulled the Suburban to the side of the road. He grabbed the bag with the melted jerry can inside and flipped it over.

Forty-six "W" zero zero.

Anson worked the numbers and letters in his head. They had to be significant somehow. Frustrated, he threw the bag back toward the passenger seat. It hit the side of the door and flipped end for end, the handwritten letters upside-down. It looked like a word now, not a combination of numbers and letters.

oomph

Anson sounded it out. "Oomph?" In an instant, everything clicked. He grabbed the melted jerry can and turned the letters and numbers back around.

Forty-six "W" zero zero.

They weren't zeroes, but Os. The answer had been staring him in the face all along. "4-6-W-O-O." He cast his mind back to the last time he had picked up Jezebel and taken her to the station. She had just forced Quinn and her friends off the road.

Anson recalled Jezebel's ramshackle house and overgrown yard right in the middle of southie territory. Woodpark Avenue.

"1-4-6-W-O-O-D-P-A-R-K." Anson spelled out Jezebel's address to himself. The jerry can belonged to the occupants of 146 Woodpark Avenue. It was circumstantial evidence at best, but it was stronger than an eye-witness account, even if that eye-witness was Nolan. Jezebel had been at the LaCroix trailer this morning. He was one hundred percent sure of it.

Anson smiled and floored the gas.

Devil's Gun

QUINN MADE GOOD TIME. She had swung by Jake's place to get his camcorder and arrived at the Starlite SuperSkate at twenty minutes past one. She pulled into the parking lot and rolled Blue Belle into the space next to Zain's Corolla.

Wynter surveyed the parking lot. She tried to conceal her anxiety, but now that they were here with their plan in action, it became more difficult with each passing minute. "It's weird to see the place so empty." She directed her gaze toward the entrance.

"Totally." Quinn shut off the engine and Blue Belle's frame began to click as it cooled.

"Maybe we shouldn't park right next to Zain's car." Jake held the camcorder case between his unbroken thigh and Cash's. "Wouldn't that seem like a suspicious coincidence? Don't forget, Jezebel's smart."

"But we're smarter." Cash caught Quinn's attention in the rear view mirror. "Moving the car's a good idea."

"Ugh. Fine." Quinn twisted the key in the ignition and revved the VW's engine. "Hold on to your hats!" She shifted into reverse, twisted to look back through the rear window, and floored the gas pedal.

The Beetle's wheels caught the pavement and propelled them across the lot in a straight line. The camcorder case shot forward, wedging itself between the two front seats.

Cash watched the fence and a line of trees on the outer edge of the lot approach the back of the Beetle at a frightening speed. He looked at Jake and saw that his face had gone white with fear. Cash gripped his seat belt with white knuckles. "Jesus Christ Quinn! Slow down. You're going to—"

Quinn watched the fence hurtling toward her with a mischievous gleam in her eye, then moved her foot to the brake and put all her pressure on it. The little car's wheels chirped twice before coming to a stop. "How's that?" she asked, a maniacal gleam in her eye.

Wynter had missed all of Quinn's shenanigans, focused instead on the figure standing just inside the main doors to the Starlite.

"Going to have to peel Jake from the roof." Cash leaned toward him. "You okay, man? You look like you've seen a ghost."

Jake took a breath and nodded. It was the lack of a verbal response from Jake that reminded Quinn of his near-death experience when he was a kid.

"Oh shit," she said to herself and turned in her seat to look at him. "I'm really sorry, Jake. I forgot."

Jake managed a small smile. "It's okay."

Cash looked at them both. "Forgot what?"

Jake took a breath and shook off his fear. "Never mind." He tapped the JVC -branded molded plastic case. "Let's do this."

Quinn stepped out of the car, took Jake's crutches, and helped him out. Cash followed with the camcorder case in hand. The three of them walked around the Beetle to find Wynter still in the front passenger seat, her eyes locked on the Starlite. Cash followed her gaze and saw Zain waiting for them. He waved and Zain waved back.

"Is Wynter okay?" Jake asked.

Cash rapped on the passenger window with his knuckle. "Wynter? You coming?"

She blinked and looked at him, then smiled and nodded. Wynter pushed open the door. "Sorry. I'm feeling a little spaced out."

"You want to do this another time?" Cash's concern was clear. "We wouldn't mind, would we?" He looked at Jake and Quinn, who were both returning nods.

"Any day without having to fight Jezebel is a good day," said Jake.

"No, I'm good." Wynter pressed the lock button in the door and swung it closed. "Let's go."

The group crossed the parking lot and took the ramp up to the front entrance of the Starlite. The deadbolt clicked and retracted.

Zain regarded all four of them, singling out Wynter. "Good to see you doing better, Wynter." He pocketed his keys and crossed his arms against his chest. "So, we're really going to do this?"

"If we're lucky." Jake tapped the camcorder case in Cash's hand. "I brought backup."

"Got to be honest with you guys," Zain began. "I'm a little uneasy inviting Jezebel back in here. She jammed a gun in my face the last time she was here. I don't want anyone to get hurt."

"Jezebel has a one-track mind," Quinn said. "She's not one to start shooting random people."

"She will if they're in her way." Cash stepped into the darkened foyer.

"So we make sure that no one is in her way." Quinn shrugged. "Easy peasy."

"Not so easy peasy. She's a loose cannon." Jake looked at the locations of Zain's video surveillance. "Can we temporarily re-aim the cameras?"

"Yeah, no problem," Zain said. "But I need to know how you're going to keep Jezebel from leaving a path of destruction."

Cash pointed toward the darkened admissions window. "Can we use your office to fill you in?"

Zain motioned toward his office. "Be my guest." He followed the four teens into his back office and flipped on the overhead fluorescents. Jake, Quinn, and Wynter took a seat on a ratty old sofa with a repeating autumn leaf motif. It was comfortable enough, but the sofa had seen more than its fair share of butts and likely would fail a black light test. Cash sat on a dirty plaid lounge chair peppered with cigarette burns.

"Sorry." Zain reclined in the chair behind his desk and propped his feet up. "I don't get many visitors back here." He alternated his gaze among the four teens. "So, sell me on this idea of yours."

Cash looked at the others and they nodded at him. "Well, it's pretty simple really. We bait Jezebel, let her know that Wynter's out and she has Ransom. Then we wait and catch her violence on video surveillance."

"She's probably going to go apeshit, so I'll be shooting video too." Jake shared a knowing glance with Quinn and Wynter. "Then we'll have some hard evidence that we can use to put her away."

Zain crossed his arms against his chest. "That's it? You call Jezebel and she comes running?" He paused to let them respond but the four of them stared back, as if their plan was perfect. Only Wynter showed any hint of doubt.

"I hate to tell you this," Zain continued, "but that's not a plan. It's a dangerous fantasy."

"It's the only way in the time we have," Quinn said. "You're already set up for video."

"There's no way I'm going to say 'yes' to inviting a psychopath into my business, risking the lives of hundreds." Zain dropped his feet to the floor and sat forward, his hands palms down on the desk top. "Even if I was crazy enough to say yes, which I'm not, there's no way I would go ahead without Anson as backup."

Cash stole a glance at Wynter, then stood and began to pace. "No police."

"You're not making this very easy," Zain said. "But that's the line. You need police presence."

"You don't understand." Cash dropped his hands to the desk

and leaned in toward Zain. "She'll know. And she'll bail. Then she'll jump us some other time. We need to stay in control." He slumped back into his chair.

Quinn sat forward. "What if we do it before you open?"

Jake's eyes widened with sudden excitement. "Great idea. We can avoid the crowds and just get the evidence."

"And no police," Cash said.

Zain eyed the teens warily. "Okay. We open at seven and the concession staff get here at six. I'll give you from five to six o'clock. No more. Will that work?"

"That'll work, won't it guys?" Jake nodded and looked to the others for approval. "You won't regret it."

"I hope not," Zain said. "But if anything goes wrong, and I mean *anything*, I'm pulling the plug and calling Anson."

Cash sat forward and massaged his temples. Wynter reached out and placed a hand on his arm.

"Are you feeling alright, Cash?"

Cash winced and scrunched his eyes shut. "Actually, no. I got a wicked headache coming on."

"Want something for it?" Zain rummaged around in a desk drawer and pulled out a bottle of ibuprofen. He shook two out into his palm and offered them to Cash. "Hold on. I'll get you something to wash them down with." Zain stepped out of the office.

Cash eyed the door, then looked at the others. "You think he bought it?"

"We're going to have to assume he did." Quinn handed him a small Ziploc baggie of zees. "This should be enough."

Zain returned to the office with a cup of water. Cash jammed the baggie under his leg.

Cash took the cup of water and washed the ibuprofen down. "Can I sit here for a second? I'm feeling a little dizzy."

Jake pulled himself up onto his crutches and pointed to the sofa. "Want to lie down?"

Cash shook his head. "No. I think if I sit for a bit, I'll be okay."

"We'll get started re-aiming the cameras," Jake said. "You can join us when you're ready."

Zain sat on the corner of the desk. "I'll go fire up the system. I'll need someone to help me with the cameras and—"

"Pick me," Quinn said, smiling.

"Okay. Queenie's with me. Good. Wynter? Want to watch the video monitor to see if we're on target or not?"

"Got it," Wynter said. "Just point me where to go."

"And Jake..." Zain paused. "What's your job?"

"The most important job of all," Jake said. "I'll be the stand-in for Jezebel so you can aim the cameras properly."

Cash looked at the floor, his head in his hands. "Don't forget your camcorder, man."

"No way." Jake tapped the plastic case with the tip of his crutch. "That's the cherry on top of this plan. I'm saving it for last."

Zain glanced at the clock on his desk. "Let's get a move on. We've only got a few hours." He led the charge out of the office.

Cash transferred the baggie to his pocket, stood, and followed everyone out of the office. "Zain, I need some fresh air. I'm going to go lie down in Quinn's car."

"Sure." Zain flipped on the power to the video surveillance system. The screen beneath the admissions window faded up with a black and white image divided into four quadrants, each showing a different camera view. Time code ticked forward at the top. "Sounds good. Need any help?"

"No, I think I got it. Except for keys." Cash walked around the rental counter. "Quinn?"

Quinn dug into her purse, pulled out her keys, and placed them in Cash's hand. "Good luck," she whispered into his ear.

"Thanks, *Queenie*." Cash winked at her. "I'm going to need it." He headed toward the front entrance and walked out into the afternoon sunshine, leaving the others to set up the first part of their plan.

The fresh air actually did feel good, but it was warm out. He would have to open Blue Belle's windows or he'd cook.

Cash popped the lock on the driver's side door, pulled it open, and rolled down the window. He closed the door, then did the same to the passenger side. Once inside, he shut the door behind him. He exchanged the keys for the baggie in his pocket and shook the little gelatin cubes into his palm.

"Sure hope this works." Cash tossed the cubes into his mouth and swallowed them with ease. They didn't even require chewing. He lay on his side as comfortably as possible on the back seat and closed his eyes.

Sleep overtook Cash in minutes. The entire plan hinged on what he had to do within the next hour and a half. Failure was not an option.

WHILE CASH SLEPT, Quinn, Wynter, Jake, and Zain prepared the Starlite for their sting operation. Quinn and Zain aimed the surveillance cameras with Wynter's guidance, finishing close to three thirty. They hit a small snag when they pointed the camera at the entrance in the opposite direction. The cable ended up too short. Zane ran new cable, but the delay put them behind. Jake cracked jokes and spouted lines from movies to keep the mood light.

When they were done, Jake stood centered in all four quadrants of the surveillance monitor and took a bow.

"Ladies and gentlemen, for my next trick, watch me conceal my camcorder in this here garbage can." Jake lifted the decorative cover and propped the camera on several stacked buckets inside.

The JVC GR-C7 came with a wired remote. Jake plugged it in, hung the control switch out of the garbage can, and put the camcorder into standby mode. When he returned the garbage can cover, the camcorder's lens pointed out the opening in the side, practically invisible to the casual observer. He pressed record on the remote and shuffled back on his crutches.

"Voila!" Jake said. "What do you think? Can you see it?"

Wynter whispered something into Quinn's ear. She smiled and nodded in response. "The record light is a dead giveaway, don't you think?" She pointed at the little red beacon inside the garbage can's side opening.

"Shit. You're right. That's a problem" Jake found Zain in the admissions booth by the surveillance monitor, loading a video tape into the connected recorder. "Hey, do you have any black electrician's tape?"

Zain paused to think, then nodded. "Probably. Somewhere. To save me a wild goose chase, would masking tape and a black pen work instead?"

"Yeah, it should."

Zain disappeared into his office for a moment and returned with a roll of tape and a black Sharpie with an extra wide tip. "Go wild."

Jake returned to the covert camcorder and set to work on concealing the recording light. He finished ten minutes later, again seeking approval from the girls.

Quinn gave him a thumbs up. "Looks good, Jake."

"I can't see a thing," Wynter added. "It's recording right now?"

"Yup." Jake smiled broadly, satisfied with his contribution to the plan. "Operation Dreamscape is officially a go."

Wynter crouched and crawled on all fours up to the garbage can. She raised her head into the camcorder's field of view. "Bang! You're dead."

"Don't even joke." Jake clicked the button on the remote. "I'm going to power off to save batteries." He reached into the garbage can and turned the camcorder off.

Quinn squinted to read the clock over the rollerskate rental desk. "Is it really quarter to four?"

Zain noted the timecode counting forward on the surveillance monitor. "It is."

"We've got over an hour to kill," Wynter said. "Any suggestions?"

Jake raised an eyebrow at Quinn, then turned toward Zain, who was still fiddling with the surveillance system. "Zain, how about you fire up the arcade?"

Zain leaned on the counter. "Love to Jake, but we should keep the place looking like it's closed. How about..." He reached under the counter, grabbed a deck of cards, and slapped them on the worn countertop. "Blackjack? I could be dealer."

He received no response from the three teens.

"Poker?"

"Oh yeah," Jake said. "Make it *strip* poker and I'm in." He flashed a toothy self-conscious grin at Quinn.

Quinn and Wynter cast knowing glances at each other, both remembering the last time they had played strip poker at the cabin with Ransom.

"No way, José," both girls said in unison.

Quinn smiled. "How about 'Screw Your Neighbor' instead?"

Jake's jaw dropped. "Um, *what?*"

Zain laughed. "You can pick your tongue up off the floor any time, Jake."

"It's just a card game, you perv," Quinn said. "But it's a good one. I'll teach everyone how to play. Come on."

They all took a seat around a table. Quinn quickly explained the rules as she shuffled the deck like a professional, never once looking at her hands.

"It's easier to explain if we just play a round." Quinn dealt everyone a card. Despite early mistakes, Wynter, Zain, and Jake caught on quickly. After the first round, Jake held the most points. In this game, just like in golf, the goal was to have the smallest point total.

After several more rounds, Jake held the dubious title of most consistent loser. "Jesus, I'm cursed or something."

"You've been totally screwed, over and over, that's for sure." Quinn caught Jake's eyes with hers, but he couldn't hold her gaze.

Zain glanced at the clock. "It's after five. When are you planning on calling Jezebel?"

"Soon." Quinn slid off the stool and watched the second hand of the clock above the rental desk tick its way around the dial. "Come on, Cash," she whispered to herself. But no matter how strongly she hoped for a better outcome, the doors to the Starlite remained closed.

THE MECHANICAL CLICKING caught Cash's attention. He opened his eyes to the back of Blue Belle's front passenger seat. It was back in its proper position, instead of pushed forward like when he had first closed his eyes. Maybe it was the wind.

The summer breeze felt good on his face, warm and fresh, but there was something else.

Popcorn? Cotton candy?

The clicking continued and the Beetle jostled in time with it. Cash turned his head to look at the roof of the car, but instead he saw nothing but sky.

"What the..." Cash sat up and realized that the entire car was tilted upward at an odd angle. He used the back of the seats to pull himself up and saw there was no steering wheel, dashboard, or glove box. He twisted to look out the back window but it, too, was gone.

Leading away from the back of the car were a pair of rails with wooden ties set underneath, twisting and turning out of sight far behind him.

No. Not behind, but below.

Cash could see Newhaven far below him, the north and south sections of town, even Stedford Plaza and Finn's Gas N Go. The height made his knees ache. He swung his legs into the footwell as the VW Beetle morphed into a roller coaster car. Gravity pressed his spine into the seatback. He felt like an astronaut waiting for launch.

The incessant clicking scratched a groove on Cash's nerves. He closed his eyes and tried to ignore it.

"You ready?"

Cash turned to find Ransom sitting next to him, looking relaxed with his hands clasped behind his head. "What the hell is this?"

Ransom leaned out the left side of the car and looked down. Cash reached out to pull Ransom back into the car but caught a glimpse of the town below him and froze.

"Looks like one hell of a roller coaster to me," Ransom said. "It's going to be a sweet ride. You up for it?"

Cash stared blankly back at him.

"You've never been on a roller coaster before, have you?" Ransom smiled. "A real one, that is."

Cash managed to shake his head slowly back and forth.

"Interesting choice."

Puzzlement won over Cash's fear for a moment. "What do you mean?"

"This is your dream," Ransom said. "Your life have a lot of ups and downs lately?"

"You could say that. You should know, actually."

"Right. Can I help?"

"That's the plan." Cash spoke in a low rasp as he gripped the seat. "We're going to reunite you with Wynter."

"Good. I've really missed her." Jealousy sparked in Cash's eyes and Ransom noticed. "I know you have feelings for her. So do I... I just don't want things to get weird."

"Too late for that," Cash said. "She's made her choice. But I'll always be there for her. You can't make the same promise."

Ransom nodded and faced forward, his smile fading from his face. "Feel that? The car's tipping. We're coming to the top." He motioned at Cash's waist. "You better get your seat belt on before…"

"Before what?" Cash noticed the absence of clicking and the horizon dipped up from below, vast expanses of grassland as far as he could see.

Ransom reclined in his seat. "Before we fall to Earth." He glanced at Cash. "What goes up must come down."

Cash's fingers scrabbled instinctively for the seat belt beside him but there was nothing there. The bench seat looked less like a part of a VW and more like a roller coaster car with every passing second. And this roller coaster car had no seat belts.

"Where are they?"

Ransom focused lazily on the scenery in front of him. "Man, that's beautiful."

"WHERE ARE THE SEATBELTS?"

Ransom shrugged. "This is your dream, remember?"

The roller coaster car tipped forward until the two of them were almost facing straight down. Newhaven dipped up into view and the car hurtled down the track toward the ground.

Cash clenched his teeth and gripped the seat and side of the car, his knuckles bone white. He wanted to scream but his voice had abandoned him.

At the last moment, the car leveled with the ground, rocketing down the track at an insane speed. Ahead he saw Wynter standing beside the track, but as he drew closer, he realized Wynter towered over him. She looked to be at least fifty feet tall, and she was waving her hands, mouthing the word "Stop!"

The car flew past her, revealing Jezebel standing behind with her pistol raised. Rapid muzzle flashes burst from the pistol's barrel. Cash looked behind to see Wynter crumple to the ground, half on and half off the tracks, red dots blossoming through the fabric of her shirt.

Cash reached for her and yelled, "NO! WYNTER!" He looked at Ransom next to him, laughing hysterically in silence.

"What's so fucking funny, asshole?"

But Ransom wasn't laughing. He was screaming without making a sound.

Cash cast his eyes forward, the track ahead twisting and turning until it headed straight up toward the sky. The roller coaster car followed on its predetermined path up, then upside-down, and finally down again, like a plane caught in a stall.

Cash watched in horror as the car headed for a pile of bodies strewn across the tracks. There were only seconds before impact when he recognized Jake's Nintendo hat and Quinn's pink FreshWhip polo shirt. And Wynter's fiery hair.

His friends. Were they all dead? Cash had no way of knowing, but being struck by an out of control roller coaster car would surely deliver an unfavorable outcome.

"STOP!" Cash yelled.

The roller coaster froze on its tracks, throwing Cash and Ransom forward into the seat backs in front of them.

Dazed, Cash looked up at Ransom. "You okay?"

"Yeah." Ransom swallowed hard. "Your dreams really suck. Why didn't you stop that hell ride sooner?"

"I forgot I could do that." Cash peered above and saw that the sky had been replaced with the roof of the Beetle. "Wait. Are you dreamwaking now?"

Ransom stuck his head up and looked out the windows. "We're in the Starlite parking lot. In Blue Belle? I guess I am."

Cash crumpled against the back seat. "It worked." He heaved a sigh of relief. "Do you know what time it is?"

"No idea."

Cash scanned the entrance to the Starlite. "Okay. You need to stay in the car, out of sight."

"Why?"

Cash placed his hands firmly on Ransom's shoulders. "Because we're going to take you to Wynter. Got it?"

Ransom nodded. "I'd do anything for Wynter."

Cash exited the car and raced toward the entrance to the Starlite. He hoped that trusting Ransom wasn't a mistake. And he hoped he wasn't too late.

THE TIME ZAIN had given them was evaporating before their eyes. Quinn couldn't take the wait any longer. Wynter felt the heat of her gaze and faced her.

"Now?" she asked.

Quinn nodded but there was no excitement in her eyes, only fear. The operation was derailing. She dug through her purse and removed a business card. Text on the front in plain hand-typed lettering said, "Say hello to your little fix." Beneath that was a phone number. She handed the card to Wynter.

"It's Monty's pager," Quinn said. "Punch in the Starlite's phone number and he'll call you back." She slung her purse over her shoulder and walked to the front doors of the Starlite. Quinn crossed her arms like a worried parent.

Wynter stood and slapped both hands on the little table. "It's showtime. I have a call to make. Where's your phone?"

Zain led Wynter to the phone in the admissions window, Jake following close behind. She picked it up, consulted the business card, and dialed. The line clicked and began to trill in her ear.

"Shit." Wynter snapped her fingers. "What's the number here? Quick."

Zain stammered for a second before listing off the Starlite's phone number. Wynter punched in the digits on the phone's push button number pad, waited, then hung up.

"Who was that?" Zain's eyes narrowed on Wynter. He snatched the business card from her hands.

"Hey, give that back!" Wynter tried to retrieve the card, but Zain turned his back and deflected her attempts.

His head began to shake back and forth, slowly. "No. This wasn't part of the plan. No way."

"It's the *only* way," Wynter said.

"Inviting Jezebel and her flunky here is dangerous enough. Adding Monty to the mix is just... *insane*." Zain flung the business card on the counter. "I trusted you guys and you fucking lied to me."

"Technically, we didn't lie," Jake said.

"Oh, really?" Zain pierced him with his stare. "What would you call it then?"

"We just left out a few... details." Jake could feel Zain's disappointment burning.

"That's such bullsh—"

The phone rang, cutting Zain off. The three alternated their gazes among each other. Zain snatched the phone off the counter and held it in his hand.

"Let me answer it. Please," Wynter said softly. "We're sorry. We were afraid you'd say no."

The phone rang again.

"Please, Zain." Wynter's irises blazed blue and almost seemed to glow within her welling eyes.

The phone's ringer echoed through the emptiness of the Starlite.

"We'll make it up to you," Jake said. "Somehow. We promise. Just let her answer it."

Zain had cooled. "Jezebel needs to be stopped. But if I see Monty, I'm calling Anson. Got it?"

Wynter and Jake both nodded. Zain handed the phone back to Wynter. She took a breath and lifted the handset.

"About fuckin' time," Monty's voice crackled through the receiver. "Who is this?"

"I got a message for Jezebel," Wynter said.

"Who the *fuck* is this?" Monty buzzed back.

"I'm out, bitch, and I got a score to settle." Wynter looked up at Zain and Jake with a gleam in her eye that almost felt evil. "And I got Ransom with me. Meet me at the Starlite. Come alone or else. You got thirty minutes."

Wynter hung up the phone, cutting off Monty's tirade of expletives mid-sentence. "Sounds like he's pissed."

"That's the plan," Jake said, but his excitement dropped when he saw anger still simmering behind Zain's eyes.

Wynter stepped out from behind the counter and joined Quinn at the front entrance. She slid a cool hand onto Quinn's shoulder.

"The rockets are flying."

Quinn managed a small smile, but her voice was low and steeped with anxiety. "*The Dead Zone*. Nice one. You can be taught."

"Everything okay?"

Quinn shrugged and glanced back at Jake and Zain, now in a lively discussion comparing the pros and cons of video recording formats. She leaned toward Wynter. "I'm worried. Cash is taking too long. We're going to miss our opportunity."

"Jezebel will show up even if Cash fails, you know that."

Quinn shook her head. "But I want the *whole* plan to work."

Wynter sighed and settled her eyes on Blue Belle in the distance. "Cash will come through. He always does. I'd bet my life on it."

"You kind of already have."

"Yeah, but it won't be real."

"Sure it will," Quinn said. "It's real for everyone who doesn't know the secret. Plus, it's going to hurt. And Zain's going to flip out."

"Maybe."

Quinn took Wynter's hands in hers. "Can I ask you something?"

Wynter nodded.

"Is he worth all the trouble?"

"You mean Ransom?"

"Yeah. I mean it's pretty obvious that you like Cash," Quinn said. "It's *more* than obvious that Cash likes *you*. So why are we doing all this?"

"We're building evidence against Jezebel." Wynter looked up at a surveillance camera on the ceiling. "That's what all *this* is for. She needs to go away. For a long time. Ransom's just a small part of everything else." She returned her eyes to Quinn's, a kindness showing through. "Here's the thing though. Ransom is a big part of *me,* and I need him back or I'll probably go crazy. Does that make sense?"

Quinn thought for a moment, then smiled. "Yeah, I guess it does."

Wynter smiled too and her eyes went distant.

"What is it?"

Wynter pointed out the windowed entrance. "I knew he'd come through for us."

Instead of responding, Quinn burst out of the Starlite's entry doors and raced toward Cash as he approached the building at full sprint.

Zain glanced back to see Quinn disappear out the door. "Hey, what's going on? Why is Quinn leaving?"

"She has to be somewhere," Wynter said.

Quinn ran past Cash without stopping. "Did you do it?"

Cash yelled back, "Yeah. He's waiting. But Quinn!"

She turned and faced him. "What?"

Cash pulled the keys to Blue Belle out of his pocket and threw them. Quinn grabbed the keys out of the air with one hand and resumed her race to the car. She hopped in and started the engine.

"Get inside! Quick!" Quinn yelled out her window before zooming out of the parking lot. "We're running out of time."

Cash ran to the door of the Starlite, pulled it open, and punched through into the darkened foyer of the building. He threw his arms around Wynter and hugged her tight. "Am I too late?"

Wynter kissed his cheek lightly, just once. "No. You're right on time."

"Jezebel is on her way." Jake smirked and waved him over.

Cash stepped back from Wynter and smiled. He gave her hands a gentle squeeze and trotted to the counter, still out of breath.

Jake looked him up and down. "Have a good sleep?"

"Yup. Just what I needed." The two slapped each other's hands.

Jake turned to Zain. "Fire up the surveillance recorder and I'll get the camcorder in standby." He grabbed Cash's shoulder and patted it excitedly. "Dude, you got to see this." He pulled Cash to the garbage can where he had hidden the camcorder.

"God help us." Zain's eyes met Wynter's, her eyes no longer the vibrant blue that they had been moments ago. "I hope you know what you're doing," he said.

"Don't worry. We do." Wynter's part of the plan was simple: Face Jezebel and don't back down. But as she took her position in the center of the foyer, her thoughts went to Quinn, because Quinn's part of the plan was even more important than hers.

MONTY SLAMMED THE pay phone's receiver back onto its cradle. "Fuckin' bitch hung up on me," he hissed through gritted teeth. He picked the handset up again and struck it three more times. The few customers in the parking lot of Stedford Plaza looked shocked by his outburst. He sent them a scowl in response.

Wynter meant nothing to him. For a fleeting moment, he thought of leaving Jezebel out of the picture entirely and going to the Starlite alone to claim Ransom for himself.

But in a small town like Newhaven, Jezebel would find out eventually. She always did. And despite the brave front Monty put up when dealing with her, Jezebel scared him. She would not let anything, or anyone, prevent her from getting what she wanted. That included Monty.

He climbed into his car and revved the engine as he worked through possible scenarios in his head. They all led to a confrontation that he would rather avoid.

Monty laid a strip of black rubber across the white outlines of the parking spots. He turned onto Main Street, fighting his desire to drive directly to the Starlite, and headed for the only place Jezebel could be: the storage shed behind Ollie's MovieTyme.

Five minutes later, Monty rolled onto the graveled space behind the storage shed. As expected, he found the Barracuda concealed under a blue tarp. He stepped out and sniffed. A faint odor of gasoline and burnt plastic hung in the air.

Monty stepped up to the door of the shed and closed his fist, ready to unleash his frustration. Instead, he chose to let calmness prevail in hopes that some part of this confrontation would play in his favor. He turned his hand and used his knuckles to rap the door.

"Jazz? You in there?" Monty paused for a second but didn't wait for an answer. "Wynter's out. She's got Ransom and I know where." He cupped his hand against the door and placed his ear next to it. There was a sound – a scraping noise – that didn't come from inside, but from above.

"Start talking," said a familiar voice.

Monty jerked his head up to see Jezebel and Roxy staring down at him from the edge of the roof. Jezebel pointed her 9mm pistol at him.

Monty raised his hand as a shield. "Use that fuckin' thing or put it away. I'm on your goddamn side for fuck's sake."

Jezebel considered his words, then swung her legs over the edge, the gravel spreading under her shoes and absorbing the weight of her landing. Roxy followed her off, clinging to the edge until her arms extended fully. Her feet hit the ground ungracefully and she took her spot behind Jezebel.

"You're only on my side because it suits you." Jezebel kept the pistol aimed at Monty's gut. "Now talk."

"Lower the fuckin' gun." Monty looked back at the Fiat. "You're runnin' out of time."

Jezebel narrowed her eyes at him, then lowered the pistol, holstering it in her waistband without taking her eyes off him.

"Wynter's at the Starlite. She said come alone or else."

"*Or else*," Jezebel said. "That's funny."

As if it was a cue to laugh, Roxy began to giggle.

"Shut the fuck up." Jezebel shot her leg back and struck Roxy's shin.

Roxy stumbled backward, her giggles replaced with a stifled cry of pain.

"You sure Ransom's there?"

Monty shrugged indifference. "Hey, I'm only tellin' you what she told me."

"You're driving," Jezebel said.

"Fuck that. I got better things to do than taxi your ass around town."

Jezebel placed her hand on the pistol. "But you're on *our* side, remember?"

"What's wrong with the Barracuda?" Monty gave her a sly knowing look. He walked over to the muscle car and lifted a corner of the tarp off the back. The smell of gasoline washed over him. "Having problems fillin' your tank? Or did you need the gas for something *else*?"

Monty watched Jezebel's face for her tell but was met with a look of stone. "I get why Wynter'd have a score to settle."

"Is that what she said?" Jezebel's body tensed as she stepped toward him, her hand still resting on the pistol's handle. "You tell me everything?"

"You torched that trailer." Monty folded his arms across his chest. "Wynter's trailer."

Jezebel spat at him. "Fuck you. Drive."

Monty shook his head and raised his hands, palms forward. "Fine. Get in. But I can only take one of you."

Jezebel strolled to the passenger door of the Fiat. "Looks like you're walking, Rox." She stepped inside and slammed the door closed. "Better get going or you're going to be late," she said, waving the pistol at her.

"Aw shit, Jazz." Roxy deflated. "Come on."

Monty took the driver's seat, started the engine, and backed out onto the road.

"Don't be an asshole," Roxy yelled after them, limping on the shoulder.

"That's what I do best." Jezebel watched Roxy shrink in the side mirror. She turned to Monty. "You better not be feeding me shit." Her hand rested comfortably in her lap with the pistol aimed at his abdomen.

Monty shook his head slowly. He knew when to keep his mouth shut and this was one of those times. *Let Jezebel relax,* he told himself. The pistol in her hand did just that. She flipped the safety on and off, on and off, like a mechanical mantra or a ticking clock winding down to an inevitable end.

NEWHAVEN WAS A SMALL TOWN. With just over two thousand people, it didn't meet the population threshold of 2,500 to be considered a city. Despite its small size, tracking down a person remained difficult, especially when that person didn't want to be found. Add the limited resources of the Newhaven Police Department, and a person of interest could elude the police for days or weeks. Eventually they would slip up, make a mistake, and be spotted in town with arrests made soon after. But Jezebel had proved to be elusive in every regard.

Anson settled on the next best thing: Jezebel's mother, Frankie.

Approaching five o'clock on a Saturday meant that Frankie was at work. The Itty Bitty Bar sat on a patch of land on the northwestern side of Newhaven, close to the intersection of 19th Street and Main. The topless bar was a favorite of out-of-towners passing through and locals who preferred to remain nameless if they could.

Anson pulled open the door, the grab handle worn smooth from years of loyal voyeurs. He entered a darkened cavern-like space where the only source of sunshine came from the door he had just passed through. The air felt moist on his skin, heavy with the smell of booze and cigarette smoke.

Free-standing tables and chairs were scattered around the front of a central stage, with the bar and kitchen running along the right side, and several booths along the left. Colored lights focused on the dancer currently performing.

Anson was careful to never let his eyes stray below faces when dealing with the dancers or servers. Working at Itty Bitty took guts and he had vowed never to minimize that effort by staring. Besides, it was impolite.

A petite blond server with "Brandi" on her nametag approached him wearing a white babydoll T-shirt and a waist apron that hung lower than her black denim miniskirt. A pen and an order pad stuck out of the front pocket. In one hand she held a circular tray lined with cork, bills and coins stacked on top.

"Hey Anson, darling. Long time, no see." Brandi had no problem letting *her* eyes drop below Anson's face and hover over other parts of his body. "Can I get you something?"

Anson removed his hat and held it in front of his chest. "I'd like to speak with Frankie, if she's in."

Brandi hooked her free thumb back toward the bar. "Yeah,

she's in the kitchen. Can I get you a brew while you wait?" She winked at him. "On the house?"

"No, thanks." Anson forced a smile and hoped it didn't look the way it felt. "I'm on duty."

"Okay. Jus'sec," Brandi said. "I'll go get her." She sauntered off and disappeared into the kitchen.

The bar had always made Anson feel uncomfortable. He was fine with the dancers making the choice to bare it all for the mostly male crowd. In fact, should he be lucky enough to have a daughter in his future and she chose to work in a place like Itty Bitty, he'd support her decision despite his misgivings. For some, this was the only way to make a living. But exposing your body to complete strangers seemed like giving away a part of your soul one small piece at a time.

Everything had a price.

"What do yah want, Anson?"

He turned to face Frankie, who on a good day looked like Jezebel transported fifteen years into the future. They had been mistaken for sisters on numerous occasions. Instead of crimping her hair to death, Frankie had pulled hers back into a brunette ponytail. She wore an outfit similar to Brandi's but preferred black bootcut jeans and kept a pack of cigarettes tucked in her apron pocket.

"Or should I say, *Sheriff Jacobs?*" Frankie scrutinized him suspiciously.

"Anson's fine. You know that." Anson glanced at the exit. "Mind if we talk outside?"

Frankie shrugged as Anson led her toward the door.

Brandi watched them leave just as hoots and catcalls erupted from the tables, alerting her that a dancer had finished her routine. It was also a good time to suggest another beer. She grabbed her tray and began collecting empty glasses.

Anson pushed open the door, squinting at the bright evening

sunshine. The change in environment didn't seem to bother Frankie.

"What's so important that yah got to drag me out of work?" Frankie removed a cigarette from the pack in her apron, lit it with a Zippo, and flipped it closed.

Anson pointed at the lighter. "That's a Zippo, isn't it?"

"Yah. So?" Frankie took a drag from the cigarette, then let loose a blue cloud of acrid smoke. She flipped the ash off the end. "This is a Marlboro. What's your point?"

"Mind if I take a look?"

Frankie gave him a puzzled look and handed over the lighter. Anson found what he was looking for within seconds. The letters "XO" were engraved on the side, just like the lighter found in the remnants of the LaCroix's trailer.

"Nice craftsmanship," he said as he handed it back.

"I guess." Frankie took another drag, propelling the fiery ember up the length of the cigarette. "Yah going to get to the point?"

"Do you know the whereabouts of your daughter, Jezebel?"

Frankie crossed her arms against her chest. "What has that little bitch done now?"

"I'm sure you've heard about the fire at Sven Dwarfs this morning."

"Yeah," Frankie said, wariness creeping into her voice. "Been some talk about it."

"We have reason to believe that Jezebel knows something about the incident." Anson held Frankie's gaze. "I'd like to talk to her."

"Don't know where she is." Frankie looked past Anson, focused on something in the distance, and took a drag from her cigarette. "She does what she wants."

"She's seventeen," Anson said. "She needs—"

Frankie's eyes darkened and settled on Anson's. "You telling me how to raise my kid?"

Anson held his hands in front of his chest, palms out, in an attempt to placate. "Sorry. I overstepped."

"Damn right you did."

"If you could keep an eye out for her, I'd—"

"Fuck you, Anson." Frankie flicked her cigarette at him. The embers at the end hit his chest and exploded in orange sparks, leaving a small burn mark on his shirt. "Find her yourself. I'm done talking."

Frankie pulled open the door and disappeared inside. She tried to slam it closed but the door stopper attached to the top slowed its arc back to a crawl.

"Smooth, Sheriff Jacobs," Anson said to himself as he brushed the ash off his shirt. He returned to his SUV and set off for the station. While he hadn't gotten the information he really wanted, the discovery of a Zippo with identical markings to the one used on the LaCroix trailer made the trip worthwhile.

He filed the exchange with Frankie in the "Screw-ups" folder of his brain and focused on better things. It was Saturday night and his shift was almost over. He could pick up some beer and a couple of steaks at the FoodXpress, and host a private barbecue with Mercy. Maybe with a little luck the night could spin into something more.

But being Sheriff rarely afforded Anson with much personal time, even when he was off the clock. Tonight would be no exception.

MONTY TURNED RIGHT onto Jones Avenue. As he approached the entrance to the Starlite parking lot, Jezebel sat up straight in her seat, her eyes focused on something in the distance.

Monty squinted ahead, then glanced at her for a moment. "What?"

Jezebel scowled at him. "If you'd take off those stupid sunglasses, maybe you'd see things better." She returned her eyes to the road ahead. "It's Quinn in that fucking VW. Another one on my hit list."

Monty slid his sunglasses down his nose to get a clear view. Ahead at the other end of Jones Avenue, a light blue VW Beetle turned left onto Main Street. "Your eyes are better than mine," he said. "Want me to follow her?"

"No." Jezebel's gears were turning. "Something's up. Those two are, like, best friends. She's always with Wynter."

"Except when you put her in the hospital."

"Wasn't my fault the bitch can't keep her balance." Jezebel raised the pistol. "Pull over."

"We're almost at the parkin' lot."

"She said come *alone,* fuckhead," Jezebel said. "Rolling in with me in the passenger seat kind of blows my cover, don't you think?"

Monty pulled over and turned off the engine.

"For a drug dealer, you're pretty stupid."

"You better watch your mouth, *Jazz.*" Monty slipped off his sunglasses for emphasis. "You're not the only one who has a gun."

Jezebel stepped out of the car and slammed the passenger door shut. "But I'm the only one who's got the balls to use one." She glanced up at the side of the Starlite. "Stay here. I'm going to need a fast getaway." She ran down the side of the road toward the entrance.

Monty stuck his head up out of the window and called back at her, "What are you goin' to do?"

Jezebel stopped and turned. "I'm going to take what's mine."

As she rounded the corner of the building, Jezebel counted five cars in the lot and performed a quick mental calculation. Thirteen bullets would have to do.

Jezebel approached the doors and stepped inside.

THE CONCESSION STAFF began to arrive at twenty to six. Zain took Wynter, Cash, and Jake aside. "The deal's off. My life is one thing, but I can't risk injuring anyone who works for me."

Wynter balled her hands into fists. "We're here too, remember."

"But you *chose* to be here." Zain's eyes flicked wildly between the three. "It's all getting too dangerous."

"Just tell them to start later," Cash said.

"They have procedures to follow. Besides, I can't afford a delay. The concession pays their salary."

"But all this work will go to waste," Wynter said.

Zain shook his head. "Sorry. I made a mistake. You're going to have to come up with a different plan."

"No," Jake said. "The plan stays."

Zain stepped toward Jake, eyes wide with surprise. "Excuse me?"

"I said we go through with the plan as it is."

Zain crossed his arms against his chest. "Oh, so *you* make the rules around here, is that it?"

Jake shook his head. "No, you do."

"Damn straight I do."

"But *she* breaks them." Jake jerked his head toward the front entrance.

Zain looked back to see Jezebel framed by the doors, a pistol gripped tightly in her right hand. "Shit," he whispered as he backed away from the group. "Stick to the plan." He hustled to the concession and stuck his head over the counter to relay what was going on.

Cash and Jake crouched behind a concession table.

Wynter took her predetermined position in the foyer. "I didn't think you'd show."

Jezebel took several more steps into the building. She detected motion through the admissions window and saw Zain talking hurriedly to his staff at the concession counter beyond. She aimed and fired, shattering the glass.

Everyone flinched and Zain dropped to the floor. The bullet deflected wide, embedding itself in the menu above the serving counter. The concession staff scattered and hid in the kitchen.

"No one fucking move." Jezebel stopped and scanned her surroundings. It took seconds for her eyes to narrow on the surveillance cameras. "You think I'm stupid?" She took out the first camera overhead with one shot, the small unit exploding into bits of circuitry, plastic, and glass.

The small foyer amplified the gunshot and caused Wynter to cower slightly, raising her hands to her ears. Jezebel dispatched the remaining three cameras with quick precision, requiring five shots in total to render the rest of them useless, hanging from the ceiling by their electrical entrails.

Jezebel's marksmanship both impressed and terrified Wynter. She resumed her fearless stance even though the Starlite surveillance system had been destroyed and would not record the rest of Jezebel's assault. Jake's camera was their only chance.

Jezebel lowered her pistol and stepped toward Wynter. "Where is he?"

"What if I said you killed him?"

"I'd say you're a lying bitch," Jezebel said with a snarl. "So cut the shit." She leveled the pistol at the center of Wynter's chest. "Where is he?"

Wynter raised her hand slowly to her head and tapped her temple with her index finger. "In here. Safe from you."

The remains of one of the surveillance cameras fell from the ceiling, struck a concession table, and bounced off the garbage can. Jake jumped in surprise from his spot on the floor and knocked his crutch off the seat.

Jezebel swung her arm wide and squeezed off a round. The

bullet ricocheted off a table top and hit the ceiling. Cash slid a chair in front of them for cover and pulled Jake behind it, but he didn't move quickly enough. Jezebel fired again, hitting Jake's cast mid-thigh.

"Stop!" Wynter grabbed Jezebel's pistol and pushed it upward. Jezebel fired again, sending a bullet into the ceiling tiles and through the roof. "It's me you want, not them."

"No. I don't want *you*." Jezebel shoved Wynter backward hard enough to make her stumble and land on her backside. "I want *Ransom*. But he's in your head. If I can't have him, no one can." She placed the muzzle against the center of Wynter's chest and pulled the trigger.

The bullet exploded out of Wynter's back in a spray of blood and bone. She collapsed to the floor.

"NO!" Cash stood in defiance.

Jezebel aimed and fired twice just as Jake took hold of the hem of Cash's T-shirt and pulled him backward to the floor. The first bullet clipped the top of his left ear and the second whistled past dangerously close to his head.

Jake glared at Cash and whispered angrily, "Dude! Don't be fucking stupid!"

From his vantage point, Cash could see Wynter already sputtering blood from her spot on the carpet. He rocked back and forth, squeezing his eyes tight to fight the flow of tears. He hadn't been prepared for everything to be so real.

Jake settled his hand on Cash's arm, grounding him. "Sorry. Didn't mean to come off harsh," he said.

"It's okay," Cash said. "It's just hard to watch and do nothing."

"I know."

Blood oozed from the center of Wynter's chest and the corners of her mouth, feeding an expanding maroon circle soaking into the carpet. Jezebel stepped over her and crouched. She stuck the muzzle of the gun into the gaping wound in Wynter's chest and twisted it. "Is little *Whiner* going to die? Yes, I think she is."

Wynter fought through the pain, narrowed her eyes to slits, and laughed through the blood in her mouth. She spat burgundy clots onto Jezebel's face. "You're so blind. And *stupid*."

Her laughter echoed in the foyer as her eyes burned bright blue. Iridescence spread across her face and over her body. In an instant she was gone, drifting in a cloud of ozone mixed with gun smoke.

"The fuck?" Jezebel stumbled backward and scanned the floor where Wynter had been lying a moment ago. The blood pool on the carpet was gone. She wiped her face with her sleeve, revealing nothing but sweat absorbed in the fabric.

She shot a glance at Jake and Cash, who were both trying to hold back satisfied grins and failing. "Where is she?" Jezebel screamed and waved her gun at them.

"Buh-bye, *Jizz-balls*." Cash waved mockingly.

Jezebel fired. The bullet went wide and ricocheted off a support post close to where Cash lay hidden. The slide on her pistol shot back, ejected the bullet casing and locked. She had emptied the magazine.

Without the pistol as her backup, Jezebel lost her nerve. She turned and ran for the doors she had walked through just five minutes ago.

Cash turned to Jake and examined his cast, noting cracks in several places at the top. "Are you hurt? Did your leg get hit?"

"No, but I think I'm going to need a new cast." Jake nodded at Cash's left ear. There was a groove running across the top of his ear and blood had made a slickened path down his neck to his T-shirt collar. "You're lucky she didn't blow your head off, dude."

Cash felt his ear and saw the blood on his fingertips and neck. "Holy shit, you're right. But when I saw Wynter get shot, I just lost it. I totally forgot she was a dreamwaker."

"Jezebel is a fucking psycho," Jake said. "But we got her. She didn't shoot *my* camcorder." He smiled broadly. "Do me a favor and grab it, will you? I don't want it falling into the wrong hands."

Cash ran to the garbage can, lifted the lid and retrieved the JVC camcorder and its remote control. He set it down next to Jake. "Let's watch it. Just to make sure."

"Nah." Jake picked up the camcorder, ejected the VHS-C cassette, and shoved it into his pocket. "I need to make copies of this master for safe-keeping before we do anything else."

Zain approached Cash and Jake. "Anson's on his way. You guys okay? You need an ambulance?" He shifted his gaze between them, focusing on Cash's bloodied neck. He drew breaths in panicky gasps, having experienced Jezebel's wrath for the second time in less than a week.

Cash shook his head. "Looks worse than it is."

"Where the hell is Wynter?" Zain scanned the area with concern. "Did Jezebel *shoot* her?"

"I don't know what happened." Cash shot a quick look at Jake. "I was ducking for cover. Maybe she ran after Jezebel when she ran out of ammo."

"Bingo," Jake said.

"That's the last time Jezebel sets foot in here. I mean it." Zain grimaced at the surveillance camera remnants hanging from the ceiling. "It's like she knew exactly where to shoot."

"She's a psycho, but a smart one," Jake said. "Dangerous combo."

Zain spotted the camcorder next to Jake and his eyes widened in revelation. "What about your camera? She didn't shoot that one, did she?"

"No, but..." Jake shared a quick knowing glance with Cash, then shook his head slowly. "It didn't record. I guess something happened to the remote or something. And since I had covered up the recording light, I had no way of knowing if it was working."

Zain deflated. "Damn. That sucks."

"You're telling me," Jake said.

"Zain?" A familiar voice floated from the Starlite entrance.

"There's Anson now." Zain disappeared for a moment and ran to the foyer. A minute or so later he returned with Anson in tow.

"Holy shit." Anson crouched to look at Cash's ear. "The grazing looks superficial. How's the pain?"

Cash shrugged. "It's not too bad."

"How did it happen?"

"Gunshot."

Anson scanned the ceiling over the concession area and foyer. "Same bullets take out the security cameras?"

Cash nodded.

"They were brand new, too." Zain scowled at the damage.

Anson glanced at Zain. "You and your staff okay?"

"Yeah. They're fine. They hid in the back of the kitchen, and Jezebel stayed out front." Zain rubbed his wrists subconsciously. "That psycho shot at me through the admissions window, but I ducked just in time."

"Yeah, I noticed the broken glass coming in. Those cameras record some of the assault?"

"They must've," Zain said. "I'll go get the tape." Zain ran back behind the counter to the admissions window.

Anson shifted his attention to Jake. "How about you? Shot as well?"

"Nicked the cast." Jake snapped off a loose piece of plaster. "It's cracked pretty bad."

"You're going to need a new one. Catch anything on that fancy camera of yours?" Anson shifted his gaze from Jake to Cash and back.

"The remote control fucked up," Jake said. "Didn't record a thing."

"Hmm." Anson stroked his beard, then stood and headed to the admissions window where Zain had gone.

"Here." Zain handed him a VHS cassette. "Should have

everything you need... before the cameras were destroyed, that is."

Anson studied the man. Zain didn't appear insincere. Instead, he displayed a desire to help, and always had when there was a dust-up at the Starlite. "Can you play this for me?"

"Uh, yeah." He slid the VHS cassette back into the recorder connected to the surveillance monitor and pressed 'play.' A jagged image of static appeared on the screen. "Sorry. Got to go back to the beginning. Forgot about that." Zain stopped playback and pressed 'rewind.'

The VHS cassette deck clicked and whirred, its internal mechanics spinning up to speed. The motor stopped with a clunk before it reached its maximum rewind speed.

"It was a brand new tape." Zain pressed 'play.' The picture on the monitor flipped and zigzagged with static before an image displayed, the screen divided into four quadrants, each quadrant labeled with the camera location. Time code showing the time and date ticked away at the bottom.

"Let me fast-forward a little." Zain worked the VHS cassette deck controls and the timecode on the screen rolled ahead at two times its normal speed.

The camera views in the four quadrants on the monitor panned and tilted one by one, centering on Jake in the middle of the foyer. The first camera went blank part way through, but then reappeared.

"Sorry," Zain said. "We had a cable issue."

"You're aiming all the cameras at Jake." Anson addressed Zain without taking his eyes off the monitor. "Is this a sting?"

"Totally. I mean it's probably obvious because you're a cop," Zain said. "Whatever Jezebel was going to do, we wanted to catch her in the act." He hooked a thumb over at Jake and Cash, who were now sitting at a concession table. "It was their idea."

"Stop."

"What?"

"The tape. Pause it."

Zain fumbled with the controls and paused the video playback. Anson leaned in to take a closer look at the monitor screen, as if getting closer to the screen would make the video image more detailed.

"We know that's Jake, that's Quinn, and that's…" Anson's eyes widened in recognition. "Wynter? Wynter LaCroix? Am I seeing this right?"

"Yup."

Anson turned to Zain. "Are you sure?"

"A hundred percent," Zain said. "Those two are inseparable. Glad to see she came out of her coma okay."

"Me too." Anson stood back. "Can you fast forward to where Jezebel comes in?"

"Sure thing." Zain stopped the playback, pressed 'fast-forward,' and watched intently as the time counter ticked forward. He pressed 'stop,' then 'play.' The monitor displayed four quadrants of black. "Oops. Just a little too far." Zain rewound the playback until all four quadrants showed a picture and let the video play back at normal speed.

The first camera view showed Jezebel face off with Wynter. She aimed to her right and fired her pistol.

"That first shot was at me," Zain said. "Through the admissions window, like I told you."

Jezebel aimed at the first camera and its image went black. In less than ten seconds, she identified and shot the other three surveillance cameras, their images on the monitor mirroring their destruction by returning black.

"So that's everything?"

"Afraid so," Zain said. "Jake's camera screwed up too. Something about his remote."

"Okay." Anson stroked his beard. "Where are Quinn and Wynter now?"

"Quinn had to be somewhere. Not sure where. And Wynter

went after Jezebel when she ran out of bullets. That's what the guys said. I was still hiding."

"Mm-hmm." Anson nodded. "I'll take that tape now, if it's not a problem."

"No, of course." Zain stopped the VHS deck and popped the tape out. He broke off the record protection tab along the edge and slid the cassette back into its protective sleeve. "No chance of it being recorded over now."

Anson took the tape from Zain and strolled back to where Cash and Jake sat. "Jezebel can't seem to stay away from you guys, can she?"

Jake flipped up his collar, crossed his arms against his chest, and beamed. "Can you blame her, really?"

"You might want to be a little more serious," Anson said. "She tends to destroy everything in her path. People could have gotten hurt. Or worse, killed."

Jake exchanged a glance with Cash and swallowed dryly. "You're right. Sorry, Sheriff."

Anson set the VHS cassette down on the table and leaned closer to the two teenagers. "You two have anything else to tell me?"

Cash and Jake stared back at Anson and shook their heads in unison, as if they had been practicing their response.

Anson met their gazes a moment longer, then stood, tucking the VHS cassette under one arm. "Alright. Let's get you guys checked out by a doctor. I'll drive you to the hospital." He escorted the two teens toward the front doors.

JEZEBEL BURST OUT of the doors to the Starlite, the pistol still gripped firmly in her hand, and took a hard left around the side of the building toward Jones Avenue. The thought of Monty being her getaway driver made her stomach clench more than it already was. Jezebel hated not being in control.

She rounded the outer wall of the Starlite. Just as she had expected, Monty stood waiting smugly beside his shitbox Fiat.

And those stupid mirrored glasses.

But behind Monty's Fiat sat the Barracuda, her black beauty. Roxy leaned against the hood, a sly grin on her face and the keys jangling off her finger.

Jezebel ignored Monty and ran to her. "Rox, I could so kiss you right now." She ran around the front bumper of the muscle car and beckoned with her hands.

"Maybe later." Roxy tossed her the keys.

Jezebel grabbed them out of the air with her free hand, pulled open the driver's door, and slid into the seat, dropping her pistol on her lap. Roxy took her usual spot riding shotgun.

"What the hell happened in there?" Monty walked to the back bumper of his Fiat. "I heard gunshots."

"Use your fucking imagination, genius," Jezebel yelled back. She twisted the key in the ignition, revved the engine, and threw the car into reverse. The vehicle jolted backward, spewing loose gravel back at Monty.

"Hey! Watch it, you bitch!"

"Fuck you, asshole." Jezebel raised her middle finger at him. "Eat my dust."

Roxy mirrored Jezebel's insult, with middle fingers displayed on both hands. She sneered at Monty as the Barracuda tore past him and down the street, leaving a strip of rubber behind.

Jezebel glanced in her rear view mirror. Monty and his ugly sports car shrunk in the distance. She tossed the pistol onto Roxy's lap. "Magazine's empty. There's ammo in the glove box."

A small smile grew on Roxy's lips at the thought of more responsibility. She popped open the door to the glove box and the box of 9mm bullets cascaded out mixed with an avalanche of napkins, straws, condiment packets, and condoms, all collecting in the footwell. The box of bullets opened on one side, spilling its contents under the passenger seat.

"Shit." Roxy released her seat belt and tried to rescue the bullets, but they had slipped under a seam in the car's carpeting. She snaked her arm under the seat, searching for anything resembling a bullet.

"You didn't fuck up, did you?" Jezebel side-eyed her suspiciously.

"No." Roxy's fingers found a bullet and she secured it in her other hand. "I didn't *fuck up,*" she said with clenched teeth.

"Good, 'cause I'm going to need that gun loaded." Jezebel slowed at the junction with Main Street and was able to hear the rhythmic rise of a police siren in the distance.

Roxy continued her fruitless search. "Sounds like the sheriff's on his way."

"You think?" Jezebel took a quick glance in her rear view mirror and saw the headlights to Monty's Fiat flip up and turn on, like a monster waking up. "Time to motor."

Roxy's sweaty fingers fumbled upon a second bullet but lost it again when Jezebel floored the gas and headed left onto Main Street, then right onto the on-ramp to the interstate headed east. The Barracuda rocked side to side on its suspension, further hiding the remaining bullets. One would have to do.

Roxy returned to her seat and buckled herself in. She used the single bullet to pretend to load the entire magazine. Once she had faked thirteen bullets, Roxy slid the magazine back into the pistol.

"Tell me something, Rox," Jezebel said. "How did you know where the keys were?"

"You bust heads. I watch. And I remember." Roxy forced a smile, trying to forget her recent failure. "You're not the only one who knew where the spare key was."

"You came through this time." Jezebel gave Roxy a brief side-glance. Her eyes dropped to the pistol in Roxy's lap, and she gave a reassuring nod. "Thanks."

Roxy's eyes widened. "Wow."

Jezebel crunched her brow in puzzlement. "What?"

"You actually thanked me for something," Roxy said. "This is a rare event. I have to remember this day for later."

"Fuck you." Jezebel punched Roxy in the shoulder a little harder than she meant to.

"No. I'm like so serious." Roxy rubbed her shoulder. "And that kind of hurt, so I guess the moment's passed already."

Jezebel shrugged as she eased the speedometer past fifty-five miles per hour.

"Where we going?"

"The hospital." Jezebel focused on the road and the early evening sky ahead. "I still got a score to settle."

Red Skies

Madeline had spent the entire morning and afternoon by Nolan's bedside. Despite the antiseptic smells she associated with a hospital, she still caught the odd whiff of gasoline. It made her stomach turn and fanned the flames of her anger each time. Surely Nolan's account of what had happened at the trailer would be enough to put Jezebel away forever. But Madeline also knew that the law and justice could sometimes work in unexpectedly unjust ways, especially for people of color.

Around five-thirty, Madeline stepped away from Nolan's bedside to grab a sandwich and a cup of coffee from the cafeteria on the first floor. She sat at a vacant table and devoured the ham on Swiss, realizing only afterward just how hungry and exhausted she had felt. Madeline sipped her coffee, then broke into sobs. She covered her face with a napkin to absorb her tears and hide her emotional display. It was no one's business but hers.

She finished her coffee and headed back to the elevators. When the doors opened going up, she stepped inside and selected the fifth floor. Just as the doors began to slide closed, she selected the fourth floor as well. It wouldn't hurt to check in on Wynter.

Madeline stepped out onto the fourth floor and found her way to Wynter's room. Her entire family, her reason for living, resided in this hospital. The building had become far too familiar to her over the past week and she hated it.

She poked her head into Wynter's room. It looked the same

as the last time she had peeked in. The cardiac monitor continued to emit a steady rhythm and Wynter lay inclined in the bed, her eyes closed. At least she was officially within visiting hours.

Madeline stepped inside the room and took Wynter's hand in hers. She kissed it lightly. "Squeeze my hand, Wynnie, love," she whispered, and held her hand against her cheek.

Wynter squeezed back. The sensation took Madeline aback. She had held Wynter's hand on multiple occasions over the past seven days, hoping for a response and receiving none. And now she had reacted. She set Wynter's hand down gently and hurried out of the room toward the nurses' station.

"Hello? I'm Madeline, Wynter's mom? She just squeezed my hand."

The nurse behind the desk stood and joined her as they returned to Wynter's room. "Was it a random flexion?"

Madeline's cheeks were moist with tears. "No. I asked her to squeeze my hand and she did. That's got to be a good sign, right?"

"It can be," the nurse said. "Which hand was it?"

"Her right."

The nurse raised Wynter's left hand in hers. "Wynter, sweetie, can you squeeze my hand for me?" The nurse waited a moment. "Wynter? Can you squeeze my hand?" The nurse met Madeline's eyes. "I'm sorry. I'm not feeling anything."

"Wait. Try her right hand."

The nurse walked around the bed and took Wynter's right hand. "Wynter, can you––"

"Let me say it, okay?"

The nurse nodded.

"Wynnie?" Madeline spoke softly. "Can you squeeze my hand again, hon?"

The nurse waited, then smiled when she felt Wynter's response. "I felt it this time. This is a *very* good sign, Mrs. LaCroix." She set Wynter's hand down on the bed. The clock in the room read ten to six. She noted the time and response on Wynter's chart.

"I'll let the doctor know about this positive development, but he may not be able to give her a full examination for another couple of hours."

Madeline placed her palms together under her chin in silent prayer. "Hallelujah."

"You can stay with her if you want, Mrs. LaCroix." The nurse stepped to the door. "She's a lucky girl."

Madeline wiped the tears from her face. She wanted to stay, to be the first person Wynter saw after coming out of her coma, but she had to share the news with Nolan. She planted a soft kiss on Wynter's forehead and hustled out of the room toward the elevators. This time she couldn't wait and took the stairs to the fifth floor. She hoped Nolan would be awake.

Quinn piloted Blue Belle east as fast as the Beetle's engine could manage. Destination: fourth floor of Halston Medical Center. Beside her sat Ransom. He had his hoodie pulled off his head and collected around his neck, allowing his curly blond hair to go free. He chewed on his thumbnail.

The two of them had barely spoken for the past thirty-five minutes. If the State Patrol caught them, it could derail their entire plan. Quinn had been lucky so far but decided not to risk fate by slowing to the speed limit. There could be no fuck-ups.

KROK 92.9 FM kept the silence from becoming intolerable. Night Ranger was in the middle of belting out "Sister Christian" when Ransom turned down the radio and broke the tension. "I still think about our time together, you know. Do you?"

"What? No!" Quinn shot him an angry glare before returning her eyes to the Interstate. "That was the worst mistake I ever made. I thank God every day that Wynter forgave me."

"Got to admit though, it was hot, right?"

"No, it wasn't," Quinn lied. Their tryst had been one of the most exciting moments in her young adult life and she would never forget it. But she also would never talk about it again with anyone, especially not with Ransom. "Don't bring that shit up again. If you must talk, then, like, stick to the plan." She looked at him, concern replacing her annoyance. "You were in Cash's head last. Do you even know what the plan is?"

"It's a jumble," Ransom said. "I've got bits and pieces. We're meeting Wynter at the hospital." He brought his hand up to his left ear and ran his fingertips lightly over the folds. "Cash is in pain. I know that for sure."

"What kind of pain?" Quinn glared at him, alarmed. "What happened?"

"I don't know."

"But he's okay?"

Ransom nodded. "Yeah. If he wasn't, I wouldn't be here, right?"

"Right. Whatever." Quinn shook her head as if that would help clear her thoughts. "Back to the plan The idea was to keep Jezebel busy while I get you back to Wynter. You kiss her and everything goes back to normal."

"Like that's ever going to happen," Ransom said. "Jezebel's obsessed with me."

"That's why we wanted to catch her in the act at the Starlite." Quinn gripped the steering wheel until her knuckles bloomed white. "Then she'd be sent to juvie, or better yet, prison."

"Catch her in the act of what?"

Quinn gave Ransom a wide-eyed stare for a few seconds before returning her attention to the road. "Wynter is going to *sacrifice* herself. As a dreamwaker, that is. That was the plan. Lure Jezebel out and make her crazy enough to kill Wynter." Quinn's own words hit her square in the heart. They sounded insane.

"It wouldn't take much to set her off," Ransom said. "The girl is fucking nuts."

Quinn glanced out the driver's side window and wiped a tear away with a quick swipe. "Do you feel pain? Like when you die?"

"Yeah." Ransom stretched his arms, then clasped his hands in his lap. "There's pain, but it doesn't last long. I doubt it's as bad as the real thing, but I have no way of knowing for sure."

Quinn tried to stem the flow of tears, but it was no use. "Sorry. I keep thinking of Wynter back at the Starlite. Jezebel's going to do something terrible to her." She sniffled and wiped her hand across her face. "It was a stupid fucking plan."

"It's okay." Ransom placed a hand on Quinn's shoulder. "Soon we'll see Wynter for real. So in a way, it worked."

Quinn nodded. Her foot sank on the gas pedal and Blue Belle responded, greedy for fuel. Fuck the State Patrol. She needed to see Wynter as soon as possible.

MADELINE RETURNED TO Nolan's hospital room on the fifth floor to find him in tears. She rushed to his side, took his hand, and leaned up next to him. "Nolan, honey. What's wrong?"

He looked at her, his eyelids red and swollen, and began to speak.

"Wait." Madeline refilled his drinking cup with ice water from a pitcher on a table next to his bed and handed it to him.

He sipped slowly, then released a long sigh. His whole body seemed to deflate a little bit.

"Better?"

Nolan nodded.

Madeline reached for a tissue and handed it to him. "What is it, hon?"

"I brought Wynter out of my dreams." Nolan spoke barely above a whisper.

Madeline eyed him with surprise. "What? When?"

"This morning, before you arrived." Nolan shook his head slowly. "I know it's dangerous. I shouldn't have done it."

"Why, in God's name, *did* you do it?"

"I don't know. A moment of weakness, I guess." Nolan sipped from his cup of water. "Having almost died, I just wanted to hug Wynter for real and never let her go. She just came out of my dream with me, just like that." His wiped his eyes.

"Sounds like your summoning power never left you." Madeline smoothed Nolan's long hair with her hand. "Where did she go?"

"Not sure," Nolan said. "We hugged and Wynter left the room. I've had this feeling of emptiness all day, probably how Wynter feels when she summons Ransom out of her head." He paused. "But now I feel whole again, but still sad. It's strange, Maddie."

"Well, I have some good news," Madeline said. "I just returned from Wynter's room and she squeezed my hand on command."

"That sounds like a good thing."

"It's a very good thing." Madeline sighed. Her family had been bent but not broken. And soon things would be right again. "The doctor will check up on her soon. In the meantime, you think you have room for me on this bed?"

"Absolutely," Nolan whispered, then shifted to his left. Madeline swung her legs onto the bed and placed her head in the crook of Nolan's right shoulder.

Within minutes, the two of them were asleep and dreaming of better days to come. But less than an hour later, the sound of a single gunshot one floor below jolted Madeline and Nolan awake.

QUINN FOUND A parking spot close to the front doors of Halston Medical Center. She turned to Ransom, exhaustion clear on her face. "How many times do you think I've driven here in the past week?"

Ransom shook his head and stammered. "I, uh…"

"Never mind," Quinn said. "The answer is 'too many.' But I'll make as many trips as it takes. Let's go. I got a feeling we don't have much time." She unbuckled her seat belt and stepped out of the car. Ransom followed her lead.

The two of them headed for the elevators. Once inside, Quinn punched the fourth floor.

"You think she's awake yet?"

Ransom thought for a moment as the floor numbers above the elevator doors counted up. "I can't tell."

"But you're connected, right? Even when Wynter's in someone else's head, you can still sense her?"

"Usually I can." Ransom paused and cocked his head to the side slightly. "But I'm feeling bits and pieces. Maybe it's the coma still clouding me."

"Soon that won't matter," Quinn said.

The elevator doors slid open, and Quinn led Ransom down the corridor to Wynter's room. She pushed open the door and tiptoed inside.

"Oh, Bug," Quinn whispered as she placed her trembling hands over her mouth. After spending time with the dreamwaker version of Wynter for most of the day, seeing her back in her hospital bed, unresponsive, hit Quinn with unexpected grief. She leaned over the bed, careful to avoid the tubes and wires connecting her to the cardiac monitor and support equipment, and embraced Wynter in her arms. "Come back, Bug."

Ransom stood on the opposite side of the bed and held Wynter's left hand in his.

Quinn stood, tears standing out on her cheeks. "Jezebel did this. We need to undo it."

"I'm so sorry, Quinn," Ransom said. "Jezebel's hold on me

stops now." He leaned over Wynter and kissed her softly and deeply.

Quinn watched the cardiac monitor for signs that Wynter might be waking. But the machine's readouts remained unchanged. "Maybe you're not her Prince Charming after all."

"Maybe I never was." Ransom caressed Wynter's cheek and stroked her red hair, still as curly as it ever was. He placed his ear gently to her chest and listened to her actual heartbeat, instead of the electronic blip from the cardiac monitor.

"Jesus, I need a coffee." Quinn wiped her face free of tears. "Want one?"

Ransom sat in the orange vinyl chair and kept his hand on Wynter's. "Yeah, thanks. I want to stay up as long as it takes to be here when Wynter wakes up."

"Okay. Back in a flash." Quinn pulled open the door and headed for the elevators at the end of the corridor. She pressed the down call button and waited.

Her thoughts floated back to Jake and Cash at the Starlite. Had their plan worked? Had they recorded video of Jezebel doing something psychotic? Had Jezebel even showed up? She hoped the answer was yes to all three.

The elevator doors slid open and Quinn stepped inside. She selected the first floor and the elevator swallowed her up.

Just as the elevator doors closed on Quinn, the adjacent doors rolled open. Jezebel and Roxy stepped out. Roxy gnawed and snapped on a piece of gum.

Jezebel noted room numbers as they walked down the corridor. They stopped a few paces from room 413.

"You know what to do." Jezebel eyed her warily.

Roxy nodded and snapped her gum.

"And spit that shit out," Jezebel said. "It makes you look obvious. And even more stupid."

Roxy took out her gum and rolled it into a ball between her fingers. She spotted a small garbage can in the waiting alcove across the corridor. She aimed and tossed the ball of gum, missing the can completely.

Jezebel pulled Roxy close. "Don't fuck up," she hissed into Roxy's ear.

"Got it."

Jezebel pushed the door to Wynter's room, opening it in a slow arc, just enough to slip inside. She pulled up the hem of her T-shirt and grabbed the pistol wedged in the small of her back at her waistline.

Roxy saw Jezebel draw her gun just as the door closed and she began to fidget, rocking back and forth on her feet and tapping her hands on her thighs. She embodied the very definition of conspicuous.

"Forget something?" Ransom gazed at Wynter's face. "That didn't take very long."

"Really?" Jezebel said. "Because it's felt like a *long* time to me." She tilted the blinds shut with a quick yank of the cord.

Ransom stood, knocking the orange chair behind him. His eyes widened in horror and surprise, and sweat began to bead on his forehead. "Jezebel. How did you—"

"I should ask you the same question."

"It's a long story."

"It's a good thing I hate long stories." Jezebel raised the pistol, aiming at Wynter's head.

"Wait, wait, WAIT." Ransom held up his palms pleadingly. "You don't want to do this."

"I don't?" Jezebel pulled the slide back on the pistol, loading a bullet into the chamber. "I started the day by soaking her dad with gas and burning him alive. I kind of want to end it with a bang."

"If you kill Wynter, I'm gone forever." Ransom stepped closer to Jezebel. "You don't want that."

"Gone forever? Sounds good to me." Jezebel held her aim

steady on Wynter. "You're a good lay, Ransom, but I've had better."

Ransom took another few steps toward Jezebel and reached toward her with one hand. "Give me the gun."

"Fuck you. See you in hell." Jezebel's trigger finger tightened.

Ransom leapt and grabbed Jezebel's pistol with one hand and her throat with the other. He pushed her across the small hospital room until her back slammed against the exterior wall and window above. "Drop... the... *gun*."

Jezebel snarled as she drove her knee into Ransom's crotch. He lost his grip on her throat but managed to keep his hand on the pistol. Jezebel used her momentary advantage to spin Ransom around, slamming him against the window.

She forced a kiss on Ransom's lips, despite his attempts to avoid it. Anger flared in his eyes. One kiss had ruined their entire plan. If he died now, he'd be back in Jezebel's psychotic prison of a mind, and he couldn't accept that.

They grappled with the gun. Ransom worked Jezebel's hand down and in front of her body. The pistol's grip had become slick with the sweat of their battling hands.

"You're going to regret this," Ransom said through gritted teeth.

"Not as much as you will."

Ransom's grasp on the pistol slipped and the barrel jutted up under his sternum.

The blast of the pistol at point blank range was deafening in the small room. The bullet ripped through Ransom's body, exited his back, and shattered the window behind him. Glass shards exploded in all directions, littering the floor.

A red blossom of blood expanded in the center of Ransom's chest. Jezebel stuck her finger in his wound and licked the blood.

"See you in my dreams, lover boy."

Ransom grabbed Jezebel by the throat as he slid to the floor.

She raised the gun to discover that the magazine was empty and the slide was locked open.

"Fucking *ROXY!*" Jezebel screamed, glancing back at the door as she flicked the pistol's slide stop and closed the chamber.

Ransom found a shard of glass on the floor, wrapped his hand around it, and drove it into Jezebel's gut. He held it there as long as he could, twisting the razor-sharp edge of the shard even as it cut through the skin of his palms.

"Fuck your dreams," Ransom whispered into Jezebel's ear. He snapped the glass shard where he held it, leaving most of it in Jezebel's gut. He hoped it was enough to end this madness.

QUINN STOOD IN the ascending elevator with a paper cup of coffee warming each hand. She closed her eyes and listened as each new floor announced its arrival with an electronic chime. She raised one cup to her lips and sipped the rich brew. It wasn't bad for vending machine coffee. She closed her eyes and felt relaxation roll over her. The sweet roasted flavor of the coffee was what Quinn loved and craved. The caffeine was a bonus.

Everything felt right with the world for the first time in almost a month. Ransom was safe with Wynter, and with any luck, her friends had captured Jezebel on video doing God knows what at the Starlite. It had been the dreamwaker version of Wynter, but imagining Jezebel's acts of violence and depravity still made the hairs on the back of Quinn's neck stand on end.

The elevator chimed and settled on the fourth floor with a gentle bounce. The doors glided open, and Quinn stepped out, taking another sip from her coffee.

Her eyes tracked up from her cup and settled on the door to Wynter's room at the end of the corridor.

"What the *fuck?*" Quinn's eyes widened on Roxy, who was

pacing in front of the door. She lost her grip on the coffees and burst into a sprint down the corridor. The cups of coffee hit the floor behind her and exploded their contents everywhere. "WHAT THE *FUCK?*"

Roxy turned her head to see Quinn barreling toward her. She fortified her stance and prepared to keep Quinn from entering.

Quinn grabbed Roxy's shirt and tried to yank her away from the door. But Roxy held her ground, using Quinn's momentum to fling her to the side.

"Let me in!"

"Sorry. Can't do that." Roxy had no intention of disappointing Jezebel again.

"Wrong answer." Quinn grasped handfuls of Roxy's shirt and pulled her across the corridor and into the waiting alcove. She threw Roxy over the back of a chair and turned to run back to Wynter's room.

Roxy scrambled on all fours toward the alcove entrance. She caught Quinn's foot with her hand and pulled her off balance.

Quinn landed sideways on the institutional tile, close enough to detect its sour smell. She rolled onto her back and kicked Roxy square in the chest. "Stay down you bit—"

A single gunshot rang out from within Wynter's room. Both Quinn and Roxy snapped their attention to the door across the corridor, their quarrel forgotten.

"NO!" Quinn turned to Roxy, her eyes ablaze with fear and rage. "What'd she do? WHAT'D SHE DO?"

Roxy narrowed a look of smug superiority at Quinn. "Evened the score."

Quinn launched herself across the corridor and burst into the room. "Bug?" She checked Wynter's cardiac monitor, which appeared to be operating normally. "Ransom?" She ran to where Ransom and Jezebel lay in a heap in an expanding circle of crimson but slid to a stop when Jezebel raised her pistol at her.

"Shit!" Quinn covered her face with her hands and arms in a desperate attempt to shield herself from gunfire.

Ransom locked gazes with Quinn, his life fading before her eyes. "Gun's empty," he gasped between shallow breaths.

"No! Ransom!" Quinn ran toward him in an attempt to kiss him, but Jezebel pistol-whipped her jaw, sending Quinn sprawling backward.

"I'm sorry." Ransom's soulful eyes glowed blue as electrical energy spread out from his face and across his body. A moment later he drifted, leaving Jezebel to collapse in a pool of her own blood. Still, she managed to train her empty gun on Quinn.

"He's back where he belongs," Jezebel hissed. "In *my* head, *my* dreams."

Roxy appeared at the door to the room, taking in the carnage against the back wall. The wound in Jezebel's abdomen soaked her shirt with dark blood. "Holy shit."

"You stupid cunt," Jezebel yelled. "You put *one fucking bullet* in my gun!" She winced as she shifted her aim to Roxy and pulled the trigger several times.

Roxy flinched at the trigger clicks, then backed out of the doorway and ran down the corridor.

"Yeah, you better run!" Jezebel's pain made it difficult for her to talk. "*DUMB BITCH!*"

Quinn inched her way backward to the foot of Wynter's bed, shaking her head slowly. Her jaw dribbled blood down her neck and into the collar of her shirt. "You...," she said low enough for only Jezebel to hear. "You ruined everything."

A nurse burst into the room. "Sweet Mary and Joseph." She checked Wynter's vitals first, then knelt beside Quinn. "What happened here?" She lifted Quinn's arm, feeling for a pulse, then checked her wounded jaw.

"I'm okay," Quinn panted and motioned toward Jezebel.

The nurse's eyes darted around the room, stopping on Jezebel.

She took a step but stopped cold when she saw the bloodied pistol in Jezebel's hand.

Quinn tugged on the nurse's pant leg. "She's out of bullets. Otherwise, I'd be dead."

The nurse made another hesitant step toward Jezebel.

"She's not worth it," Quinn whispered. "We'd all be better off if you let her die."

The nurse looked back at Quinn, her face ashen. "I'm afraid I can't do that, miss."

"Can't say I didn't try."

Jezebel raised her middle finger at Quinn. "You're next, *bitch*."

The nurse backed to the door and lifted the handset from the push button phone on the wall. "Code silver, rapid response required, room 413. Repeat. Code silver, room 413." The nurse stepped out of the room and ran down the corridor, her hurried footsteps fading as the door closed.

Quinn slid herself to the orange chair by Wynter's bed and pulled herself up into it. After confirming Wynter's vitals on the cardiac monitor again, Quinn stroked Wynter's left arm with gentle fingertips.

Tears cascaded down Quinn's cheeks. If she hadn't gone for coffee, none of this would have happened. Or maybe it would have been worse. She wished she had taken that bullet instead of Ransom.

They were back at square one. Jezebel was down, but not out, and she had won again. But Jezebel's injury allowed time to gain an advantage. Quinn closed her eyes and busied her mind with plans for payback. Because one thing was certain: Jezebel had to pay. Her reign of terror had to end. The question was how?

∞

CASH HAD TAKEN the front passenger seat in Anson's Suburban to allow Jake to stretch his leg out in the back. Neither of them had uttered more than a few words the entire trip, which raised an immediate red flag in Anson's head. Add to that their omission of Wynter being at the Starlite, and he knew something was up. It had to be big if Jake wasn't talking.

Back at the Starlite, Anson had decided to delay his questions for later, to see where things would lead, but after entering the Halston city limits, his need for the truth got the better of him.

Anson caught Jake's eye in his rear view mirror. "You okay back there? How's the leg? Any pain?"

"My leg's aching a bit, but I'm okay," said Jake.

"Not surprising. Your leg hasn't had much of a chance to heal yet. What's it been, a week? Refracturing it now wouldn't be a good thing." Anson shifted his eyes back to the road. "How about you, Cash? How's that ear of yours?"

Cash held a folded wad of gauze on his left ear. Dots of blood had begun to soak through the loosely woven fabric. "It hurts way more than it did when we left."

"We'll be at the hospital soon, get you both looked at." Anson handed Cash the remaining roll of gauze from the center console. "It's soaking through. Maybe change the dressing."

Cash took the gauze with his right hand and shoved it into his pocket.

"So, guys," Anson said. "I have this burning question I need to ask you both."

"Shoot." Jake winced at his choice of words. "Sorry."

"Can either of you tell me why Wynter was at the Starlite this evening when I know for a fact that she's lying in a coma right now at Halston Medical Center?"

The interior of the Suburban fell into silence again. Anson glanced at Cash, then at Jake in the back. They kept their eyes forward as if they hadn't heard a thing.

"No point in denying it," Anson said. "It's all recorded on

Zain's surveillance tape. Until everything goes black, that is." He picked up the tape from the center console and gave it a shake to punctuate his words.

"You wouldn't believe us if we told you," Jake said.

Cash twisted in his seat. "Shut up, man!"

A subtle grin spread across Anson's lips. It was working. The first chink in the two teen's armor of silence had broken. It wouldn't be long now.

"Why? He might actually be able to help us."

Cash sneaked a peek at Anson as he returned his gaze forward.

Jake waited for a moment. "So, are you going to tell him or am I?"

Cash closed his eyes and rolled his right hand into a fist. "Shit." He glanced at Anson. "The Wynter you saw was a dreamwaker acting as a decoy to lure Jezebel to the Starlite."

"Wait. Hold on." Anson scrunched his brows in confusion. "What the hell is a *dreamwaker*?"

"Wynter, Quinn, myself, and unfortunately Jezebel, and maybe Roxy, can pull people from our dreams into waking life," Cash said. "Those people are what we call dreamwakers."

"I haven't had the chance to try it yet," Jake added.

"So, these... dreamwakers... they look just like the real thing?"

Cash nodded and gave Anson the abbreviated version of dreamwaker rules. "You're going to find it hard to believe, but it's the truth."

"I want to believe you, but I need proof." Anson shrugged. "What can I say? I'm a cop. It's in my blood." He flipped on his turn indicator and moved into the off-ramp lane.

Jake tapped Cash on the shoulder. "Tell him about Ransom."

"Wait," Anson said. "I've heard that name before."

"No surprise." Jake nodded at Anson in the rear view mirror. "He's the root of everything that's going on."

"So, who is he?"

"He's Wynter's boyfriend." Cash spoke through a clenched jaw.

"I thought *you* were Wynter's boyfriend." Anson said.

"Fantasy's better than reality, I guess." Cash released a heavy sigh. "Not going to stop trying though."

"The problem is Jezebel wants him," Jake added. "And she's been doing whatever it takes to get him back."

"When Wynter fell off the 19th Street Bridge..." Cash tensed up at recalling the events of a week ago. "Ransom was there. Remember?"

The lightbulb clicked in Anson's head. Ransom *had* been there. Then he wasn't. In an instant. "Right. I remember."

"A lot of shit's gone down over the past few days," Jake said.

"Now that you remember Ransom, do you still need proof?" Cash asked. "Or is your memory good enough?"

"More evidence never hurts." Anson's smile melted away when he saw the oscillating blue, red, and white lights of emergency vehicles in the distance outside the main entrance to Halston Medical Center.

Cash looked at him. "What's going on?"

"I don't know." Anson pulled the Suburban past the front entrance into the hospital parking lot and secured a spot.

"Wynter." Cash was out of the SUV in a flash, the gauze stuck to his left ear forgotten and unraveling in the wind of his sprint.

A Halston police officer stopped Cash from entering the building.

"What's going on?" Cash tried to push past but the officer held him at bay.

"We have reports of shooting inside," the officer said. "For your own safety, you need to stay outside until we get the all clear."

Cash's eyes widened as he saw Roxy push through an exit door and run toward the parking lot. Pointing at her, he yelled, "Arrest her! She knows what happened."

"Stand back, son," the police officer said.

"Do something!" Cash glared at the officer. "Fuck this." He turned and raced after Roxy, tackling her amidst the parked cars.

Cash flipped her over, straddled her, and shook her shoulders against the asphalt. "What did she do, you bitch! TELL ME!"

Roxy fought against Cash's assault, blocking his grasp with her forearms. "Get off me, asshole!"

Anson grabbed Cash's shirt and yanked him off Roxy. She scrambled to her feet and continued her sprint into the night.

Cash flew backward. "What are you doing? Let me go!"

Anson pulled Cash nose to nose. "Stop. And *listen*. She's not worth an assault charge on your record."

"Suck it!" Roxy yelled from the middle of the parking lot. She raised her middle finger at them, turned and continued across the lot.

Cash pointed and struggled to break free of Anson's grasp. "She's getting away. Do something!"

"She might be escaping now," Anson said with a calm, level-headed voice. "But she'll be easy to find. Jezebel's the brains of their little operation."

On the opposite side of the parking lot, Cash spotted Roxy bound up a short embankment lined with hedges and disappear.

Anson matched his gaze. "Let it go, Cash."

Jake hobbled up next to Anson and Cash. "Shit. Missed the good stuff. This damn cast is cramping my style. But Anson's right. We'll get her, Cash. Hell, I live right across the street. I could set up video surveillance."

Cash shifted his eyes between Anson and Jake and appeared to have understood them without hearing a word. "Wynter..." He glanced at the hospital's front entrance and the cop who had held him back before. "Anson, you got to get me inside. Something's happened to Wynter. I can feel it."

Anson studied Cash closely, then nodded. "I'll see what I can do."

"Get me in, too." Jake shrugged. "I can't raise shit. I'm on crutches."

"We got to get you two looked at, too. Hold on." Anson strolled toward the officer guarding the entrance.

Cash and Jake watched Anson introduce himself to the officer and begin a conversation.

"You think he'll get us in?" Jake asked.

"He's got to." Cash tapped his foot nervously. "I need to make sure Wynter's okay."

"Hey, dude. Sorry about spilling the dreamwaker stuff back there."

"No problem," Cash said, his eyes locked on Anson and the Halston police officer. "It was going to get out eventually. But still, I don't think Anson believes it."

"Even though he actually *saw* Ransom disappear?"

"Maybe too much time has gone by. Maybe he thinks his eyes played tricks on him. I don't know."

Jake patted the VHS-C cassette in his pocket. "We've got definitive evidence *right here*."

Cash faced Jake. "Let's keep that to ourselves for now."

Jake nodded. "Totally. Got to make a dub of it first anyway." He motioned at Anson walking back toward them.

Cash stepped forward to meet Anson halfway. "What'd he say?"

"I got you in to the ER to get your injuries looked at," Anson said. "That's it. No funny business. My reputation's on the line."

"Got it," Jake said. Cash nodded for emphasis.

"Good. Let's go." Anson led the two teenagers past the Halston police officer and towards the sliding front doors of the hospital.

"Take care of that ear and that leg," the officer said.

Cash nodded as the doors slid open. The three of them followed signage toward the Emergency ward.

"I wonder what the wait times are like," Jake said.

"Sorry, guys." Cash broke from their group and raced toward the elevators.

"Cash! Stop!" Anson turned to Jake. "Shit. You going to be alright on your own?"

Jake gave Anson a serving of side-eye. "What do you think?"

"I think you're going to follow us."

"You'd be correct." Jake watched Cash plow through the door to the stairs. "You'd better go. He's got quite a lead on you."

"Right." Anson ran toward the elevators, veering toward the stairs.

"Here comes Jake, bringing up the rear." Jake glanced back at the entrance to make sure his path was clear and crutch-walked to the elevators. He pressed the up call button, but nothing happened. The floor numbers above each elevator remained unchanged.

"I should just get my cast looked at," Jake said to himself. But the fear of missing out kept him pressing the call button relentlessly for a couple more minutes.

"Aw, shit." Jake pushed through the stairwell door and began his four floor ascent, one concrete step at a time.

CASH DIDN'T CARE about his ear. He didn't care if it looked normal again or if it had gotten infected. He rarely broke promises but this time he had no choice. He felt compelled to make sure Wynter was okay. Wynter was all that mattered.

"Sorry, guys." Cash made a break for the elevators, leaving Anson and Jake behind. He thought he heard Anson call out his name in protest but the sound of air moving past his ears drowned out most of the noise around him. His legs pumped furiously and carried him across the foyer toward the elevators and stairs.

Elevators will take too long.

He veered toward the door to the stairwell and hit it with a solid *thump*. Cash pushed the door open and began bounding up the stairs, two steps at a time. By the third floor he switched to one step at a time.

Breathless, Cash arrived at the fourth floor landing and pulled open the door to the corridor that had taken a permanent spot in his memories. He felt as if he could navigate it with his eyes closed.

A stitch in his right side, like a piece of hot glass pushed through his body, caught him off guard. Cash gasped and massaged his abdomen. He slowed his pace but did not stop.

At the entrance to Wynter's room stood a throng of medical, security, and police personnel. An officer spotted Cash's approach and drew his gun.

"Stop!" the officer called out.

"Wait! I'm a friend," Cash said through panicked breaths. He raised his hands and continued running, but he slowed his pace.

The security guard stepped behind the officer and pulled out his weapon. Doctors and nurses scattered, some back into Wynter's room, others toward the waiting alcove across the corridor.

"Stop! NOW," the officer ordered.

"I need to see Wynter." Cash slid to a stop within a dozen feet of Wynter's door. The medical staff inside her room closed the door but not before he spotted Madeline. "Mrs. LaCroix?"

The officer fortified his stance, his gun trained squarely on Cash's chest. "On your knees. Hands behind your head. Now."

Cash followed the officer's orders and sank to his knees. Hitting the hard institutional tile made his teeth rattle.

The officer stepped behind Cash, placed his gun in his holster, pulled out his handcuffs, and secured one of Cash's wrists. He motioned at the security guard. "Holster your weapon." The officer brought Cash's other wrist around behind his back and locked it in the remaining cuff. He pulled Cash up. "On your feet. Now."

"MRS. LACROIX!" Cash yelled.

The door to the stairwell flew open and Anson stumbled out, panting. His eyes assessed the situation in seconds. "Cash."

Cash turned his head. "Anson! Get him to let me go!"

The security guard had yet to holster his weapon and instead aimed it at Anson.

Anson reduced his run to a brisk walk. "Sheriff Jacobs, Newhaven Police," he said through heavy breaths. "Uncuff him. The kid's with me." He shifted his gaze to the security guard. "And get that gun out of my face, if you know what's good for you."

The security guard complied at once. The officer appraised Anson with a wary eye. Medical personnel stepped out from their hiding places.

"You're a little far from home, aren't you Sheriff?"

"Kid was shot," Anson said. "No hospital in Newhaven. Was taking him in to be checked out."

The officer glanced at the caked blood trailing down the left side of Cash's face. He brought out his keys and removed the cuffs from Cash's wrists.

"Cash?" Madeline poked her head out of Wynter's room. "Anson?"

Cash broke free of the officer and ran across the corridor to Madeline and wrapped his arms around her. "I'm sorry, Mrs. LaCroix. I'm so sorry."

"Cash, hon. Your ear."

"Is Wynter okay? Can I see her?"

Madeline looked back into the room. The doctor nodded without words. "Of course."

Cash released Madeline and entered the hospital room that would forever haunt his dreams.

Quinn sat in the orange chair by the bed. She stood and let Cash side-step by her. He picked up Wynter's left hand, warm to his touch. She moved her fingers against his palm.

Surprised, Cash looked at Quinn, then up at the doctor going over Wynter's chart. "Her fingers, they moved. Is she going—" He stopped cold when his eyes shifted to the nurses and doctor in the opposite corner of the room. They were tending to Jezebel and securing her onto a gurney.

Jezebel's eyes bore into Cash like an evil parasite. Her malevolent smile felt as if she held his fate in her hands, a fate that she'd gladly snuff out if she could. Cash's heart hammered in his chest, and it took all his will to force himself to look away.

Cash cleared his throat and again faced the doctor by Wynter's bedside. "Is she..." He squinted at her name tag. "Is she going to be okay, Dr. Cornell?"

Dr. Cornell nodded. "It looks like it. We've been seeing good GCS response... in layman's terms, Wynter's body is slowly coming back. But it may be a few days, weeks, or months before we know the true outcome of her brain injury."

Quinn placed her palms together under her nose. "Thank God."

Tears welled in Cash's eyes as he leaned over and lightly kissed Wynter's forehead. A single tear breached his eyelid and splashed on her cheek. He wiped it away with the back of his hand and placed his lips next to her ear.

"Come back to me, Wynter," Cash whispered. "Please." He stroked her long, red curls and imagined seeing her eyes once again, open and clear and full of life.

As if she had heard him, Wynter's eyelids opened a crack, then wider. "Cash," she said faintly, almost inaudibly. "You found me."

"Holy shit, she just talked to me." Cash glanced at Dr. Cornell with excitement, then returned his attention to Wynter. "Yes, I found you. But I had help." He glanced at Quinn, then continued his whisper. "*We* had help. Especially from you, you as a dreamwaker."

Wynter's eyes focused on the opposite side of the room. The nurses and doctor tending to Jezebel rolled her toward the door, the wheels of the gurney leaving bright red wheel tracks halfway across the room.

Quinn, Cash, and Wynter locked their gaze on her exit. Jezebel turned her head toward Wynter. Her smile, full of hatred and fury, peeled back over her teeth and she narrowed her eyes. She used her middle finger to draw a slow line across her throat then directed her gesture at the three friends.

"*Whinerrr...*" Jezebel's grating whisper caused goosebumps to break out across Cash's body and sent a chill up his spine. Wynter squeezed Cash's hand. She must have felt something too.

"Not on my watch," Cash said under his breath. A nurse setting up a cardiac monitor on Jezebel blocked his view and he let out a sigh of relief.

"Not on mine, either." Quinn patted Cash's shoulder in solidarity.

"Don't touch anything." Anson blocked Jezebel's gurney. "Everything in this room is part of an ongoing investigation, including whatever you find in her gut."

Jezebel's doctor narrowed her eyes at him. "You and I both know this scene is compromised," she said, forcing the gurney past him. "Get out of our way. We have a life to save."

Anson crouched to the floor, hooked Jezebel's pistol with the tip of his pen, and followed the gurney out into the corridor.

Dr. Cornell let her eyes wander past the chart in her hand to Quinn, Wynter, and Cash. She had sensed their unease when Jezebel was in the same room with them. "I take it you all know that girl?"

Cash nodded. "You could say that."

"Did you see who she was shooting at? Or who stabbed her?"

Cash glanced at Quinn, then met the doctor's gaze and shook his head. "No idea." Lying was becoming too easy.

Madeline entered the room, Anson and Jake following behind her. "Wynnie, honey! You're awake." She scurried to the side of the bed opposite Cash and Quinn, leaned into Wynter and hugged her, burying her sobs in Wynter's hospital gown.

Dr. Cornell hung Wynter's chart on the end of her bed. "I don't want to alarm anyone, but this isn't going to be like what you see on TV. People don't just wake up and everything's fine. Wynter's progress may be slow. She'll forget things. She'll need time and rest."

Madeline dotted her eyes with a tissue. "But my baby's going to be okay though, right?"

"I'm optimistic," Dr. Cornell said. "This is just the first step." She glanced at the clock. "In fact, visiting hours are almost over. I would suggest everyone go home and get a good night's sleep. I know that's what Wynter will do." She smiled warmly, then left the room.

Madeline turned to Wynter. "Wynnie, honey? Would you like us to stay a bit longer?"

Wynter looked at her mother and blinked slowly. For a moment she looked lost and confused, then her eyes cleared and she nodded. She turned to Quinn, Cash, Jake, and Anson and nodded at them as well.

"Dad?" she said hoarsely.

Madeline stroked Wynter's head. "He's fine. And I'll tell him you're fine too."

Wynter eased her eyes closed, a small smile on her lips. "He knows already."

"Ransom?" Wynter directed a concerned gaze at Quinn. Cash shifted on his feet uneasily.

Quinn shook her head slowly. "Jezebel got him. Again."

Wynter looked away, deflated. Tears welled in her eyes.

"Don't worry, Wynter," Jake said. "We'll find him."

As Saturday night's visiting hours wound down, Wynter lay surrounded by those she loved, everyone except Nolan. But she felt his presence. He was close and that reassured her, even if she couldn't see him or remember why. The world finally felt right again for a fleeting moment.

Jezebel was somewhere in the hospital. She had Ransom. And more than ever Wynter wanted him back for good.

AS HALSTON POLICE handcuffed Cash on the fourth floor, Roxy flagged down a taxi and hopped in.

"There's an extra twenty in it for you if you can get me to Newhaven in less than an hour," Roxy said to the taxi driver.

"Sorry, kid. I don't leave the city."

"How about an extra fifty?" Roxy displayed a wad of bills.

The taxi driver looked at her with tired, distrusting eyes. "A'ight. I'll make an exception just this once but you gotta give me the fifty now."

"What if you dump me on the side of the road?"

The taxi driver returned a sly smile. "Guess yer gonna have to trust me."

Roxy considered the driver's words for a moment before Jezebel's voice interrupted her thoughts, criticizing her for not sticking to the plan. She handed the driver the money. He reset his meter and within minutes the taxi merged with traffic headed west on I94, chasing the sun as it drifted toward a blood red sunset.

Was Jezebel alive or dead? Roxy had no idea. She watched the taxi's speedometer push past fifty-five miles per hour and found that she didn't care. Instead, she reveled in being free of Jezebel because Roxy knew it wouldn't last. Her whole body vibrated with excitement.

Knowing Jezebel's track record for surviving, Roxy wagered that she was alive. She'd find out soon enough.

Roxy heard the radio playing up front. "Hey, turn it up."

KROK's eight o'clock news update was just finishing up, with no news of a shooting at Halston Medical Center.

Jazz just might get away with it again.

The power chords of "Jailbreak" by Thin Lizzy broke through the car's speakers. The taxi driver turned the volume down.

"No," Roxy said. "Play it loud. I've had one hell of a day."

The driver raised the volume again and Roxy pressed herself into the back seat. She couldn't think of a more perfect song to drive to at that moment.

The taxi rolled up to Roxy's house just before nine o'clock. She paid the driver and hopped out.

The house was empty. Being a Saturday night, her parents were out somewhere living it up. How they managed to party in a town like Newhaven was anyone's guess.

Roxy pulled off the smelly hand-me-downs Jezebel had given her that morning and took a quick shower. Cleaned up and in her pajamas, she wandered into the kitchen. Her stomach growled hungrily. Too tired to fix herself anything nutritious, she settled for a bowl of Cap'n Crunch.

Roxy returned to her bedroom and slid her body under the cool sheets. Sleep overtook her swiftly. Dreams of driving followed soon after. This time Roxy sat behind the wheel of Jezebel's coveted black beast. With a never-ending supply of gas and an infinite stretch of highway in front of her, she floored the accelerator and the muscle car responded with enthusiastic anger.

"Pull over."

Startled, Roxy glanced to her right. Jezebel sat in the passenger seat. There was a large red circle of blood centered over her gut.

"Uh..." Roxy stammered.

"You deaf? I said pull over."

Fucking Jezebel. A buzzkill even in my dreams.

Roxy slowed the Barracuda and eased onto the shoulder. She shifted into park.

"A fucking *buzzkill,* huh?"

Jezebel could hear her thoughts too. "What? No. I meant—"

"Never mind." Jezebel reached into her gut wound and pulled out a six-inch shard of glass, the jagged edges dripping with blood. The maroon stain on her shirt shrunk until it was no longer visible. "I'm coming home. And I'm going to be unstoppable."

Roxy returned a puzzled look. "But how? You looked pretty bad at the—"

"Never mind how, just be ready." Jezebel reached across the middle console and thrust the shard of glass deep into Roxy's belly. "And don't drive my 'Cuda again."

The pain radiated through Roxy's body and jolted her awake. She sat bolt upright, her pajama top sticking to her skin like she had been in a torrential downpour. Her fingers dropped to her abdomen instinctively, searching for the glass shard and its entry wound. But her skin was damp and smooth.

Roxy's bedside clock read quarter past four in the morning. Despite her six hours of sleep, any feelings of freedom had evaporated. She resumed her role of servant to a psychopath and began the wait for Jezebel to arrive.

October 11, 2021
Victoria, BC, Canada

With Jezebel injured and Ransom still in her grip, the plan to reunite Wynter with Ransom has shifted into uncharted territory. Time is short and Wynter's sanity erodes more with each passing day. How will her friends turn the tables on Jezebel and set their world straight again? What if Cash's unrequited love stands in the way? Find out in "Lucid Fate," book three in the Dreamwaker Saga.

Available November 30, 2022.
LeeGabel.com/dreamwaker-saga

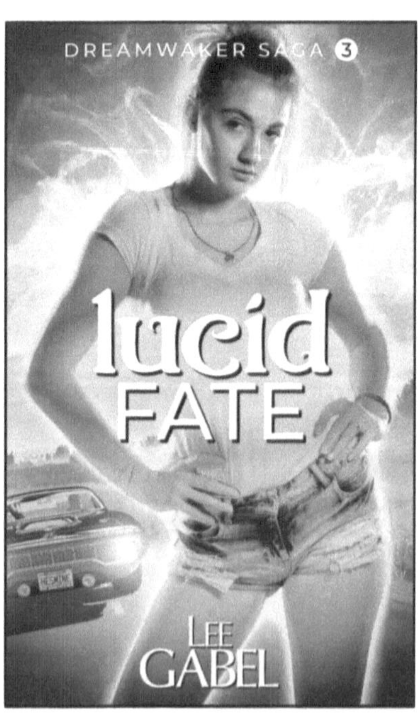

*Note from the author: If you liked this book, may I ask three things? **First,** please rate this book. I appreciate your opinion and what I focus on next depends on you, the reader. **Second,** please consider joining my reader group at LeeGabel.com/join. Once a month I share little details of my life (the fun stuff, that is) and keep you informed of future books. Plus, I'll give you a **25% discount** on all my ebooks. **And third,** if you liked this book, please recommend it to your friends. You can also ask your local library to order it for you if they don't have it yet. My sincere thanks.*

One more thing: This book features music from the 1980s and earlier. For a playlist of all music referenced, please go to: LeeGabel.com/music

Titles by Lee Gabel

DREAMWAKER SAGA
Lucid Bodies
Lucid Revenge
Lucid Fate

DETEST-A-PEST SERIES
Vermin 2.0
Arachnid 2.0
Molerat 2.0

STANDALONE
David's Summer
Snipped
Tied

Afterward

Like it? Rate it. Share it.

If you enjoyed *Lucid Revenge*, please rate it and spread the word. With your rating, you take part in this book's success. If you're interested in joining my Reader Group for fun chit-chat and advance notice of upcoming releases, please sign up by going to LeeGabel.com/signup.

Note from the author

Whew. What a journey 2021 (and part of 2022) was. I began this three-book saga in January 2021, smack in the middle of the COVID pandemic. The idea of lucid dreaming had remained in the back of my head for a number of years. I've tried to direct my dreams and have never been able to. But the few dreams I remember are usually quite vivid and I thought, "What would it be like if I could make a dream real?" I refined the idea further by focusing on making a single person from a dream real. It seemed like a cool idea and, if really possible, probably one that would get me into a heap of trouble. Perfect story material. The Dreamwaker saga was born and it represents my seventh, eighth, and ninth novel.

I decided to write all three Dreamwaker books back-to-back, unlike writing and publishing stories one at a time, like my earlier books. Stories change as they're written, although the Dreamwaker saga did stick largely to my outline. Writing the books back-to-back allowed me to refine details in earlier books to reflect the minor changes that had worked their way into the story later on.

The Dreamwaker saga takes place over the summer of 1986 and contains many pop culture references. I give sincere thanks to the many creators of the film, television, music, and magazines of the era that helped enhance the fictional world I constructed for this story. I hope you enjoyed the indirect ride down memory lane. I certainly did.

I am eternally grateful for my wife and editor Sheila. I couldn't do this without her, nor would I want to. MJ Mumford, while spinning your own time travel suspense novels, your eagle eyes and honest feedback elevated this book to a higher level. And I owe a debt of gratitude to David Hoselton for his feedback on my earlier work as a screenwriter. He helped me gather the courage to take on this novel writing journey on my own. Watch David's work on *The Good Doctor,* which airs on ABC. And to my family and friends who supported my decision to quit my job to write full-time, you were right. I am your number one fan now.

About the author

Lee reads practically any genre. Plus, he's a movie junkie. That's a dangerous combination. Traditionally trained as a screenwriter, Lee moved to writing multi-genre books in 2016 and is the author of nine novels.

Lee once walked **63.5** kilometers in thirteen hours. Why? Ask him. He loves to hear from readers. Past lives include working within the visual and dramatic arts landscape as a graphic designer, illustrator, visual effects artist, animator, and screenwriter. In 2005, he contributed to an Emmy award (LOST; "Pilot; Part 1 and Part 2") for Outstanding Special Visual Effects for a Series.

In reality, Lee lives on an island in the Pacific Northwest with his wife and son. In his head, he lives wherever his characters are.

Find Lee on the Internet:

Want to join Lee's Reader Group or find out more about Lee and the books he writes? Please go to:

LeeGabel.com/links

An infestation of supersized vermin with a hunger for raw meat? CHECK.

An estranged son staying for the summer? CHECK.

An intense fear of rats? DOUBLE-CHECK.

Sam Shaw's life has flipped upside down. Pets and tenants in his Bronx brownstone begin to disappear. Left behind is a wake of carnage.

All evidence points to a hybrid colony of vicious white-tailed rats that has moved into the basement – genetically superior with intelligence to match.

When his ex-wife dumps his son Bradley on his doorstep, Sam must switch into protection mode, if his son will let him.

Faced with impossible odds, Sam hires Bertha O'Connor from Detest-A-Pest Exterminators Inc. She runs the only outfit brave enough – or crazy enough – to take the job.

With help from the Detest-A-Pest crew, Sam must face his fears or the white-tailed mutants will eat him alive. Because this horde of super-rats are smarter than anyone had bargained for...

Detest-A-Pest #1 (304 pages)

Spiders. Over 35,000 species. Every person on Earth eaten in one year. Now there's one more... a ravenous eight-legged hybrid thousands of years in the making and bigger than a dozen burritos.

After a summer of exterminator training in New York, Bradley returns home ready to face his senior year with renewed confidence. But fate gets in the way of his grand teenage plans – especially when eight legs attack instead of four.

And these aren't your typical, everyday spiders. Their newly acquired taste for raw meat has them casting a wide net over Bradley's sleepy San Fernando suburb. It doesn't take them long to scramble up the food chain.

Add a vengeful ex-girlfriend casting a web of lies into the mix, and things get downright sticky.

But Detest-A-Pest can't resist a challenge. Sam and O'Connor rejoin Bradley and his inventive friends as they wage war on an infestation of spiders poised to swallow not only the high school, but the neighborhood and everyone within...

Detest-A-Pest #2 (504 pages)

A playground for the rich. A genetic mutation a thousand years old. A relentless hunger for human flesh. What could go wrong?

Harry Harcourt has a problem. People are dying at exclusive golf resort Mar-A-Verde. As head greenskeeper, it's up to him to "fix" the problem and keep the course open... or face termination. But it's not one problem, it's a vast network of vicious problems, all under the turf.

As bodies pile up, resident doctor Daniela Trejo joins Harry in the fight. Together, they capture a creature unlike anything on Earth – acid skin and razor-sharp fangs with agility that matches its appetite. But the creature escapes.

Outmatched and outnumbered, Harry seeks outside help. No one wants to touch the job – no one except Detest-A-Pest. O'Connor, Sam, and Hope hit the road for what looks like an easy payday in a tropical paradise. What awaits them is a journey through hell that has gruesome death hiding in every shadow...

Detest-A-Pest #3 (340 pages)

A family in crisis. An impossible choice. A race against time.

An unplanned pregnancy turns the lives of Deanna, her husband Max, and her teenage son upside down. But there's something else wrong...

After baby David receives a cancer diagnosis, Deanna drops everything to focus on finding a cure. Max has other ideas.

Based on his own troubled past, Max challenges Deanna to consider quality of life versus quantity. Their opposing opinions throw their marriage into chaos and Deanna seeks treatment options alone.

Caught in the middle, Alex must navigate this family crisis on his own. An unexpected friendship with a cancer survivor may offer the perspective he needs.

With the clock ticking, Deanna stops at nothing to save baby David's life... but her relationship with her family may not survive the process.

David's Summer (310 pages)

Two sisters. One wants in. One has a plan. But gang loyalty cuts family ties...

Jess works, spends time with friends, and earns good grades in school. But she's also sole provider for her drug-addicted mother... And she hates it.

Her sister Nova holds a high-profile position in the Dynamite Queens. Within her turf Nova enjoys fame, fortune, freedom, and respect – at a cost of family life.

But Jess wants what Nova has and is willing to do anything to get it. After one explosive argument, Jess joins a rival gang, a decision that leads her down a path of brutal consequences.

South Central L. A. erupts with violence as two gangs – two sisters – wage war on each other. For the winner, victory could be unforgiving...

Tied is a fast-paced look at family, friendship, betrayal, and revenge through the lens of tough Los Angeles girl gangs.

Note: This novel contains strong language and gang violence.

Tied: A Street Gang Novel (316 pages)

"Get snipped," they said. "It will solve all your problems," they said. Unfortunately, Ted listened...

Five years ago, it was love at first sight. Now, it's life on autopilot as tumbleweeds roll through Ted and Iris's bedroom. Their lackluster love life is driving Ted nuts. Iris's solution to their bedroom blues: get snipped.

Kunal and Ray, Ted's best friends and sworn enemies of Iris, agree with her for once. All roads seem to lead to a surgical solution, but Ted's not going there... until an explosive argument changes everything. A vasectomy seems like Ted's only play to win Iris back.

The antics of his precocious next-door neighbor complicates matters. Ted's ill-conceived decisions jeopardize everything important in his life, including his nuts.

But life was about to throw Ted a romantic curve-ball aimed straight at his heart...

Snipped: A Cutting Comedy (300 pages)